D1158851

Dell Books by Christopher Newman

**KILLER
THE DEVIL'S OWN
HIT AND RUN**

HIT AND RUN

CHRISTOPHER NEWMAN

A Dell Book

Published by
Dell Publishing
a division of
Bantam Doubleday Dell Publishing Group, Inc.
1540 Broadway
New York, New York 10036

ISBN: 0-440-22263-X

Printed in the United States of America

Published simultaneously in Canada

December 1997

10 9 8 7 6 5 4 3 2 1

OPM

This one is for Ann and Danny.

Acknowledgments

The author wishes to thank the following people for their help, without whom his task would have been vastly more difficult: Don Penrod and Tom Rose of Penrod & Co., Gordon Kato, Knox Burger, and Susan Newman.

"But because fraud is a device peculiar to man, it more displeases God; and therefore the fraudulent are placed beneath, and more pain assails them."

DANTE'S *Inferno*,
CANTO XI

ONE

Bruce Webster's thoughts were three thousand miles away when Vivian Hoag slid close to place a hand on his thigh and squeeze. He started with surprise.

"Pour us more champagne?" she purred.

As she made her request, she focused an intent scowl on the dance floor, where her husband held a tall, slender brunette and swayed to an easy mambo. Bruce saw hatred in Vivian's glare.

"How obvious is it to you?" she growled. Her hand lingered, gentle pressure still applied by those fingers as Webster reached to pull the bottle from the bucket.

"What's that?" With her hand in his lap, his mind was no longer a continent away. He filled her glass.

"That they're having an affair. Bill and that slut, Andrea."

Bill Hoag was the CEO of Telenet, a telecommunications maverick eager to acquire a revolutionary new technology developed by Webster's San Jose, California, firm. Bruce was Hoag's guest at this gathering; the annual Telenet New Year's Eve bash at the Doubles Club, in Manhattan's Sherry-Netherland Hotel. There were some problems with the deal right now, but Bruce still wanted it to happen as much as Hoag did. He reminded himself to remain cautious, but Mrs. Hoag's substantial breasts, threatening to spill from the confines of her plunging neckline, weren't any help to him. She was so close that her warmth radiated through the sleeve of his dinner jacket. He would swear he could almost feel her heartbeat. In spite of himself, his own pulse had quickened.

"Speculation or known fact?" he asked in reply. When he'd first met Hoag's dance partner that evening, he was struck by the contrast between Andrea Hill's porcelain white skin, the almost-black helmet of her short, straight hair, and a pair of huge blue eyes. The effect seemed anything but sluttish.

Mrs. Hoag sighed, sipped from her glass and leaned more heavily into him. "I don't have photographs, if that's what you mean. But wives know these things. Bill hasn't laid a hand on me in months."

This was more than Bruce wanted to know. Yet his eyes wandered down to those swelling breasts, their full weight at rest atop his forearm. Christ. "He's been pretty busy with this merger," he countered. "Back and forth to the Coast a dozen times since Thanksgiving. That's a fair-size distraction."

Her face, upturned just inches from his, showed a

hardness around its edges despite the pert, upturned nose and wide, sensuous mouth. He guessed her to be about his own age. Andrea Hill might be a year or two younger.

"We've been married five years, Mr. Webster. The first three, he couldn't keep his hands off me." Her fingers drifted as she spoke, her nails raking the fabric stretched tight across his inner thigh.

A host of images flashed through Webster's mind, all of them carnal and all involving Vivian Hoag. Divorced at twenty-eight, he'd found it difficult to reattach. After drifting in and out of several relationships, he'd decided to give it a rest. This merger had kept him extremely busy. Enough so that his self-exile from the dating pool had taken no great effort. Until now. It was five months since he'd been with a woman. Only inches from Vivian's coaxing fingers, he had an erection that begged to be allowed back in the swim again. To force his attention toward safer ground, he regarded Bill and Andrea on the dance floor and shrugged. "If they're having an affair, I think they're being pretty obvious. Don't you?"

Vivian leaned close again to respond when the band fell suddenly silent. All heads turned to focus on television monitors as Bruce recognized the scene onscreen. Times Square. Suspended on a brightly lit pole above the throng that jammed the streets below, the famous ball had begun its descent.

"Seven! Six! Five! . . ." The old year expired as the new one approached.

Bruce had joined the countdown when his breath caught in his throat. Beneath the table, hidden from view, Vivian Hoag's fingers had found his erection.

"Two! One! Happy New Year!"

His face hot with sudden, flushed embarrassment, Webster felt Vivian's eager arms encircle his neck and her surging tongue fill his mouth.

TWO

Before Vivian Hoag gave his attention new focus, Bruce Webster had been preoccupied with a monkey wrench thrown just two days ago into the guts of the deal he had working. A group of Telenet engineers was in San Jose to run Webster's breakthrough digital subscriber technology through final tests. Friday, they'd turned up a theoretical flaw in the mathematics. Though the problem was thought to be minor, thirty-six hours had passed and it remained unsolved. This was not the best of times for the new boss's wife to grab his cock . . . or climb into his lap. Mortified, Bruce could only hope that Bill Hoag had been too distracted with his own romantic pursuits to see it. As soon after midnight as he could make his excuses, Bruce collected his coat and hurried through the Sherry Netherland lobby toward the street.

Webster hadn't consumed enough champagne to be drunk, yet his mind reeled as he emerged from the hotel onto the Fifth Avenue sidewalk. All day, he'd argued with Hoag for a delay in the merger announcement and failed to budge him. Now, as a frigid winter wind forced his hands deep into his pockets, Bruce tucked in his chin and tried to focus his attention on that problem once again. Instead, all he could see in his mind's eye were Vivian Hoag's breasts, and the tapered elegance of her fingers beneath their table, closed on his throbbing ardor.

Absorbed in his thoughts, Webster didn't notice that there were no cabs outside the usually busy hotel. With a quarter-million revelers cramming streets to the south, traffic was using streets east of him to avoid the midtown jam. Bruce started absently toward the corner of East 60th Street. He remembered that Mrs. Hoag hadn't seemed disappointed when he'd moved to depart, despite her earlier advances. Any port in a storm, he supposed. But her tongue, all that body heat, and the way her perfume had filled his nostrils? They had been real, and persisted to haunt him.

He stepped from the curb into the avenue as the *Don't Walk* sign started blinking. There were no more than a dozen pairs of headlights as far uptown as he could see, and he guessed he had a long wait before the next available cab. Residual ice from a Christmas snowstorm made footing treacherous as he eased past the bumper of a parked car to get better vantage. Shoulders hunched to ward off the cold, he shifted from foot to foot, trying to stay warm.

His back to it, Bruce didn't see the car that eased from the curb, fifty feet behind him. Its back-up lights suddenly flared as the car shot in reverse toward where he stood. The squeal of tires got his attention and he spun in time to see the rear end of a late model Saab. Too late, he tried to leap from harm's way. The force of impact flung him across the hood of a parked Jaguar XJS. His head collided with the windshield, snapping his neck, while the Saab lurched to a stop. Its driver shifted into drive and sped off into the night.

Seven blocks west of where Bruce Webster lay draped across the hood of that Jaguar, Lieutenant Joe Dante, NYPD, watched the gyrating throng on the Copacabana dance floor as he traced patterns in the dew on the outside of his champagne glass. His lover, Rosa Losada, was off in a corner somewhere, huddled up with her new political mentor. Their host this New Year's Eve, Rosa's uncle, was on the dance floor with that mentor's loud, self-impressed wife. Together, they chugged without grace through a hot, peppery salsa.

For Dante, the festive mood he could have been in was wrecked earlier at dinner. Uncle Tico had toasted his niece and informed his guests that next November, Rosa hoped to be elected New York's Twelfth District representative to the United States Congress. Dante knew that the current congressman, Roberto Isabel, faced indictment for misappropriation of funds and would announce Tuesday that he will not seek reelection. To replace him, Manhattan's Hispanic Democratic Coalition needed a candidate so squeaky clean that any attempt to smear them would only look offensive and ugly. Captain Rosa Losada, commander of the Manhattan District Attorney's investigation squad, was the perfect aspirant.

A much-decorated street cop, she'd recently survived an ordeal at the hands of a homicidal psychopath in Florida that had grabbed national headlines. The HDC, an organization founded and run by barrio barrister Jaime Ruiz, had tendered an offer of unqualified support. To Dante, who'd had run-ins with Ruiz, it looked like a sleazebag's opportunistic grandstanding. When he told Rosa that, they'd wrangled.

A light touch on his sleeve roused Dante from his reverie. He looked up to see Rosa's aunt Esmerelda, on her feet and smiling down at him.

"Ask me to dance?" There seemed to be a hint of sympathy in the way she said it.

Since the case that had taken Joe and Rosa to Florida that past Thanksgiving, Dante had been nursing a badly sprained right knee. Just this past week, it finally felt good enough to allow a return to active duty. He looked back toward the dance floor. The Tito Puente Orchestra was launching into yet another salsa number. Why not? He nodded and rose.

With familiar ease, Esmerelda hooked a hand through his arm and leaned close as he led them toward the floor. She and Tico had been his hosts in Florida, too, at their opulent home in the Miami suburb of Coco Plum. "You looked a million miles away," she observed.

"At least that far. Sorry," he apologized. "No woman as beautiful as you are, in that dress, should be left stranded with a moody cop on New Year's Eve. There's no justice."

He could feel the sweet heat of her breath in his ear as she laughed. "If you dance half as smoothly as you flatter old ladies, there's justice enough, Lieutenant."

As well as she'd gotten to know Joe during his stay in Miami, Esme still addressed him by his title rather than his name. He supposed it was either a conscious or unconscious defense mechanism, meant to enforce a formal distance between them. She might be the mother of college-age twins, but this was no old lady by any stretch of the imagination. Probably close to Dante's own age, she looked like her daughters' big sister, not their mom. But she was married to a much older, extremely wealthy man and there were politics involved that Joe, as an outsider, couldn't hope to fathom. Her husband clearly doted on her, and in Joe's presence she was always cautious to avoid any behavior that might incite even the slightest jealousy in the man.

On the dance floor, Dante watched his partner's hips roll and sway with the salsa's liquid sensuality. As she danced, Esmerelda regarded him with a kind of bemusement he'd never seen in her eyes before.

"You look very handsome tonight, Lieutenant. Dinner clothes suit you."

"You flatter old men pretty smoothly yourself," he replied. It was difficult for him not to stare at her body, encased in thousands of shimmering black and silver sequins.

"You disagree with my husband's interference in Rosa's career," she observed. "Strongly, to judge from the expression I've been watching on your face."

"Jaime Ruiz sucks the blood of his community." He spoke bluntly, with no attempt made to sugarcoat it. "For the past ten years, Congressman Isabel has been his whore."

Her eyes widened, not in shock but more in amusement. "Tell me how you really feel, Lieutenant." She laughed. "You've no idea how refreshing it is to hear such frankness. Whether I agree with your assessment or not."

"That means you don't?"

She kept her expression neutral. "I didn't say that."

"There's a side of Ruiz I'll bet you or your husband have never seen. But Rosa has, and I can't believe she's still climbing into bed with him."

"An unfortunate turn of phrase, don't you think?" As she danced, she closed her eyes and appeared to shudder. "I believe bed is the last place she would go with him. All that soft, pudgy flesh is so . . . unappealing."

Joe felt the familiar vibration of his silent paging device, clipped to the strap of his cummerbund. He reached for it, their conversation interrupted. A summons at that late hour was never good news. If events ran true to course, he wasn't likely to get home before sunup. Esme watched him scan the display to see a number he knew by heart. The Operations Desk, at the Big Building, downtown.

She stepped to his side as the music died. "Problem?"

He took her hand, tucked it beneath his arm, and started them back toward their table. "Sorry it was only one dance," he apologized. "I need to find a phone."

"You're leaving us?"

He patted the back of that hand. "Just when I'd

almost gotten up enough nerve to ask you to run away with me."

She laughed a soft, musical laugh, her fingers tightening on the inside of his biceps. "Careful, Lieutenant. Maybe I should wear this dress more often."

Rosa had returned to their table with Ruiz. She saw the look in Joe's eyes and leaned back in her chair to make contact. "What's up?"

"Just got a call. Borrow your phone?"

Her tiny cellular unit was about the only thing she carried in her black velvet clutch bag. She handed it across. Joe punched in the Op Desk number while he paced the floor behind her. The fingers of his free hand drummed impatiently against his left thigh.

"Operations. Lieutenant Crowell."

"At one in the morning, on New Year's? Whose parade did you piss on, Dick?"

"Drew the short straw," Crowell growled. "Lissen. Lieutenant Busby just called. Knew you'd want word. Diana Webster's brother was killed half an hour ago. Hit and run, corner of Fifth and East Sixtieth."

Melissa Busby, the Chief of Detectives' executive officer, was a former Dante protégé. She knew of Dante's friendship with rock singer Diana Webster and her sculptor husband, Brian Brennan. Joe froze as he absorbed this news. Diana's brother, Bruce, had been in town since Wednesday and was staying upstairs from Dante, in Brian and Diana's loft. "Who's on the scene, Dick?"

"Manhattan North Homicide. Crime Scene Unit. The C of D is en route."

Joe wasn't surprised by Chief Gus Lieberman's reaction. He'd been the chief's go-to guy in sticky, problem situations for years. They'd been close friends for all of Dante's plainclothes career. Gus knew how tight Joe and the dead man's sister were.

"Do me a favor?" he asked Crowell. "Get Beasley Richardson. Tell him what's happened, and that I'll meet him there." Lieutenant Beasley "Jumbo" Richardson was Dante's partner of six years.

As Joe handed back her phone, Rosa frowned up at him. "You look like you've seen a ghost. What is it?"

"Some drunk hit Diana's brother, Bruce. Right outside the party he went to tonight at the Sherry. Killed him."

Her hand went to her mouth. "Oh, Jesus. What can I do?"

"Meet Gus and Beasley there." Joe dug his car keys from his jacket pocket as he spoke, and searched for his coat claims. "Brian and Di should be home. That's where I'm headed. I'll hook up with you at the scene, soon as I can."

Rosa stood to face him as he spoke, and took the claim check he pressed into her palm. "You sure you don't want me to come along?" She was also a friend of the dead man's sister, and her sculptor husband.

"I'd rather do this alone, I think," he replied. An involuntary contraction squeezed his gut, knotting it like a fist. What he needed was the time alone to figure *how* to tell them. "You and Beasley get every detail you can collect. I want to know what the hell happened." Her run for Congress temporarily forgotten, he leaned to kiss her quickly. Full of dread, he hurried from the club into the frigid New Year's night.

* * *

When the call came at one-oh-five on that first morning of the brand-new year, Lieutenant Beasley Richardson and his wife, Bernice, had been asleep for almost three hours. The man whom other cops called Jumbo enjoyed quiet nights at home with his librarian mate more than he did splitting hangovers. He had fashioned his life accordingly. He and Bernice had turned down half a dozen invitations to parties, preferring to celebrate alone that night. Earlier, they'd had champagne to toast the fourth anniversary of Beasley's vow to lose one hundred pounds. He'd accomplished that feat in twelve months, and had managed to lose an additional ten over the three years since.

They'd also toasted the fact that, in May, the younger of their two children would graduate from the State University at Binghamton. That put them in the home stretch. No more tuition and board at twelve grand a year. After dinner, they'd pored over maps of England and France. This coming summer they would finally take that long-anticipated trip. At ten o'clock, they'd gone to bed and made love.

When Richardson arrived at the scene of Bruce Webster's hit-and-run homicide, his head was clear and his mind sharp. That put him in yet another minority. He was a black male, situated well up the NYPD command chain, a middle-aged survivor of the East New York, Brooklyn, meat grinder, and had been an accustomed member of minorities all his life.

Homicides were never a walk in the park, but when they involved a friend or relative of a friend, the atmosphere at a scene was less of a going-through-the-motions routine. Chief Gus Lieberman,

Rosa Losada, and the members of Joe Dante's Special Investigations Division squad all knew Diana Webster. They knew her before she became the sort of celebrity she was today, and hadn't seen it change her very much. They knew that Joey, her neighbor in the big warehouse loft building that she and her husband owned, was the closest friend that either Brian or Diana had. None of them envied Dante his current mission.

Richardson spotted Rosa huddled up with the chief, the whip of Manhattan North Homicide, and the Crime Scene Unit commander. She extricated herself to cross and dip her head in a quick, familiar nod. Seconds later, Gus joined them.

"Half the job is drunk on their asses tonight," the chief grumbled. "Aside from the regular duty guys, you two are the only clear heads in the crowd." A former all-city linebacker, Lieberman shared Beasley's burly build. His wife had been on him to quit smoking for years, and the cigarette that waggled at the corner of his mouth remained unlit. At least for the moment. The best he'd been able to do was cut back.

Jumbo watched a pair of Emergency Medical Services attendants load a blue rubber body bag onto a stretcher. "Joey intends t' bring Brian and Diana here?"

"I imagine," Rosa replied. "Depending on what sort of shape she's in. Napier is here with Mel. They're inside the hotel lobby, working the party guests. With this icy wind, even the doormen were all in, off the street. So far, they haven't found anybody who saw anything." Napier was Detective Guy Napier, one of Dante's squad. Mel was Lieutenant

Melissa Busby, his girlfriend and Lieberman's new X.O.

"Who's workin' the neighborhood?" Jumbo asked the chief.

Gus plucked the cigarette from between his lips and scowled at it. "The Nineteenth's got every available warm body doin' door-t'-door. Most'a their uniforms on the clock tonight are all midtown, workin' crowd control."

Shoulders hunched against the cold, Rosa turned away from the spectacle of the body being loaded to stare north up Fifth Avenue. "The Crime Scene Unit has recovered broken taillight fragments. Judging from them, and the direction Diana's brother flew, they and the Medical Examiner's man concur. Bruce Webster was hit by a car moving in reverse. How bizarre is that?"

To Richardson, it sounded downright crazy. Who got thrown fifteen feet by a car rolling backward? "Movin' how fast?" he asked.

"Had to be flying," she replied. "The people he sat with at the party all say he left sober. If that's true, the speed of the car might explain why he didn't get out of the way. It probably blindsided him."

"Any make and model?"

When she shook her head, and her mass of thick, lustrous black hair shimmered, Beasley vividly recalled the time, six years ago, when he'd first met her. It was hard for him to imagine why any woman this good-looking would choose to be a cop. But that was before he got his first glimpse of the ambition in her, and knew the story of her parents' brutal unsolved murder. She hadn't wanted to be just any cop back then. She'd wanted to be New York's first female police commissioner.

"Nope. They've sent the taillamp shards to the lab. And some paint chips they found."

"Your night at the Copa must've just been gettin' into full swing," Beasley mused. "What kinda shape's Joey in?"

A rueful expression crossed her face as she stared off into the distance again. "It wasn't gearing up to be that sort of night, I'm afraid. It's too long a story to get into right now."

Gus finally lit that butt. He gestured with it toward his Crime Scene Unit commander, now talking to a couple of his techs. "They think them flecks of paint can be positively made in the lab. Car and model year." His well-worn Zippo lighter went back into a pocket of his pants.

"How soon?" Beasley asked.

"Depends. It bein' a holiday weekend and all. A domestic car, maybe a day. Foreign job could take longer."

Richardson thought about what he'd heard, glanced at Captain Losada, and then back at their boss. "Considerin' the odds against Homicide clearin' any case like this, unless the perp turns himself in, how about me an' Joey turnin' our guys loose on it a while?"

Lieberman shrugged. "Regardless of the fact that it's Diana's brother, I don't like the car-in-reverse angle. No more'n you do. Maybe if Webster was asleep in the street, passed out drunk. But cold sober? Standin' upright?"

"The driver could have seen an empty parking spot in his sideview and not looked over his shoulder," Rosa reasoned. "How often have any of us al-most hit a car like that, changing lanes?"

"Or got it in reverse by mistake," Gus supposed. "And just gave it too much gas. I realize there's plenty of possibilities."

"So why didn't he stop, once he hit him?" Jumbo argued. "Why'd he just leave him there t' die?" He was surprised by how much anger he felt as he spoke. Diana's brother was someone he'd heard Joey talk about, but a guy he'd never met. A high-tech hotshot of some sort. Whenever he traveled to New York on business, he'd stay with his sister in her West 27th Street loft. Joey and Bruce had gotten friendly. Shared some good times.

"Most likely he was so drunk he shit his pants," Lieberman supposed. "And once he realized what he'd done, he couldn't get outta there fast enough."

"And when he sobers up, he might get an attack of the guilts," Rosa added hopefully. "And turn himself in. Either that, or the body shop where he takes his car calls us. There's bound to be plenty of press cov-erage, considering who his sis—" She stopped, her attention drawn to a distraction up the way.

Beasley turned to follow her gaze. He saw Joey's car pulled to the curb on the opposite side of East 60th Street. His partner had emerged to shield Diana Webster from news photographers as he hustled her and her husband, Brian, toward the sanctuary of the cordoned-off crime scene. "This is the fuckin' part I hate the worst," he murmured, and moved to inter-cept them.

* * *

Diana and Brennan had eaten dinner at one of their favorite neighborhood restaurants. Then they'd headed up to Central Park for a couple hours of skating on Wollman Rink, early enough to avoid the thickening Times Square horde. Dante had found them enjoying brandies in front of a crackling living room fire. When he arrived, they'd thought it was Bruce, returning home early from a less than scintillating corporate fete. But no such luck.

It was four o'clock before Joe and Rosa got the distraught couple home again and finally said good night. Now, one floor down, Dante loosened his bow tie and poured himself two fingers of Black Bush Irish whisky over cubes. Emotionally drained, he splashed a little water into his glass, then carried the drink into his cavernous living room. Collapsing onto the sofa, he kicked off his shoes and scratched his affection-starved cat, Toby, beneath the chin.

Still in her heels and her backless silver lamé cocktail dress, a restless Rosa wandered the perimeter of the room. She stared vacantly at the titles on his book-crammed shelves, trying to look distracted.

"I know this might not be the best time to talk about it, but you treated Jaime Ruiz like a piece of shit tonight, Joe." She tried to make it sound casual, but Dante knew her too well.

He studied the sculpted muscles of her back, down to that provocative curve of hip and haunch. Moments ago, in the bathroom, she'd put her hair up with one of those big shark-jaw clips. All that flesh, bared from the nape of her neck to the sacral dimples at the base of her spine, was having a predictable effect on him. "He is a piece of shit," he replied. "And before you found out that he and your uncle are swimming in the same cesspool together, you used to think so, too."

She spun on him. "Cesspool? And just what the hell is that supposed to mean?" Her eyes flashed fire. "Go on. Say it!"

He took a considered sip of his drink and warned himself. Control this, before it escalates. "Look at Congressman Isabel's voting record, Rosa. He's in Big Sugar's pocket. He cares more about price supports for Tico's Florida grower pals than he does for school lunch and prenatal care programs in his own district."

"Ah. Roberto Isabel is a thief. Ergo, I accept this offer, I'm a thief, too." There was ice in Rosa's tone to match her stone-cold expression. "That is what you're implying, is it not?"

He met it head-on. "You accept Tico's money, and Jaime's backing, they'll expect they've bought something. It's how the game is played."

He saw her blink, just the slightest crack appearing in her confidence, only to close an instant later. "I already have accepted, Joe. Ruiz and I were discussing when the announcement will be made while you were out on the dance floor, playing footsie with my aunt."

He smiled, a sadness at the edges of it. "That's one thing Washington won't have to teach you, babe. How to fight dirty. So when's the big date?"

"The congressman will be indicted Tuesday. The HDC already has a fund-raiser scheduled for Wednesday night, at Roseland. Ruiz thinks it would be as good a time as any."

Joe drained his drink. "Timely, even."

"I'd like you to be there."

He heaved himself to his feet. "I don't think so, Rosa. You want to throw in with the likes of Jaime Ruiz, count me out. His brand of clusterfuck, I can do without."

From the kitchen, as he dumped ice from his glass and set it in the dishwasher, he heard the gate of the elevator squeal open and then slam shut. Wonderful. The street below was full of hookers and drunken johns. It was bitter cold. Where did she think she'd find a cab at this hour? As the elevator car descended toward the lobby, he and his stiff right knee headed for the back door, and three flights of stairs.

More than a little drunk after his company's New Year's party, Telenet CEO Bill Hoag was regretting his fondness for Maker's Mark bourbon. A night meant to be festive and celebratory had ended in tragedy. Bill's guest, Bruce Webster, had been killed by a hit-and-run driver, leaving the party. A horrible mess, and a situation that demanded he say something to the press. He only hoped his responses to those questions from reporters, answered with a pretty serious buzz-on, had been dignified and appropriate.

As Vivian emerged from her dressing alcove, Bill reached to switch off the bedside lamp. Backlit by the glow of the bathroom light, she stood hipshot, arms folded beneath her breasts. At hardly more than five feet, she had the long, slender lines of a much taller woman, and Bill still couldn't get used to the so-called enhancement surgery she'd had done last year. Not because it made her look grotesque; just different. Indeed, though they were a bit large for his taste now, her new upswept breasts were still in fair proportion to the rest of her.

"So tell me just one thing, you self-serving prick." She fired it point-blank, with no preamble. "What is it she's got that I don't have?"

Hoag flopped onto his back, his end of the room now plunged into relative darkness. He adjusted the pillow beneath his head to better face her, and considered the path that had taken them to this juncture. It was a mere five years long. And a rocky one. When he'd met Vivian, he was about to be named the youngest president in Telenet's thirty-year history. It seemed prudent that he take a wife; to demonstrate stability on the domestic as well as the business front. Vivian was a promising lawyer at a major midtown firm. She'd gone to all the right schools. She had a great ass. So what if they didn't really love each other?

"I'm tired and drunk, Viv. Let's go to sleep."

"I asked you a question. Answer me, goddamn it."

"What's she got that you don't have?" He heard a hollowness in his voice. "Eros, I guess."

He'd needed a smart, attractive, socially presentable wife. His marriage to Vivian was a deal they'd struck, with benefits to both parties. Even if uninspired, the sex had been okay for the first three years. During that time, by virtue of their alliance, her stature in the eyes of her firm had grown. She'd since been made junior partner.

"You humiliated me tonight, you bastard."

"How's that?" He forced himself to keep a measured cool in his tone. "By leaving you with my honored guest? A single, handsome guy, all alone in this big, hostile city?"

"You're fucking the bitch, Bill. Don't deny it."

In the gloom, he raised his gaze to the ceiling, sucked a breath deep, and sighed. "Who'd you get the new tits for, Viv? You think I'm stupid? I know it wasn't me."

"I've never rubbed anything in your face," she shot back. "Never trotted anything out in public like that; paraded it around where the whole world could see."

He couldn't contain the sharp bark of a belly laugh that surged past his lips. "Paraded? Gimme a break. She likes to dance. So do I."

He shifted to get a better view of her as she stood rooted, her face frozen in cold fury. "Right after the ball dropped? I happened to glance over at the table, Viv. Just think. That poor bastard might still be alive, you hadn't scared him off like that."

Just as she reached for the vase atop his highboy, the alcohol-fuzzy edges of his perception saw her intention. He managed to get an arm up. When she let fly, the impact sent a hot, searing shock of pain from his elbow to his shoulder. Tulips flew as the vase shattered. A sharp shard of ceramic grazed his temple. He and the bedclothes were drenched with water, his forehead cut deep enough to draw blood.

The tangle of sodden bedclothes thrown aside, Bill roared with pain and outrage. He found his feet, tripped on the corner of a twisted sheet, and went down on all fours. The numbness in his left arm frightened him almost as much as the cut that ran blood into one eye. He had a news conference scheduled for first thing Tuesday morning. The televised business media would be there, and he would look just great, one arm in a cast and his head swathed in bandages.

"You'd better hide, bitch!" he screamed. His head swam as he struggled to his feet again. "I catch you, you're fucking dead!"

THREE

Joe Dante was an accustomed early riser, no matter what hour he'd gotten to bed. New Year's morning, with only three hours sleep, he was up and showered by seven-thirty. He'd just poured himself a cup of coffee and pulled up a chair at the kitchen table when a soft knock came at the back door. It was Diana, eyes red from crying, clad in old jeans and a sweater.

"Heard the pipes," she explained as he hugged her. "Figured you were up and around."

"Get any sleep at all?" He turned and grabbed another cup from the cabinet.

"Not that I know of." Diana pulled up another chair as Joe poured her cup full. She glanced around as she sat. "Where's Rosa?"

"Home, I expect. We had a spat."

"Oh good. I guess that means she's gonna go for it, huh?"

He looked up in surprise as he set the cup before her. "You knew?"

"She called and wanted to have lunch last Wednesday. That guy Ruiz was making overtures and she wanted to talk about it."

Dante sat in the chair opposite. Diana looked rough, her short-cropped hair rumpled and the remnants of last night's eye makeup smudged beneath her eyes. "What she needs is a shit-filter overhaul," he complained. "Jaime Ruiz has the ethics of a grave robber."

"I bet that's just how you put it to her, too."

"I think I called him a piece of shit, first."

She reached across the table to click her cup with his. "Good one, Copper. And a happy new year to you, too."

He eased back in his seat and grimaced. One floor up, Diana and Brian had a guest room full of her dead brother's travel clothes. It wasn't hard to imagine how much she had to be hurting right now. Tomorrow, there would be a Medical Examiner's inquest to face. Then funeral arrangements to make. "I'm gonna give this investigation I'm launching everything my guys and I have got, Di," he promised. "But I hope you realize what a long shot it is. Without us in your corner, the odds would be nil. Unless this asshole turns himself in. Even with us, they're still slim to none."

"You trying to make me feel better?"

He took one of her hands in his. This was a woman he cared for. Deeply. Once upon a time, he'd saved her life. It had created a mystical bond. She and Brennan were now two of his closest friends in a world where cops don't have many, if any, civilian confidants. "Just don't hate me if I fail," he replied.

"I couldn't. I know how hard you'll try."

He lifted that hand to his lips, kissed it and set it on the surface between them. "I'll cut through as much red tape for you as I can. Use what weight I've got to speed up the autopsy. What else? Anything you can think of?"

She took a noisy slurp of her scalding coffee and shook her head. "Not really. My sister's flying in, sometime today. I've got to work out a pickup, soon as I know which flight."

Dante had never met her sister, and knew only the thumbnail-sketch details. She taught college somewhere in the Midwest. Missouri, he thought. Messy divorce, a year or so back, and some bad blood of one sort or another between her and Diana. They'd been estranged until only recently.

"You want, I can give you a lift," he offered. "As long as I'm free at the time. Why not give me a call on my mobile when you know more?"

"I wouldn't mind the company," she admitted. "So what'll you do about Rosa, Joe? Sounds to me, her hat's in the ring."

"Not much I can do. I'd like to break her uncle's legs for putting her up to this, but I like his wife and kids too much."

"And things were going so well between you two."

It was true. Theirs was an often turbulent relationship, but lately the sailing had been smooth. "You know I'm nuts about her, Di. But I won't help her campaign. For her, that could be a deal breaker. She runs, I'll run the other way. Fast as I can."

* * *

Accustomed, after twenty-six years on the job, to being called out often in the middle of the night, Lieutenant Beasley Richardson still felt surprisingly rested as he stepped off the elevator onto the eleventh floor of One Police Plaza. He chalked it up to having initially crawled into bed at so reasonable an hour. As Dante's partner on their five-man SID task force, he and Joe shared a tiny, partitioned cubicle tucked behind the Major Case squad's offices. When he entered it on that quiet holiday morning, he found Detective Guy Napier propped on the edge of his desk. A full six and a half feet tall, Napier held an interdepartmental envelope in one huge hand, and fidgeted impatiently with the string clasp.

"What're you doin' here?" Richardson asked in surprise.

"Same thing as you, Lou. Where'd you expect me to be?"

Napier had handled most of the interviews with guests at the Telenet party last night. So far as Beasley knew, he'd come up empty-handed. He pointed to the envelope Guy held. "What's that?"

Contents removed, the younger man handed them across. "I'm waiting on a list of everyone on the Telenet guest list. We'll run it through Motor Vehicles and see if any of them own this make and model of car. On my way here, I stopped by the lab."

"That fast?" Richardson couldn't conceal his surprise. Gus must have lit some pretty hot fires. Most of the personnel who worked for NYPD's Scientific Research Division were civilian employees who got weekends and holidays off. Only skeleton crews worked those eight-hour shifts. Someone had burned the midnight oil.

"A Saab 9000. Dark green," Napier said. "They used the same taillights on both the '95 and '96 model years. But that only gets us halfway there," he cautioned.

"Why halfway?" To Beasley, the make and model of the car got them a lot closer than that. "How many could there be? Even in the tri-state area? A couple hunnerd?"

"You'd be surprised. That's why I'm hoping the guest list from that party will help. That, and one from the hotel, of everybody registered there last night."

"We need to call Albany, anyway. Get that ball rollin', huh?"

Napier stood to stretch the kinks out of his lanky frame and yawned. He looked beat. "Done. And to Hartford, Trenton, and Saab North America. We need an estimate from the manufacturer of how many green ones they've sold. Soon as the lab finishes spectrograph analysis, they'll fax their paint chip findings to Stockholm. They hope the factory can pin down the exact production run for this."

"Gonna be as slow as cold molasses, this bein' a worldwide holiday," Richardson supposed. "That could take days."

That morning, when Telenet's chief financial officer, Greg Nichols, awoke, he had trouble making any sense of the information his pounding head was trying to process. It was daylight. That much was obvious. But how and when he'd gotten where he was,

was *not* obvious. His last recollection was of his company's New Year's Eve party in Manhattan. Now, he was in a guest room of his pal Dennis Bennett's weekend retreat, clear up north in Pound Ridge. He'd had what? Two, maybe three drinks? Perrier Jouët and framboise. The way his head hammered, it felt like he'd had a few dozen.

Gingerly, Nichols eased aside the bedclothes and experimented with movement. Legs over the side of the bed. Toes to the oriental carpet underfoot. When he tried to stand, all equilibrium abandoned him. He lurched. The room suddenly swooped and swirled as he made a desperate lunge for the bath. He didn't quite make the commode for that first round of retching, but when he finished, five minutes later, he had a shaky hold on the edges of the bowl. His stomach heaved dry, the room ceased to spin. Good God. He'd had so much to drink, he'd blacked out. But how was that possible? He'd even slept in his clothes.

A long, hot shower later, Nichols emerged to finish mopping up his mess. He tossed the towels he'd just used into the tub, still trying to figure out what had gotten into him last night. Not since his frat days at Yale had he tied one on like that. And never in his life could he remember being so drunk that he'd suffered a total memory loss.

Wearing an ill-fitting sweat shirt, old khakis, and moccasins he'd found in the closet, Greg descended the stairs. He heard noises emanating from the kitchen, and on the landing, he paused to peer out a window into the drive. It was a gloomy, bleak day. A blanket of snow from last weekend's storm still covered the landscape. He was surprised to see his fiancée's Land Rover Discovery pulled up before the front stoop, skis and poles clamped to the roof rack. Thursday, Phoebe and a group of women from the brokerage where she worked had rushed off to Stowe for the long holiday weekend. Powder and parties. So what was she doing here?

When he pushed his way past the swinging kitchen door, he found Dennis and Phoebe seated across from each other at the breakfast table. They drank coffee and were deep in earnest conversation. Bennett, a Wall Street fund manager and former boyfriend of hers, had been Greg's guest at the Telenet party last night. He and Phoebe looked over as Greg entered. Phoebe had her lower lip clamped between her teeth, her brow furrowed in an expression of distress. Greg headed straight for the liquor cabinet.

"What's going on?" he demanded. Once he located a bottle of Absolut, he shuffled to the refrigerator and found store-bought Bloody Mary mix. "You're supposed to be skiing, Pheeb. And what the hell am I doing here?" Glass from an overhead cabinet. Ice. His hands shook as he built himself that much-needed eye-opener.

"You don't remember any of it?" Bennett asked.

"Any of what, goddamn it? I go to a company party, have three drinks and feel like someone tore my head off." Ingredients poured, he plunged an index finger to mix them, then took a gulp. The moment it impacted with his knotted gut, he knew he'd made a mistake. One hand flew to his mouth as his stomach lurched. "Damn!" he gasped.

Phoebe stared openmouthed at him. "You killed a man last night, Gregory. Or don't you remember? You hit him with your car."

She might as well have punched him flush in the

face. His drink nearly drained, Greg lowered it from his lips, stunned speechless. He turned to Bennett, full of questions he was too paralyzed to voice.

Dennis shrugged and nodded. When he spoke, his tone was almost apologetic. "I got us out of there, quick as I could. Never should have let you have the wheel, mate. Not in the shape you were in."

Nichols finally produced enough moisture around his tongue to form words. How could anyone not remember getting behind the wheel of a car? Let alone killing someone. Overwhelmed, he was forced to grip the edge of the kitchen counter to steady himself. "Where?" he croaked. "My car. Where is it now?"

"Hidden in the garage," Bennett told him. "Can't believe my luck, getting us all the way up here. With only one taillight, no less."

For Greg, the attempt to think with any clarity was like trying to run on ice. "Taillight?"

"I imagine you thought you were in drive. Had it in reverse instead. The man you hit was in the street, trying to hail a cab."

Nichols searched to find reason or sense in any of this and repeatedly stumbled into the same memory void. If his car did, indeed, have only one taillight, it was nothing short of remarkable that Bennett had managed to drive more than thirty miles upstate in it. On New Year's Eve, the most heavily patrolled night of the year. "How did you find Pheeb?" he asked.

"Damned lucky, that. Another of the girls at work mentioned the name of the place they were staying."

An expatriate Brit, Bennett managed a group of mutual funds at Pierce, Fairbrother, the same brokerage house where Phoebe Michel worked as an analyst. Immensely successful from the earliest days of his career, he was a Wall Street legend. He and Phoebe had remained friends after their breakup three years ago. It was through Dennis that Greg had met his future fiancée.

"He called me, a little after three," Phoebe added. "I just got here an hour ago."

Greg wondered if he dared hope what he found himself thinking. "You said hidden, Den. It can't be possible that no one else saw what happened. I mean, can it? On Fifth Avenue?"

"It's what the news reports are all saying," Bennett replied. "There was little or no traffic. And it all happened so fast. Apparently, the police have been unable to locate any witnesses."

There was a hollowness in Greg's tone now when he spoke. "Killed who?"

"Another fellow who attended the same party we did. Name of Webster. Guest of Bill Hoag. And get this. He's the brother of Diana Webster. The rock star."

Greg gaped, and not because of who his victim's sister was. He'd spent the last six weeks in close contact with Bruce Webster. Telenet was poised to announce Tuesday a merger with Webster's firm that would marry the telecommunications innovator with Omnicom's revolutionary new digital subscriber technology. It was an advancement that would quadruple the speed of Telenet's real-time video-imaging capability and give them dominance in the international teleconferencing arena. Both companies expected their stocks to skyrocket, once the announcement was made. Greg quickly tried to weigh the impact of Webster's untimely death against the impact of the merger news. Speculators who knew anything about the high-tech field were a hard-hearted pack of jackals. A hit-and-run death was not loaded up with the same clouding intrigue as an outright murder. The Omnicom technology was real, and the current market, starved for it. Nichols forced himself to face his old business school classmate directly.

"I can't get away with this, Den. You know that. God, how will investors react when they find out it was Telenet's own CFO who hit the poor bastard? The longer I hide, the worse it will look."

Bennett's reply was startling in its vehemence. "The hell you can't, mate. I'm in this as deep as you are. We both left the scene. I shoved your drink-sodden arse into the passenger seat, took the wheel, and drove the damned car myself."

Greg let go of the counter and pushed off from it. He collapsed into an empty chair at Phoebe's side to cover his face. As hard as he tried, all he could remember of events last night was his arrival at that party. He and Dennis had sat at their table only briefly, then headed off to sit at the bar. Bennett liked to mix and mingle. Always had. He'd been the one to suggest framboise with their champagne. Tiny bubbles mixed with the subtle essence of raspberries.

"I can only remember three drinks." His voice was muffled by his hands as he said it. He heard Dennis snort.

"Three? You're joking. After your second bottle of PJ, I stopped counting. You were having too good a time."

Dear God. What had he done?

* * *

Joe Dante entered his eleventh-floor SID cubicle to drag out his desk chair and drop into it. Still in his topcoat, he pushed aside debris on the corner of his desk and put his feet up.

"You look like the sandman used ground glass," Jumbo commented. "How's Diana?"

"It's not shaping up to be one of her better years. At least not so far." Joe tilted his coffee mug toward him to inspect it for filth. It needed a rinse. "But you consider what she'd been through, the past eight hours, I'd say she's hanging in there." He motioned toward their Mr. Coffee. "Who drank all the java?"

"Napier's been here since dawn. Hit the lab. Picked up what they've got to date."

Another commander might have been surprised, but not Dante. With the chief's blessing, he'd hand-picked the members of his squad. Guy Napier, the youngest of them, was as fiercely loyal as he was te-nacious and smart. For his boss, tragedy had struck close to home, and he was closing ranks, just like any family member would.

On cue, Guy arrived outside the cubicle, a yellow legal pad and wad of fax transmissions in hand. "Morning, Lou," he greeted Joe. Then he turned to Richardson. "Telenet's still dragging ass, getting us that guest list. Something about the holiday and someone they can't seem to reach. Meanwhile, I just got off the horn with the duty captain at the Nine-teenth."

"No luck, I take it?" Beasley was reading the younger man's expression.

"Nuh uh. The neighborhood canvass drew goose

eggs. Cold as it was last night, only two doormen on Sixty-first Street were outside at time of impact. Both saw something late model speed away. Dark-colored. No plate, no occupants, no make."

"Couldn't have been worse timing," Dante observed. "At that hour, the Geritol set is all in bed, but it was still too early for most parties to break up."

"Watch it with the Geritol set shit," Richardson growled. "I was in bed by ten."

Napier went on to bring Joe up to speed with the details he'd already learned about the car. "The way I see it, there's hope in the hotel guest register and party guest list. Meanwhile, we need to start contacting every parking garage, lot, and body shop in the five boroughs."

"You ran the hotel list by Motor Vehicles?" Joe asked.

"Yep. Nada from New York, but I'm still waiting for Jersey and Connecticut to check in."

"Any idea how many dark green, late model Saabs are registered in the tri-state area?"

Napier glanced down at his yellow pad. "Eight hundred thirty-seven registered in the downstate New York region, alone. Eleven hundred six, statewide."

That Bloody Mary had kicked in sufficiently to hold the worst effects of Greg's abuse in check. Still, as he stood with the cold from Bennett's concrete garage floor seeping up through the soles of his moccasins, he felt as though his brain had been run through a meat grinder. The left taillight of his car was missing entirely, the lead wires and a plastic connector socket left dangling. The Saab's crumpled skin looked like a stomped soda can. The impact had come dangerously close to crippling the back wheel, the fender bent so far in that it missed the tire by less than an inch. As Greg saw what must have transpired, the image flashing before his mind's eye, another wave of nausea hit him. He thanked Christ the car was leased to the investment corporation of which he was the sole proprietor, and not to him in his own name. If the police did have a make and model, they were sure to check a list of New Year's party guests for possible owners.

"How could I?" he murmured. It was more to himself than to either Phoebe or Dennis. "I've never driven drunk in my life."

With Bennett at Greg's side, Phoebe wandered slowly around the car. Dennis laid a consoling hand on Greg's shoulder. "It's as much my fault as yours. If I hadn't been so squiffed myself, I surely wouldn't have let you take the helm. Frankly, I'm amazed I managed to get us here."

Greg turned, stiff-necked, to face him. "Bruce Webster, of all people. What am I going to do, Den?"

Heartthrob handsome and taller than Nichols, Bennett had an almost spellbinding gaze. It penetrated to the core of its subject and sank hooks. "For starters? We need to give ourselves a day or two to cool off. I, for one, need at least that much time to organize my thoughts."

"Thoughts about what? I killed a man."

"And I was in the car with you." Once Bennett had the hooks sunk, he would cut no slack. "You need to get your head straight, mate. Need time to look at your dilemma from all angles. You might be tempted to flush your own future down the commode, but I'd rather you didn't flush mine along with it."

Across the car, on the opposite side of the garage, Phoebe contemplated a rack of brooms, mops, and a shelf containing cleaning supplies. "You still have that housekeeper who comes during the week, Den? That could be a problem."

"She's in Orlando. Visiting her sister. Not back until Sunday next."

"I'd make damned sure," she warned. "If she's the same one you had three years ago, she's got to be the nosiest woman on the planet." Phoebe completed her circuit of the garage as she spoke. Then, eased up next to Greg, she let one hip make soft contact and slid an arm around him to pull close. "I'll drive you back to the city, lover. How do you feel now? You still look awful."

A year had elapsed since they'd started dating, and Nichols still marveled at his great good fortune. Aside from the fact that it was high time for a man in his position to find himself a wife, he loved everything about her. The clarity of her thinking processes, her laugh, how she smelled, and how they fit together while making love.

"What am I going to do, Pheeb? I've never felt this helpless."

"You're going to do just what Den suggested, honey. Get some distance. Then think about your options. You might decide to do nothing." She lifted her face to kiss him. "Think about us, too. There's nothing you can do that will bring that man back to life."

"I realize that," he complained. "But I still feel like I'm on the deck of a sinking ship. Without a lifeboat in sight."

For Sid Cooperman and Leo Swift of Cooperman & Swift Investments, New Year's Day was a time for prognostication. Stockbrokers to the plodding but surefooted, neither man much enjoyed football or the usual pressing hordes of family. Both men loved their work, valued the opinion of the other, and liked this quiet time at the office, once a year, when no one was around to bother them. As partners, from the downturn of 1959 through two serious recessions and the crash of '87, they'd both played it safe and tight to the line. In a world where hunch bets and rash speculation were all too usual, Sid and Leo had always done their homework. Each New Year's morning, they tried to look into the future; to see beyond the tips of their dicks, and thereby avoid stepping on them in the months to come.

The partners were in Cooperman's office, on the third floor of the brokerage's 44th Street midtown building. They had coffee, cream cheese, lox, and bagels on the low table between them, and piles of printout strewn within easy reach. A head taller than Sid, Leo Swift relaxed in a comfortable leather club chair and listened while his friend of over thirty years spoke. Sid was their detail man, while Leo had an earnest, eager beaver manner that made him the better front man for their garment district and midtown office worker clientele. Mostly from the outer boroughs, their clients seemed to like Leo's easy familiarity, and how his craggy visage was perpetually knit in an expression of deep concern for their financial well-being.

"You remember that new client, I told you called middle of last month?" Cooperman was saying. "Character who threw the huge numbers around?"

"Sure," Leo replied. "We both figured he was fulla shit."

Bald as a gazing globe, Sid paused to rub the top of his gleaming head. He had an account activity report in his lap and was frowning down at it. "Well, maybe not. Check this out."

Leo took the offered report and scanned.

"Late Friday, he transferred a million six into that account," Sid continued. "Said it was a gesture of good faith; to show he's serious about the play he wants to make this week."

Sure enough, the account opened in the names of Randall Andrews and his wife, Veronica, was showing a $1.6 million transfer from Pierce, Fairbrother, one of the bigger downtown houses. The standard Cooperman & Swift commission on any large securities purchase was one half of one percent. The simple fact that Andrews had put this money into play meant that they stood to earn eight thousand dollars in fees.

"So who the hell is this guy?" Leo murmured. "We know anybody at Pierce, Fairbrother we could call?"

When Cooperman got anxious, his naked scalp prickled. After the lousy quarter they'd just had, they needed this one to be real. "Who cares, Leo? Andrews and his wife could be fronts for the Michigan Militia for all we care. He's claiming there will be thirty million in that account by Wednesday, and right now I'm inclined to give him the benefit of the doubt."

"This is a fair-size gesture of good faith," Swift agreed. He handed the report back across. "I guess I don't give a rat's ass, he's a direct descendant of Genghis Khan."

Sid nodded his agreement. "Only thing that matters to us is whether we can get our hands on thirty million worth of bearer bonds. I called. The Federal Reserve Bank downtown has over two hundred million worth in their vault. It shouldn't be a problem."

Bearer bonds were considered antiquated instruments in this age of electronic interest payments, but Leo could understand their appeal to some. Less bulky than bundles of hundred-dollar bills, and more easily disposed of than gems, they were as convertible as cash. "Just make damned sure we get all his dough up front," he warned. "Anybody this eager t' get his hands on that much liquid cash? He ain't gonna be around, tryin' t' find a chair once the music stops."

FOUR

Most workdays, Detectives Don Grover and Rusty Heckman carpooled into Manhattan from Queens. Their morning commute this New Year's Day differed from the usual in that traffic through the Midtown Tunnel was almost nonexistent. Heckman had the wheel. Grover slouched against the passenger door, his color off.

"You know that asshole in those commercials?" Don asked. "The one so thrilled he's drinking Ballatore?"

It got him a blank look.

"You know. The one who goes around asking everyone how the name of this wonderful sparklin' wine in his glass is spelled?"

"Vaguely," Heckman murmured. One of those nifty new BMW M-3 roadsters was coming up fast on his tail as he passed a lumbering cab. He cut over to make way. "We don't watch much TV."

Grover grunted. "Well I wanna find that asshole

an' carve how it's spelled into his fuckin' forehead. Then maybe his head'll hurt as much as mine does right now."

Rusty watched the rear end of that gorgeous little roadster as it scooted away, and dreamed of owning one himself. He chuckled. "Serves you right, Donnie. All that sweet, sparkling crap is headache in a bottle."

"Never again," Grover swore.

Heckman had his doubts. His partner was in the throes of midlife crisis. Ever since his divorce, three years ago, he'd dated a long string of Generation X'ers, most young enough to be his daughters. It was yet another of their parties that Donnie had attended last night, with yet another child. Decent champagne was as alien to that bunch as dry martinis.

"So who was last night's prize?" he asked.

"I don't wanna talk about it."

"Sure you do. You always do. The tungsten tits, steel wheels, and what a wonderful sense of fun she has."

Grover leveled an unfriendly glare at him. "Gimme a break, Rust. I'm dyin' here."

"I take it you didn't score."

"Fuck you."

Fifteen minutes later, as they pulled into a slot in the Big Building's parking garage, Rusty glanced over once again at his green-gilled partner. This time, he had the needle retracted. "You gonna be okay?"

"Jury's still out. I hadn't planned on workin' t'day."

"And it ain't written anywhere you got to."

Don waved the notion away. "It's better I be

movin'. Them doughnuts I ate helped. I'll be aw-right."

Heckman tugged at the door release and retrieved his keys from the ignition. "Okay, but you insist on drinking at the kiddie end of the pool, I suggest you start bringing your own bottle."

Upstairs, they found Joe Dante and Jumbo Rich-ardson in their SID cubicle, with Guy Napier stand-ing in the doorway. They and Napier dragged over chairs from adjacent offices, and the five of them crowded into the tiny space. Dante asked the team's junior member to give them an update. By the time he finished, everyone was aware that, unless the car proved to be stolen, the Saab 9000 would be the quickest route to discovering who had killed Bruce Webster.

Dante referred to a page in his notebook. "I just got off the horn with Central Records. Asked them for the thefts of any late model Saabs during the past seventy-two hours. They've got nothing in dark green, but then it's early yet. Most borough com-mands are slow reporting, because of the holiday."

"You put it over the teletype when?" Grover asked.

"Little more than half an hour ago."

Don shrugged. "Any station house that's got somethin' suspicious, that's more'n enough time for them t' report back. Still, there's the chance the owner ain't discovered it missin' yet. Half the city's still in bed."

Dante flipped to another page of his notebook. "I'm not sure how this fits, or if it does at all, but I've gotta mention it. This morning, Diana told me her brother had run into some sort of problem with the deal he was working on. He was so distracted yesterday, he almost forgot to pick up his tux."

Heckman frowned. "What's that got to do with him getting hit?"

"Probably nothing," Joe admitted. "But she wondered if his head was still in the clouds somewhere, when he stepped off that curb last night."

"Don't really matter much, does it?" Grover countered. "Where his head was? His ass was in the path of a car. Dude behind the wheel drove off."

"I'm curious t' know how drunk he might'a been," Jumbo piped up. "Joey called Rocky Conklin. Asked him to do the autopsy personally."

"When?" Heckman wondered.

"Said he ain't much for parades on TV. Things at the morgue are pretty dead most Sundays, anyway."

"Don't do that to me," Grover moaned. "I'm suffering here."

Guy Napier had put together an organizational chart. He cleared his throat to get their attention and propped it up on one knee. "I think we should split it up like this. I'm already running with the forensics end. Rust and Donnie?" He focused on the paunchy, frizzy-haired redhead and his slouched, rail-thin partner. "We need to kick off a precinct-by-precinct check of body shops. And parking garages. Get them on the lookout. Which would free you two up, Lou," he told his boss, "to do the morgue, and chase whatever else comes our way."

Greg Nichols noticed the Ryder box van parked at the end of Bennett's driveway when he stepped outside the Pound Ridge house for the journey back to the city. A big one, at least twenty-five feet long.

"What's that about?" he asked his friend. Dennis was hardly the do-it-yourself mover type. The presence of such a vehicle, parked on his property, struck Greg as odd.

Bennett had a back door of the Land Rover open as he paused. He located the object of Greg's attention, waved a dismissive hand at it, and continued on into the car. "My next-door neighbor asked if he could leave it there. They had a party last night. Needed the space in their drive."

"He's moving?"

Dennis smiled, apparently amused by the notion. "With one of those? I hardly think so. He collects folk art. There's a show that he's taking some of his prize pieces to, somewhere in Massachusetts, I think."

An impatient Phoebe was ready to roll. "C'mon, Gregory. The garage is locked. Your car is safe, right, Den?"

"I should think so," Bennett agreed. "My neighbor is a retired insurance company executive with two bad knees and the curiosity of a tree stump."

With reluctance, Nichols climbed into the front passenger seat. He didn't like the idea of anyone on the property while Dennis was away. "No one else has a key?" he asked.

"We've already been over all that," Phoebe snapped. She certainly had less at stake legally than Bennett, but she had much more, emotionally. Greg's jumpiness was an irritant. Once she got them down the drive and out onto the road, headed south, she glanced over at her fiancé again. Her earlier scowl was still fixed on her face.

"You need to think long and hard about what more damage can be done, Gregory. If you wind up serving time for manslaughter, who would ever give you another job? You've worked all your professional life to get where you are."

That, and so much more, had already occurred to Greg. "The police never tell the media all they know," he argued. "What if there *are* witnesses?"

"Then that would be our rum luck, wouldn't it," Bennett growled from the backseat. "We have no choice but to roll the dice, and hope we don't crap out. There's really no alternative."

The trim, athletic Phoebe sat stiff in her seat, jaw set and eyes locked on the road ahead. "Think about what it would mean to actually go to prison, Greg. It changes people. Never mind the fact that my biological clock is ticking and that, by the time you got out, it would be too late for either of us to start a family."

He shot her a sharp, sideways glance. "You're saying you wouldn't wait. I understand that. I wouldn't ask you to."

"I'm saying you need to think about being branded a felon for the rest of your life. And to think about poor Dennis. It's a miracle he didn't get caught last night. He fetched your fat from the fire."

Convinced long ago that dead men *do* tell tales, Joe Dante and Jumbo Richardson had developed a solid relationship with the forensic pathologist considered by many to be the best slab man in the country. Dr. Rocky Conklin's basement office in the Medical Examiner's First Avenue and 30th Street headquarters was familiar turf. Over the years, they'd collaborated on a number of notable homicide investigations where Conklin's insights were instrumental in bringing them to resolution.

Dr. Conklin washed his hands at a sink outside his glass-partitioned office as the two detectives entered. He dried with paper towels and grabbed a clipboard, his greeting spoken past teeth clamped around one of his ever-present cigars. "You and your buddy grab chairs, Cowboy. Be wit' ya in a sec." Stripping his soiled lab coat from his pallid, bony body as he hurried off, he tossed it into a laundry cart.

Joe and Jumbo stepped behind the glass, not at all offended by the brusqueness of the man's manner. Conklin hardly bothered to give most cops the time of day. But Dante? Joe had thrown too much good business his way.

"Be a while before I get the whole blood tissue workup back from the lab," he said as he entered in a rush. His clipboard tossed onto his blotter, Rocky eased into his desk chair and put his feet up. "Had a few minutes, so I put one sample through a few paces of my own. Blood alcohol, point oh-seven-six. Hardly drunk, huh?"

"Not by a long shot," Dante agreed. "Anything else strike you as odd?"

"Not really." Rocky dug out a fresh cigar from his humidor and found a clipping tool in his top desk drawer. "So who was the dead guy's girlfriend?"

"Girlfriend?" Joe asked.

"Took a date to this gig, correct? So where was she when he gets whacked? You said there are no witnesses."

"Whoa," Joe slowed him down. "Back up. You say he had a date like it's a fact. But he didn't. At least not that Diana or anyone else mentioned. What makes you say that?".

With cheeks puffed quickly in and out, Rocky set fire to his new smoke. He spoke with his head wreathed. "Lipstick. Smeared on his cheek, neck, and back of his left hand. Heavy odor of perfume on him, too. Looks to me like he'd been in a heavy clinch. Traces of that lipstick on one of his front teeth, too."

Puzzled, Dante reached for the phone on Conklin's desk and punched in Diana's home number. After four rings, he got their machine. "Diana. Brian. It's Joe. Pick up if you're there."

A brief squeal down the line was followed by a muffled, "Hold on." He heard the machine click off, and then Diana's voice, now sharp and clear. "Sorry about that. We're monitoring. What's up?"

"Did your brother take a date to that party last night?"

"I'd think he would have mentioned it. Why?"

"Just one of those routine questions I never asked." She was under enough stress, he didn't need to feed it. "You got any idea who he sat with?"

"His host, I imagine. The Telenet CEO. Somebody Hoag. That's who invited him. What's this about, Joe?"

Dante jotted the last name in his notebook. "Me, just trying to establish a time line," he lied. "Who might've seen Bruce last. You know what flight your sister's on yet?"

"I was just going to call you. TWA. Number five

thirty-six. St. Louis to La Guardia. Gets in at four-oh-eight."

"You still want the company?"

"Love it. If it's not too much trouble."

He told her to look for him around three-fifteen, and cradled the receiver. "No date," he told Conklin and Beasley.

"Makes you wonder who laid that lip-lock on him, don't it?" Jumbo mused. "Come midnight, New Year's Eve, people get friendly. You think that's what it was?"

"Real friendly, by the sound of it," Joe replied. "His host was the Telenet CEO. Let's get an address on him."

When Greg Nichols arrived at his East 75th Street apartment building, he complained to Phoebe that he still wasn't feeling well; that he needed to sleep. She had Dennis to drop off, farther south, on Sutton Place, and asked Greg to call her later. Greg's thoughts were jumbled and confused, threatening to unravel his sanity, and what he really wanted was to be alone. He kissed his fiancée on the cheek and told her not to worry. He'd get a handle on his feelings, once he managed to get some rest and his head stopped pounding. Then he thanked Bennett for what he'd done, all too aware of how hung-out-in-the-breeze his friend was feeling. This was crazy. Things like this didn't happen to people like them. They were pillars of the community.

Nichols was alone in his apartment for about twenty minutes, three more ibuprofen under his belt and still nowhere near ready to sleep, when he began to have serious second thoughts about what he'd been told. He just couldn't believe that he'd hit and killed a man, without any recollection of the event. God, he didn't even remember the process of getting drunk.

From where he'd flopped atop his bed, still dressed in those borrowed street clothes, he rose again to pace with the nervous aimlessness of a caged animal. It was over fifteen years since he'd last consumed alcohol to any regrettable excess, but the hangover he suffered now felt like nothing he could recollect. His knowledge of drugs was limited, never having done any, but still, he would swear that this was what the aftermath of a drug binge would feel like.

He forced himself to sit on his sofa, curtains drawn against the gloomy day outside, and thought hard about what the presence of drugs in his system might imply. He had no idea how he could have ingested them, or what motive anyone would have for playing such a dirty trick, but it was the only reasonable explanation for how he felt, and how he could have done what Bennett was claiming. He was still searching for answers to those questions when an idea came to him. His parka collected from the entry hall closet, Greg headed for the door. The Lenox Hill emergency room was just two blocks away. He was going to get himself a blood test, and put at least one question to rest. The answer to it might lead to other answers, and help prevent him from going off his nut.

* * *

The address of Telenet CEO William Hoag was on East 81st Street between Madison and Fifth. When Dante and Richardson arrived there, they were informed by the doorman that Mr. Hoag was out.

"There happen to be a Mrs. Hoag?" Jumbo asked.

The uniformed man allowed that there was, and that she was in, so far as he knew. After a brief conversation with her, via intercom, the doorman offered the receiver to whichever detective wanted to take it.

"Wants to know what it's about. Says she's in the middle of a business call."

Dante stepped up. "Mrs. Hoag? Lieutenant Dante," he introduced himself. "NYPD Special Investigations."

"What is this about, Lieutenant?" The female voice was low and husky. He pictured the post-Bogart Bacall, maybe a little heavier.

"My partner and I would like to talk to you; about last night."

"What about it, Lieutenant? My husband and I went to a party."

"We understand Bruce Webster sat with you, at your table." He took a flyer there, not having had that fact confirmed.

The woman's tone became more sympathetic. "That poor man. I'm not sure what I can tell you, but sure. Come on up. I'm on the phone with one of my partners. I should be off by the time you get here."

Three minutes later, Joe and Jumbo stepped off the elevator into the dark paneled vestibule that separated the sixteenth floor's only two apartments. The door to 16-B had been left slightly ajar. When Richardson rang the bell, Mrs. Hoag called out and invited them to enter.

They found her in a living room to the left of the entry hall. With large windows that overlooked mid-Manhattan to the south, it had the kind of dramatic view no cop could afford, but most presidents of major corporations and their wives could. What looked like legal briefs were stacked neatly on the coffee table before a woman who looked nothing like her intercom voice. She was blond, with thick, straight hair of shoulder length, worn back from her face with a wide black band. Dressed casually in an oversize denim work shirt, she had its cuffs turned back from slender, delicate wrists. Bare feet protruded past gray leggings. Her face was striking, with a wide, sensuous mouth. She glanced up, raised a finger to indicate she'd be off in a moment, and waved them toward empty chairs. Joe wandered over to take one, and sat while Beasley continued to stand.

With some forceful persistence, she managed to conclude her telephone conversation. When she hung up the phone, she did it with a flourish. "I do apologize, gentlemen." On her feet, she swept across to Jumbo, hand extended. "I'm Vivian Hoag."

"Lieutenant Richardson," he introduced himself. "Lieutenant Dante spoke with you."

Joe felt her intent hazel eyes appraise him as he unfolded his lanky frame from the chair. He was surprised to see how tiny she was. While she'd been sitting, the long, slender lines of her build were deceptive. Now, he towered over her by at least a foot. "We appreciate your time, ma'am," he said. "We're trying to understand what happened outside the

Sherry Netherland last night. We've had trouble locating witnesses."

She returned to her place on the sofa as he spoke. Perched there, with her feet tucked beneath her, she spread her hands in a gesture of helplessness. "I can't tell you how terrible I felt when I heard. I was still inside at the party when word reached my husband."

"He was your husband's guest, correct?" Jumbo prodded.

"Oh yes. It's probably no secret now; that his company and Telenet are about to merge. The announcement won't be made until Tuesday, but Bill invited him to the party as a sort of celebration."

"Who else was at your table?" Joe asked. "Did Webster bring a date?"

Something flickered behind her eyes before she forced a smile his way. "Bill thought Bruce might enjoy Andrea Hill. She's one of the managers of Telenet's pension fund. I wouldn't call her Bruce's date, though. Not per se."

"How did they hit it off?" Jumbo asked.

She pursed her lips and shook her handsome head. "I can't say, really. They were pleasant enough to each other, of course, but I don't think she was his type. Or vice versa, for that matter. And to tell you the truth, he seemed a little preoccupied all night. I imagine it was the deal."

"So they didn't leave together," Richardson guessed.

The notion appeared to amuse her. "No, Lieutenant."

"Did he talk to or dance with anyone that you can recall?" Joe wondered.

"After dinner, Bill took him around to some of the other tables. He danced with me a few times."

Beasley leaned forward in his chair, elbows on his knees and fingers steepled beneath his broad, square chin. His was a face that could turn mean and nasty when the purpose served. Right now, it looked intent. "Where were he and Miss Hill at midnight? You remember?"

She smiled outright. "You mean when everyone indulges in twenty or thirty seconds of unrestrained hedonism? She was on the dance floor, with my husband. He was at our table."

Dante looked directly into those wide, frank eyes. "With you?"

She nodded.

"The Medical Examiner found traces of lipstick on his cheek and collar."

"Ah." She might have colored slightly. It was difficult to tell with her deep, midwinter tan. "You want to know if we indulged in some of that unrestrained hedonism ourselves." Her gaze remained steady, refusing to falter. "We'd both had quite a bit of New Year's cheer, Lieutenant. We probably did."

Mystery solved. No date, just a little alcohol-fueled friendliness on the part of the host's inebriated wife. To judge by what Rocky Conklin had determined about Bruce's condition at the time of his death, it sounded like Mrs. Hoag probably had more of that cheer than the target of her affections. Looking at her, Joe doubted that Webster had much minded.

"Was Mr. Webster's preoccupation with somethin' that your husband might know about?" Beasley asked.

"This merger was very much on both their minds, Lieutenant. They'd worked on it together for months."

"You expect him home soon?" he pressed.

If she was worried that her husband might learn she'd slipped his honored guest a little tongue last night, Dante saw no evidence of it. She faced the question openly. "He left for the office, early this morning. I'm sure he needed to monitor reaction to news of last night's tragedy, and manage damage control. I've got no idea when he'll be back." She unfolded her legs from beneath her and got settled again with her bare feet stretched out beneath the coffee table. "You'll see the bandage sooner or later, so you might as well get it from me, first. We had words after the party. When they escalated, I threw a vase at him. He spent a few hours at Beth Israel emergency, getting stitches."

On the sidewalk outside, Beasley Richardson paused to crane his neck and stare upward toward the sixteenth floor. "Hot damn, partner. You see the body on that woman?"

"No, buddy. I'm blind," Joe retorted. "A woman like that came on to me? I doubt I'd run off quite as fast as it sounds like Bruce did."

"I dunno," Jumbo reasoned. "I doubt that kinda merger was quite what his new boss had in mind."

FIVE

When a rare parking place manifested itself across from Dennis Bennett's Sutton Place building, he suggested that Phoebe come up with him for a nerve-calming drink. While she'd been up half the night and was dead on her feet, she still rode the tail of an adrenaline high. A drink sounded like a good idea.

Bennett's apartment had once been Phoebe's second home, but that seemed a lifetime away now. Back then, she'd just started to make a reputation for herself at Pierce, Fairbrother, analyzing public offerings in the fast-paced high-tech field. Dennis—already an assets manager of some renown—had recently signed on there to run a new group of mutual funds. It was her analysis acumen that first attracted him to her. Romance came later, with the typical whirlwind characteristics she now associated with all of Bennett's undertakings. In time, it had simply blown itself out.

"You've changed your furniture again," she observed. "Who's the lucky gal this time?"

Dennis took her ski jacket to hang it in the entry closet as he chuckled. "You know me too well, Phoebe love. But actually, this one I did myself. The last was so dreadful, I called the decorator the afternoon she packed her bags."

Phoebe wondered if the urge was actually primal; for one woman to thoroughly loathe the tastes of her predecessor. She'd succumbed to it herself. But then the tastes of her predecessor *had* been atrocious. And Dennis had made it so easy. With a net worth of thirty to forty million dollars, he could afford to indulge these petty jealousies. And unlike Greg, he had no strong decorating tastes of his own. Evidence this current layout. Expensive, without a doubt. But it had all the individuality of a set-piece from the Maurice Villency showroom. Nothing about the occupant of this apartment was betrayed anywhere; not by even one solitary object. How like Dennis, she thought. Physically, he was a tall, fit, truly beautiful specimen. In his appearance and in his occupation he was all the component pieces of an ideal mate. In reality, he'd proven less than the sum total of his parts.

"So what will it be?" he asked. "I think we should beg the gods for a change of luck, and toast them with a pair of Bennett's famous Pimm's Cups."

"A Bloody Mary might sit better, thanks," she begged off. "If it's not too much trouble." Phoebe selected an end of a cream leather sofa and eased herself into it. Not until she'd sunk six inches deep into its soft embrace did she realize how truly exhausted she was. She yawned.

"You look as tired as I feel," he observed as he approached with her drink. "Spicy, love. Just the way you like them."

Phoebe accepted the glass and took a grateful sip. "Perfect."

Forgoing the Pimm's, Dennis built a second Bloody Mary for himself, and lifted it in salute. "To an upturn, my dear. In your immediate fortunes, and mine."

She watched him over the rim of her glass as he eased onto the cushion beside her and took a first sip. "I'm worried about him, Den. He's more honorable than either of us."

Bennett snorted. "And just what is that supposed to mean?"

She fixed him with as direct a look as she'd ever given him. "You know exactly. People like us bend when the chips are down. Or the odds are against us. I'm not sure Greg will. The only thing that matters to him about all this is the fact that he killed a man."

"Surely he won't go to the police." Dennis said it with an edge of horror in his voice. "Not once he's had a chance to think about it. He's not that stupid."

She shook her head. "It has nothing to do with stupidity. It's his moral makeup. Sometimes it astonishes me that he's managed to get as far in this world as he has. There's not a ruthless bone in his body."

Bennett grunted and threw back half his drink. "Wonderful. And I was fool enough to take it on myself to help him. Where does that leave me? Is he going to hang me out to dry?"

She eased a steadying hand onto his knee. "I didn't say that, Den. I said I'm worried. That's all."

"What a comfort." His voice dripped sarcasm. "If

I hadn't been so drunk myself, I might have considered my options more clearly."

Her fingers on him tightened almost involuntarily. "Don't say that, Dennis. Please. You did the right thing."

He snorted. "Did I? I'm an accomplice to felony vehicular manslaughter. If that lily to whom you're engaged wilts, I may well go to prison."

Phoebe set her drink aside and leaned forward as a fresh wave of panic washed over her. One hand went to the side of Dennis's face. She could recall a time when she'd thought him almost too pretty, and herself too ordinary but fortunate to have been singled out as the object of his affections. Time had tempered so much of that. She liked to think she'd gotten better-looking with age. The baby fat of her twenties had melted away to sculpt her face. And over that same span of time, the host with the most had seen alcohol and stress etch tiny lines in his boyish beauty. She caressed that older, time-tempered visage, her fingers tracing the crow's-feet at the corners of his eyes.

"He won't wilt, Den. I swear it. I won't let him."

Then, without really knowing why, she kissed him, oh so tenderly. Their lips met for little more than an instant. An expression of her gratitude? Or perhaps some lame attempt to put his mind at ease; to get it off the dilemma at hand? She wasn't prepared for the spark it ignited, and had barely begun to pull back when she felt his body begin to move toward her. That one hand, still at rest on his leg, felt the flexing muscles of his thigh. The hand on his cheek sensed his eagerness. Rather than retreat in the face of it, she let it come to her. Their mouths met again, both hungry this time. He fumbled to get rid of his drink, and nearly upended it on the coffee table before it was set to rest. That gave her only an instant's pause; to wonder what she thought she was doing.

Because it was a Sunday, in the middle of the three-day New Year's weekend, the Telenet executives who'd gathered inside the Telenet Tower on 47th Street and Lexington Avenue were not dressed in their customary work attire. However, nothing else about the atmosphere there was casual. According to the ex-cop security guard who escorted Dante and Richardson upstairs from the lobby, Bill Hoag and his management team had been joined by the company chairman and half the board of directors for the emergency meeting now in progress. When Dante and Richardson were announced, they were asked to wait. Twenty minutes into it, Jumbo could tell that Joey was getting irritated.

"Feels like a council of war, don't it?" Beasley observed.

Dante tossed aside the copy of *Fortune* he'd been thumbing as the door that separated them from the interior of the conference room swung open. A slender, dark-haired man of medium height stepped through to approach. He had a two-inch square of gauze taped to his right temple. Otherwise, the most notable thing about him was his apparent youth. This guy hardly looked thirty.

"Gentlemen. Sorry to keep you waiting. Bill Hoag." He extended his hand.

Dante presented his gold lieutenant's shield and

I.D. "We appreciate your time, sir. Your wife told us we'd probably find you here."

Beasley saw the man grimace. "The news about Bruce Webster came as a terrible shock. To all of us."

"I understand," Dante acknowledged. "We're investigating the circumstances of his death. His sister tells us there was some sort of business problem that was pressing. It seemed to be heavy on his mind, all yesterday. Any light you could shed there would be helpful."

The Telenet CEO sat in a chair that faced theirs, clearly puzzled. "I don't understand. I thought it was a simple hit-and-run."

"Probably was," Dante replied. "But the car was in reverse, moving at speed, which is odd. There's also the question of why he didn't see it coming."

"He'd just come from a New Year's party, Lieutenant. You don't think that alcohol was a factor?"

Joey gave him that, with a nod. "But his blood alcohol levels seem to indicate he wasn't drunk. Not even close. So we're wondering what was troubling him, and if that might have been a factor."

Hoag took a moment to consider what he would say next. "This is a touchy area," he said at length. "If you talked to Webster's sister, you might have heard of the merger pending between Telenet and her brother's company."

Dante nodded, and then gestured toward the conference room door. "I imagine you're a little concerned about what his death will do to your stock price. And Omnicom's, too. Gotta have you a little edgy, I'd think."

Hoag scowled and sat a little straighter. "It isn't going into the tank, if that's what you're implying,

Lieutenant. Yes, Bruce had agreed to stay on as president of the new Omnicom subsidiary, but it's the technology we're buying that will spark real investor interest. Omnicom's new digital processor is so revolutionary, we're talking about a decade of global dominance in teleconferencing and all other real-time video image transmission."

Jumbo listened to this spiel, still trying to decide what to make of this guy. The casual weekender khakis Hoag wore had starched, razor-sharp creases. The loafers were hand-stitched Italian. His demeanor was so stiff that Beasley would bet Vivian had thrown that vase at him, just to see what would shatter: it, or his head. "So what was this thing his sister talked about, that preyed so heavy on his mind?" he pressed. "The picture she paints don't look quite so rosy."

Hoag fidgeted with the cuff of his golf sweater. "You're forcing me into delicate territory again."

"Hit-and-run or not, this is still a homicide investigation," Dante reminded him.

"I understand that." There was defensiveness in Hoag's tone. "But you've got to understand that no matter what you've heard, this new Omnicom technology is real. Telenet is a far cry from buying a pig in a poke, no matter what reservations Bruce was having. Our test engineers found a tiny numbers flaw. That's all."

"Which means what? Exactly?" Dante pressed.

Hoag tried for nonchalant. He shrugged and pushed a disarming smile at them. "As far as Telenet is concerned? Nothing. We've seen the processor work with our own eyes. Maybe not quite as fast as Omnicom claimed at first, but quick enough to blow away our competition. Even after our Tuesday announcement, there will be plenty of lead time to iron out that one little kink."

Beasley held up a hand to stop him. "There's somethin' I'm missin' here. This wonderful new technology is so remarkable, it don't matter who dies or gets arrested for baby rape, investors from all over the globe are gonna beat down your door, tryin' t' buy a piece of your action. So what could have had Mr. Webster so twisted sideways?"

Hoag appeared to be losing patience with them. "Bruce Webster is—or, uh, was—that irksome type of perfectionist who makes a wonderful visionary and engineer, but the worst kind of businessman. He wanted us to delay our Tuesday announcement, not because the technology doesn't work, but because it doesn't work as perfectly as he'd like. Considering the amount of money that Telenet has invested in press conference preproduction, he was not being reasonable."

"Preproduction means what?" Joey asked.

"Contacting the business media. Our marketing staff has gone to great lengths to hype this event. If we canceled a press conference that has this much hoopla preceding it, the marketplace would interpret it only one way. Investor confidence could collapse overnight."

"In other words," Beasley concluded, "you cancel that announcement, your stock takes a header."

Hoag nodded. "I and the other officers here have a responsibility to our stockholders, Lieutenant."

Dante shifted in the chair alongside Beasley and moved to change the subject. "We appreciate your candor, sir. And realize that this is a difficult time.

There's one other item we're hoping you can help us with. Your guest list from the party last night."

It caught Hoag with his mind in the clouds somewhere. He blinked. "I'm sorry. Our guest list? What could . . . ?"

"The taillight fragments and paint chips we recovered from the scene are from a 1996 Saab 9000," Joey explained. "We need to run that list past Motor Vehicles."

Now Hoag looked troubled. "You think that one of the guests from our own party could have . . . ?" He let it dangle.

"It's a possibility. One we can't afford to overlook," Dante assured him. "And one of my men, a Detective Napier, has had trouble locating anyone from your company who can get that list for him. It being a holiday and all."

"I'll give my secretary a call. If you'll leave me this Detective Napier's number, she'll get it sent right over." He paused to frown again, looking to Beasley like a man who might have had too much to drink last night, and was kicking himself for it right now. "I, uh, would appreciate it if you'd keep this aspect of your investigation up your sleeves, unless some name on that list bears fruit. That kind of publicity, Telenet doesn't need. The media pricks smell the faintest possibility of trouble like a shark smells blood."

The physical aspects of Phoebe Michel's relationship with Dennis Bennett hadn't changed much since they'd last made love. If the British had a reputation for being remote, dispassionate lovers, Dennis defied it. He'd always been right there; energetic, attentive to her expectations. The sex was glorious, a frenzied coupling between two healthy, vital beasts. Her problem with Dennis had always been afterward, in where he went and who he became *out* of bed. Today's stroll down memory lane was delicious, just as long as the groping, the kisses, and the naked writhing lasted. The instant her climax came, Phoebe was planning her escape.

"Away so fast?" Dennis murmured. His hand reached out from where he lay, sprawled atop his bedclothes. The tips of his fingers traced the curve of her bare fanny as she stooped to gather up her clothes.

"I shouldn't be here in the first place," she replied. "Count your blessings." She moved out of reach to step into her panties, then slipped into her brassiere.

"I'd forgotten what a great fucking bonk you are, Phoebe love. Surely you can stay for another drink."

She clipped her brassiere in place and stepped into her slacks. "One word of this to Greg and I'll kill you, buster. Not a smirk. Not anything."

"Please," he protested. "What sort of boor do you take me for?" His voice had that dreamy, drugged quality it invariably got in the aftermath of sex.

"Your word not mine. The sort of man who calls a woman a great fucking bonk." She jammed arms into her turtleneck and tugged it over her head. "It was fun. Let's not make any more of it than that, Den." Her boots and socks in hand, she started for the door. "Don't bother getting up. I know the way out."

* * *

From Bill Hoag's point of view, Bruce Webster's being killed by a drunk was a sort of blessing in disguise, and Joe Dante wondered how much that should bother him. Dante thought he might expect to see more empathy flow from the man. Then again, he reasoned, Hoag and Bruce Webster weren't friends. They were only business associates, and Hoag appeared to be one of those automatons whose veins were filled with hydraulic fluid, rather than blood. It made Joe think of Hoag's wife, and the anger he'd seen there, boiling just beneath her surface. He wondered if this starched-stiff character, seated before him, was capable of expressing any emotion other than impatience.

"We understand there was a fourth party at your table last night, sir," he pressed the man.

Clearly eager to return to his meeting, Hoag had started an unconscious tapping of the carpet with his left foot. "That's correct. Andrea Hill. I can't imagine what she might be able to add."

"Did she and Webster know each other?"

"No. We needed a fourth at our table. I thought they might enjoy each other's company."

"She works for you?"

"Not directly. No. She's one of three assets managers engaged to oversee our employee pension fund."

"She and Webster talk at all?"

Hoag frowned at his wristwatch and shook his head. "I can't imagine they spoke in any depth, Lieutenant. Not at a party like that. I performed introductions. They sat next to each other through dinner." He started to rise.

Joe looked to Jumbo, then rose to offer his hand. "We thank you for your time, sir."

Even while his grip was firm, Hoag was already out of there. "I doubt I've been much help," he said distractedly.

"We appreciate your frankness, all the same," Dante reiterated. "The more information we can get, the better view of the field we have."

Hoag shrugged it off and started to move sideways toward the conference room door. "Everyone's got his shorts in a bit of a twist around here today. If you want to know what Webster and Andrea talked about, why not ask her?"

Joe nodded. "We'll undoubtedly do that, sir." He gestured to the bandage on his subject's forehead. "Nice tape job. Looks professional."

"The graveyard shift at Beth Israel. I recommend them. Banged my head, getting into a cab."

At home in her apartment on Central Park South, Phoebe Michel checked her machine for messages, and wondered why she felt no particular guilt about what she'd done that afternoon. Yes, she was engaged to be married, but it wasn't like she and Dennis had never fucked before. Once the ice was broken, the old familiar rhythms came easy. And there was no denying that she'd enjoyed herself. She was a woman of strong sexual appetites, one who had little use for moralistic self-flagellation.

Greg hadn't called. Perhaps he'd managed to nap, after all. Considering the shape he was in when she left him, she wondered about the wisdom of trying to wake him now. Then she lifted the receiver and dialed his number anyway. He picked up on the second ring, and to judge by the tone of his voice, he hadn't been dead asleep. He was filled with anxiety.

"I'm starting to think I'm going crazy," he complained. "I keep pinching myself, but can't get this nightmare to go away."

"It won't, Gregory," she assured him. At least he didn't whine. She hated that more than anything in a man. "It's real. The sooner you face that fact, the better."

"That's my problem, Pheeb. I can't. There's too much that doesn't make sense."

Maybe he *was* going to whine. She felt her anger build in anticipation. "You're in denial, Greg. Don't you think it's time you snapped out of it?"

"I said it earlier, and I'll say it again. I've never driven a car drunk in my life. Last night I'm supposed to have gotten so blitzed that everything from eleven o'clock on is a blank. Baloney, Pheeb. I think I was drugged."

She grunted in exasperation. "By whom? G. Gordon Liddy? Now you're talking like a fool."

"Am I? How long have you known me? Have you ever seen me drunk? Or even close?"

He had a point. Over the year that they'd dated, Phoebe had never known Greg to have more than a couple glasses of wine with dinner. A few beers while watching a ball game, maybe, but never hard liquor. He complained that it bothered his stomach.

"Never once," he insisted. "I'm at my wit's end, Pheeb. I've even tried to imagine why Dennis might have wanted to kill him."

"That's preposterous!" she snapped.

"Maybe, maybe not. He's got so many sources, it's

possible he knew about the Omnicom deal, and how Webster was threatening to derail it. But not from me. I never said a word about it."

What Omnicom deal? Phoebe wondered.

"But that's the only reason I can imagine," Greg continued. "That he's got a lot of money at risk, and ran Webster down on purpose."

Phoebe felt a wave of dizziness wash over her. What on earth was he going on about? "I can't believe I'm hearing this," she protested. "About a friend who helped you out of a jam. It's not just preposterous, it's perverse." The memory of Bennett's strong hands, their grip tight on her buttocks, was still vivid. She squeezed her eyes shut, barely able to control her anger as she spoke through clenched teeth. "Gimme a break, Greg. Please. This is crazy talk."

"Not so crazy as you think. The way it stands, he's as much as accused me of murder."

"Manslaughter."

"What's the difference?"

"Quite a bit, actually."

"You think so? Either way, I do felony time in jail. And if I do that, I'm ruined."

"You go around making accusations like the one you just made, you'll live to regret it, Gregory." She'd seen Bennett angry and knew how he could lash out. He was rich. He could bury an enemy under an avalanche of libel litigation that might drag on for years.

"I didn't kill anyone, Pheeb. And if I didn't, your old boyfriend is working some angle. One way or another."

Abruptly, Greg hung up. Left alone with her thoughts, Phoebe hugged herself and stared out at the barren treetops of Central Park. That roll she'd taken down memory lane seemed a lot less harmless to her now. Good God. What if Greg was right? What if Dennis *did* know something about a deal cooking between Telenet and Omnicom? As an analyst in the industry, she knew too well what the implications of such a deal were. Omnicom had developed some breakthrough technology that Telenet desperately needed to keep its head above today's turbulent telecommunications waters. If Dennis knew about it, he was in a position to make a royal fortune. It made her shudder to consider how freely she'd taken that ruthless bastard into her mouth. Her skin crawled.

But if Dennis would go so far as to kill a man, there had to be a reason. Phoebe couldn't imagine what it was. He had done all his jockeying for position, and fought his power battles a decade ago. His reputation was made. For a man in his position, there was too much money to be made, playing by the rules. It was his damned game.

The Omnicom deal. Greg had said it like it was a fait accompli. He'd been furtively working his fanny off for weeks on some project and never said a word about it to her. Something had crossed her desk at the brokerage about a press conference Telenet had called for Tuesday. Having heard no intriguing rumors, she'd ignored it. Now that she considered the kind of marriage those two companies would make, she kicked herself for missing all the obvious indicators. They were right there in front of her face.

SIX

Aware that Dante had offered to give his grieving neighbor a ride to the airport, Beasley Richardson suggested he and Guy Napier locate Andrea Hill, while Joe headed for home. When Dante arrived outside his building, Diana was waiting inside the front door, out of the cold. On the sidewalk, a handful of hookers were huddled around a flaming fifty-five-gallon drum. The holiday traffic in their trade was sparse.

Circumstances considered, Diana looked to have pretty much pulled herself together. Dressed in one of her bulky, incognito outfits, she wore wraparound sunglasses to hide the redness of cried-out eyes. She raced across the sidewalk, jerked open the passenger door and jumped in. "You don't know how much I appreciate this," she thanked him, and leaned over to kiss him on the cheek.

"I think I do," he replied.

La Guardia was north and east of where they

were, but the quickest route between two points in New York is rarely a straight line. Dante headed them west toward Twelfth Avenue, his intention to go south around the bottom of the island. "What's Brian up to?" he asked.

"I gave him a bye. I think he's grateful. Packing up my brother's stuff shook him up pretty good."

"He ever met your sister?"

"Nope. But knows our history, chapter and verse."

"Sounds ominous." From the intersection with West Street at Twenty-third, Joe went with the green light to ease them into the flow of southbound traffic. "Bring me up to speed on this sister. I'm flying blind here."

Diana eased a bit deeper into her seat, removed the sunglasses, and massaged the bridge of her nose with thumb and forefinger. "It's a long story."

There wasn't much traffic. If their luck held, they'd be at the airport inside half an hour. "We've got nothing but time on our hands," Joe replied. "Try me."

Diana stared off across the Hudson toward the old Maxwell House coffee plant, and nodded. "Okay. You remember me talking about Sandy getting that divorce last year?"

"Not the details, but yeah. You weren't exactly heartbroken."

"Guy she married is a scuzz bucket. She got her first teaching job that same year they tied the knot. My junior year at Oberlin. When I went to visit them over Christmas break, he climbed into my bed one night and tried to fuck me."

"Nice."

"The asshole thinks he's irresistible. Sandy didn't

want to believe my side of the story when I told her what happened. She said I'd led him on. He fed her some bullshit story about me pulling a seduction number, then freaking out when he called my bluff."

"So you made a scene." Joe could just see the unsuspecting academic trying to force the issue, and what he probably got for his trouble. Joe and Diana sparred together on the karate mat in his loft, several times a week.

"He did all the screaming, not me. After I kneed him in the nuts."

"Ouch. What about the fact that he was in your bed? How did your sister rationalize that?"

"I doubt she ever did. Not completely. But the dickhead was a full professor. At the same university. Over the years, stories kept trickling back about him and other women. His teaching assistants and students."

"And she lived in denial, right?" How many times had Dante seen it? Wives of guys on the job who buried their heads in the sand, rather than face the fact that they'd married some pogo-prick.

"It only works for so long. In this case, she kinda got it shoved in her face."

"How's that?"

"He dumped some student he'd been screwing. She tried to commit suicide. The academic senate first called in the police, and then brought him up on charges. Stripped him of his tenure. Sandy complained the cops were just persecuting the easiest target at first; that the girl had a reputation. Then some letters he'd written came to light."

"In which he said more than happy birthday, I'll bet."

She grunted and pulled open her coat to shrug out of it. "It's what finally opened her eyes. While she was packing her bags to leave, he freaked out and kicked down the door to their bedroom. She called the cops, but before they arrived, he beat her up."

"Where'd she go when she left?"

"She quit her job at Illinois. Took another one at Southwest Missouri State."

"How do you two get along now?"

The singer turned to face Joe directly, her pale blue eyes set more with resolve than doubt. "Remains to be seen, doesn't it. We haven't been face-to-face in twelve years. But at least we're talking again. Not often, but some is better than none."

"She got a problem with the star thing? You being famous and all?"

Bruce hadn't seemed to mind, but then he'd been a star in his own right, in the rarefied world of cutting-edge technology.

Diana smiled wistfully. Her gaze returned to distant objects as they drove past the Battery. "Believe it or not, we've never even talked about it. Closest we've gotten was this past fall. She called to say she'd seen an exhibition of Brian's work at the Nelson Gallery, in Kansas City."

"Twelve years," he mused. "You sure you'll recognize her?"

For the rest of the ride to the airport they talked about the logistics of Diana's upcoming week. She had cremation arrangements to make, her brother's estate to contend with, and was scheduled to go back into the studio with her band that Friday. Even if she postponed the recording session, there would be rehearsals, last-minute consults with producers, and other business she couldn't avoid. Joe offered to do what he could to help. She said that until she could go through her brother's personal effects at his home in California, she wouldn't know how he'd left his affairs. He'd never mentioned a will. He wasn't religious, and had never said anything about a service. Dante supposed it wasn't the sort of thing that weighed heavily on the minds of most thirty-four-year-olds.

There was no means of flying directly from Springfield, Missouri, to New York. Sandy Pruitt had accomplished her journey in two hops, the longest, a TWA flight between St. Louis and La Guardia. Her plane arrived only ten minutes late. Dante used his shield to bypass security, and stood waiting alone with Diana as passengers disembarked.

Joe had a picture in his mind's eye of Diana's sister that ran toward the thickset, tweedy image of a middle-aged female academic that he'd carried away from his own college experience. The woman who stepped from the line of passengers to embrace the singer was so different from that image that Joe had looked right past her. He was still sorting through the crowd.

Taller than Diana by a good four inches, this woman had short-cropped hair, its reddish tones the color of old mahogany. Rather than Diana's slightly squinting blue eyes, she had large, expressive green ones. They did share that tiny, upswept nose, but the facial similarities stopped there. Still, the body-type resemblance between the two sisters was uncanny. Clad in a short skirt, sensible flat shoes, and a crisp white cotton blouse, this sociology professor had her shorter sister's tiny waist, sculpted legs, and long, square-shouldered torso.

"You must be Brian," she said, her hand extended to him.

Caught off guard, he took the hand and shook his head. "No, Joe." The hand, cool to the touch, didn't linger long.

Sandy Pruitt looked with confusion to her sister.

"Sorry," Diana apologized. "Joe Dante, Dr. Sandra Pruitt. Sandy, this is my neighbor, and one of our closest friends. Brian's home, getting your room ready. Joe was good enough to offer us a ride."

Dante was being scrutinized now. The open trust of a moment ago had been replaced by wariness. He saw her look quickly to the ring finger of his left hand. Another look lingered for a moment on the whitened scar from his right cheekbone down across his jaw to the collar of his shirt. Joe rarely thought of himself as a rough customer, but was reminded at times like this that it was an impression he sometimes gave.

"I see," she said.

"C'mon." Diana took her by the elbow. "Let's get your bags."

An awkward stiffness prevailed as the three of them moved toward the gate. Downstairs in the baggage area, Joe moved to Diana's side as her sister waded into the crowd in search of her carousel.

"Not the usual effect you have on women, eh, Copper?" she murmured.

"Maybe this wasn't such a good idea."

"Bullshit. You think I'd rather be standing here alone right now?"

He watched the proud, almost defiant way that

Sandra Pruitt carried herself. She located her flight number on the electronic carousel board and strode toward it with purpose. "Given what you've told me about her, she's probably a little apprehensive about my kind of male."

"Gimme a break. You're a pussycat."

"You bet I am. Meow."

Diana's presence in the baggage claim area had started to draw attention. Joe slid a protective arm around her shoulders as a gushing teenage girl rushed up, brandishing pen and paper. The singer scribbled an autograph, a forced smile glued to her face. As soon as she handed the paper back, Joe started to edge her toward her sister's position, alongside the carousel rim.

"You never mentioned how good-looking she is," he muttered.

"It's been twelve years. People change."

"Sure they do. I bet she used to be a dog."

"Down boy," she growled. "Don't forget how stupid you look with your tongue hanging out."

Weary from the long night and unsettled day he'd had, Dennis Bennett had showered after Phoebe left, and crawled back into bed. When his doorbell awoke him at four-thirty that afternoon, he'd been asleep for close to three hours. As he drifted up out of a deep slumber, he tried to ignore the insistent ringing. But the spell had been broken. He was awake.

Bennett wondered who could have gotten past the doorman, as he slipped into a robe and tugged the sash tight around his waist. In the entry hall he paused to check his appearance in the mirror, and gave his hair a quick finger-comb. Once white-blond, he was a few shades darker now, his hairline considerably higher as he stared down the barrel at middle age. Most of his boyishness was gone, replaced by a distinguished masculine beauty that he prized even more. Dennis's looks, combined with his faux-upper-class British accent, had opened untold doors for him. He was a man who stood out in a crowd.

The bolt retracted, he swung his front door open to discover Andrea Hill on his threshold. She held her winter coat thrown over one arm, a fur hat and leather gloves in hand.

"Where've you been?" she greeted him as she advanced. "I tried to call you twice."

"Asleep. I got home terribly late." He accepted the coat and a buss on the cheek. "Greg Nichols and I took a run up to my place in Pound Ridge, after the party."

That earned him a bent eye as she tossed her hat and gloves onto the entry table. "You, Greg, and who else? Last I saw of him, it was doubtful he could walk, let alone seduce some young lovely."

He patted that trim backside of hers and led the way across the front room toward the bar. "You've got a terribly suspicious mind, Andy, love. How do you think I felt, watching that fool Hoag drool all over you? I'm the one who should be jealous." He grabbed a gin bottle and two martini glasses as she barked a quick, merry laugh.

"Right, Den. You don't have a jealous bone in your body. People with hearts of stone rarely do."

He removed his shaker from the freezer and started to pack it with ice. "You wound me to the quick," he protested.

"Rhymes with prick. What a coincidence."

He laughed as he filled the shaker with Boodles and a splash of vermouth. Three quick shakes and he strained the concoction into their glasses. Andrea dropped in two olives and picked hers up. He raised his own in toast. "To the finest protégé a man could ever wish for."

She sipped as a smile deepened her dimples. "Lucky you, lover. Bruce Webster got himself killed last night. Did you hear?"

"Indeed? How?"

"Walked in front of a car, right after you and your play pal left the party. Put to rest any qualms that Bill had about making that announcement, Tuesday. I was worried at first about how it could affect Omnicom's price, but the market is so hungry for this development, I think we're home free."

"You didn't make your relief too obvious, I hope."

She fixed him with a baleful glare. "Who taught me everything I know?"

"Easy." He stepped close, the front of his body brought into full contact with the heat of hers. "Frankly, I can't tell you how good that news is to hear. We pull this off, everything is right as rain again. I am grateful, Andy."

"You don't have a grateful bone in that beautiful body, either." The warmth of her breath caressed his cheek as she spoke. "But you do owe me, Den. Big time. Every time that lovesick jerk puts his hands on me, it makes my skin crawl."

His fingers probed beneath the hem of her sweater to find the taut, cool flesh of her back. They pushed on to explore up the length of her spine. Discovering no brassiere strap, he felt a heat in his loins begin to build. "His seduction was your idea, Andy dear," he reminded her.

"My ass," she whispered, her mouth close to his ear now. "You all but dared me." With her hungry mouth in search of his, she ground her hips against him.

Bennett grabbed the hem of her sweater with both hands to pull it over her head. She barely let go of him long enough to let it slip free before she was on him again, fingers loosing the tie of his robe.

"Why am I so nuts about you, you ruthless son of a bitch?" she panted. One hand occupied with his erection, she used the other to grab a fistful of his hair. She was toe to toe and eye to eye with him, and her smile was full of challenge.

"Because we're two peas from the same pod, love." Bennett knew the facts of Andrea's real motivation for climbing into Bill Hoag's bed. She was driven by greed, pure and simple. There was an abundance of competent assets managers in the marketplace today. But the one thing that set her above the rest in the Telenet pension fund sweepstakes was how desperately Bill Hoag wanted to screw her. He was hooked, the first time she batted those baby blues at him. They'd agreed on a two percent management fee, half a point kicked back to him. Still, Andrea had known she could do better. What she aimed to garner was a bigger share of the whole pension fund pie, and three months into his affair with her, Hoag had persuaded his board to increase the size of her chunk by double. To two hundred million dollars. Even after the kickback, her fees still ran to three million dollars a year.

"You're as ruthless as I am," he growled.

She had his right earlobe between her teeth and gently tugged at it as she squeezed his cock. "Take me to bed, you opportunistic bastard. I need some real sex. Now."

He jammed himself up against her and grinned. "Now? I thought you might want to finish your drink."

She twisted away, unzipped her skirt, and hooked thumbs into her waistband. "Heel, buster. Or I'll dump it on your head."

Home after his trip to the airport, Dante fed his cat, changed into a sweat shirt and jeans, and played back the messages on his machine. Beasley had called. He and Napier had struck out, trying to find Andrea Hill. According to her doorman, she'd left her apartment, late afternoon, and not returned. The lab had faxed to Sweden results of the spectrography on those paint chips from the killer car. They awaited a reply. Grover and Heckman proposed to expand the scope of their search for the car to nearby counties in New Jersey, Connecticut, and upstate. Though Monday was a holiday, Richardson suggested they meet first thing in the morning at Ms. Hill's building, and hope she wasn't out of town. He concluded with mention that the Colts had beaten Oakland for a trip to the next round of the AFC playoffs, in Pittsburgh. Dante owed him twenty bucks.

Seated in his living room, his cat in his lap and some vintage Coleman Hawkins on the sound system, Joe thought back over his trip to and from the airport that afternoon. The moment that Diana's sister approached his job-issue sedan, I.D. card on the dash, he'd watched her stiffen. It could be she still resented the police in Urbana for failing to protect her from her irate ex-husband. When he'd shed his jacket for the drive back into town, she'd stared at his service weapon as if he had a growth instead of a gun on his hip. As a rule, Joe hated generalizations. He hated them even more when they were aimed at him.

"Christ. You're a cop," she'd murmured with clear contempt.

"Detective lieutenant, NYPD," he replied.

She looked to her sister as if searching for explanation.

"Does that make him subhuman?" Diana protested, reacting to her sister's tone.

Then her sister had taken offense. "That's a terrible thing to say."

Diana stood her ground. "Nuh uh, Sand. It's an asshole thing to imply. You don't know this man."

"But . . ." Sandy had sputtered, flustered. Joe guessed it had been some years since anyone had called her an asshole.

"No buts," Diana cut her off. They were standing on a sidewalk in front of the main arrivals terminal, a biting wind swirling around them as darkness fell. "It seems to me, you make a habit of treating good people badly. Your ex-husband would have raped me, if I hadn't fought him. And you stood up for him, not me." Diana's celebrity was at work again, attracting passersby who stopped to gawk. She didn't give a damn. She jerked a thumb over her shoulder at Joe. "This man is my friend. Once upon a time, he saved my life."

Her mortified sister stood rooted. Speechless. Diana got into the car and slammed her door. Hardly a word was spoken during the half-hour ride back into Manhattan. Dante left the two of them to ride upstairs together while he parked his car. He could only imagine the icy atmosphere that prevailed upstairs right now, and pitied his pal, Brian. Twelve years of sibling discord had just been dropped, full-blown, right in his buddy's lap.

Dripping with the sweat of her exertion, Andrea Hill sucked smoke from a cigarette deep into her lungs and picked a long blond hair from the back of her hand. "Hmmm. I'm amazed you had anything left."

Dennis had started to doze. Men. They *were* predictable. "Beg pardon? Any what?"

"Steam, lover." She drawled it, and extended her hand to let that strand of hair drop. It landed in his face. "That wasn't the most spectacular fuck I've ever had, but I've had worse. Blond. Just about Vivian Hoag's color. I saw how you eyed her in that dress last night."

He rolled over onto one hip, head propped against his hand. "For crissake. What are you on about?"

"Not what. Who? You had the decency to shower, but the stink of that cow is all over the bed. And it's familiar."

He opened his mouth to protest. She gently closed it with a finger. "Shush. I know it wasn't poor little Vivian, but I sort of wish it was. Turnabout's fair play."

Dennis smiled and wiggled his eyebrows. "You think she'd be my type? Got a wonderful arse on her, that woman."

"It wasn't her arse you were staring at, boyo." She planted a hand on his chest to shove him onto his back. "I hope you're using your rubbers, whoever your little whores are. I get some galloping crud from one of your playthings, I'll kill you before it kills me. I swear to God."

He threw his arms above his head to stretch, luxuriating in it. "So charming, Andy love. Your rhetorical gifts never fail to astound. What about your sweet William? What are you using with him?"

"He's my latex meal ticket," she sneered. "Not the future father of my children."

It seemed like an eternity since Dante had undertaken a graduate course in criminal psychology at John Jay College. He thought he might like to teach, once he retired, and the criminal mind held endless fascination for him. His course work was long since completed, but the writing of his thesis had hung up his doctoral pursuit. His subject was the documented correlations drawn between adult sociopathological behavior and demonstrated tendencies in early childhood.

This past month, his sprained knee and the time off it forced him to take had driven him back to his desk. He'd made encouraging progress that he was now determined to continue. That night, after dinner, he went into his study to push ahead. He managed four hours of work before the sound of the elevator stirred him out of his intellectual labyrinth. The car stopped at his floor. A moment later, the mesh gate in his living room rolled back, and Rosa called out.

"Joe?"

"In here." He punched the power button on his laptop and screwed fists into his eyes.

Rosa was dressed for an evening out. She smelled of cigarettes, though she herself didn't smoke. "I didn't realize you'd be working," she apologized. "I should have called."

He swung around in his desk chair and heaved himself to his feet. "No problem. Ready to quit. Just trying to keep my momentum, is all. Where've you been?" As soon as he asked it, he saw her jaw muscles tighten.

"Not really material. I'm here now. To talk, Joe. We need to get a few things straight."

"Something to drink?" he offered.

"I don't think so. Thanks. Let's go sit." She turned toward the living room.

The woman was achingly beautiful. Her hair was done up in a French twist. She wore a short, black knit dress that was both modest and outrageously flattering at the same time. Dante didn't think he'd ever met a woman more physically desirable, and often wondered how much it was their physical attraction that kept him coming back, and vice versa.

She sat in her favorite chair. He found a spot on the sofa, and got right to the point.

"I can imagine what it is we need to talk about. But you know how I feel about Jaime Ruiz, why, and that my opinion isn't going to change. Ten years ago, nobody did a major-weight dope deal in Spanish Harlem that Jaime didn't know about."

"I think you exaggerate," she countered. "By then, he was already deep into politics. He'd have to have been a fool."

"Fifteen years ago he was a wanna-be power broker with no financial base," Joe persisted. "Then, presto, he had one. Almost overnight. He went from barrio barrister defending drug scum to rubbing elbows with the likes of your uncle."

"He had the ear of the people," she insisted. "That made him a force. Any Hispanic who wanted to hold office had to reckon with him."

Dante shook his head, his memory harking back to those days when he'd roved Manhattan night haunts as an undercover skinhead. "He bought the ear of the people, Rosa. I remember those block parties he and his cronies used to throw, like it was yesterday. Free food, up and down both sidewalks. Separate salsa bands at either end of the street. I was there. I watched how he worked those crowds."

The tendons in her neck tightened as she came forward in her chair. Her hands spread, she grabbed at the air between them. "I've spent hours over the past two weeks, talking to the man, Joe. Of course he's a politician. I won't deny that, and neither would he. But he has so much he can give back to his community. They need that. He's their champion."

"Your uncle isn't even a New Yorker. What's his interest?"

"The plight of the underprivileged goes further than New York."

Joe grunted. "Right. And Tico Losada bleeds pity for some poor bastard trying to raise a family in a half-boarded-up building on ten grand a year."

"He gives more money to charities than both of us make in a year," she retorted. "Combined."

"And how much to the political action committees funded by him and his sugar-grower pals?"

She stood abruptly and stalked across the room to grab her coat from the elevator alcove rack. "Attack Jaime Ruiz and Roberto Isabel if you want." She jammed her arms angrily into the coat sleeves. "But don't you dare attack my family!"

Whether he was unable, or just unwilling, to back down, Joe didn't know. He stayed where he sat. "Your uncle and his partners have two thousand acres planted in sugar, Rosa. They're destroying the Everglades. He implied that much to me, himself, bitching about environmentalists one night. You take his money, are you gonna vote for any clean water acts? Or vote against sugar price supports?"

Rosa yanked open the elevator gate and stabbed her key at the control panel. A moment later, she was gone. Dante watched the top of her head disappear, and shook his own. An agitated Toby trotted over and leapt into his lap, always able to sense trouble when it was afoot. He looked directly into Dante's face, and yeowled.

"I know, little buddy," Joe murmured. "I know. What have I gone and done now?"

When Brian Brennan stepped through the access door onto his roof and into its winter-barren garden, a light snow had started to fall. He wandered toward the east-facing parapet wall and stood in his heavy parka and scarf, relieved to be breathing the crisp, strife-free night air. Whatever had happened between Diana and her sister during that ride home from the airport, had made dinner at a neighborhood restaurant a chilly proposition. Being no party to their ancient squabble, he was of no use to Diana and was only in the way. Clearly the two sisters needed time to sort out whatever they had to resolve, and he needed to make himself scarce.

A snowstorm did something magical to New York. It was not the city of his birth, but was a place he'd grown to love with something close to a passion over the twenty-six years he'd lived there. On a night like tonight, under different circumstances, he and Diana might have grabbed their skates and cabbed it to Central Park. There was nothing quite like skating on Wollman Rink in a light snowfall. Old lovers did things like that—at least the ones who didn't let their love grow old.

But Bruce was dead, and that had changed everything.

The roof access door swung open and Joe Dante stepped out into the cold, also bundled against it.

"Didn't know you were home," Brennan greeted him. "Thought I heard the elevator."

"Rosa. Leaving."

Brian could read Dante's face. "Shit. The Congress thing, huh?"

Joe stood shoulder to shoulder with him and stared ahead into the snow. All the distant lights were fuzzy at the edges. "Might be a deal breaker, buddy. You know how she is, once she's dug her heels in."

"A whole lot like you. It's scary."

"Her sponsor's dirty."

"What politician isn't?"

"That's fatalistic. I'm a cop. I'm dead if I buy into that."

Brennan knew he was right, and apologized. "Guess I'm a little out of sorts. Been a rough day."

"No need to explain. How are Diana and the ice maiden getting on? Or is that a stupid question, you being out here?"

Brian glanced sideways at his friend. Both of them were roughly the same height, but Dante outweighed him by a solid twenty pounds. Theirs was an unlikely friendship: the sculptor and the cop; one from Oregon, the other from Brooklyn. Brennan was a man of imagination and creative ideas who expressed himself in clay, wax, and bronze. Dante's imagination and creativity were focused on the job, through action.

"What the hell happened between those two tonight? The atmosphere at dinner was so cold you couldn't melt it in a blast furnace."

Joe attempted to relate what had transpired. "If I hadn't been there, it might have been different," he concluded.

Brian doubted it. "This has been festering for more than a decade. Crap like that isn't resolved with a happy hug hello. They need time."

"How much time? You could freeze to death out here."

Brennan looked skyward. The snowfall had intensified. His hair was wet. "Much as it takes. Invite me down for a drink. We could make a pot of coffee, and dump in some of that good Irish I gave you for Christmas."

Joe frowned at him. "Thought you'd sworn off the hard stuff for good."

"I thought I had, too," Brian replied.

SEVEN

Bill Hoag had been trained not to expect Andrea Hill to answer her phone after ten at night, or before eight in the morning. She contended that it was a selfish little isolation quirk she indulged. In fact, it was her device meant to buy ten hours of privacy each night. As long as she was either home or at the office to answer his calls after eight, he couldn't question her whereabouts. She'd lost count of the times he'd phoned at eight-oh-one.

This Monday morning, Andrea had forgotten to set an alarm at Dennis Bennett's place, and overslept. She knew she had to look like hell, but had skipped her shower and hopped into a cab for the fourteen-block trip uptown to her place. Thank God she wore her hair short.

"Miss Hill?" It was the concierge who hailed her as she rushed across the lobby of her York Avenue building toward the elevators.

She skidded in her heels and nearly fell on her ear

as she turned toward the voice. "What?" she gasped, irritation in it.

He indicated two men, seated on the lobby sofa. One was black, the other, white. Both were big. "These gentlemen are waiting to see you. They're from the police."

A self-conscious hand flew to her hair as her gaze met the white cop's. He had intent, slate-blue eyes that seemed to almost bore through her. Breaking the unsettling contact, she looked quickly to the other. He had the size, thick neck, and scowl of a middle linebacker. Suddenly dizzy, she forced herself to take a deep breath.

"Andrea Hill?" the white cop asked as he rose. He was almost as tall as Dennis, and Bennett was nearly six-two. As handsome, too, but in a different way. This one was more rugged. "Lieutenant Dante. Special Investigations Division. This is Lieutenant Richardson. Can we have a minute?"

"I don't understand," she said.

Lieutenant Dante looked across the lobby to where elevator doors had opened. A half dozen of her neighbors were disgorged. "We'd rather explain upstairs. It has to do with the party you attended New Year's Eve."

A wave of relief washed over her. "Sure," she agreed, suddenly on solid footing again. "I'm sorry. You caught me a little off guard." She turned to lead the way toward the open elevator. When the doors began to close, Lieutenant Richardson darted ahead with surprising quickness, to grab them.

One of the lessons she'd learned from Dennis while working for him at his Foray Fund Group was to keep her mouth shut and observe. Apparently these cops had taken lessons at the knee of their own master. It made for an awkward ride to the twelfth floor.

Outside her door, she finally broke the silence. "My cleaning lady had the weekend off. You'll have to excuse the mess."

It was likely that a couple of middle-class public servants like these two were knee deep in rug rats, toys, and dirty Tupperware at their houses. The fact that the plate glass table in her otherwise immaculate dining room had gone undusted for three days would doubtless go unnoticed. They'd be too busy gawking at her East River view.

"We're investigating the hit-and-run homicide of Mr. Bruce Webster," Lieutenant Dante told her. They'd entered her living room and he got right down to business. He hadn't even paused to glance out toward Queens. "We understand you sat at the same table with him, Saturday night?"

"I did," she replied. "Would either of you like coffee? I'm dying for a cup."

They told her they were all set, but to go ahead and start some. She excused herself for as long as it took to fill the reservoir and grind beans.

"I was shocked, of course, when I heard," she told them on her return. "News of it spread through the party like brush fire. Really put a damper on things."

"Had you ever met Webster? 'Fore that night?" Lieutenant Richardson asked.

"I hadn't. No. I'd heard of him, of course. From Bill Hoag."

"Mrs. Hoag thought he seemed preoccupied," Richardson continued. "That your read?"

The smile that Andrea flashed him was meant to

disarm. "She'd know better than I would, Lieutenant. In my line of work, a party like that is always so much business. Mr. Webster and I hardly talked, I'm afraid."

"Mr. Hoag says Webster was nervous. About some test results they'd gotten out west," Richardson pressed. "Y'did know about this merger they were workin' on t'gether, correct?"

It caught her by surprise. "I do. But how do you? It's supposed to be very hush-hush."

His return smile was indulgent. "This is a homicide investigation, Miss Hill. Till it's concluded, we're privy to everything. Too bad I can't call my broker, huh? It bein' a holiday and all."

She wasn't amused. It was doubtful that even Bill's wife, Vivian, knew the details of this deal. He must have told them himself. Damn. Dennis had twenty million of her dollars riding on his current gamble. Or at least twenty million of the two hundred she was entrusted to manage. Either way, her career was on the line. If the Omnicom stock he'd purchased with it didn't at least double in value once the Tuesday announcement was made, and her twenty million, plus a nice chunk of interest, wasn't tucked back in the pension fund all safe and sound, she was out on the street. She'd be looking for a job as a cocktail waitress. God only knew how many of his cop buddies this joker lieutenant had already tipped.

Lieutenant Richardson read the look of fleeting panic on her face and sobered. "Only kiddin', ma'am. Seriously. We're tryin' t' determine if there might'a been a motive for someone wantin' to see Webster dead; to determine if it was or wasn't an accident."

"The news reports are all saying it was probably

some drunk, aren't they?" A few years back, when a mugger stole Andrea's handbag and punched her in the face, they had been nowhere near this diligent in their efforts to find *her* attacker. She suspected that this extraordinary thoroughness was motivated by pressure brought to bear on City Hall by Webster's rock star sister. Neither the *Post* nor the *Daily News* had missed that connection. Andrea doubted the mayor's office had, either.

Richardson paused to regard Dante. "That's prob'ly the best guess, still. But understand. We've gotta chase down every lead comes our way. This merger's put a little different twist on things. Him askin' Telenet t' postpone their announcement of it until he could get these problems ironed out."

Andrea felt her guts do a backflip. If Bill were in the room right now, she doubted she'd be able to refrain from an attempt to strangle him. "You can't possibly suppose that someone might have hit him on purpose," she protested. "That's ludicrous."

Together, as if on some prearranged signal, both detectives stood to leave. "You're undoubtedly right," Lieutenant Dante said. "And we're sorry to have bothered you, but in a case like this, we wouldn't be doing our jobs if we didn't talk to everyone he saw, right before he died." He extended a hand. "Thank you for your time. We appreciate it."

The way he looked at her made her think again about what a mess her hair was. Thank God she'd taken a moment to put on a little makeup. "Sure you won't have a cup of coffee?" she asked. Why? Did she really want him to? Handsome or not, he was a policeman, for crissake. Probably made fifty a year and lived on Staten Island.

"Smells good," he begged off. "But we've got a busy day. Thanks." His smile did a little flirting of his own. "Maybe some other time."

Because it was a holiday, the Pierce, Fairbrother building in Manhattan's financial district was all but empty when Phoebe Michel arrived there, Monday morning. She'd been troubled all night by what Greg had blurted out over the phone to her yesterday. It was true that the Foray Group of funds hadn't done as well as many others had of late. Bennett certainly hadn't scored the kinds of victories and racked up the prodigious profit percentages that had made him famous. Indeed, there were some nagging rumors circulating that he'd been trying too hard, taking wild gambles based more on his hunches than on solid analysis. If this was true, he was playing with fire.

As a senior analyst in the brokerage's high-tech securities section, Phoebe had a window office that faced south into New York Harbor. There were days when she was astonished that this was where she'd landed. A bright, ambitious former cheerleader—God, how the thought of that embarrassed her now—from Loogootee, Indiana. Here in New York, with her own private view of the Statue of Liberty. Last year she'd made $268,000. She was thirty-four years of age, and the sky was limit. She might eventually wind up with an assets manager career of her own. That was where the really big bucks were. Or a partnership in an independent analysis firm, where all the players had a piece of the investment strategy pie. She might write and publish her own newsletter. Big money could be had there, too.

Seated at her desk, she got rid of the little roosting vultures of her screen-saver format, and clicked into the house's main database. The menu popped up on her monitor, and she began to scroll through until she landed on her ex-lover's Foray Fund Group. Five of those funds were overseen by Bennett's submanagers. A sixth was managed hands-on by Dennis, himself. Ultimately, he was responsible for the performances of all six, but Phoebe suspected that if there were any problems, they would lie with Foray Hi-Yield Growth. That was Dennis's exclusive turf, the fund with the most disappointing numbers in the group in recent months. It was also the biggest of the six. Investors tended to gravitate toward marquee names. In the eighties, Peter Lynch had built the Fidelity Group into a colossus, to a great extent on the basis of his own reputation.

It wasn't too hard to unearth what Phoebe feared she might find. Bruce Webster had been president of Omnicom. Given that fact, and that no securities analyst in the Pierce, Fairbrother high-tech stable had recommended an Omnicom buy in better than a year, the two-point-two-million shares that Dennis had acquired since December 10 stuck out like a sore thumb. He'd be crazy to think it would escape the attention of a routine internal audit, which could only mean he intended to flip those shares. Fast. She cursed her fiancé for being such a tight-lipped company man. The news media was reporting that Webster had been in New York all last week, but Greg hadn't said a word. From what Phoebe saw on her screen, it didn't take a genius to figure this out. Telenet was engineering an acquisition. That meant Webster's Silicon Valley firm had developed something hot; something Telenet needed desperately to reestablish itself as a communications industry leader.

Phoebe needed more information. She was determined to get it from Greg if she had to choke it out of him. Like where the Telenet–Omnicom negotiations stood at the moment. What terms were being discussed. And perhaps most important, how soon would an announcement be made. Was it still on for Tuesday? When she'd seen that last Telenet press release cross her desk, she'd thought it more empty hype, and tossed it. If it *wasn't* just hype, Dennis was positioned to make a major trade, and probably a sizable fortune. It was a move that had to be based on insider information, and that notion pointed to something unthinkable.

Once Andrea left Bennett's apartment that morning, Dennis had an errand to run. It was after nine before he finally managed to get himself into a cab and head downtown. Dennis was irritated he had to make this journey. Such running around was beneath him. Not that he dared complain to anyone.

The stone-and-glass canyon that was William Street was enveloped in a hush that was typical of weekends there. Almost as though ghosts had been at work in the early hours, the sidewalks out front of Pierce, Fairbrother were swept clean of the snow that had fallen last night. One lone uniformed guard manned the security desk in the lobby. When Dennis paused to sign the weekend log, he noticed Phoebe's name among the dozen or so there. The woman was a workaholic. He made a mental note to pop up and see her. Say hi. Perhaps she'd join him for a drink. He smiled to himself, savoring the memory of yesterday. Her backside, he'd noticed, was still nearly as firm as her commitment to her work.

The Foray Group occupied one entire floor of the brokerage building. There, Bennett operated beneath their umbrella with relative autonomy. They provided him access to their various market analysis sections, to their accounting and bookkeeping departments, and to their pool of support personnel. In compensation, Foray paid one-half point off the top of all monies invested in its six funds, and split all commissions charged for the purchase and sale of securities.

Bennett's cut of the pie at Foray was substantial. Last year he'd been compensated $11.7 million. Of that, he'd paid his staff of five young submanagers an average of $1.5 million each. His own net was less money than he'd made in any of the last ten years, by nearly half. The salaries were more than he'd ever paid a group of managers before. Dennis had slipped badly in recent years and was now forced to pay for that high-dollar talent out of necessity. On Wall Street, the best management skills and savvy came at a price. In the early nineties, Bennett had gotten greedy, tried to take the lion's share of the pie for himself, and good talent like Andrea—as much as she professed to love him and to owe him for teaching her everything she knew—had accepted offers elsewhere. When equity invested in his funds began to fall off from the billion and a half dollars it had once approached, Dennis had been forced to scramble. He had less than eight hundred million invested in his six funds today, and the young talent he'd bought had cost him dearly. Still, their numbers were only on a par with other middling performers. Investor confidence in the Dennis Bennett name was no longer what it once was. For the Foray Fund Group, in general, that spelled trouble.

At his desk, in his lavish corner office, Bennett switched on his computer. Last month, when Andrea had infused twenty million dollars into his Foray Hi-Yield Growth Fund, he'd moved immediately to purchase two-point-two-million shares of Omnicom preferred stock. He knew that Telenet needed four million more shares, in addition to those controlled by Omnicom's president and its board of directors, in order to gain control. The takeover was friendly. With those other shares already pledged, Telenet would move quickly to acquire the rest. Tomorrow, after the announcement of intent to acquire, Dennis would be first in line. Through Pierce, Fairbrother's direct NASDAQ connection, he had a choice. He could dump the entire two million-plus shares on the market as a block, or deal it off piecemeal. In a two-for-one swap, with Telenet currently trading at twenty-six, and Omnicom at a shade under nine, he could realize an instant profit of nine million dollars. Or be patient, and make even more. Not bad for a month's work, either way. Hit and run.

As engrossed as he was with making sure all his ducks were in a row, Bennett guessed he'd been online for better than fifteen minutes before he saw the notation in the upper right-hand corner of his monitor screen. He had no idea how long it had been there. A feature of the Pierce, Fairbrother internal security system were the so-called firewalls with which all of their databases were equipped. They made note of terminal assignment and time of day when one department accessed another's files. For the most part, such incursions were innocent. But this time, the advisory made Bennett's fuse flare. He'd been invaded by Phoebe, from her office in High-Tech Analysis.

Bennett's pulse thundered in his ears as he switched off his terminal and leapt to his feet. He wouldn't ride the elevator and risk the attention its bell might draw to his arrival. He opted for the stairs. Though he worked out regularly at the New York Athletic Club, he was still panting hard by the time he reached Phoebe's level, four floors above. Ready to charge ahead like a bull in a rodeo ring, he forced himself to pause on the landing and recover his breath. He didn't necessarily want to confront Phoebe. At least not here. He wanted to see exactly what she was up to.

Breath held, Bennett opened the door onto the twenty-eighth floor. He knew that one greeting from anyone on the floor would blow his cover, but all the way down the hall, and around the corner to Phoebe's office, all was holiday quiet.

The drone of what sounded like either a fax machine or an ink-jet printer reached his ears as he approached Phoebe's open office door. Within, she stood with her back to him. It was her printer he'd heard, as the data that scrolled past on her monitor screen was systematically turned into hard copy. Phoebe moved from keyboard to out-tray, selecting the sections of data she wanted, then retrieving and stuffing them into her briefcase.

* * *

The five members of Joe Dante's SID task force met for an early lunch in their favorite Vietnamese restaurant in Chinatown. Located on Mulberry Street, the eatery was just a short walk from headquarters on a nice day, and a shorter ride by car on a bitter cold day like this one. After they'd ordered, Rusty Heckman reported on the progress he and Grover had made.

"So far, we've chased after three Saab 9000's, all brought to body shops with rear-end damage. Not a live one in the bunch. Two owners filed police reports right after their accidents. The third one backed into a brick wall in Fort Lee, Friday night. Wife says he was drunk as a skunk."

Napier, half slouched in his chair, toyed with his chopsticks. "Somebody in Stockholm didn't mind a little holiday overtime," he told them. "The lab got a fax back this morning. Early. Saab's found us a match. It's from a production run in the early months of '96. January to March."

"You've contacted Motor Vehicles?" Joe asked.

"Ours. Connecticut's. Jersey's. Even Pennsylvania," Guy replied. "Should have something back by this afternoon."

Food started to arrive. After the chaos of finding room on the table for the different dishes subsided, they began to pass them around. Beasley reported on what he and Dante had learned from Telenet CEO Bill Hoag, and his wife, yesterday, and Andrea Hill, that morning. "I think the Hill broad kinda likes Joey," he concluded. "Legs up t' here." He used the side of his hand to indicate a spot midchest. "Course a woman like that'd flirt with a squirrel, it had nuts she wanted."

Dante pretended to almost dump a bowl of fried rice in his partner's lap. "We've got nothing else to support it yet, but what we have now is a possible motive for murder," he told them.

Richardson made circles in the air with his chopsticks, as if to keep the idea rolling. "Seems t' me, the number of suspects'd be fairly small. Limited to people who had access t' this merger information. That, and news of the second thoughts Bruce was havin'."

"Could be a lot bigger circle than you think," Grover warned. "Think about it. Lotta people wanna make a quick buck off a deal like that. Some dipshit in marketing leaks word to a broker buddy. Maybe Hoag's secretary tells her boyfriend. He sticks his neck out, buys a whole lotta Omnicom he can't afford."

"So this boyfriend waits outside the Sherry and runs Webster down?" Heckman asked. "Not fucking likely, Donnie. I still say it was some drunk."

"I'm inclined to lean Rusty's way," Dante agreed. "But there's still that big 'what if?' As much as I want to shake it, I can't. It sits there staring at me like a pig in a fucking prom dress."

Grover leaned forward, chopsticks jabbing the air. "That secretary's boyfriend ain't a bad direction t' hunt. Somebody who's bet his whole wad. And maybe a friend's money, too. If it wasn't a drunk, I'd look for whoever had the most t' lose." He ignored his food—a rare event—as he warmed to this notion. "Somebody with access onna inside. Someone who hears, once he's placed his bet, that Webster can screw up his whole fuckin' play."

"Slow down," Dante cautioned. "Your food's getting cold." Not that Grover wouldn't consume it, no matter its temperature. "Any minute now, you'll have this secretary's boyfriend tried, and strapped into the chair."

"But you see where he's headed," Napier insisted.

"I do," Joe admitted. "I've been over that ground a few times myself."

"Speakin' of headed," Richardson rumbled. "We're on our way up t' the M.E.'s office again, t' look over the toxicology workup Rocky's done. That'll give us a definite fix on what kinda shape our victim was in."

"In the meantime," Dante told the others, "I want you to keep chasing that phantom Saab. It's still our only lead. What about the Telenet guest list? That ever arrive?"

"Finally. Just this morning," Napier replied. "Didn't take long to run it, once we got it. But no luck."

It took effort to sound resolute, but Dante tried. "We're playing the odds here, just like a bookmaker does. And the odds say we're looking for a drunk."

EIGHT

Bill Hoag had already left a message on Andrea Hill's phone machine by the time those two cops intercepted her in the lobby of her building. After she emerged from her shower, she discovered another message. He was anxious to hear from her. He was at his office. It was ten-thirty by the time she called him back, and by then she'd managed to get a handle on her anger. Bill was essential to her plans, at least for the immediate future. She couldn't risk any sort of blowup, but it had taken the morning to cool off; to collect her thoughts.

The mess Dennis found himself in was none of her doing. More than once this past week, she wondered if she should have her head examined for being so easily suckered into bailing him out. He was the one who'd taken those risks. He was the one who'd crapped out. So what on earth, she wondered, did she think she was doing? And why? To repay an old debt? Because she loved him? Any motivation that approached gratitude would be the old Andrea Hill's; the motivation of someone she hardly knew anymore. Bennett could blame himself for the tough-minded, heartless businesswoman she'd become. He'd created her.

Bill Hoag was another story. Bill could make her rich; as rich as Dennis had been, before his house of cards collapsed. When she called Bill back, she explained that the first time he'd called, the cops were there. The second time, she was in the shower. She suggested he come to her place, around noon. She would fix them something simple for lunch, and tell him all about her meeting with the police.

Andrea knew Bill's basic agenda and answered the door to him, dressed accordingly. It wasn't so much that he needed a road map. Andrea just preferred to occupy the driver's seat. What looked to him like submission was, in fact, her taking control of the game. He became blind to everything but what she wanted him to see.

"Wow!" he gushed as he stepped into her entry hall.

"You like it?" A silly question, of course, but asked with just the right measure of hunger for approval. When the doorman announced her guest's arrival downstairs, she'd rubbed ice on her nipples. They jutted hard against the shiny silk of her jade green chemise.

Still in his overcoat, Bill was suddenly all over her. One hand reached toward her breast as his other arm encircled her waist.

"Easy, baby," she cooed. "Slow down." She disengaged, both hands planted on his chest. "We've got all afternoon. C'mon, let me take your coat. What on earth happened to your head?"

Suddenly self-conscious, he touched the bandage at his temple and winced. "Vivian had a fit after the party the other night. Threw a vase at me. Said she knows I'm fucking you."

"Good aim." She took his coat and hung it in the closet. "How bad is it?"

"Sixteen stitches."

He started toward her again, and she backpedaled, determined to keep the upper hand.

"God, you look good enough to eat, Andrea."

She dipped her chin and pretended to blush. "I was hoping you'd say that. Come on. Let me get you a drink. We need to talk. If you're hungry, I'll fix you a sandwich."

"I can't think about eating," he complained. "Not with you prancing around in that outfit."

"I'll put on a robe."

"No! I'll eat. I swear."

She turned to an antique secretary, set along one wall, and lifted the top. From beneath, she extracted an envelope. "Friday was the end of the quarter. A good quarter for me. It's time to settle up." On her way past him toward the liquor cabinet, she placed the envelope in his hand. "Scotch?"

He stared tentatively at the envelope, but didn't open it. "Still pretty early, isn't it?"

"We're celebrating. That's an electronic transfer acknowledgment. From your bank in Nassau. It informs you that two hundred eighty thousand dollars were wired into your account, Friday afternoon."

Corporate titan that he was, Bill could appear terribly resolute when he wanted to. The severity of his long, thin face lent itself to seriousness. He shook his head with the sort of firmness that always scored him points in an acquisition negotiation. "I don't feel right about this, Andrea. Not in the face of our current, uh, relationship."

Poised to mix water with the Scotch in his glass, she paused. "What's changed, Bill? We've been sleeping together for over a year."

"That's true. But . . ." He was at a loss for words. "It didn't feel right the last time, either. Or the time before that. Just having this envelope in my hands feels . . . I don't know . . ." He groped again, and then shrugged. "Tawdry, I guess."

She kept the glow of her satisfaction buried deep, eyes averted lest he catch the gleam of triumph. "That's terribly sweet, William. But you see . . ." She looked up to nod at the envelope. "It's already a done deal." She carried their drinks across the room and handed his to him.

"Give me your account number. I'll transfer it back," he offered. "Please, Andrea. I insist."

Beautiful. When the Telenet board considered the handsome thirty-one percent return she'd gotten them on her $200 million chunk of their fund, Bill would have no trouble convincing them to swing another $100 million her way. Combined, the assets she would manage then would net her a fee of $4.5 million, no more kickbacks attached. To think, there were Neanderthals who still insisted it was a man's world. Meanwhile, she was building a reputation as one of the top-performing assets managers in America. Once that rep was made, guys like Bill Hoag could go jerk themselves off.

She lifted her glass in toast. "To us, then."

He sipped, smacked his lips, and smiled at her, the contented proprietor. "You don't watch out, I might make you rich." And as he spoke he took a step closer to drag a thumb across her left nipple. "What an utterly magnificent creature you are."

"I hope you're prepared to back that up," she growled. "It made me crazy, to watch Vivian leave with you the other night."

"She threw a vase at me later," he reminded her. "So tell me. What did the police ask you that they didn't ask me?"

Andrea wasn't home yet. She needed this creep for at least another year. She leaned into his fondling hand. "How would I possibly know?" she purred.

He took another sip of his Scotch, his thumb still pressed against the tip of her nipple. "You know how the police are," he said. "They knew that you, Viv, and I all sat with Bruce at the party. Bruce was staying with his rock star sister. She told them he was worried about what a team of our engineers turned up at his plant, out in San Jose. Just a minor glitch, but Bruce was a stickler."

So *that* was where the leak had originated. Andrea supposed she should be relieved. It wasn't Bill who had opened his mouth first.

"Did Vivian add anything to that?" she asked.

He shrugged. "How much did she know? She mentioned how preoccupied Bruce seemed to be. They put the rest together from things I and others said."

Andrea let that admission slide. "She mention how she tried to comfort him by crawling into his lap?"

"I very much doubt it."

"You tell her you saw it all?"

As if the subject were some bothersome insect, Bill lifted his hand from her breast to wave it away. "She knows I couldn't care less. That's what infuriates her." He moved closer to nuzzle the side of her neck. "But let's not talk about her anymore. Let's talk about us."

Andrea set her drink aside, slipped her arms around his waist and eased up against him. "I think we've had enough talk. I've been dying to fuck you, ever since you walked through the door."

He caught a fistful of her short black hair and kissed her hard. When at last he came up for air, his hands helped hers with the buckle of his belt. Panting, he pressed his lips close to one ear. "I had this wild dream about you last night. Took me forever to get asleep again, once it woke me up. Want to hear it?"

Oh, do tell, she thought.

"I was on my back, where you insisted I lay perfectly still. Then you teased me for hours with your tongue. It was like water torture."

He was so primed, she figured he might last three minutes. Tops. She'd learned to count her blessings.

After a night of pacing his living room, alone with his thoughts like a trapped animal, Greg Nichols finally fell into a fitful sleep on his sofa. He didn't awake until noon, the dazzling winter sunlight eventually flooding his living room to hit him full in the face. His neck cramped as he tried to sit upright.

The nurse practitioner who drew his blood at Lenox Hill yesterday had said it would be at least twenty-four hours before his tests results came back. Meanwhile, with a much clearer head, he wanted to have another look at his car. His night of reflection had convinced him that, drunk or sober, there was no way that Bennett had driven the car thirty-six miles upstate with only one taillight. Not on a night as heavily patrolled as New Year's Eve, unless he'd devised some alternate means of transport. Last night, as Greg wandered his apartment, unable to sleep, he recalled that box van parked at the end of Dennis's drive. What was it really doing there? Was it big enough to accommodate his Saab? Could that be how Dennis had accomplished the seemingly impossible?

No matter how Greg looked at it, the conclusion was always the same. Bennett had killed Bruce Webster in an act of premeditated murder. The fact that it seemed to make no sense was immaterial. Dennis had a net worth in excess of thirty million dollars. There must be something here that Greg couldn't see.

It was early afternoon by the time he showered and was ready to hit the road. Phoebe had elected to spend the night at her place, and still hadn't called. Before he left, he tried her apartment and didn't get the machine. Just no answer, which was uncharacteristic. On Lexington Avenue, a half block from his building, he bought copies of the *Post* and *Daily News* before flagging a cab. On his way toward the car rental agency where Telenet had a standing account, he read recent news of the Webster killing. The dead man was the brother of a celebrity, and the story was getting more ink than most hit-and-runs. Apparently, police still had no reliable witnesses. The *Post* ran photographs of rock singer Diana Webster and her husband leaving the Medical Examiner's office yesterday. The *News* carried a picture of her outside the arrivals terminal at La Guardia, yesterday afternoon. She was accompanied by a man identified as a New York police detective, and a woman believed to be her sister. There was no way that NYPD was just going to go through the motions, the way cops loved to rub elbows with the rich and famous. Greg's nightmare got worse by the hour.

With most major shopping centers open, and retailers eager to squeeze every last dime from the holiday season, there was a fair amount of traffic as Nichols drove north into Westchester County. En route, he tried Phoebe again, from his cellular phone. Again, no answer and no machine. Where the hell was she, he wondered? At work? He tried her office number and couldn't reach her there, either.

A comforting, staid kind of affluence was in evidence everywhere along the winding, wooded roads that led to Dennis Bennett's Pound Ridge driveway. Until now, Greg hadn't given it much thought, but it seemed as though the poor and middle classes didn't exist in eastern Westchester. It made him wonder where the people who cleaned, mowed lawns, fixed leaky faucets, and plowed driveways lived. For four miles before he reached Bennett's place, he hadn't seen a dwelling that even a plumber could afford.

As he turned into Bennett's driveway, he noticed someone had plowed it clear of last night's snow. Of course. Home or away, Dennis would have someone on retainer to do such things. Greg then noticed the absence of that rented box van, supposedly left there by one of his buddy's neighbors. There were tire tracks in the fresh snow where it had been parked.

It seemed odd that every bit of snow had been cleared from in front of only two of the three garage doors. On either side of them, it was shoveled into thigh-deep piles. Greg parked, put on his gloves, and stepped out into the cold. A day and a half after Saturday night's blackout, he still didn't feel quite himself. He took a moment to gulp several lungfuls of icy air and waited for a wave of nausea to pass. When he spit, his saliva froze almost as soon as it hit the ground.

He had to assume that Bennett's alarm system was wired to protect the garage as well as the house. That would mean a motion detector inside, and magnetic contacts on the doors. He hadn't really thought about how he would get inside once he arrived here, and decided he would knock on the neighbors' doors and ask about the van, instead. If one of them had rented it, then he was back to square one. But first, it couldn't hurt to walk the perimeter of the garage; see if he could catch a glimpse of the damaged rear end of his car through a window. He'd been so muddled yesterday, he hadn't absorbed a lot of what he'd seen. It was all like a terrible dream. If he could stand on tiptoe and see his car, maybe some of what had happened Sunday morning might jar loose.

Snow hadn't been shoveled around the side of the garage. After that Christmas weekend snowstorm, and now this most recent one, the going was a bit of a slog. With the aid of an extension ladder found half buried in a drift, he finally gained access to a window set up high on the south-facing garage wall.

As bright as the day was, with brilliant sunshine

reflected off the surrounding snow, it took a moment for Greg's eyes to adjust to the comparative gloom of the garage interior. When they did, another wave of dizziness and nausea swept over him. The side where his car had been parked was empty. In one of the other two slots, vacant just yesterday, sat his old B-school buddy's turbo Bentley roadster.

Patrol officers Ernesto Rodriguez and Timothy Ryan had been forced to work the eight-to-four shift that Monday while most of their pals from the Four-Five station house were home watching bowl games. Such was the luck of the draw. But at least they were in a nice warm cruiser, and not working foot patrol. It was nasty cold out, despite all the bright sunshine, with a stiff, biting wind that swept the Bronx from off Long Island Sound. The wind was even colder here, where they patrolled the deserted southern section of Pelham Bay Park.

This remote, waterside stretch of the Bronx was always quiet this time of year. To patrol it generally meant a quick cruise through, to make sure vandals hadn't hit the public rest rooms, and the homeless hadn't built shelters beneath the picnic tables. No matter how much cardboard an individual could collect, or how many blankets, a person could die of hypothermia on a day like this. Ernesto Rodriguez knew. He'd been raised in a cold-water flat where the boiler was broken more often than it ran. To sleep in a box, in weather as cold as this, a man had to be crazy.

From the passenger seat, Ernesto nodded toward a late model sedan, dark green, parked down near the water at the end of one access road. "What do you think that dude is up to?" he asked his partner. "Goin' for a swim, maybe? Or gettin' his pipe cleaned?"

Timmy Ryan peered through the windshield across a cluster of snow-covered picnic tables. "No snow. At least it ain't abandoned. We should prob'ly have a look, huh?"

To do so, Timmy had to swing north around a wide, flat play area before he could catch the road going east. None of those secondary spurs had been plowed. The going was slick. Rodriguez noted a single set of tire tracks going in, and what looked like a solitary set of footprints going back out again. He pointed at the prints.

"Don't think it's been abandoned for long. Who parks his wheels out here, and leaves them?"

"Unless he's ditching them," Timmy supposed. "Or stalled." Not that he cared. Right now he was more concerned with getting stuck as he searched for a place to turn around. Rodriguez paid more attention to the car itself as they rolled by.

"Wait a minute, Timmy. What's that car everybody's lookin' for? You know. The hit-and-run wheels."

"Saab 9000." Ryan had slowed to ease the cruiser into a careful three-point turn. A glance back over his left shoulder got him his first glimpse of the parked car's rear end. The left quarter panel was stove in, the taillamp missing. "SID bulletin said they're lookin' for a late model. Ninety-six, I think."

"This one's gotta be almost brand new, bro. Same color, too."

"Let's call it in," Ryan murmured. "I think we just hit pay dirt, partner."

By the time Dante, Richardson, and Napier arrived at Pelham Bay Park, Don Grover and Rusty Heckman had already been on the scene for twenty minutes. They'd been in Queens, on Northern Boulevard, checking out a lead at a body shop. It was a straight shot across the Whitestone Bridge.

Uniforms from the Four-Five station house had cordoned off the area with yellow tape, then retreated to the warmth of their cruisers. The mercury loitered down around eighteen degrees, with the windchill in negative numbers. Joe wished he'd worn long underwear that morning as the wind bit through the fabric of his wool slacks. He approached Don and Rusty with shoulders hunched, his gloved hands plunged deep in the pockets of his overcoat, and surveyed the abandoned Saab.

"Doesn't look like it's been parked here long," he observed. "What've we got?"

"Plate registered to a Wooden Nickel Investments, Inc.," Grover told him. "Sole proprietor, one Gregory Nichols. Address on East Seventy-fifth. The Nineteenth's got a unit headed there now. You'll be interested, what we found in the trunk."

"It's too cold for three guesses," Joe complained. "Surprise me."

"A single, blood-smeared latex glove and a bloody gym sock. Wedged behind a road safety kit like someone in a hurry might'a missed 'em."

* * *

Nightfall was fast approaching when Greg Nichols returned his rental car to the midtown agency and stopped at Dennis Bennett's building on Sutton Place to confront him. The doorman contended that Bennett had left an hour earlier by cab, with luggage. He'd said he was off to meet friends in Acapulco for two weeks vacation. No longer willing to believe anyone, Greg tried Bennett's home number from his cellular phone. It got him Dennis's voice mail. On his way uptown to his own apartment, he called Phoebe again. Still no answer. For a panicked moment he recollected how chummy the former lovers had seemed yesterday. He started jumping to the assumption that they'd run off together, then forced himself to calm down. His fiancée was a bona fide workaholic. She wouldn't do anything to jeopardize her job. Not once in the two years he'd known her had she even called in sick.

Nichols was so distracted as his cab pulled up to his East 75th Street building that he was halfway across the sidewalk before he saw the police car double-parked just up the street. A surge of fresh panic got hold of him as two men in overcoats, talking to the doorman, suddenly turned to start in his direction. One of them looked directly at him, and nodded.

"Gregory Nichols?" The heavyset man produced a gold police shield and I.D. "Detective Bommarito. Nineteenth Precinct. This is Detective Cowan. You're under arrest, sir. For suspicion of vehicular manslaughter. You have the right to remain silent, the right . . ."

Nichols had watched enough movies and television shows to know the rest of it by heart, and didn't hear. Too much rage deafened him. That bastard Bennett. He hadn't just moved the car. He'd left it somewhere the police would be sure to find it. Good God. The worst of his nightmare was suddenly reality.

Greg didn't see the two uniformed policemen, from the parked patrol car, until one of them grabbed him to spin him around and jerk his hands behind his back. He didn't see the several pedestrians who stopped on the sidewalk to gawk as cold steel clamped shut around his wrists. Hands frisked him for weapons.

"He's clean, Rocky."

"Then haul his ass in," Bommarito replied. "We'll be along, soon as we're finished, upstairs."

Telenet was one of those trademark names that anyone at all tapped into the contemporary consumer culture knew. Neither Dante nor Richardson was clear on what exactly they produced, but both had heard the name associated with a number of communications products and services. Dante thought he'd seen hardware with the Telenet name on it, but couldn't recall just what it was. That the suspect arrested in the Bruce Webster homicide was this multinational corporation's chief financial officer seemed unlikely on first meeting. Gregory Nichols, white male, didn't have a gray hair on his head. Born in Brattleboro, Vermont, he'd earned a B.S. from Yale in economics, and an MBA from the Harvard School of Business. Before Telenet, he'd worked for Sun Microsystems in Mountain View, California, and Hewlett-Packard in Palo Alto.

"Quite a resumé," Jumbo Richardson growled as he stared across the table at their subject. Nichols was seated with his attorney in the Nineteenth squad's interrogation room. "You did attend your company's New Year's Eve party at the Doubles Club, correct?"

Nichols's attorney cleared his throat. "I don't care how obvious or innocent a question sounds, you answer nothing without my okay," he warned his client. A prematurely gray partner at one of the big downtown firms, the man had reportedly roomed with Nichols at Yale. No expert in criminal defense, he was pinch-hitting here until he had some idea of how strong the evidence against his client was. He nodded. "Go ahead."

"Yes," Nichols replied.

"And what time did you leave?"

The accused man got another okay from his counsel, then shifted in his chair with obvious impatience. "Like I told Detective Bommarito when he arrested me. I don't know. I have reason to suspect I was drugged."

"Hold it," the attorney ordered him. He reached out to grab Nichols's arm and stop him, but not quickly enough. "Just answer the questions, Greg. Offer nothing. I'm begging you."

Indignant, the accused man shrugged his hand away. "This is insane, Jay. I haven't done anything." He turned back to Dante. "Sometime around eleven, after consuming no more than three drinks, I passed out."

Beasley grunted and looked Joe's way.

"Drugged how?" Dante asked.

Nichols ignored his attorney's scowl to plunge

ahead. "Most likely? By something dumped into one of my drinks. I'll have a better idea once the toxicology report I requested at Lenox Hill emergency comes back."

The lawyer threw his pen at his pad in anger, sat back in his chair, and covered his face with his hands. Dante tried not to register the same amount of surprise as the counselor did anger. Either this was pure bullshit, or truly odd. "Requested it why?" he pressed.

Nichols looked at him as though he were dim. "I just told you. I thought I'd been drugged."

"And when did this test take place?"

The attorney growled through his hands. "Why don't you douse yourself with gas and light a match, Greg?"

"Almost as soon as I got back into town," Nichols replied. "Early Sunday afternoon."

From the briefing that Rocky Bommarito had given them on arrival, Joe knew that Nichols had denied driving his car that night. He claimed he'd been drugged somehow, and was trying to implicate a friend he'd invited to the party. Someone he'd gone to business school with.

"You told Detective Bommarito that this friend whose house you woke up in . . ." Joe checked his notes. "Dennis Bennett. Had called your girlfriend?"

"This interview is ended, gentlemen," the attorney announced, hands planted on the edges of the table before him. "I insist it be terminated before my client further incriminates himself. He's clearly distraught. Anything he said to Detective Bommarito is not admissible."

"Not my girlfriend, my fiancée," Nichols corrected

Dante. He refused to make eye contact with his counsel as he spoke.

"And she drove down from Stowe?" Joe asked.

Suddenly animated, Nichols leaned forward. "At least that's what they're claiming she did. For all I know, she was waiting for him at his place, when we got there."

"That's a pretty nasty thing t' say about your fiancée," Jumbo observed.

Nichols's face got hard around the mouth and eyes as he shook that judgment off. "Dennis moved my car and left it right where you people couldn't help but find it. He's left the country. What am I supposed to think? I've tried to reach Phoebe all day, and can't."

"So you think what?" Beasley asked. "She might've run off with him?"

"What else can I think?"

"But why? You sound like you think this Bennett killed Webster on purpose. Why would he do that?"

Behind Nichols, his counsel was on his feet, his face red with anger and the knuckles of his fists white.

"And whose blood is on the glove and gym sock we found in the trunk of your car?" Dante hit him right between the eyes with it.

The suspect blinked. "Beg your pardon?"

"Wait a minute!" the attorney all but yelled. "There's evidence against my client of yet another crime? One you haven't even charged him with? This is ludicrous. And borders on entrapment."

A knock came at the door. Guy Napier poked his head in. "Talk to you a minute, Lou?" he asked Joe.

Dante rose to join him in the hall, with Richardson close on his heels. "What's up, big guy?"

"Don and Rusty checked the garbage cans up and down his block while the lab boys were tossing his apartment." Napier eyed the agitated suspect through the glass as he spoke. Nichols and his attorney were having heated words. "They found a shopping bag in one, three doors down. The other glove and sock were in it. Along with a gray sweat suit, blood all over it, and a six-inch Sabatier Professional kitchen knife. Blood on it, too."

Dante felt his stomach tighten. Jesus. When he looked at his partner, he saw Jumbo staring back. "I believed that reaction we just saw in there. You?"

Beasley nodded, and glanced through the glass to where Nichols sat. "Seemed genuine t' me. But it could'a been the surprise of learnin' he'd left them things behind."

"Possible," Dante admitted. "But I don't think so. Something's out of whack here."

"The weight of the physical evidence is damning, Joey. Especially if we turn up a corpse. We got an address on this fiancée?"

Dante looked to Napier.

"Bommarito's report says Forty Central Park South," Guy replied.

Joe watched Beasley's expression as his partner stared in at their suspect. "Don't think it, buddy. I can't tell you how much I want her to still be alive."

NINE

Don Grover and Rusty Heckman arrived at 40 Central Park South ahead of any other response. It was almost six o'clock as they rode the elevator toward Phoebe Michel's floor. Grover had a date later, and both cops were tired. Heckman doubted he would be able to stay awake for the entire Fiesta Bowl, if he got to see any of it in the first place.

"You still haven't told me who the lucky child is, you intend to molest tonight," he chided his partner. Each of the nine floors drifted past with a paralyzing slowness; a journey best filled with idle chatter. "Same one you struck out with, New Year's Eve?"

"Hope you realize what an asshole you can be sometimes," Grover complained. "For your information, it ain't. It's her mother."

Heckman realized his mouth was agape and clapped it shut. "You're shitting me."

"Nuh uh. Trina lost her wallet on the floor of my car. When I couldn't get hold'a her, I found her mom's number on a card. Called and took it over there."

Rusty didn't know quite what to think of this. For any mother to fit Donnie's midlife crisis criteria, the daughter would have to be twelve. "And?"

"Woman opens the door is a stone-cold knockout. I think she must be Trina's sister at first."

"But turns out she's Mom."

The way Grover straightened the front of his coat and squared his shoulders, it looked like he was re-living the moment. A trace of that surprise enlivened his face. "It's amazin', Rust. I thought she was maybe thirty-two or -three, but she's gotta be closer t' forty. Had Trina when she was sixteen."

Forty? For the past sixteen months, Rusty had heard nothing but how women over thirty were too bitter, too set in their ways. Without exception. "I don't get it," he said, bewildered. "So what's this gleam I see in your eye?"

"Pure fuckin' lust, partner. She offers me a cup of java, I wind up spendin' over three hours."

"Doing what?" Donnie wasn't prone to embellishment, but this was too radical a shift. Rusty was determined to coax it out of him.

"Talkin'. Hell, I ain't spent three hours talkin' t' any broad in twenty years. Ever, maybe."

The elevator doors opened onto Phoebe Michel's floor. Heckman stepped out and paused there. "Talking."

Donnie scowled at him. "Yeah. " 'Bout how Trina's dad ran off, joined the navy, an' left her alone t' raise the kid for six years. Then the dude feels threatened, when she decides t' finish school."

"Did she?"

"With a fuckin' vengeance. Get's accepted t' City College, dumps the fuck, and goes on t' get her master's at Columbia. In audiology. Works for some hotshot ear surgeon, on the faculty at University Hospital."

In the wake of his own ugly divorce, Grover had channeled his anger into sexual aggression. He'd been badly used and was going to give back some of what he'd gotten. But it had lasted way too long, and right now, Rusty felt relief. At heart, Donnie was a great guy. But lately he'd been a real asshole with women. When Rusty reached out to grip his partner by the shoulder, Grover looked at him with puzzlement.

"What?"

"I dunno. It's just good to have the old Donnie back. I was starting to worry about you, partner."

"Fuck you."

Heckman grinned, released him, and nodded toward the hallway ahead. "Let's do this. If it's ugly, you go on and cut out once the cavalry arrives. No reason we should both hang around all fucking night."

"What about the ball game?"

"Tape it for me."

Phoebe Michel didn't answer her door. Heckman tried it and found it unlocked. That familiar gnawing feeling at the pit of his stomach started. The moment he pushed the door inward, his apprehension was justified. Stale air from the apartment interior hit him in the face. Dead air. With the extreme cold outside, the boiler in the bowels of the building had been cranking all day. A constant seventy-two or so degrees had hastened decomposition just enough that he knew, the moment he inhaled, that something had died in there.

"Holy Mother a ' God," Grover murmured as they entered the master bedroom. It looked like a slaughterhouse. The flowered wallpaper behind the headboard of a queen-size bed was spattered black, clear to the ceiling, where great gouts of blood had landed and dried. The mattress, also soaked a mottled rust and black, was stripped of bedclothes. The stink of death was so strong in there that both cops covered their noses with handkerchiefs.

Rusty approached the open bathroom door, where a blood-streaked bedsheet was left lying across the threshold. He could hear the buzz of flies in there, and knew what he would see, even before he flipped on the overhead light. The corpse of Phoebe Michel had been dumped in the bathtub, along with the comforter the killer had likely used to transport her. The knife slash across her throat was so deep that she'd been all but decapitated. The corpse was fully clothed; leggings, bulky sweater, and Doc Marten boots all in place. Her killer had come here with just one purpose.

One good look and Heckman turned to head back through the bedroom at a dead run. He managed to get to the tiny galley kitchen before he threw up. He even managed to hit the sink. He was wiping his mouth when he saw the set of Sabatier Professional knives.

Booked on suspicion of vehicular manslaughter, a practically numb Greg Nichols was transported to the city's downtown Manhattan lockup to await arraignment. The holding cell he was confined to was populated by six other men: two Hispanic and four black. All of them looked like hardened street criminals. When the door banged shut, and he found himself locked in with those leering miscreants, Greg felt his first wave of soul-shaking fear. Nothing up to that point had been real; the fingerprinting, the interrogations, the talk with his frat brother attorney, Jay Olgilvie. Jay was angry, but still promised to find someone to defend him. The concept alone threatened to smother Greg. Why defend himself? He was innocent. But now, shut up here with this gruesome crew, he forced himself to snap out of any sense of the surreal.

For two hours, Nichols sat huddled in one corner of the cell and tried to mind his own business. With even his belt and shoelaces removed, there was nothing tangible his cellmates could want from him, yet they were able to see and smell his terror. Twice, when the guard at the end of the block was distracted, they kicked him in an attempt to provoke. In his pressed khakis, buttoned-down oxford-cloth pink shirt, and bright yellow golf sweater, he was a clearly defined target and easy meat. Their keepers had thrown these predators a frightened rabbit, to tear apart for sport.

When Greg refused to respond to the second vicious kick—this one to the ribs—his tormentor squatted down at his level and got right in his face.

"Whassamatter, *blanco* boy? You like to get kicked? You got no fucking *cojones*?"

Greg looked up to stare into those flat, lifeless eyes and felt the blank nothingness send a shock wave to the core of his being. He'd never seen eyes like that, with no emotion, or anything else in them. Not even hatred.

"Wha'. You can' say nothing, *hombre*? Maybe you just too good, huh? Won' talk to no shitbird like me." That leering face broke into a broad, evil grin. "Man. Some big black dick gonna stretch that little pink hole of yours so big, you can park a fucking bus in there."

"Sounds like you speak from experience," a voice commented from beyond the bars.

The voice came from behind Greg, and above his head. He watched the face before him go rigid, plenty of hate there now, and saw those eyes rise.

"I don't take dick. I stick it. You wan' some?"

"Not my brand, Chico," Lieutenant Dante replied. "Let's take a walk, Greg."

When Nichols turned to look up, he found Dante outside the cell, a guard at his side. Tall and ruggedly built, the lieutenant had a whitened scar on his face that Greg had noticed earlier. It ran down across his cheek, from jaw to neck, to end less than a quarter inch from where the jugular vein in his muscled neck pulsed.

The jailer opened the cell door and beckoned Greg to his feet. Bewildered, the prisoner struggled upward, his cramped legs half asleep. "What's this?" he asked Dante. "My attorney can't be here. He was going to the opera." The wall clock said nine-thirty. Jay wouldn't leave Lincoln Center any earlier than an hour from now.

Dante led him toward a door at the end of the cellblock without explanation. Then, once they passed beyond it, he turned to Greg, his tone businesslike and matter-of-fact when he spoke. "You don't have to say a word, you don't want to. But this one is off the record. No tape recorder. No one else in the room. Just you and me."

Suddenly suspicious, Greg squinted back at him. "I don't understand."

"Just wait. You eat tonight?"

Because of the hour when he arrived, Greg had missed the evening feed here. He admitted to being hungry as Lieutenant Dante led him into an empty office, not an interrogation room. When they were both seated, the detective handed across a white deli bag, retrieved from the desk.

"Chicken salad on whole wheat." He picked up one of two paper cups, peeled back the lid, and nodded toward the other. "Coffee. Black. I could probably scare up some creamer. Help yourself."

Greg said it again. "I still don't understand." He opened the bag as he spoke, removed the wrapped sandwich, and flattened the paper sack in his lap. What the hell. He *was* hungry. He hadn't eaten all day. And though he hadn't eaten anything from a Manhattan deli case in years, how bad could it be?

The lieutenant gave the unnerving impression of not seeming to blink as he bore into his subject. It felt as though there was nothing those eyes would miss; like a rattler's, keeping vigil outside a rodent's burrow.

"Tell me more about your fiancée, Greg. About why you think she might've run off with this buddy of yours. The one who moved your car."

"I never said that!" Nichols snapped. Or had he? Jesus, the events of that afternoon and evening were such a confused jumble now.

"To the best of my recollection, you did. Or at

least implied it," Dante countered. Cool. No measurable heat in it at all.

"Was she involved with this guy?"

Greg waved a hand at the notion, dismissing it once and for all. "I was angry. Talking crazy. Phoebe wouldn't run off with Dennis, but I do think he used her. That's the only way I can figure it."

"Used her how?"

Greg thought that was fairly obvious. "To reinforce the bullshit story he fed me. By calling her down to Pound Ridge from Stowe, and feeding it to her, first."

Dante eased back a bit in his chair, overcoat falling open to reveal the empty holster on his left hip. A precaution, Greg supposed. A cop comes to talk to a criminal such as himself, no sense in taking the chance of having his weapon wrested away and turned on him.

"Is there any reason you can imagine why Bennett would want to see Bruce Webster dead? We've done a little checking. By our accounts, he doesn't sound like the cold-blooded killer type." Dante sipped at his coffee. Conversational. Relaxed.

"I don't know why," Greg replied, then leaned forward, his sandwich ignored. "But I've had the past four hours to think plenty about how."

"I'm a pretty good listener. Try me."

Animated, with much of what he'd been mulling for the past few hours suddenly in sharp focus, Nichols started to draw a word picture, as clear as he knew how. "There's no way he drove my car to Pound Ridge. Not New Year's Eve with all the cops on the road, and only one taillight. Even if he could, I know Dennis too well. He just wouldn't risk it."

"You're telling me you believe he had this all planned?"

"It's the only way it makes any sense," Greg insisted. "Whether I know why he wanted Webster dead or not. Phoebe saw that Ryder truck in his driveway, too. The one he must have used to transport the car. Ask her. He told us some story about a neighbor parking it there. I'll bet next year's stock options that Dennis parked it there himself."

Dante held up a hand as he jotted in the notebook now opened in his lap. "Ryder truck. Not U-Haul. Not Penske."

"That's right. A fairly big one. Plenty big enough to hold my Saab. Like I said. Ask Phoebe. We both saw it sitting there, plain as day."

Dante closed his notebook and set it aside, his hard-ass demeanor softening some. "I want you to think hard now. You claim you rented a car from that agency on Fifty-third Street around one this afternoon. We checked. It was one-twenty. You claim you never left your building before you caught that cab to go get the car. We're checking that, too. When was the last time you talked to your fiancée?"

Greg shrugged. He didn't have to think hard about it at all. "Yesterday evening. I told her a lot of what I just told you."

"And how did she react?"

"I think she thinks I'm crazy. But I tell you what. You want to know why Bennett might want to see Bruce Webster dead, she could probably give you a better idea of that than I could. She works as an analyst at the same brokerage where Dennis manages his funds."

Dante frowned, clearly not following. "Care to elaborate?"

Greg dug the sandwich out of his lap and took a first bite. It wasn't bad. "Sure. He got rich taking gambles that paid off big. There were people who claimed it would catch up one day; that his luck would eventually turn. Phoebe is one of them. She thinks he doesn't rely enough on the kind of information she and other analysts can provide; that he flies too much by the seat of his pants."

"So when you told her what you told her last night, how did she react, Greg?"

Nichols took another bite and shook his head with his mouth full. "Like I said, she thought I was crazy."

"You think she might've checked it out anyway?"

Another bite and another shrug. Now the sandwich was disappearing fast. "Ask her. It wouldn't be the first holiday she spent at the office. I tried her there when I couldn't find her at home, but struck out both places. My attorney can't find her either."

Dante came forward in his chair, those big hands of his with the scarred knuckles folded before him. Greg wondered how a man got hands like those. It looked like he'd been punching walls. For years.

"I don't know how else to say this to you, Greg. We found your fiancée in her apartment tonight. The Medical Examiner puts her time of death at sometime between ten this morning, and noon. Right now, that's all I can tell you. That, and I'm sorry."

What remained of his chicken salad sandwich hit the floor as Nichols grabbed at his midsection and doubled up, choking. A hot, hard lump formed in his throat, and his eyes filled with sudden tears. "No," he moaned. "Oh Jesus God, no." He rocked, eyes squeezed shut while tears of grief, helplessness, and rage poured down his cheeks. "I'll kill him," he heard himself snarl. He'd trusted a man he thought was his friend. Phoebe was the best thing that had ever happened to him. Smart, witty, vivacious. He forced himself to look up at the cop.

"How?" he demanded.

Dante shook his head. "You don't want to know, Greg. Believe me."

Jumbo Richardson was beat and wanted to be home, headed for bed. Instead, he was out here in the wilds of Queens, trying to track down a doorman who, more than likely, wouldn't be able to tell him dick. The damned homicide was eating at him and dragging him down into a dark mood. He could go the rest of his career without ever seeing another corpse like Phoebe Michel's. Homicides sucked, but sometimes there was an extra, predatory element that set certain killers apart. This guy Nichols, for all his buttoned-down crispness, was one of them. It made Jumbo wonder why he was bothering to go through the motions of hunting down a possible alibi for the guy. The evidence against the little preppy prick was overwhelming.

Aram Basralian was supposed to live on Elder Avenue in Flushing, off Kissena Boulevard. It wasn't far from the Queens Botanical Garden, but Beasley had taken a wrong turn and circled for ten minutes before he finally located the red-brick apartment building of the doorman's address.

The guy who opened the sixth-floor apartment door was still dressed in the satin-trimmed wool slacks of his uniform. His burly torso, clad in a sleeveless undershirt, was matted with thick black hair. He glanced briefly at Richardson's I.D. and shield, and then at him. "What you wan'?"

"You know a resident of the buildin' where you work, name of Nichols? Gregory Nichols?"

Basralian shrugged. "Sure. Misser Nickel. Good tipper." He grinned, a gold tooth showing.

"Nice guy?"

Another shrug, less committal this time. "Not as bad as some. Okay. Sure."

"You see him today?"

"Sure."

"Remember when?"

The off-duty doorman had to think about it, distracted by two squabbling kids who rushed past, one chasing the other and demanding the return of a toy. "After lunch?" He nodded. "Sure. I get back from break, he come down in elevator. Ask me, I got any newspaper?"

"He leave the buildin' then?"

"Later. Maybe ten minutes. He come back down, wearing coat."

That pretty much jibed with the story Nichols had told during his interrogation. Beasley looked for some other hole in it, not convinced he'd gotten the whole story here. "What about his girlfriend? She leave with him?"

"Today? No." The man seemed pretty positive on that point.

"When's the last time you saw her?" Beasley pressed him.

The kids ran past again and Basralian turned to yell something at them in a language Richardson didn't think he'd ever heard before. When he turned back, he scowled with impatience. "Yesterday, she drops him off. In her car. Land-Rover."

"She alone?"

"No. Another man. Misser Nickel, he look sick."

Nichols was claiming he'd spent the night at his buddy's house in Pound Ridge. that his fiancée and this buddy had dropped him off around noon, Sunday. The doorman's story seemed to bear that out.

"You ever get any complaints about them fighting? Ever hear 'bout him hittin' her?" Beasley asked.

That earned him a quick, derisive snort. "Heck no. They going to get married. All happy about it." He stopped to think about the implications of Richardson's question. It brought on another scowl. "What this about? Misser Nickel in trouble?"

"Maybe, maybe not." Beasley said it thoughtfully. "I appreciate your time, sir. Sorry to interrupt your evenin'." Maybe he'd been hasty in his rush to judgment, too eager to let the most obvious evidence tell the story. Less obvious was the fact, pointed out by those two cops who'd discovered the Saab in Pelham Bay Park. It hadn't stopped snowing until seven that morning. The Bronx had gotten three inches, and yet the car was clean. Joey had wondered why anyone would abandon a car there, unless he ultimately wanted it found, and didn't want to be seen leaving it. As Beasley started down the hall toward the elevator, he considered that question. It seemed like an awfully good one.

Once he parked his car in his neighborhood garage, it occurred to Dante that a couple of beers might make life more tolerable. He knew he should eat something, hungry or not, and stopped at a Ninth Avenue bar that did a fair burger. The place was crowded for a work night, with the weather as cold as it was. Joe hung his coat and scarf on a rack near the rest rooms and spotted an empty stool down near the end of the mahogany. He'd just settled in, ordered a pint of Guinness, a burger, and fries when a woman's hand touched him lightly on the shoulder. He turned to find Sandy Pruitt behind him, a coffee drink cupped in her hands. She wore a sheepish expression that was almost a smile.

"If you're still speaking to me, I think I owe you an apology," she said. "I behaved abominably yesterday."

"You'd had a rough one," he replied. Abominably was putting it mildly, but she was Diana's sister. He'd cut her some slack. "Here. Take my stool. I'll scare up another."

She tried to protest as he hopped down. He returned quickly with another stool and wedged it in next to hers.

"What are you drinking?" he asked.

"Irish coffee. I was out for a walk. Got cold."

"Another?"

She glanced at her near-empty glass and shook her head. "Not yet, thanks. Interesting crowd here. I feel like someone's grandmother."

That got a chuckle out of him. "I owned this town when I was a kid. Now it's this crowd's turn. I guess that's life."

She shifted on her perch to better face him. "Diana says you're from Brooklyn. You don't sound like it."

"Canarsie. Born and raised. I moved here straight outta high school. City College and construction jobs, to pay my way through."

With her gaze turned on him, those strange green eyes shone like polished malachite. Her wide mouth had the same intriguing downturn at one corner that Diana's had. "They're saying on the news today that you caught the man who killed my brother."

"I wish I could be sure," he replied, caution in it. That recent interview with Gregory Nichols was still so fresh, he could almost taste the man's grief, outrage, and tears. "Innocent until proven guilty and all."

Some of the anger he'd seen yesterday flared again. "He was at the same party, right? And it was his car? What more do you need?"

"We've found a few discrepancies, need to be resolved," he explained. "Another man was with him. There's a question about who was driving."

When she opened her mouth to press him for more, he checked her with an upraised hand. "But . . ."

"I shouldn't even have told you what I did," he said. "Sorry."

She forced a smile and made an effort to look grateful. "I appreciate the candor, Lieutenant. You don't know how infuriating all this is. Some drunk runs your brother down, then just drives off. I want you to catch the bastard and nail his balls to the wall."

"Just want to be damned sure it's the right pair."

"I understand." She swallowed the last of her drink, then signaled the bartender to order a Dewar's and water. "I suppose, in your line of work, if you're going to err, it better be on the side of caution."

He shrugged. "The mayor and city have a real thing about costly lawsuits. So how are you and your sister getting along?"

She looked hard at him, as though trying to determine what the question really meant. Apparently willing to accept it at face value, she sighed and looked away. "I was feeling pretty defensive last night. We've still got things to work out, but at least we're talking now."

From Brennan, Joe had a good idea of how rough the sailing had been. "Must be strange," he offered. "Getting to know a sibling all over again, who you haven't seen in twelve years."

The smile she forced wasn't as cheery as she probably intended it to be. "I assume you know all about what happened, way back when?"

He nodded.

"At this late date, I suppose it rang a little hollow, but last night I admitted I was wrong. I'm not proud I took my ex-husband's side. Other than my own insecurity, there was really no excuse."

Joe could imagine how hard it must have been for this woman, now a full professor and head of her own department, to swallow her pride like that. He also knew how badly Diana had been hurt. "Cliché or not, these things take time. But your sister doesn't have a victim's personality. She'll get past it, quicker than most."

Sandy studied Dante's face with new interest. "You're just about the best friend she has, aren't you, Lieutenant?"

"She calls me Joe. Most of my friends do. And no. Brian's the best friend she has."

"Joe." She tried it on for size.

"I'm that other guy-friend some women need. The one who can walk away, when the bullshit gets too deep."

"And how often does that happen?"

"Hardly ever." He grinned at the thought. "She likes having me around too much."

As Izzy Bristol slammed his pick down hard across the strings of his new Fender Stratocaster, the little Pignose amp on the table before him snarled back. Straight G-major chord, lots of hand action on the neck. Stretch it out and force it to scream.

"Thisss iss the year," he rasped, eyes squeezed shut. God, he could feel all that vibration, clear down to his balls.

D-minor, C. *"Gonna make them kneel and pray / For mercy. From me. Do anything I say."*

The guitar was an *old* Strat, actually. From the sixties. Just like Hendrix used to play. And Willie Scaife, from Alice Cooper. Izzy had scored it over Christmas. Swapped it for a couple dime bags with this hype on Avenue C. Ripped off from a van parked out front of CBGB. Sweet Jesus, it felt good in his hands; all that awesome history; all the miles it must have traveled before it came to him.

This was the year. Izzy had been chanting it like a mantra since New Year's Eve. Dick Ring and the Scroats was gonna break out; take the downtown Manhattan club scene by storm. Izzy would quit his shitty mailboy job at the brokerage house, get his tattoos finished, sign a record deal, be mobbed by a million babes, all dying to ride his bone. Move out of this East Village hole into something fine. Fifth Avenue penthouse. View of the park.

Like a man possessed, Izzy had locked himself in his two-room Avenue D apartment three days ago, and played his fingers raw. Two of the other guys in the band had gone home to the Midwest for the holidays. Sentimental assholes weren't back yet. But not Izzy. Fuck Mom and Dad. They weren't the future. Not *his* future. Ric Ocasek hadn't landed a babe like Paulina, and Tommy Lee hadn't grabbed Pam Anderson, by running home to mama every Christmas. Naw. Izzy was pretty sure. They'd stayed in the trenches. Fought the guitar wars.

When the phone rang, Izzy was so deeply entrenched, it took a moment to realize the noise wasn't emanating from his Pignose. Pissed at the interruption, he grabbed the receiver, full of surly.

"Fuck is this? I'm workin'."

"Sorry to bother you, Izzy. Your music, I presume?"

Holy Christ. It was Mr. Bennett. Calling him here. At home. Bristol answered cautiously. "Uh, yeah." Demeanor change time. This was a dude had partied with Bowie; had pictures on his office wall to prove it. A rich guy, could bankroll the whole Dick Ring thing. "Sorry 'bout that, Mr. B. Guess I was kinda deep into it."

"Not a problem, Iz. I admire that. Good weekend?"

"Two new songs," Izzy replied. "Both awesome." He'd given Bennett a demo cassette of six tunes, a couple months back. For an older rich guy, the dude wasn't such an asshole. Not like most of them at work. He talked to Izzy about his music. About other shit, too. Deliver his mail, drop into a chair for five or ten, and rap back. Dude knew Rage Against The Machine, Nine Inch Nails, Subdudes. Until now, Izzy had no idea that Bennett also knew his phone number.

"I'd like to hear them sometime," Bennett told him. "Another handful like those six you gave me, we'll have to find you fellows a producer. Very good, hard-edged stuff."

Anybody but Bennett, Izzy would figure: stroke job. But Bennett had the weight. Fucking *Fortune* did articles about this dude. "Thanks, Mr. B. So whas-sup?"

"I was thinking, if anyone could do me this favor, you could. But I'm reluctant to ask. It's rather un-usual."

Jesus. Mister Mutual Fund was looking to score.

"I told you, Mr. B. I'm your man. Anything you want. Except babes, a'course." Izzy chuckled. Ben-nett did pretty well in that area, all by himself. Shit, Bennett's parade of women, the three years Bristol had worked at Pierce, Fairbrother, was legendary. Man had proven something to Izzy with that display. The bulge of a fat wallet in a dude's pants beat the bulge of his dick, any day.

"I'm taking a vacation," Bennett explained. "Bonefishing. In the shoal waters off Quintana Roo and Belize. There have been recent reports of bandit trouble, one place I'll be. I thought some protection would be a good thing to have along."

Ah. So it wasn't dope. Interesting. Man wanted firepower. "Why me, Mr. B? Why not a gunshop?"

"Time is why not, Izzy. I only just heard about the trouble down there from a friend, and my flight is at six in the morning." Bennett paused. When he continued, his tone was hesitant. "There's an extra couple hundred in it for you, Iz. But if it's too much bother . . ." He let it hang long enough for Bristol to grab it if he wanted it. Izzy grabbed.

"Might take a couple hours, Mr. B. I'll have t' hunt around some." He was trying to think what he'd have to trade for something decent. Nothing he was willing to part with. "I'm, uh, a little short at the moment. Once I find what you want, you think you could, uh, meet me? Front me the cash?"

"Whatever you think is reasonable," Bennett told him. "I'll give you a number where I can be reached."

Bristol grabbed pen and paper.

"And Izzy," Bennett finished up. "I'd prefer you didn't mention this to anyone. When I return from my vacation, we'll see what we can do about setting you up with some record people."

By the time Bristol hung up the phone, he had to swallow hard to force his heart from his mouth. Scratch his back tonight and the dude who had partied with Bowie would turn the magic key. So what if Tommy Lee already had Pam Anderson? Izzy Bristol would step up to the pump, nail down Yasmine Bleeth.

When Dante had finished eating, and both he and Sandy had finished their drinks, he walked with her across 27th Street toward his building. Along the way, they talked about her move last year from Urbana, Illinois, to Springfield, Missouri. She admitted to missing the proximity to Chicago, once only two hours away. On the plus side, she had her own department now; something that had always been a dream.

"Nightcap?" he asked as they stepped aboard the elevator.

Her smile was easier now than it had been just an hour ago. She nodded. "That would be lovely. But aren't you awfully tired?"

"We had a nasty one this evening," he replied. "You'll read all about it in the papers. I never sleep well after something like that."

"Want to talk about it?"

He shook his head. "I'd rather talk about what you're doing. There's more hope in your line of work."

Inside his loft, he fixed them drinks. Sandy met Toby the cat and read a feeding note her sister had left. Of course, Toby tried to lie about that. Joe relented with a compromise handful of Pounce. When he emerged from the kitchen, a glass in each hand, he found his guest perusing the titles on his book-crammed shelves.

"It's true then?" she asked. "About the doctorate in behavioral psych?"

"Someday. If I ever finish my thesis." He handed her drink across.

She clicked her glass with his. "Cheers. You'll hate yourself if you don't, you know."

He took a slurp of his whiskey and smacked his lips. "Just do it, huh? Is it my imagination, or has the woman I met at the airport yesterday decided it's safe to lighten up a little?"

"Tall redhead? Big chip on her shoulder?"

"That's the one. If it wasn't politically incorrect to say so, I'd contend she was the best-looking social scientist I've ever met."

She registered surprise. "That is definitely politically incorrect. Watch it." Then, for the first time since he'd met her, she laughed.

Bennett thought the little blue Dodge Neon he'd rented under his new name pitifully underpowered and so cheaply constructed that executives at Chrysler should be ashamed to sell it. Crank windows rather than power. A suspension that jolted his molars each time he hit a pothole. Not exactly the turbo Bentley roadster he'd left parked in his Pound Ridge garage, but then what sort of statement would that car be making right now, on the Alphabet City streets of Manhattan's Lower East Side? Dennis needed to do this quietly, and that ragtop Bentley fairly screamed target.

The address Bennett had gotten from Izzy Bristol was on Avenue D, just south of 2nd Street. Izzy was the punk kid who delivered the Foray Fund mail every day he managed to show up for work, aspired to be a rock star, and liked to brag about the weight he carried on these neighborhood streets. Dennis wasn't surprised to see what kind of a dump the kid lived in.

On a night this cold, there wasn't much to fear about the rented Neon being stolen. Bennett left it at a hydrant to cross the ice-encrusted sidewalk to the door of Bristol's building. In a lobby strewn with empty malt liquor bottles and crumpled cigarette packs, he found a shiny new intercom panel, so recently installed that tenant names had yet to be placed alongside the corresponding apartment buttons. He pushed twelve.

"Be right down," Izzy's eager voice responded.

Back in his car, Bennett checked the time on the digital dash clock. Less than two minutes had elapsed before the mailboy appeared to scoot out the front door of his building, the collar of his black leather jacket pulled up and shoulders hunched against the icy wind. Dennis reached across to pop the passenger-door release. Once Izzy negotiated the ice, he jumped in.

"What's this?" There was definite disappointment in it. "I thought you drove a Rolls or some shit."

"It belongs to my housekeeper," Dennis explained. "I couldn't very well come here to purchase an illegal weapon in my own automobile, could I? And it's a Bentley, Izzy. Not a Rolls-Royce. Same manufacturer; whole other philosophy."

Most of that went right past Bristol, but he wasn't about to let on. He nodded sagely. "Once our first album goes platinum, I guess that's shit I'll hafta know, huh?"

"Without a doubt. And so much more. But you're a bright lad. You'll pick these things up. Just keep your eyes and ears open." Dennis reached to an inside pocket of his coat and produced a sheaf of seven one-hundred-dollar bills. "There's two there for you," he said. "But don't you think five a bit steep? For a street weapon?"

Bristol took the cash and tried to look like he wasn't counting it. "Not on short notice. You can get a piece'a shit for less, but this is a Browning nine.

Comes with an extra box'a cartridges. Hollow-points, dude tells me. Tips scored. Tear a guy's heart out."

Dennis smiled. "Let's hope it never comes to that, shall we?"

"Course not." Izzy had warmed to his subject now, and turned in his seat to get conversational, just like he did in Bennett's office. "But lemme ask you this," Bristol pressed him. "How you gonna get this through Customs down there? Them Mexican pricks catch you, they'll throw the key away."

Bennett gave him a quick, not-to-worry pat on the knee. "Diplomatic pouch. I have friends in high places, remember? Now. Shall we?"

Bristol straightened, stuffed the cash into a pocket of his jeans, and started to let himself out. "Prob'ly take ten or fifteen. Y'might wanna run the heater. I'll be back."

Left alone, Bennett contemplated the surrounding well-worn urban landscape and stifled a yawn. How crazy was this? he wondered. To give some deadbeat seven hundred dollars and expect a return on his investment. But then Dennis had spent months figuring out what this kid's buttons were, and how to push them. That picture of him and Bowie, snapped backstage at a concert twenty years ago, had done half the trick. The other half was his promise to use record label connections to help launch Izzy's career.

The weapon Bristol returned with, ten minutes later, was far better than anything Bennett had hoped to acquire off the street. A nine-millimeter Browning automatic with a five-and-one-half-inch barrel. In excellent repair.

"Nicely done," he complimented the mailboy.

Sprung, the magazine proved fully loaded with fifteen hollow-point rounds.

"Them two new songs'll be tight, time you get back from your trip," Izzy told him. "And I got ideas for at least two more. You think ten'll be enough t'go with?"

Bennett slapped the magazine home and toyed with the slide to test the strength of the spring action. "I should think so. You get those new numbers sounding like the others, I might pay for the studio time; to get you a proper demo mastered. Nothing lost in putting your best foot forward."

"Fuckin' A, Mr. B." Izzy told Bennett to have a nice trip and opened the door to head back across the sidewalk.

Left alone, Dennis racked a shell into the chamber before he started the car. The mailboy had almost reached the lobby of his building when Bennett tapped the Neon's horn, caught his attention, and waved him back. Smiling with the thought of his impending good fortune, Izzy stopped and turned. Dennis leaned over to crank down the passenger-side window. He didn't wait until the lad reached the car. No point in getting it messy with blood. When Bristol was ten feet off, Dennis raised his new purchase and shot him in the middle of the chest. He was forced to lean out the window a bit to get a second shot off. This one was at the head of Izzy's madly twitching corpse. Then he drove off to disappear around the corner onto Avenue B.

TEN

By Tuesday morning, the first official workday of the New Year, the Special Investigations probe into the death of Bruce Webster was already two days old. At nine forty-five that morning, Dante and Richardson met with Chief of Detectives Gus Lieberman in his office to discuss progress. Earlier, they'd stopped at State Supreme Court on Centre Street to watch Greg Nichols being arraigned. Guy Napier had been dispatched to the labs on East 20th Street to prod along the staff there, the analysis of evidence obtained from the Nichols and Michel apartments being a priority now. Don Grover and Rusty Heckman had headed off to see what they could learn at Ms. Michel's place of employment, down in the financial district.

"I don't get it," the chief complained. He closed the file folder he'd been scanning and tossed it onto his desk. "Why ain't this clown been charged with his fiancée's homicide, too?" A large-boned man, Gus

looked substantial behind his huge blond oak desk.
He had Joe and Beasley facing him, the thirteenth-
floor view of the East River and Brooklyn off to their
right.

"There's too much that doesn't add up," Dante
explained. He'd gotten a solid six hours sack time last
night and felt fresh for the first time since Saturday.
The report on his boss's desk included results of the
Nichols toxicology tests from Lenox Hill Hospital,
where blood work showed significant traces of GHB
or "Liquid X," the latest odorless and tasteless date-
rape drug. It also contained a summary of Jumbo's
conversation with the accused man's doorman last
night. "True, he could have dosed himself after the
fact. And the doorman might have had his head up
his ass. But there are other things, too." Joe had his
notebook open. He referred to it as he spoke. "For
instance. The Michel woman's time of death is estimated between ten and noon, yesterday. Her doorman says she left early, carrying a briefcase, and
hopped into a cab. Returned about ten, with the
briefcase again."

"What's this crap about the pizzas?" Lieberman
asked, gesturing toward the file.

"We think it was a diversion," Richardson replied.
"The killer blowin' smoke t' cover his arrival."

Yesterday, the doorman at Phoebe Michel's building had reported that six large pizzas were delivered
to a tenant who hadn't ordered them, sometime
around eleven. The deliveryman had been none too
happy about being stiffed, and had made a scene.

"While the pizza guy and the doorman were
arguin', this jogger in a stocking cap and sweat suit

comes in carryin' a laundry bag. He was in the elevator before the doorman could stop him."

"What about people comin' back down?" Gus wondered.

"Nobody he could I.D. The killer could'a let himself out the service entrance. Door there only locks from the outside."

"We searched the apartment," Joe added. "Couldn't find a briefcase anywhere." He had a picture of the bewildered and shaken Greg Nichols in his mind. Last night, he tried repeatedly to imagine Nichols with that Sabatier knife in his hand, cutting his fiancée's throat. And try as he might, he just couldn't conjure it. "While Napier's at the lab, he'll get the results of the blood analysis from the sweat suit Rusty found. It's an XL. Be loose on Nichols, the way he's built."

Gus fidgeted with a plastic cigarette and studied Dante for what Joe hadn't said. "I know that look you're wearin', Joey. You don't think Nichols is our guy."

Dante tossed an uneasy glance at Beasley, then met his boss straight on. "All of us have misgivings, Gus. Not just me. But I had a long talk with him last night, before I headed home."

"Where was counsel?"

"I told him it was off-the-record. Nothing admissible."

"Jesus."

"I know. But we were at that point. And based on our earlier interrogation, I already felt he didn't do it."

The chief flipped that little plastic cylinder end over end in his right hand and raised his eyes to the ceiling. "If the D.A. knew about this? She'd fry your balls for breakfast."

"No question."

"So?"

"He told me about a truck. In his pal Dennis Bennett's drive. Big rental van, with room enough for a car in it. Says his fiancée saw it, too. Told me to call her and have her confirm it, before I told him she was dead." Joe watched Gus's face. It stayed impassive. "Later last night, I asked the State Police to swing by Bennett's place in Pound Ridge. They made casts. Of tracks they found in the snow."

"Truck tires?"

Dante nodded. "They also found a Bentley roadster, parked in the garage just like Nichols said. I asked the Crime Scene Unit to send someone back to Pelham Bay Park. They found truck tracks there, too."

Gus held up a hand to stop him. "Why ain't any of this in the file?"

"I just got both reports back, right before we came up here. They'll send faxes, as soon as they do the write-ups."

"That truck at Pelham Bay was parked underneath an overpass, at the intersection of I-95 and the Pelham Parkway," Beasley added. "There's one set'a tracks from the bigger rig, an' one from a car."

Gus had stuffed that bogus butt between his lips. He spoke around it while patting his pockets for his lighter. "They doin' cast comparisons 'tween them an' the tires on the Saab?"

Joe pointed at the Zippo that had materialized in Lieberman's hand. "Don't light that thing, boss. I.D. on the separate sets of tracks in the park is positive.

We should have word on the State Police casts, up-state, any minute."

Gus threw the plastic cigarette across the room in disgust. He then swiveled from side to side in his chair, deep in thought. "I've met Dennis Bennett."

Lieberman's wife was heir to a Wall Street banking fortune. Therefore he often traveled in the same circles that Bennett would. The chief's access to that world was the source of some jealousy and resentment among other Big Building brass. Most of them couldn't imagine why any cop, eligible for maximum retirement benefits, would continue to work.

"Man's a wealthy guy. Kind of a legend," he continued. "What could his fuckin' motive be?"

Dante had asked Greg Nichols that same question. "Nichols thinks it's money." He took a moment to describe what Telenet CEO Bill Hoag had told them about the Omnicom deal, and explained that Bruce Webster was having misgivings the night he died. "If we can establish that Bennett had his neck out, with too much to lose if Bruce pulled the plug, we'd have all the motive we need."

Lieberman had turned to stare out his window while he listened. On a clear winter day like this, the weblike strands of the Brooklyn Bridge stood out black against the background of sun-bleached buildings beyond. The windshields of cars that crossed the bridge glittered like gemstones. "But why Nichols?" he asked. "Why frame him?"

Richardson grunted. " 'Cause he was handy. Sounds t' me like Bruce's doubts were pretty recent, based on bad test results only thirty-six hours old. That wouldn't give Bennett much time t' plan."

"Look at all the loose ends we've found," Joe agreed. "I doubt he had any time at all."

The Zippo still in his hands, Gus snapped it shut, open, and shut again. "I'd be damned sure where I was goin', if I decided t' crawl up that particular character's ass. You start slingin' mud, it better hit the mark, and stick."

"We're gonna need help, locating that truck," Joe pressed ahead. "It's probably one of the bigger move-it-yourself rigs Ryder rents."

"No problem. You get me the tire casts, I'll have Central Investigations find some warm bodies t' put on it."

Restless to forge ahead, Jumbo heaved his bulk from his chair to wander toward the window. He leaned against the sill and stared out at the borough of his birth. "Nichols told Joey that Bennett lives on Sutton Place," he said. "I'd be curious t'know where he parks his car. And what time he left his garage with it, yesterday."

When Telenet CEO Bill Hoag stepped to the press conference podium to announce acquisition of Omnicom, his company's stock was trading at twenty-six dollars per share. That was down nearly ten dollars from the fifty-two week high. The deal he announced meant a giveaway to Omnicom shareholders of four dollars per share, but Hoag was confident. His financial office staff had projected gains far in excess of any immediate outlay.

But that was *before* news of Bruce Webster's death and the arrest of Telenet's CFO for the crime. Fears that both stocks would go into the tank were rampant as Hoag took the podium, and he knew he had his work cut out for him. For a full thirty minutes he extolled the virtues of this merger in terms that could leave no doubt about the effect it would have on the telecommunications marketplace well into the next millennium. Rather than ignore those tragic developments now dominating tabloid headlines, he took pains to mention them, and then to separate the announced deal from them. Telenet was acquiring a revolutionary new technology, already real and ready to go on-line by early autumn. He was confident that investors would see this unique opportunity to participate in a development as revolutionary as the fax machine, for what it was.

Hoag felt his speech had gone well. God knew he'd come prepared. Yesterday, he and the marketing department's audiovisual staff had rehearsed every slide change, run every computer graphics effect, and checked each foot of videotape projected onto the screens behind him for over six hours. While he described an advancement that would allow computer users to receive super-crisp, real-time video images, transmitted station-to-station over their phone lines, beautiful images created by the new technology paraded across the huge screens behind him.

To confirm the astonishing performance and capability claims Telenet made, trim showroom models in blazers, silk blouses, and short skirts handed out brochures jammed with glossy, full-color support documents. A lavish breakfast buffet was being catered in an adjoining room, to get the media in a receptive mood. It seemed to be working. Despite the news of

Greg Nichols's arrest, the fax machines and phone lines provided in the press room were jammed.

Earlier that morning, before Grover and Heckman had left for Pierce, Fairbrother, Dante had recapped his conversation with Greg Nichols for them. That, together with other statements the suspect had made in the wake of his arrest, put a discomfiting twist on some assumptions the investigation had made. For the hour they spent in the company of the brokerage's Analysis Section chief, the connection between the dead woman, Phoebe Michel, and this fellow Dennis Bennett nagged at Rusty Heckman.

The murder victim's office was a spartan affair, consistent with the sort of personality that Rusty imagined a good securities analyst would have. The room was spacious, with a big south-facing window that overlooked New York Harbor. There was no clutter. While Donnie had concentrated on the physical layout, riffling through drawers of computer printout all neatly labeled, personal effects in the woman's desk, and the reference materials on her bookshelves, Rusty toyed for a while with her computer work station. Before joining SID, he'd spent three years in the Organized Crime Control Bureau's Fiscal Section and had become an information-processing wizard. Now, having been granted access to the main Pierce, Fairbrother data banks, he explored the most recent activity on Phoebe Michel's hard drive.

A light knock came at the door frame and Ms. Michel's secretary, Donna Meehan, poked her head into the office. "I'm gonna take my break. You guys

want anything from the cafeteria? Croissant? Bialy?"
Still stunned by the news of her boss's murder, she
asked it softly. To judge from her short skirt, Day-
Glo pink nail polish, and teased mass of red hair,
Rusty guessed that such sobriety was not her usual
demeanor.

Never one to refuse food, Grover reached for his
wallet. "Bialy with butter'd be great, Donna. Maybe
I'll fire up the coffeemaker, huh?" As he said it, he
moved to the credenza where the unit was perched
and removed the filter drawer. The grounds left
there from the last pot looked damp. He probed
them with a finger. "I'd say she was here awhile yesterday, settled in t' do some serious work," he told
his partner.

"How's that?" Rusty asked. He glanced over.

"Grounds here are wet." Don turned back to the
secretary. "You dump the pot?"

She shook her head. "It was empty."

Rusty wondered why, if Phoebe Michel had spent
two hours working here yesterday, he could find no
evidence of it. At least not on her computer. The
only thing that was clear was the time she'd logged
in. Nine-oh-eight.

Ten minutes later, when Donna Meehan returned
with Grover's bialy, Rusty decided it was time to take
a break. By that time, the new coffee in the carafe
was almost ready. He stood to stretch the kinks out
of his lower back.

"Why don't you pull up a chair?" he suggested to
the young woman. "You might be able to help us."

Tall, at nearly six feet, she was all gangly angles,
with nary a curve, lots of freckles, and a tiny pug
nose. In the face of Rusty's invitation, she was hesi-

tant. "I gotta warn you, I don't know anything about stock analysis, Sergeant. I just answered her phone an' made her appointments."

Heckman patted the seat of the chair he'd been sitting in, then crossed to fill a foam cup with coffee and offered her some. She sat, and nodded.

"Sure. Thanks. It's kinda nice t' get outta that office. Everybody walks by acts like I got the plague. It's creepy out there."

Rusty carried her cup to her, then eased up alongside Donnie, propped against the front edge of the desk. "Tell us what kind of mood your boss was in, Donna. The last time you saw her before the holiday weekend."

The redhead sipped at her coffee and shrugged those wide, angular shoulders. "In a great mood. She an' some'a the others was all going skiing. Up in Vermont."

"You ever met her fiancé?" Grover asked.

"Greg? Yeah, sure. Lotsa times. You ask me, it's crazy, anybody thinks he done this. He was nuts about her."

Heckman stared out at the brilliant winter day and Miss Liberty, the gilt on her torch gleaming bright with reflected sunlight. He tried to picture the woman he'd found in that bathtub last night as whole and vibrant; excited about life and the skiing trip she would take. "No Mr. Hyde side then?"

Donna Meehan scoffed at the idea. "I worked for Miss Michel four years, Sergeant. The past year and a half, I ain't never seen her more happy. Contented. I don't think they'd even had their first fight yet, which is weird, considerin' the kinda guys I meet."

"The log downstairs says a man named Bennett

was also in the building yesterday, same time as her."
Donnie said it with his mouth half full as he
munched contentedly on that bialy. "You know
him?"

"Dennis Bennett?"

He nodded.

"Sure. Everybody here knows him. Miss Michel
was pretty serious with him, once upon a time. I used
t' see him up here quite a lot."

Greg Nichols had mentioned that his fiancée and
Dennis Bennett had been involved once. An old
B-school chum of Nichols's at Harvard, Bennett had
introduced him to Phoebe Michel. Even so, Rusty
wondered how Bennett had known where to find her,
Sunday morning. In Vermont, no less.

"Those two were still friendly then?" he asked.
"Your boss and Mr. Bennett?"

That earned him one of her expressive shrugs. "A
guy as hunky and fulla silver-tongued blarney as him
is prob'ly hard t' stay mad at for long."

"Mad at? For what?" Donnie wondered.

Up to that point, she'd been at ease with their
conversation. Now, turtle-like, she decided it was
time to pull her head in. "I don't think I should talk
about that. It's really none'a my business."

"This is a homicide investigation," Donnie reminded her.

Clearly uncomfortable, and having second
thoughts about what she'd already said, the secretary
shook her head. "It don't have anything t'do with
that. Mr. Bennett's got some serious weight around
here. I ain't gonna be spreadin' gossip about him."

Rusty eased away from the desk to approach her,
his attitude easy and nonconfrontational. "I don't

know if this information is important, Donna, but it might be. Understand, you tell us, it's not gossip. And that you don't have to fear for your job." He gestured for her coffee cup and carried it to the machine to refill it. "We need to know about Phoebe Michel's relationships. It's an important part of this murder investigation." He used the word *murder*, rather than *homicide*, on purpose. Civilians tended to react more emotionally to it.

Ms. Meehan sighed and stared blankly ahead, rather than at either detective. "She caught him screwin' around. Found out he'd been doin' it for months. And when she found out with who, she had a fit."

"That made a difference?" Grover asked. "Who?"

"I guess. Her bein' direct competition and all. Maybe if it was just some bimbo, she wouldn't have got so uptight."

"So who was it?" Rusty pressed her.

She started to look like she might get cautious again, clearly not liking the spot she found herself in at all. "Lady used t' work for him." She said it hesitantly. "As one'a his submanagers."

"At Foray?" Donnie asked.

She nodded. "Uh huh. Andrea Hill."

Well, well, Rusty thought. He glanced quickly at Grover and saw the same thought running through his head. What kind of a coincidence was this? Cops learned to hate coincidences. Neither Don nor Rusty had met Andrea Hill, but according to Beasley Richardson, she was some sort of package. Interesting.

They thanked Ms. Meehan for being forthright with them. As she scurried back to her desk, relieved to be away from them, Rusty returned to that hard drive. He'd barely had time to switch the machine back on when the Analysis Section chief reappeared.

"How you getting on, Officers? Has Miss Meehan helped you find everything you need?"

"Doin' just fine," Donnie told him. "She's been a great help. By the way. While we're here, we'd like t' have a word with an old friend of Ms. Michel's. Guy who works here."

"Certainly. Who would that be?"

"Dennis Bennett. Could y'point us toward his office?"

The section chief frowned. "Won't do you any good, I'm afraid. Mr. Bennett's on vacation, this week and next. He left last Friday for Mexico."

"Friday?" Donnie looked confused. "You sure? We saw his name on the sign-in log downstairs. It says he was here just yesterday."

The section chief pursed his lips as he thought about it, and ultimately shook his head. "I don't see how. I distinctly recall a memo that crossed my desk, last week. He's out of town until mid-month. I'm sure of it."

Dante and Richardson tuned to WINS radio—all news, all the time—while Joe drove them from headquarters to Sutton Place, east of midtown. They were curious about what sort of play the Nichols arrest was getting, and almost as interested to know when this current cold snap would break. They caught the broadcast's hourly business update, first. The Telenet Corporation had announced their acquisition of West Coast telecommunications innovator Omnicom, in a two-for-one stock swap. Together, they would produce a revolutionary new video teleconferencing technology, scheduled to be on-line by the fall. Initial investor response to this news was mixed, most likely affected by news of Telenet CFO Greg Nichols's arrest. His being charged with vehicular manslaughter in the death of Omnicom's president, Bruce Webster, saw the prices of both stocks tumble for the first hour of trading after the announcement was made. Then, astute investors, recognizing profits to be reaped through the announced deal, had flooded in with a frenzy of buying. Both stocks had made big moves since, with Omnicom up nearly five dollars a share, and Telenet up three. If that trend continued, the five million dollars' worth of Omnicom stock in Webster's estate might be worth twice that, by day's end.

The lead news item at the top of the noon hour was the indictment of Congressman Roberto Isabel. He was charged with misappropriation of administrative funds, and in a statement released by his Twelfth Congressional District office, he'd proclaimed his innocence. While he swore to fight those charges, he also announced he would not seek reelection in November.

"One possible replacement candidate, already being mentioned by sources inside the Hispanic Democratic Coalition," the announcer droned on, "is Manhattan District Attorney investigation squad commander, Captain Rosa Losada."

"Fuckers work fast, don't they?" Jumbo marveled.

Dante gripped the wheel in frustrated anger and shook his head. "Shit. It's already started. And Ruiz swore to her, no one would mention her name before tomorrow night."

"That asshole told me the earth was round, I'd be sure t' double-check," Richardson sneered. He pointed at an awning on the East River side of Sutton Place. "That's Bennett's address, there."

Dante pulled to the yellow-striped curb out front. Their arrival attracted the attention of the doorman, who hurried out waving his hands and shaking his head. Richardson ran down his window.

"Can't park here, fellas. Gotta keep this clear."

Jumbo tinned him. "Lieutenant Richardson, Special Investigations. Just need t' ask a couple questions."

The doorman scrutinized the shiny gold shield, and then its owner. The corners of his mouth creased deep, he eyed Beasley with a measure of caution and suspicion. His responsibilities included a first line of defense against all manner of inconvenient intrusions. A sheaf of crisp Christmas hundreds lined his pockets as a recent reminder of how vigilant his well-heeled handlers expected him to be. "Such as?" he growled.

Jumbo took the most useful tack. He lied. "One'a your residents reported vandalism done to his car." He glanced into his lap, at a nonexistent note. "A Mr. Dennis Bennett. Drives a Bentley roadster. Dude must have pull. The call t' investigate came from the mayor's office."

"Yeah? And?" Like everybody here knew Hizzonner on a first-name basis.

"We need t' talk to him. All we got from some assistant at City Hall is this address. Nobody knows where his garage is s'posed t' be."

"You're outta luck, you wanna talk to him. Left on vacation, yesterday. But I can tell you where he parks, no problem. Aroun' the corner on Fifty-ninth. Couple doors down, onna south side."

The garage was an establishment typical of an affluent Manhattan neighborhood. Its hourly and single-day rates were so prohibitively high that transient traffic went elsewhere. It prospered by offering pampered service to its regulars, the monthly clientele who tipped handsomely and expected prompt access to their cars in return. Dante parked at a hydrant across from the entrance ramp on 59th. Together, he and Richardson waited for a break in traffic, then sauntered across.

The kid in uniform shirt and matching chinos who lounged in the heated office watched their approach without rising. No tip here. He waited for them to come to him, which didn't bother either cop one bit. It was cozy in his office, and brass-monkey cold outside.

"What can I do for youse officers?" He asked it before they produced tin or I.D. The name patch over his shirt pocket read: *Willie.*

"Man name of Bennett parks his Bentley roadster here," Dante replied. He didn't state it as a question, and showed his lieutenant's gold to the kid anyway. "We'd like to have a look at it."

Willie lifted his hands from his lap in that classic gesture of helplessness. "No can do, Officer. Took it out, 'bout this time yesterday. Ain't been back since."

So, he'd left *after* Phoebe Michel was killed, and an hour before Greg Nichols and his doorman said Greg had left his building. Dante reflected on how close those two must have come to running into each other, upstate.

"Nice car; that turbo Bentley," Joe ventured.

"Never had the pleasure, myself. It handle as nice as they say?"

Willie gave him a slow, sly smile. "Wouldn't know, Officer. All I do is park 'em."

With Donna Meehan gone off to lunch, Grover and Heckman were left to their own devices inside Phoebe Michel's office. Don continued to work his way through the physical layout of the office, while Rusty remained seated at the computer terminal. All his expertise notwithstanding, Heckman at last gave up trying to resurrect yesterday's work file.

"Too weird," he complained, and rubbed his face with open hands in frustration.

"What is?" Grover was back on his knees before another open file drawer, his tone distracted.

"She did work yesterday, I'm sure of it. But it's gone."

Don rose to amble over. He was well acquainted with his partner's computer background, and had even played with the sophisticated setup Rusty had assembled in the basement of his Woodside, Queens, home. The damned thing had cost a fortune. Not that Don minded. It cost him nothing but a phone call from his own home computer to access the World Wide Web, using Heckman's brawny system as his server. "You think there's any backup?" he asked. "Don't most'a these big outfits do routine file copying, matter of course?"

Rusty hit a key and the dead woman's screen-saver images reappeared. Vultures. Probably something she'd created herself, or bought in some information superhighway curio shop. Dozens of them, roosting on branches and peering hungrily into the electronic void. "Not likely," he replied. "Not over a holiday weekend."

"So one tap of the delete key and what? It's history?"

Heckman continued to stare at the buzzards. His mind flashed to the scene in the bathtub in Phoebe Michel's apartment again. The dead lady had possessed a sense of humor; slightly twisted. "Whoever tried to erase it probably thought so," he allowed. "Might have been Ms. Michel herself, to keep her co-workers from snooping."

"You say that like maybe it wasn't, Rust."

"Not necessarily. But there's a program we can use to un-erase it. Norton Utilities. Just as long as nothing's been written over the old data, since."

"Un-erase?"

Rusty reached behind the machine for the power cord, yanked it, and coiled it in his hand. "Exactly. Could be, we'll only get fragments. Still, some of it will be there." He disconnected the monitor, keyboard, and modem lines from the computer, then lifted it to wrap the power cord around it. "It's like when a teacher erases a chalkboard. The writing pretty much goes away, but you get up close, generally you can still read the ghosts."

ELEVEN

As Dante and Richardson left Dennis Bennett's garage, Joe got on his cellular phone with Gus Lieberman, downtown. He gave the chief an update and asked him to generate a warrant to authorize a search of Bennett's apartment, based on what they'd learned. Lieberman told them to sit tight, so they found a hole-in-the-wall Chinese joint a few blocks north on First Avenue, and settled in to have lunch. Almost an hour passed, and both men had consumed enough green tea to float a small boat, before Gus finally called back.

"The judge saw whose name was on the request and got cold feet," he apologized. "Wall Street celebrity and all that crap."

"He sign it?" Dante asked.

"Took a little persuadin'. Napier went over with an assistant D.A., t' help plead our case. He's got it in his pocket, now. Him and the legal beagle are both on their way."

The moment Dante disconnected, and raised his hand for the check, his phone rang again. This time it was Grover.

"Where are you, Donnie?" he asked.

"Still at the dead lady's office. Just gettin' set t' leave. We talked t' Napier. He says you're gonna toss Bennett's place."

"You available?" Joe wedged the phone between shoulder and ear to dig for his wallet.

"We'll be there. And get this. Bennett's name is on the Pierce, Fairbrother security log for yesterday mornin'. Showed up an hour after the dead broad, an' left only a couple minutes after."

"Woman, Donnie."

"Either way, she's dead, boss. Rusty's impounded her computer. We'll see you, soon as we can drop it at the Big Building."

Rusty Heckman had that computer tucked beneath one arm and waited for an elevator to take him and Grover to the Pierce, Fairbrother lobby when the doors opened and Steve Reynolds walked out. The big, crew-cut homicide detective from Manhattan South was followed by Dave Gibson, another member of his squad.

"Hey," Reynolds greeted them. "Fuck're you two doin' here?"

"Michel homicide," Grover explained. "Someone got our wires crossed?" It happened on occasion, early in an investigation. Two squads each went to work on the same case, unaware that one or the other had caught it.

"Naw," Reynolds dismissed his concern. "Some

punk dweeb mailboy caught a couple on the sidewalk outside his buildin' last night. Looks like a Lower East Side drug hit t' us. We're just goin' through the motions here."

Two employees of the same brokerage, victims of homicides in separate Manhattan locations, on the same night? Coincidences were piling up, and Heckman wanted to know why. "A mailboy, you say?"

A nod. "Some grunge-rocker freak named Bristol. Body tattoos, nose ring, the whole bit. We're headed down to Personnel, now."

Heckman turned to his partner. "Get on the horn, Donnie. See if you can touch base with Joe. I'm going to tag along with these guys."

"Why?" Reynolds asked, his interest piqued. "Y'got somethin' we don't have on this yet?"

"Just one big puzzle and a lot of loose pieces," Rusty explained. "This dead guy of yours may or may not fit, but we'd be crazy not to check it out."

Not long after Guy Napier took the wheel to drive himself and Deputy D.A. Stephanie Gilchrist from the courthouse on Centre Street to Dennis Bennett's Sutton Place apartment, the petite counselor looked over to study his profile.

"You've got the same last name as my favorite teacher in high school," she told him. "Any coincidence?"

"Bayside, Queens?" he asked.

She twisted suddenly in her seat, her expression animated. "I knew it! Phil Napier. Is he your uncle or your father?"

"Dad."

"Damn. I don't think there was any girl I knew in school who didn't think he was the sexiest man alive."

Guy shot an uncomfortable glance her way. This small, curly-headed blond was just a little too attractive to be talking about his father like that.

"Not as tall as you, but still. What a hunk. God."

"You mind?" he complained. This wasn't the sort of thing he wanted to hear from one of his father's former students. A history teacher, the old man was in better shape than most of the P.E. coaches at Bayside High.

When she turned further in her seat to face him, her overcoat flopped open to reveal a stretch of leg, bare from ankle to mid-thigh. "Sorry. Am I making you uncomfortable?" She saw him look toward where she sat on the seat, and grinned. "Relax. He never did anything about it. Maria Borelli was the hottest girl in our class. She tried to seduce him and he just said no."

"You enjoying yourself?" he growled.

"Mmmm. Where'd he hide you?"

"Howard Beach. I was the Gottis' paperboy."

"Post or *Daily News*?"

"Neither. *The Wall Street Journal.*"

They found a doorman out front of Bennett's address, hands on hips, giving Dante's double-parked Taurus the evil eye. Guy pulled up to park directly behind, just as Dante and Richardson emerged from their car. Inside the building, the doorman summoned the superintendent. Shown the warrant, the super left to fetch Bennett's front-door key. Dante cornered Guy near the elevators.

"Lab make any progress?" he asked.

"Some. The tread casts the state cops made of the truck tires in Bennett's driveway match the ones our guys made at Pelham Park. Still no luck finding the truck, though. Safe and Loft caught it. They've got five guys working all the rental locations."

Guy saw his boss sneak a look at the curly-headed prosecutor, and found her slyly regarding him in return. Hormones. Everyone had them.

"What about hair and fiber?" Joe asked.

"No match. At least not between Nichols and anything on the gloves, socks, or sweat clothes. His hair and prints are all over the homicide scene, obviously." He paused to think back. "Oh. One other thing. They found an empty condom wrapper in her purse. Still damp with nonoxynol-9 spermicide."

"Why in her purse?" Dante wondered. "They analyze the hair follicles vacuumed from her bed?"

"Just hers. And the fiancé's."

Once the super returned, they all climbed aboard an elevator for the ride upstairs. The assistant D.A. was paying all her attention to Dante by then. Not that Guy minded. Telling a man how hot she thought his father was? As a turn-on, it left a lot to be desired.

Initial investor response to the Telenet acquisition announcement had Andrea Hill in a panic for a while. Then she saw on the NASDAQ board that a turnaround had occurred, and felt her excitement rise. She spent the rest of the morning returning phone calls from venture capitalists and bond merchants. It was a new year in a brave new world, and everyone had something to sell her. At eleven-thirty, she'd tried Dennis at his office, only to be informed he was on vacation. She wondered what that was about, and tried him at home, where she didn't even get his voice mail. At one, she'd broken for her lunch with Bill Hoag. Elated over the reception the Telenet–Omnicom merger seemed to be getting, he was in a mood to celebrate. Even her mention of Greg Nichols's arrest yesterday hardly seemed to faze him.

On her way back to her midtown office from Le Bernardin, Andrea wondered if Dennis had heard the news about Phoebe Michel. It would be just like him, not to be bothered much at all. He could be a coldhearted son of a bitch sometimes. Maybe it was just his British reserve, but Andrea didn't think so. She wondered why he hadn't called her today, after she'd put her fanny on the line for him the way she had. *He* was the one who should have invited her to lunch today, and dinner, too, for that matter. It wasn't just a fire she'd fetched his fat from. It was a goddamned inferno.

Back at her desk, Andrea had worked up a pretty fair peeve before she tried Bennett's apartment again. This time, an unfamiliar voice picked up.

"Hello?"

"I'm sorry," she apologized. "I must have the wrong number." And as she hung up, she realized that was impossible. She'd used the speed-dial button.

Most of the messages her secretary had left stacked on her desk were from more hot-deal merchants. The only one that intrigued her had been left by that good-looking police lieutenant, Dante. The one with the delicious dueling scar. He'd left his number and asked her to call. They'd already arrested Greg Nichols, so she wondered what it could be about. No wedding ring. Great body. Maybe he wanted to ask her out. If that was the case, and Dennis didn't watch his step, she might just accept.

"Lieutenant Dante," he answered when she dialed the number. The connection sounded cellular.

"Andrea Hill, Lieutenant. I have a message here from you."

"You at your office?" he asked.

"I am. What's this about?"

"Gonna be there awhile? I'd like to come by in an hour; ask a few more questions."

She told him she'd be there until five, cradled the receiver, and licked her lips. Dennis had sorely tried her good nature. At three million a year, she was a force to be reckoned with already. And by year end, it might be closer to six million. She'd saved Bennett's ass, and dammit, he was playing games with her.

Guy Napier and the other cops involved in the Bennett apartment search were a little over an hour into it when Guy elected to try the basement, to sort through Bennett's trash. A distasteful enterprise, it was nonetheless an integral part of any thorough search.

After the long, party weekend, all ten of the building's rolling Dumpsters were filled to overflowing with empty liquor bottles and fetid food scraps. It was a mild stroke of luck that most of the residents employed white garbage bags with drawstrings, while

Bennett and only one other resident used the handle-tie variety. Guy was a half hour going through each Dumpster to separate them from the rest. That task completed, he was left with just six sacks of trash. Neither Bennett nor the other handle-tie user was pulling his weight in a consumer economy, it seemed, but then Guy couldn't imagine a home much less lived-in than the fund manager's sprawling digs.

Three of the six bags were easy to eliminate. They contained junk mail and magazines addressed to the other tenant. A fourth bag had empty Ensure cans and a Depends carton mixed in, a fair indicator it was not Bennett's. The last two contained pieces of mail addressed to the suspect, various empty bottles, scraps of food, empty take-out cartons, a pair of wet sneakers that smelled of ammonia, and dirty tissues wrapped around two spent condoms. Guy found it curious that a man would scrub a brand-new pair of sneakers, then throw them away. He remembered the torn condom packet in Phoebe Michel's purse, and made a mental note to ask the lab techs to vacuum Bennett's bed.

Dennis Bennett had converted a stateroom aboard his sixty-foot Baia luxury cruiser into a study. In it, his face lit by the glow of the computer monitor screen, he watched with satisfaction as the Omnicom and Telenet turnarounds progressed. At eleven that morning he'd used the margin buying power of his own Foray Hi-Yield Fund to stop the skidding of both stocks before it got any worse. Once prices leveled off, he'd begun to use what paltry cash reserves he had left in a half-dozen personal brokerage accounts to buy both stocks, fast and furious. It took the entire two million to start those securities inching up. All the while, he'd cursed other investors for failing to jump on board his bandwagon any sooner. And then, in a mere thirty minutes, the surge of new interest was on. Foray Hi-Yield had bought big at six and twenty-one. His other phantom investors had provided just the right impetus to touch off the buying frenzy he witnessed now. At noon, Omnicom was trading at twelve and a half, up nearly five points from what it opened at, and now Bennett was feeding that frenzy. At twelve-fifteen he dumped his first hundred thousand shares. At twelve-thirty, another quarter million. Now, as industry analysts began to look past the death of Bruce Webster and could start to quantify what this merger meant to Telenet's profit picture, the per-share price was skyrocketing. This play would net Dennis at least thirty million off the twenty-two he'd invested. It was possible he might make eight or ten more than that. Either way, it would be enough to sustain a life of luxury, lived in relative obscurity, far, far away.

When Grover and Heckman finally put in an appearance on Sutton Place, Dante had just sent Napier with the evidence he'd recovered in his search, to nudge along its analysis at the lab. Joe quickly brought them up to date on progress made at that scene, then turned to the reason for their delay.

"What's this about another Pierce, Fairbrother employee getting whacked last night?" he asked. "You say Manhattan South Homicide caught it?"

"Reynolds and his partner, Gibson," Rusty replied. "Somebody shot one of the mailroom guys outside his building near the corner of Second Street and Avenue D. Twenty-two-year-old kid, moved there three years ago from Sioux City."

Dante watched the forensics people pack their equipment. "Hype?" he asked.

"No tracks," Heckman reported. "A little reefer and some pills recovered from inside his pad. They're waiting for toxicology."

"It ain't the who, but what he did that's piqued our interest," Grover interjected. He'd spotted the pretty prosecutor and watched her in earnest conversation with one of the lab techs. "Turns out his main duties at the brokerage included delivery of the Foray Group's mail. Bennett's secretary says this Bristol used to hang around her boss's office. Even gave Bennett a demo tape of some songs he and his rock band put together."

Those sneakers and used rubbers that Napier had found in Bennett's trash had pretty much iced it for Dante. He was convinced that the fund manager had killed Phoebe Michel, and had been driving Greg Nichols's Saab, New Year's morning. What he still couldn't get a handle on was why. This Lower East Side homicide did nothing but further muddy the waters. "You think this kid might have seen or overheard something in Bennett's office?" he speculated. "I suspect he fits in somewhere, but I can't see how."

"Rusty thinks it might be whatever the Michel broa . . . uh, woman was workin' on," Grover told him. "Either she or someone else went to the trouble t' erase it from her hard drive, an' two hours later, she's dead."

Dante turned to Heckman, while outside the apartment door, some sort of commotion erupted between the two uniforms guarding the door and a white-haired guy in a suit. "On the phone, Donnie said that you think you can get whatever it was, back."

"I intend to try," Rusty said distractedly. His attention, too, was drawn toward that ruckus at the apartment door.

Together, they moved toward it, Dante in the lead. The white-haired man in the company of the super was worked up to a pretty good state of indignation. He was blustering in the face of the young uniform who blocked his path.

"What do you mean I can't go in there, sonny?" the white-haired man seethed. "I'm the president of this goddamned co-op."

"There a problem?" Joe asked it with a directness that caught the older man off guard. He also stepped directly into his space and forced him back a step.

"Who the hell are you?" the guy demanded, clearly annoyed that he'd been forced to give ground.

"Lieutenant Dante, Special Investigations. The officer wasn't trying to be rude, sir. He has his orders. From me. Until we clear this scene, it's sealed." Joe was firm, but not belligerent. The president of a Sutton Place co-op building was not a person to be trifled with. He probably had mountains of money, and a fair amount of political clout. This one wore a few thousand dollars' worth of tailored wool on his back and had very faint face-lift scars. Joe wanted to mollify him, not mix it up. "But I'd be happy to answer any questions you might have, Mr. . . . . ?"

When Dante offered his hand to shake, the co-op

president wasn't sure how to react at first. He wanted to stay angry, but was intelligent enough to understand there was no percentage in it.

"Carr," he replied, and engaged Joe's hand for the briefest moment. "What on earth is going on here, Lieutenant? Where is Mr. Bennett?"

"A good question, sir. We'd like to know that, too. You understand, I can't discuss my investigation. Suffice it to say, we wouldn't be here if it wasn't serious."

"May I at least ask how serious, Lieutenant? And how long you intend to keep the apartment sealed?" Carr looked distressed. "The new owner is due to take possession on the fifteenth of the month; and he isn't likely to be happy about this. Nor are any of our other tenants."

"New owner?" Joe asked. "Are you saying that Bennett has sold the place?"

The president seemed surprised that Dante didn't know. "Absolutely. I assume your investigation has something to do with Mr. Bennett's, ah, difficulties at the moment? Whatever led his bank to threaten foreclosure here?" He appeared to shudder inwardly at the thought of such unpleasantness.

Caught flat-footed, Dante tried not to reveal his surprise. The man who drove a turbo Bentley, had a lavish spread in Pound Ridge and an apartment on Sutton Place, could be broke.

Andrea Hill had hoped the tall, good-looking cop would come alone this time, without his partner in tow. But no such luck. The two of them showed up in tandem outside her office door. Ah well. She greeted them in stockinged feet, her shoes and suit jacket in the closet, and invited them to dump their coats and scarves on the sofa where they sat. She returned to the chair behind her desk.

Lieutenant Richardson seemed more interested in the view here than he'd been during his visit to her apartment. Twenty-eight stories up, her office commanded a vista of all midtown, from Third Avenue, west. "Nice," he complimented.

"I took a risk," she admitted. "Spending so much on an office when I'm just starting out. But this whole business is as much about appearances as it is about performance. That's one of the first things I learned."

"Classic Calvinism," Richardson mused. "I never thought of it in them terms before."

"Beg your pardon?"

When he smiled, that tough-guy face turned gentle. "You got a nice house, good standin' in the community, God clearly loves you."

Andrea beamed her best professional smile back at him. "The institutional investor is god in my world, Lieutenant. Would either of you like coffee?"

They said thanks, but no, and Dante moved to steer the conversation toward what was uppermost on his mind. "I understand your mentor in this business was Dennis Bennett."

She saw him watching for her reaction. But she was a pretty fair poker player herself. The picture of cool graciousness, she kept her expression cordial but essentially blank. "I was lucky in that regard, Lieutenant. I can't imagine a better teacher." Clearly, this wasn't about being at the table with

Bruce Webster anymore. Her mind raced. Where was this going?

"You worked as a submanager for him at Pierce, Fairbrother, correct?"

Okay. They undoubtedly knew other things, too. "At the Foray Fund Group, actually. Technically, the two are autonomous."

Richardson leaned forward, elbows planted on his knees. "We understand you were romantically involved with Mr. Bennett at one time. Same as a woman named Phoebe Michel once was. You know her?"

Andrea nodded, more confused than ever now. "Professionally, at any rate. Foray had access to the Pierce, Fairbrother analysis section. She worked for them, specializing in high-tech issues."

"Were you aware that Mr. Bennett was seeing her at the time you started to date him?" Lieutenant Dante asked.

She colored slightly, in spite of herself. What the hell were they digging at? "I don't see what any of this has got to do with what happened Saturday night, gentlemen. And if it's not pertinent, why are you asking about it?" There was ice in her voice, despite her determination to remain nonplussed.

Richardson grunted and glanced at his partner. "I take it you ain't heard that Ms. Michel was found murdered last night?"

"What?!" So much for cool. "When? Where?"

The black lieutenant ignored the question, boring in, instead. "When did you last see Mr. Bennett, Ms. Hill?"

Still trying to comprehend what was going on, and what could possibly have precipitated Phoebe's murder, Andrea was unable to find foothold anywhere. "Good God. You can't possibly think I had anything to do with it."

"The concierge at Bennett's building recognized Ms. Michel when she drove him home, New Year's Day," Dante told her. "He says she went upstairs and spent over an hour there. Gave a pretty good description of her Land-Rover, too."

Lieutenant Dante was looking a lot less appealing to Andrea, all of a sudden. She knew what was coming next and didn't like what she saw, at all. As she struggled to maintain a blank look, she winced inwardly and braced herself.

"The concierge recognized you, too, Ms. Hill. Later that afternoon, you walked past the desk and waved, just like you always do."

Andrea propped her elbows on the edge of the desk, arms folded, and regarded Dante with calm disdain. "I am not Dennis Bennett's keeper, Lieutenant. I haven't seen Phoebe Michel in two years. If he's seen her more recently than that, other than at work, it's news to me."

"Did you know he'd stopped making payments on his co-op mortgage nearly a year ago?" Dante asked. "That six weeks ago, his bank foreclosed on it?"

Those words landed like so many sucker punches. She felt like an outclassed fighter, losing badly in the late rounds. "I don't see how that's possible, Lieutenant. Dennis is worth millions."

"Did y'know he told his doorman, an' associates at work, that he was takin' two weeks vacation in Mexico?" Richardson pressed the attack. "We'd like to talk to him, Miss Hill. We want to know if he's really left town or not."

She snorted. "Believe me, so would I."

"So you've got no idea how we might reach him?" As he asked it, Richardson extracted a little leather case from inside his jacket and removed a card.

"No, Lieutenant," she replied, her tone brittle now. "No idea whatsoever."

He handed the card across. When she didn't reach for it, he left it on the front edge of her desk. "Withholdin' evidence in the investigation of a capital crime is a prosecutable offense, ma'am. Don't let personal feelin's cloud your judgment here."

After the two detectives left her, Andrea realized the entire back of her blouse was soaked with cold sweat. Dennis broke. Jesus Christ. He'd claimed that all he needed was to get himself past some temporary setbacks. Out of love and blind faith, she'd given him twenty million dollars. Now she wondered if she even knew who he was.

Suddenly sick to her stomach, Andrea rushed through the outer office into the hall. When she reached the washroom, she locked herself in a toilet stall, fell to her knees, and threw up.

Back on the street, Beasley Richardson buckled his seat belt and glanced over at Dante, behind the wheel. "She'll try t' contact him. Guaranteed."

"I'd say so," Joe agreed. Prior to their visit here, and feeding Andrea Hill what they had, Gus Lieberman had sent that assistant D.A. back downtown to obtain a wiretap warrant for Ms. Hill's residence and place of business. Dante checked his watch. "Let's hope they get that fucking wire hung in time to do us some good. That's one hell of a needle we just stuck in her. You saw how the color drained from her face."

Richardson nodded. "Be nice t' know what her end in all this is."

TWELVE

Once Guy Napier hand-carried the evidence he'd found at the Bennett apartment to the police lab on East 20th Street, he was prepared to hang around until those sneakers, spent condoms, and hair follicles vacuumed from the bed were processed. At least one technician didn't mind him breathing over her shoulder. Doreen Wilcox was a single mother who liked working overtime, and also had a thing for the tall cop.

"You still datin' the chief's XO?" She asked it as she took scrapings from the left shoe and prepared slides for her microscope.

"Living with her," he corrected. "Going on two years."

She gave him the bent eye. " 'Bout time t' pop the question, ain't it? You too cheap to buy a ring, or what?"

"Nope. Gave her one, Christmas Eve. All we need now is the time to elope." Napier's lover, Melissa

Busby, would rather have the money her parents would spend on a big wedding to help pay off the house she and Guy hoped to buy.

"At least y' both know the drill, goin' in," Doreen supposed. A first slide mounted, she hunched forward to peer into her lens. "Most gals who get involved with cops, it's because they think there's glamour in it. I did. Ain't much glamour in sleepin' alone."

"He was gone that much?" Guy had never met the robust technician's ex. Still in uniform, and likely to retire that way, the guy worked somewhere down in the wilds of Staten Island.

She looked up as if he'd just fallen off the pumpkin truck. "Not like he wasn't gettin' laid, the prick. Home or not." She beckoned Napier closer. "If it's blood you're lookin' for on them sneakers, how's O-negative suit you?"

Guy breathed a great sigh of satisfaction as he peered into the lens and saw the unmistakable cellular structures of red and white corpuscles. When he'd found those shoes, and smelled the cleaning agent on them, he'd know. Better yet, Phoebe Michel was O-negative.

"Mind if I use your phone?"

"Help yourself, handsome. Y'know, you're different than my ex. Maybe it'll work for you an' her."

He crossed to her desk. "How do you figure? You hardly know me, Doreen." He lifted the receiver and dialed Dante's cellular number.

"You kiddin'?" she scoffed. "I know all I need t' know. You been here a whole hour. And you ain't once put your hand on my ass."

* * *

Beasley Richardson left for home shortly after he and Dante returned to the Big Building that evening. Bernice, his librarian wife, had a Reading Is Fundamental fund-raiser that he'd agreed to attend with her. Grover and Heckman had plans to haul Phoebe Michel's impounded computer to Rusty's basement in Queens, to work some arcane electronic voodoo on it, the specifics of which were beyond Dante's comprehension. What Joe did know was that Heckman had a state-of-the-art setup at home, that he did a little innocent hacking in his spare time, and could probably find those ghost images if anyone could. Those two had just departed when Napier called to report his progress at the lab. Blood that matched Phoebe Michel's type had been identified on the sneakers recovered from Dennis Bennett's trash.

As he hung up the phone, Dante's thoughts turned to Greg Nichols, languishing in some drafty, noisy cell on Rikers Island. As the state's prime suspect in the Michel homicide, the law allowed the D.A. to hold him without bail for forty-eight hours. It was time to call Gus and set the wheels in motion to get him cut loose.

Before he could dial Lieberman's home number, the phone on his desk rang. "Special Investigations," he answered it. "Lieutenant Dante."

"It's Vivian Hoag, Lieutenant. Remember me?"

Either the question was rhetorical, or she thought he was dim. He hoped it was the former. "Sure, Mrs. Hoag. What can I do for you?"

"I think we should talk, Lieutenant." She sounded

hesitant. "There's something I didn't mention, the other day."

"You've got my full attention," he assured her.

"Could we meet face-to-face?"

"Now?" It was six o'clock. He had a hungry cat to feed.

"I've got my nerve up now, Lieutenant. If Bill knew I was having this conversation with you, I'm not sure what he might do."

She didn't sound like she'd been drinking, but who knew? Dante always considered the best places for a clandestine meeting to be the most public places in town. New Yorkers tended to pay less attention to each other in crowds. "Mezzanine bar at Grand Central?" he suggested. During rush hour, he didn't want to drive anywhere he didn't have to, and Mrs. Hoag lived all the way up on East 81st Street. "I can get onto the Lex line, be there in twenty minutes. You?"

"Fine," she agreed. "I'm meeting my husband for dinner, at eight. On Fifty-second, between Park and Lex."

The Four Seasons. Had to be a nice life.

Joe hung up the phone, checked his pocket change for a subway token, and found two. At least he wouldn't have to stand in line. On his way to the train, he tried Diana and Brian on his cellular phone. He got Sandy, and asked if she would feed Toby.

Andrea Hill was at home, a stiff gin and tonic in hand, when Dennis finally called. Since the two detectives had left, her office that afternoon, she'd been unable to think of anything but what they'd told her, and the money that the son of a bitch owed.

"Andrea, love." He sounded altogether too smug and cheerful "I forbid you to believe a single thing you've heard today. Lies. All of it, lies."

"You screw me, I'm going to carve your goddamn heart out, Den. Where the hell are you?"

"Now, now, love. I'm right here in town. So is your money. Relax."

She took a gulp of her drink. "That's one of the problems I'm having. It's not my money, Dennis." It occurred to her that her phone might be tapped, but right now she didn't much care. If he ripped her off on this deal, she was ruined.

"Beg your pardon. My mistake. The money under your stewardship. I've got it, and it's yours, with interest."

"When?" she demanded.

"Patience, my dear. Things have gotten a bit sticky for me. We need to talk."

"So talk. I'm all ears."

"Not on the telephone. You're no doubt aware that the heat is on, as they say."

"I trusted you, Dennis," she snapped. "What's this about the bank foreclosing on your apartment? You said the problem you were having was temporary."

"They never actually foreclosed," he countered. "I was forced to sell for quick cash. To keep my other assets intact. I swear to you that I've done nothing wrong, Andrea. Other than engage in a bit of insider trading."

"The police think you killed Phoebe Michel."

"Oh, please," he scoffed, his tone still impossibly cool. "Why not Jimmy Hoffa, too? Just because I was in the car when that bloody fool Nichols killed Webster? What I should have done was get out and walk away. He was so drunk, I doubt he knew I was there."

"So why didn't you?" she challenged him.

She could hear him snort. "We're old school chums, for the love of God. So what do I do? I try to save his pathetic arse."

"It was her perfume on your pillow, wasn't it, Den."

Now he chuckled. "Can you believe it? The little slut actually tried to blackmail me; into hiring her as one of my submanagers. All because she knew I'd left the scene of a crime."

"So you fucked her instead?" Andrea couldn't believe his gall. "You expect me to believe this bullshit? Get serious, Dennis."

"You never asked for an exclusive, love," he reminded her. "And fucking her, as you so crudely term it, is not quite the same as killing her. I'm quite certain Gregory did that."

"Certain's a strong word."

"We had breakfast together, yesterday, and I told him what a silly slut his fiancée was. I owed him that much."

She felt sick for the second time that day. "You didn't."

"I need to see you, Andy. This has all become a bit of a mess."

No kidding, she thought. "You have such a quaint way of making all problems sound solvable, Den. I don't want to find myself in the same damned canoe with you."

"All the more reason for us to put our heads together. And I do need to return your gracious loan."

"Where are you? I'll meet you."

"Not the best idea. Might not be safe here. You know the hotel we used to check into, downtown? Why don't you take a room there?"

The charming bastard played the game by only one set of rules. His own. Whoever he'd conned into harboring him, Andrea was sure she was just attractive enough to keep him amused, and lonely enough to be flattered by his attentions.

"I suppose," she relented.

"Good. I have to run. Leave a message for me at the desk."

The Vivian Hoag who met Dante in the packed mezzanine bar above the main concourse floor at Grand Central Station was as nervous as a first-time adulterer. Joe arrived to spot her seated alone on a stool, dressed for an evening out. She had a drink in a tumbler at her elbow, and fidgeted with the strap of her handbag, while a hopeful commuter had moved in on her left flank, attempting to break the ice. Joe froze him with a glare, and apologized to her for being late.

"Train got held at Union Square," he explained.

She surveyed the press of bodies all around them. "Think we could stand? Or sit somewhere else?"

He saw people leaving a tiny table in one corner, took her elbow, and headed them in that direction. As they sat, she asked if he wanted a drink.

"No thanks. I'm still on the clock," he fibbed. "What's on your mind, Mrs. Hoag?"

This was just the second time they'd met, and tonight, she had her thick, flaxen hair up in a French twist; a style that flattered the good bones and leanness of her face. At the bar, she'd left her evening coat on. Now, she began to unbutton it. The dress beneath had a neckline that plunged halfway to her navel. Her ample breasts were barely contained within. If you've got it, flaunt it, Dante supposed.

"I'm not being a very loyal wife," she said. The fingers of her left hand went to a large single-diamond pendant around her neck. "But then Bill hasn't been a very loyal husband." She toyed with the pendant nervously, a gesture Joe found distracting. He forced himself to watch her face, not her fingers.

"Where's this headed, ma'am?" he asked. "You led me to believe it pertains to the case I'm investigating."

"You remember I told you I threw a vase at Bill, after that party?"

He nodded.

"Well, it's because he's having an affair. With the other woman who sat at our table that night." She forced it out in a rush. "I've eavesdropped on phone conversations between them, and known about it for over a month."

Dante took a mental step back. Dennis Bennett, *and* Bill Hoag. "Adultery may still be a crime, but it's not what I investigate, Mrs. Hoag."

Vehemence flashed in her hazel eyes. "You don't understand. Bill is how Andrea Hill got the Telenet pension fund account. She pays him kickbacks of some sort. I don't know how much, but it's my impression they're sizable."

It sounded like sour grapes. A husband who was playing out-of-bounds, and withholding large sums of cash from a wife who was in the mood for divorce. Dante wasn't about to get in the middle of it. "I'd say you need a good attorney, more than you need a cop, Mrs. Hoag. Fraud isn't easy to prove, but you might be entitled to half of what the courts recover, after taxes."

"You're not listening to me!" she snapped. When she leaned abruptly forward to grab hold of his sleeve, her cleavage threatened to swallow her glass of Scotch. "They've conspired to defraud the fund, Lieutenant. Last week, I overheard them talking about twenty million dollars. Money that Bill authorized Andrea to invest, outside normal channels. Bruce Webster's name came up."

"Hold on," he stopped her. "Came up how?"

She eased back away from him, her composure regained. Eyes closed for a moment, she lifted her drink to sip from it. When she opened them again, she looked smug. "It was all fairly cryptic. I got the impression that Mr. Webster could really screw things up for them. Andrea said that if he didn't rock the boat, they would double their money. If he did, it could be a disaster."

Dante was a lot more comfortable with this woman pulled back to that safer distance, no longer crowding the table and her drink like that. "I'm still not clear on why you're telling me this. Why not take your husband to task, instead of taking it to the police?"

She sat a little straighter in her chair, chin lifted in defiance. "Because the second the smoke settles, I intend to divorce the son of a bitch," she snapped. "I don't need a good attorney, Lieutenant. I am a good attorney. My husband has put my entire financial future in jeopardy."

"And you don't want to be implicated, should

there be an arrest. Correct?" He was starting to understand now.

"Damn straight, Lieutenant. I want to be as far removed from him as I can get. He may be forced to make restitution, but not with my money, he won't. If Telenet wants to sue him, they'll have to stand in line."

Andrea Hill had one habit she wished she could break; her tendency to jump too quickly to a conclusion. She often took things too literally at first, which was, in a way, an asset in her business. Many of the decisions she made had to be either black or white. The hot investment that got away because she'd said no too quickly was never so damning as the one that went sour because she'd overthought a decision.

Now, as she waited in the room she'd taken at the Vista Hotel, Andrea thought about that unfortunate habit. As she'd listened to those detectives that afternoon, she'd jumped directly to the conclusion that Dennis was a murderer. She hadn't considered any other scenario that could explain what they'd found, and that made her angry with herself. What they thought they had on Dennis ran contrary to everything three years of intimate contact had taught her about him. Yes, he could be ruthless. What good businessman couldn't? If she didn't have her own set of very sharp fangs, she wouldn't be where she was today. Dennis was adept at manipulating a situation to his advantage. It was he who'd introduced her to Bill Hoag in the first place, and advised her on how to proceed with him. If—and only if—she could see her way clear to exploit it, there was a weakness that she could profit by. In fact, her decisions in that direction had created a new, delightful kind of balance in her relationship with Dennis. It seemed to give him a rush to know she was doing Hoag. And she enjoyed a feeling of power, knowing that she had something none of Bennett's other women had. She knew him; his motivations and deepest desires.

Lost in thought, Andrea was startled by the knock at her door. She leapt up and hurried to the security peep to see a transformed Dennis in the hallway. When she opened the door to him, he stood smirking, hands on hips.

"What's this?" she demanded.

Beneath a cashmere coat, Dennis wore slacks, a T-shirt, and black wool blazer. His hair was brown, not blond, and long enough to be tied back in a ponytail. He hadn't shaved in several days and sported an eleven o'clock shadow look. "Good God. You look more like a record producer than an assets manager."

"The new me." He advanced to take her chin lightly in hand and kiss her. It scratched. "Until those inept apes at the police get this mess straightened out, I'd rather avoid jail. It's hardly my style, Andy love."

A pang of jealousy stabbed at her. "Where are you staying, Den?"

He stepped further into the room to shed his coat and scarf. "In a port in the storm, as it were. With someone I will have totally forgotten by month's end."

"All snug and warm, I'll bet."

"Please, love. I'm here now. That's what is important, is it not?"

"Damn right." Andrea closed the door, and stood with her back to it. "If that twenty million I floated you isn't back where it belongs by Thursday, plus interest, they'll have my ass. There's a routine internal audit, first Friday of every month."

He reached inside his jacket to withdraw a folded sheet of paper, and his confident smile broadened. "You have such a lusty way with words. But we can't have them having your ass." With a flourish, he handed the sheet of paper across. "I took the liberty of ordering champagne. Cheers."

Printed on the single page was a computer-generated electronic transfer confirmation. It indicated that twenty-five million dollars had been shifted from the Foray Fund Group back to the Telenet Employees Pension Fund. As Andrea scanned it, Dennis stepped close to cup one cheek of her backside and pull her up against him.

"Perhaps you'll be able to relax now, hmmm?"

A wave of relief washed over her. She let go of the confirmation and let it float to the floor. With the side of her face pressed against his shoulder, she nuzzled his scratchy neck. The way the market had gone that afternoon, he'd made a cool five or six million, easy. With other monies of his own, like that from the quick-sale of his apartment, he'd undoubtedly made more. It might not be the entire ball game, recovery-wise, but he'd had a very good inning.

"Tell me about your visitors today," he murmured. "Your pair of police lieutenants."

"They're barking up the wrong tree, Den. Heck, they aren't even looking in the right forest. The one who scares me most is the white guy. He's on a vendetta."

"How's that?"

"The papers say he's a friend of Bruce Webster's sister. The rock star. The *Post* ran a picture of them together."

"Ah. And how formidable a chap does he seem to be?"

Hard up against him now, she savored the heat generated by one of his muscular thighs, thrust between her legs. "Oh, I'd say he definitely means business. One of those rugged types. Almost as tall as you, and maybe a little heavier. I'd steer clear, Den. He can probably get nasty."

"Believe me," he assured her. "I intend to. They're predictably Cro-Magnon, that whole lot. Give them a badge, they think it's a club. Let's just hope our friend Gregory comes clean before long. This silly disguise could get tiresome."

She ran her fingers through the length of that ponytail. "I don't know. I think it's sort of cute."

"That's the slut in you, love."

"Mmmm. I've never had a record producer before."

He stroked her backside. "I imagine that visit this afternoon must have scared the hell out of you, hmmm? I apologize."

"I'm quaking in my boots."

His hand left her fanny to sneak up beneath her sweater. She felt the measure of his desire intensify as his groping fingers failed to find a brassiere strap.

"I thought you'd ordered champagne," she reminded him, before he got too carried away. Andrea felt secure again; back in control.

He'd managed to work that hand around between

them, to cup her left breast, when a knock came at the door. "Ah yes. So I did."

"Room service," a muffled voice called out from the hall.

"What say we skip it?" Dennis asked, his sights set.

"Relax and answer the door," she commanded. "Don't worry. You'll get yours."

THIRTEEN

On arrival home from his meeting with Vivian Hoag, Dante found a message on his machine from Rosa. She hoped they could have dinner and talk. He was famished, but there was little doubt about what was on her mind. Issues he was too preoccupied and tired to discuss. He dialed her number and she answered, sounding irritated.

"I've tried your cellular number for the past hour and a half," she complained. "You didn't have it switched on."

"Battery was dead. So was my backup. Busy phone day."

"Are you available for dinner?"

"I was kinda looking for a break," he replied. "Quiet night. Maybe order in Chinese."

"My treat," she pressed. "We really do need to clear the air, Joe. Someplace upbeat. Cheerful."

Cheerful sounded good. Not that he believed any conversation with her would remain upbeat for long.

The developments of the past few days had left him in a dark mood, not the least of which was the public announcement of her political candidacy. "Where you got in mind?"

"Trattoria dell'Arte." She knew the popular midtown eatery was a favorite of his, when he was feeling festive. It was always crowded and noisy, and served some of the best antipasto in town.

Dante realized he wouldn't be able to avoid this next conversation for long. He agreed to meet her in an hour, and broke the connection to call Beasley. For the next ten minutes he gave his partner the update on his conversation with Vivian Hoag. Once he wrapped it up, Richardson asked the obvious next question.

"So where to from here, Joey?"

"We need to find Bennett. That's still our priority. I'm thinking that Bill Hoag's got an awful lot to lose. Maybe we can use that to our advantage; put his feet to the fire."

"What about Andrea Hill?"

His eyes closed, Joe visualized the tall, slender assets manager. She seemed to have a keen, amoral intelligence, which was something that fascinated the psychologist in him. "Gus tells me they finally got authorization to hang that wire about an hour ago. We sure as hell gave her enough rope, Beasley. Maybe she'll figure a way to hang herself."

Cristal champagne was the appropriate choice for so momentous an event in Andrea's life. Dennis believed that such a bright, beautiful creature deserved no less. He'd savored her eagerness as she consumed her first glass, one mouthful after another exchanged with him in passionate kisses as they disrobed. Then he'd filled his mouth with the crisp, chilled nectar and kissed her nipples. They continued this champagne play in bed, as he drank a thimbleful at a time from the depression of her navel. He wanted this to be perfect, and that was how she told him, again and again, that it was.

Finally, with the dead soldier upended in its ice bucket and neither of them thinking anymore about champagne, he took her ever so gently. With his gaze locked with hers in sweet communion, she bit her lower lip, her body now in perfect sync with his. When his slow, gliding thrusts became more vigorous, she was with him. Her back arched suddenly off the mattress as she grabbed his heaving buttocks and sank her nails.

"Yesss!" she hissed. "Yes, Dennis!"

His own moment was still a delicious, aching instant away when her entire being went rigid, to vibrate like a plucked cello string. It *was* perfect. With no interruption of his rhythm, he shifted his weight from one arm to the other, grabbed a pillow, and pressed it to her face.

"Sorry, love," he apologized.

She flailed in a sudden, muffled panic beneath him. With both hands on her head through the pillow, he jerked hard enough to snap her neck.

He'd withdrawn himself just before he killed her, and was surprised when he began to ejaculate anyway. Those hot spasms coincided with her death throes, and sent a shiver of revulsion down his spine. By the time her body ceased to twitch, she'd voided her bowels and bladder. His own body was covered with a sheen of cold, clammy sweat.

After a quick shower, Dennis remembered to wipe his prints off the bottle, the bucket, and his glass. Before he left the room, he retrieved the phony transfer confirmation from the carpet. On his way out, he hung the *Do Not Disturb* sign on the outside knob.

Monday night, Don Grover's date with Katrina Sasser's mom had gone so well that he'd asked her to have dinner with him again, Tuesday. But now that the Bruce Webster investigation had picked up momentum, it presented a problem. Though Rusty was more knowledgeable about the inner workings of the electronic world, Don couldn't leave him to break the current deadlock alone. At least not while he ran off to play. That wasn't how a partnership worked.

It was Heckman's wife, Barbara, who had the bright idea of inviting Wendy Sasser to have dinner with them, at their house. She figured that if Grover was going to fall for this woman, then a dose of what a cop's life was like was in order, right up front. Grover called Wendy to explain the circumstances, and put Barb on the phone. Somewhat to his surprise, Wendy accepted the invitation.

That was two hours ago. Now, the partners were seated together at a table jammed with computer equipment in Heckman's basement, while Barb and Wendy drank coffee and talked, upstairs. Wendy worked as an audiologist and Barbara was a surgical nurse at St. Vincent's in Greenwich Village, which gave them the medical profession in common. And both had kids who'd recently flown the nest.

"I can't believe this sudden display of good taste," Rusty said as he worked to set up the equipment. His Norton Utilities program loaded, he'd linked the computer impounded from Phoebe Michel's office through the processor in his own powerful Macintosh system. "One night you're Ballatore Bob. Three days later, you're dating a drinkable red wine."

Grover watched his partner's deft fingers fly over the keyboard. He was always amazed at the grasp Rusty had of this arcane science. Different bits of data flew across the monitor screen too quickly for Don to comprehend what they were. "She kinda blindsided me," he admitted. "My defenses were down."

"Imagine that," Rusty murmured.

"Kiss mine. But y'know what I mean. She's not one'a these divorced bro . . . uh, women who's stuck in that bitter fuckin' backwater. She even likes her job."

"Nice butt. Good brain. Barb likes her, too." Heckman was still glued intently to his screen. "That's a good sign."

"I know. It kinda scares me."

Rusty nodded toward the monitor. "Check this out. That ghosting you see? It's whatever Phoebe Michel was working on that morning, after she logged on."

"So it's not gone, just like you said."

"Watch this." When Rusty tapped a key repeatedly, the images on-screen became sharper. Some were in brighter focus than others. Some characters were gone entirely. "There are fragments missing, we'll probably never get back," he grumbled. "But what the hell. It ain' a perfect science."

Grover read what had been preserved; a spread-sheet of some sort. It seemed to detail portfolio hold-ings, with shares in huge numbers, worth megabucks. "Some kinda fund?" he speculated.

"Think so," Heckman agreed. "Let's see if we can find a heading somewhere."

In all, there were more than eighty pages of docu-ments hidden on that hard drive. All of them dealt with transactions made by, or with the overall hold-ings of, the six individual funds inside Dennis Bennett's Foray Fund Group: Dividend Growth, Hi-Yield, Blue Chip, Future Value, Aggressive Growth, and Global Equity. Most of the transaction docu-ments appeared to focus on recent activity just be-fore, and after, Christmas. Two hours disappeared as the partners enhanced and then printed each page in turn. By the time they'd completed their task, both men were bleary-eyed.

Rusty switched off the monitor and rubbed his face with open hands. "Whatever she was looking at points straight to Bennett, Donnie. But there's still something here we ain't seen yet."

Grover shuffled the printed pages into a neater pile. "Sleep might help. Pick you up at what? Seven?"

"No plans to try for an all-nighter, huh?"

Don scowled. "Another thing I've discovered, these past few days? How old I really am. Besides, this one's not some perfume counter clerk. She's got a real job. Ain't neither of us can call in sick."

"I can't stand it," Rusty complained. "We're talk-ing about a woman, and you're being sensible."

"Sensible? Hell. You don't know the half. I ain't even tried t'kiss her yet."

The Trattoria dell'Arte had a huge replica of a Da Vinci proboscis hung from the facade out front, hence its nickname, "The Nose." It was as busy on a Tuesday as any other night of the week, which suited Dante just fine. He'd always enjoyed the people-watching here as much as the antipasto. Tonight, as he waited at the bar for Rosa, the watching was as good as ever. The eatery was close to the Broadway theater district, and attracted a variety of New York's beautiful people, all dressed and playing the roles of their lives to the hilt. A woman on the stool alongside him had long, flowing hair and the flawless face of a soap queen. Her attitude suggested she believed herself the absolute center of her universe. Joe couldn't tell if she was waiting for someone, or had just come to pose. And he didn't much care. He was content to sip his whiskey and enjoy the show. Manhattan. He loved this town.

Another casual observer, seated at the same bar, would have watched with equal pleasure as the raven-haired Rosa Losada entered the restaurant. With the face of a Castilian contessa, and the crisp, businesslike demeanor of a diplomat, it would be impossible to guess that this was a New York police captain.

"Our table's ready," Joe told her as she offered him her cheek. It was a bad sign, that gesture. Twice in the past she'd told him she needed some distance, and then walked away. Both times, she'd constructed an impenetrable emotional barrier. He knew the feel of that exclusion by heart, and he felt it now. It was like the cold breeze from a draft.

"Did you use your considerable charm, or just strong-arm them?" she asked. "The place is mobbed."

"I called ahead." He wasn't a cop who used his tin like that, and Rosa knew it.

They followed the hostess to their table and Joe held Rosa's chair while she sat. She nodded toward another table, in the center of the room, as he took his own seat.

"Nice to see the escort services are doing a brisk business."

A group of eight was seated around one of the bigger tables. Three of them were women, all wearing provocative cocktail dresses, hair teased and sprayed into various caricatures of steamy glamour. Blondes all. The five men seated with them were well-dressed, dark-complected Caucasians. Two might have been bodyguards, Joe thought, judging from the cold, stone-faced looks they wore.

He shrugged. "You read those ads in the Yellow Pages, you'd think they sold dates with Princess Grace." His attention turned back to Rosa, he spoke with blunt directness. "So. You said you want to talk. I thought we were already past that. Wrong?"

Rather than reply immediately, she caught the attention of their waitress. "Could we get a drink first? Before we get down to disemboweling each other?" She ordered a margarita. Joe asked for another Black Bush and water. Once their server moved off, Rosa returned to the issue at hand. "I suppose you've heard the news."

"I thought they were gonna hold off a few days," he replied.

She ignored the implications of that statement. "Thursday, the *Times* runs its first story on me. I did the interview this afternoon. I'm in the race, Joe."

He reached out to run the tip of an index finger over the back of her left hand. "Beasley thinks you'll win by a landslide. Me too. This time next year, you'll be living somewhere in Washington."

"That's where congresswomen live, Joe."

"True enough."

"But not dedicated New York cops. Correct?"

"There are those words. Dedicated and New York." He eased his fingers beneath the hand to take hold of it. "By the way. I didn't intend to impugn your integrity the other night. I meant to play devil's advocate. And to express my grave concern."

She gently removed her hand from his. "I don't want it to end, Joe. My life might be about to change, but I can't imagine you not being a part of it. Not anymore."

"I can only be in one place at a time, babe."

"I understand that. We may need a little space. And time to figure out our alternatives. But I hope we can work something out."

Those words again. How many times, since he'd met her, had he heard them pass her lips? Time. A little space. They were as much a part of their history as the words *I love you* were. He'd thought he was prepared, but still he felt the stab of them.

"I'm not sure what 'alternatives' means, Rosa. Like maybe I'll take trips to D.C., couple of times a month, to jump your bones?"

"Okay. Make it sound coarse if you have to." He

saw her struggle to keep her anger in check. "I know you're pissed off at me, but I'm telling you, I don't want to lose you. Not over the way I vote on a bill. Not over some other man or woman who happens along. We spend that much time apart, I know it's bound to happen."

"It's happened when we haven't spent time apart, Rosa. You can't ask me to commit if you won't."

Her eyes pleaded with him now. "I know that."

Three years ago, Rosa had become involved with another man. One who was from a prominent family and who had been mentioned in certain circles as having mayoral potential. It was her ambition, back then, to become the city's first female police commissioner. Joe could remember the pain and helplessness he'd felt, though time had dulled it some. But time had done nothing to dull his awareness of what a politically motivated animal his lover was.

"Something has already changed between us, Rosa. It changed the minute you agreed to entertain Ruiz's offer, knowing how much I loathe the bastard."

She shrugged. "I've never changed, Joe. From the first day you met me, and way before that, this is what I've always wanted. It's an opportunity of a lifetime."

When their drinks arrived, Joe realized how hungry he was and proposed one of the restaurant's antipasto platters as a place to start. Rosa agreed. Once they were alone again, he raised his glass in toast.

"Next stop, Capitol Hill."

"It's not a done deal yet."

He sipped his whiskey. After the day he'd had, that beer at home and the whiskey at the bar had started to loosen his knots. "I hate this," he admitted. "But I won't be a total asshole about it. You boil it down, the alternatives seem pretty simple. I can either have some of you in my life, or all of you, out of it." He stopped and grinned. "I'll take 'A,' Bob."

"That mean I can keep your key?"

He took another slug of his drink, unable to contain a bemused smirk, and shrugged. "Long as you call ahead first. And promise I'm the first guy gets to fuck you, on top of your new desk."

She clicked her glass with his. "Done."

A sudden change in her expression confused him for an instant, when it went from lusty smile to frown of concern. Then he realized her attention had turned to the middle of the room. "Damn," she murmured. "He did that on purpose."

Dante twisted in his chair to see a waitress bend over to retrieve the utensil dropped by one of those suits at the table for eight. In her short black skirt and ankle-high boots, she exposed the backs of her long, shapely legs in the process. The leering Middle Easterner, a bit unsteady from drink, had turned to get the best possible vantage. The instant her long legs were at full extension, he reached between them to paw a handful of thigh.

The waitress shrieked, came bolt upright, and swung to defend herself. The fork now in her hand flashed as its tines grazed her attacker's forehead, above his left eye. With a roar of pain and outrage, he leapt from his chair to strike back.

Dante came to his feet out of reflex and saw that his initial assessment of the group was correct. Those two stone-faced characters were indeed bodyguards. By the time he closed the distance in three quick strides, their boss had slapped the waitress hard, and staggered her. They came out of their chairs as Joe grabbed the outraged Arab and shoved him back into his seat. One of them was close enough for Dante to hook him with a vicious right cross, just as the body-guard reached inside his jacket for a weapon. The mandibular joint of the guy's jaw gave way beneath Joe's fist, and his target let out an anguished scream of pain and surprise. The second bodyguard had just produced a machine pistol when Dante launched across the table at him. Not more than four or five seconds elapsed from the time Joe grabbed that drunken, bellowing man, mid-swing, and now, when he drove a shoulder into the gun-toting bodyguard's midsection to drive him toward the floor.

Glasses, tableware, and plates laden with food flew toward all points of the compass as Dante landed atop his opponent and drove a knee hard into his groin. The impact with the floor, all two hundred pounds of Dante landing atop him, drove the air from the bodyguard's lungs. The knee-shot made sure he wouldn't get back up for a while.

From the corner of his eye, Joe saw another of the men from the table now on the attack, one foot drawn back to aim a kick at his head. He rolled hard, out of harm's way, just as the muzzle of Rosa's off-duty weapon touched the back of that man's head.

"Down, boy," he heard her growl.

Pandemonium reigned as Dante struggled to his knees, and then to his feet. The terrified waitress, fork still in hand, stood hugging herself, wide-eyed and trembling. The patrons at adjacent tables had run for cover the instant the first firearm appeared. The man with the broken jaw was still moaning while his partner on the floor continued to writhe and fight for air. The original perpetrator sat with a hand pressed to his forehead, blood oozing between his fingers.

Her weapon still trained on her target, Rosa backed off a step. "You okay?" she asked Joe.

Dante stopped to retrieve the fallen machine pistol. "Fine. Your phone in your bag?"

As Rosa dug her phone out with her free hand and tossed it across, the one unscathed man at the table began to jabber indignantly about this outrageous affront. Dante circled the table to see what other artillery they'd captured, and dialed 911. Once he reported his shield number and requested backup, he broke the connection and leaned down to remove a weapon from the shoulder rig of the man with the broken jaw. It was another Czech-made Skorpion machine pistol. Thirty-two-shot clip.

"Who the hell are these guys?" he asked Rosa.

"That is what I am telling you!" the jabbering man screeched. He had his passport out, and waved it where all could see. "You cannot do this. We are diplomats." He pointed to the man with the cut above his eye. "That is Sheikh Saad al-Mohmed as-Sabah."

Dante was in no mood for anything about diplomatic immunity. "And who, pray tell, is that?"

"We are Kuwaitis," the man replied. "He is our minister of finance. A prince. Second son of our emir."

FOURTEEN

The ordeal with the Kuwaitis dragged on for hours. By the time Dante was finally able to break away at half-past midnight, those events at Trattoria dell'Arte had become a full-blown international incident. City Hall and the State Department had been called into the act. Every media organ in the city had come running. The final gauntlet Dante was forced to run, as he left the Midtown North station house, was a battery of TV lights, cameras, and talking heads with microphones. He was curious to know how Jaime Ruiz would react to all this free publicity for his new candidate.

Brennan was at work in his studio upstairs when Joe stepped off the elevator into his living room. Dante was halfway to his bedroom when the phone rang. Thankfully, he maintained a separate, secure line to the Operations Desk. If he wanted to get any sleep tonight, he would have to leave his regular phone unplugged.

When the answering machine picked up, Diana's voice came over its speaker. "We just heard you come in, Copper. Looks like you're famous again. Pig Punches Prince. I can see the *Post* headline now."

He crossed to the machine, switched it off, and grabbed the receiver. "Hi. Meant to check in with you, then Rosa called and wanted to have dinner."

"Some dinner. What the hell happened?"

"Long story." He loosened his collar and stripped off his necktie. "Some jerk grabbed a waitress's ass. It all went south from there."

"A Kuwaiti prince-type jerk, no less. How about a nightcap?"

"Maybe one. I'm still pretty keyed. How's Toby?" Dante shed his jacket and hung it, phone wedged between his cheek and shoulder. Next came the shirt.

"You'd better check my sister's luggage when she leaves. I think she wants to take him home with her. See ya."

Joe changed into old jeans, beat-up Top-Siders, and a sweat shirt, and pushed past the back door of Brennan's studio a few minutes after one. He found his pal at work applying patina to a three-quarter-scale bronze of intertwined lovers. The details of the piece were so real and expressive that the figures seemed frozen in life.

Joe pulled a cold Harp lager from the six-pack he carried, opened it, and handed it across. "Take a break."

"Hey," Brian greeted him. "What was it the Kuwait embassy spokesman called you?" He grinned as he paused to formulate it. "A policeman who uses the Gestapo tactics of Saddam Hussein's Republican Guard. Good stuff. Powerful imagery."

"A bit heavy-handed, don't you think?"

"In a world where Joe Camel spouts philosophy? Why split hairs?" Brennan started to clean up his tools and work space. "All we've gotten is the news reports. A few eyewitness accounts, and the Kuwaiti side of the story. You gonna tell us yours?"

Dante opened a bottle for himself and took a long, soothing pull. It had been only forty minutes since his knees had finally stopped shaking. His nerves were still raw. "Gimme a minute. I've done so much explaining tonight, my throat feels like Bill Clinton's after the '92 campaign."

They found Diana and Sandy on the sofa in the loft's huge living room, a backgammon game on the cushion between them.

"It's the infidel dog himself," Diana greeted Joe. "Demon alcohol in hand. Got one of those to spare?"

Dante pried off another cap, handed the bottle across, and offered one to Sandy. She had a brandy working, and declined.

"We want to hear everything," she told him. Together with her sister, she lifted the game board onto the adjacent coffee table. "The Kuwaiti spokesman claims you broke Prince Whatzizname's elbow."

Between intermittent sips of Harp, Joe was forced to tell the story all over again. "I can't see how I managed to break his elbow," he finished up. "All I did was grab his wrist and shove him back into his chair."

"The waitress thinks the mayor should give you a medal," Diana reported.

"Anybody mention the three hookers they had

with them?" Joe wondered. "And how drunk that princely paragon of Islamic virtue was?"

"The Kuwaiti embassy has chosen to take a slightly different tack," Sandy replied.

Dante grunted. "So I heard."

"They've called for your immediate dismissal, and demanded full apologies from the U.S. government and the City of New York," she told him.

Joe drained the last of his beer and chuckled. "God, I can't wait until tomorrow. The P.C. is gonna have a field day with this."

Sandy looked to Diana, puzzled. "P.C.?"

"Police commissioner," Diana explained. "This one hates our buddy's guts." She turned back to Dante. "So. Before all the excitement. How'd dinner go with Rosa?"

"She thinks it would be wonderful, if we could stay friends."

"Oh no," she groaned. "Not that again."

"Could be worse. Sounds like I'll have conjugal rights this time."

"She tell you she wants us to sit with her at her coming-out tomorrow night?"

It was a fund-raiser at Roseland. The Democratic Coalition's big kick-off-the-New Year shindig.

"Didn't ask. Probably because she knows I wouldn't go."

Diana paused to puzzle something. "So if this Ruiz is so bad, why is Rosa's uncle Tico involved with him?" she asked.

Dante thought about another beer, figured what the hell, and reached for one. He was so tired now, his exhaustion was like a high. "I probably sound ungrateful, saying this. Tico has never been anything but generous to me. But I wouldn't trust him and his Florida Cuban cronies any further than I could throw them. Rosa's playing with fire."

"So where did you and she leave it?" Diana pressed.

Dante opened his beer as Toby emerged from wherever he'd been hiding to jump into Joe's lap. "We've got a nosy neighbor," he told the cat. Scratched vigorously behind the ears, the animal got a craven look on his face. "Shit. I've got no idea, Di. It's different now. That's all I know. I'm probably lucky I haven't had any time to really think about it."

Sandy yawned, stretched, and rolled her eyes. "I've been down on the farm too long, I guess. And a social scientist, no less. Is this the latest in urban love?"

"More like urban survival," Brian supposed. "Our friend here is a perfect study."

Sandy smiled at Dante. "An idea not without appeal. I'm stranded tomorrow night, Lieutenant. What are you doing for dinner?"

"Got something in mind?" he asked.

"What say I buy? And write it off as research."

Wednesday morning, Don Grover and Rusty Heckman were at their desks, coffee made, by eight o'clock. Grover had insisted they stop en route for his usual box of doughnuts. Heckman, his New Year's dieting resolve already in tatters, had eaten one in the car. Now, as he removed from his briefcase the eighty pages of printout they'd generated last night, he contemplated having a second.

"Do me a favor," he begged Grover. "Get that fucking box out of here. Put them around the corner, where I can't look at them."

Don complied reluctantly as he muttered something about Napier eating them all. On his return, he had a jelly-filled wrapped in a napkin, which he set lovingly in his top desk drawer. For later.

Rusty had made additional progress after Don left last night, and now spread his results across the surface of his desk. He pointed to one sheet of the printout with his pen. "What it looks like to me? Bennett knew, from one source or another, that Telenet was on the verge of acquiring Bruce Webster's company. Monday, the fifth of December, he received a twenty-million-dollar liquid cash investment into his Growth Fund from somewhere. By Tuesday, the twenty-seventh, he'd bought two-point-two-million shares of Omnicom preferred stock with it."

Grover leaned close to study the figures. "He made them acquisitions over a long time-span, like he didn't want t' rock any boats. Check it out. Price per share barely inched up six bits."

"Until yesterday." Rusty had a copy of today's *Wall Street Journal* opened to the NASDAQ stock tables. "Yesterday, it went on a roller-coaster ride. Took a dive into the tank early, then rallied through the roof. I've run the numbers, Donnie. It would depend on when he started to dump, once the market heated up, but he probably made somewhere between thirty-two and thirty-eight million. On an investment of twenty. It's inspired."

Don wandered back to his own chair and dropped

into it. Outside their cubicle, the rest of SID had started to come alive. One of the Major Case guys stuck his head in to say good morning. He was eating a doughnut. Grover put his feet up and gave his partner the evil eye.

"Any idea at all, where that twenty mil came from?" he asked.

"Not yet. Or where the cash he's made has gone."

"How fast could he clear it? Turn it into somethin' negotiable, or transfer it offshore?"

Heckman removed a copy of the Barron's *Finance and Investment Handbook* from his briefcase, and grinned. "Funny you should ask. The standard clearing time is the trade, plus three days. But that doesn't mean it couldn't happen sooner." He tapped the cover of the book with his pen. "It's one of about a dozen questions I want to ask a woman I used to work with. The Security and Exchange Commission's liaison with our Organized Crime Control Bureau."

"Callin' them in at this point's a big step. We ready for that?"

"We need all the help we can get," Rusty countered. "Without the SEC's involvement, we risk seeing everything we've uncovered here just dry up and blow away. Bennett *and* all his cash."

"You wanna clear it with Joe first, or just do it?" Don understood the urgency, but they had a chain of command to consider.

"After last night? Could be hours before he shows his face," Rusty reasoned. "Let's run it by Richardson, see what he thinks." He dragged over his Rolodex to dig for SEC Investigator Marsha Hensley's number. "By the way. How'd it go with Wendy, after you left our place last night?"

Grover had already half dialed Beasley Richardson's mobile number when he stopped, index finger poised over the keypad, and got cagey. "She asked me t' tell you again, how much she enjoyed the evenin'. How the rest went ain't none'a your fucking business."

There was no question in Dante's mind what Wednesday morning had in store for him. He arrived at work at nine, later than he liked, and had barely sat down with his task force when word came down from the fourteenth floor. Commissioner Anton Mintoff wanted to see him. Forthwith.

Grover and Heckman already had their work for the day lined out. They'd gotten the okay from Beasley, reached Marsha Hensley at the SEC, and set up a late morning meeting. Meanwhile, Joe wanted Richardson and Napier to concentrate on Andrea Hill. Last night's wiretap had failed to snag a single phone conversation. After what Vivian Hoag had revealed to Dante, her husband could wait until they got Ms. Hill's version of that story. There was a strong possibility that a woman-scorned motivation had twisted some or all of what Mrs. Hoag alleged. Andrea Hill's response had to be carefully weighed before any rash move was made against him.

"Scorned or not, it looks like what she told you is right on the money," Rusty told Joe. "The figure she gave you is twenty million, and here it is." He pointed to the top page of data recovered from Phoebe Michel's hard drive. "Same amount that Bennett received, on December fifth. That's too big a coincidence."

"You think Andrea Hill would have the authority?" Napier asked. "To make an investment that size, without any oversight?"

Dante wondered about that too. He looked to Grover and Heckman. "Unlikely, isn't it? What do you guys think?"

"It's on my list of questions to ask my pal Marsha," Rusty replied. "I imagine there are safeguards in place. But for all we know, Hoag's authority might be all she needed."

Joe checked his notes, assembled in haste over a cup of coffee in his kitchen that morning. He turned to Napier. "You've contacted the credit card companies? About Bennett's recent activity?"

"The past couple days, there's been nothing," Guy reported. "But one place, I did hit pay dirt." He picked through a pile of paper in his lap and came up with a fax copy of an Amex charge. "According to this, he rented a twenty-seven-foot box van from Ryder, on East Seventy-sixth between First and York. Detectives from the Nineteenth squad impounded it last night."

Dante saw the look on Beasley's face and knew what he was thinking. "If the lab can put the car that killed Bruce inside the van, the D.A. don't have no choice, Joey. She's bein' stubborn, but now she's gotta spring Nichols."

Joe had contacted Gus to set the wheels of Nichols's release in motion late yesterday, and as of that morning the Telenet CFO was still behind bars. If a move wasn't made soon, Dante reflected, Greg was going to have one hell of a good lawsuit on his hands. "Bennett's definitely our guy," he agreed. "But other than to buy some time, what's his motive for wanting to see Nichols on ice in the first place?"

"He's Hoag's opposite in the Telenet power structure," Rusty reminded him. "If what Vivian Hoag says is true, Nichols might have been in Bennett's way. Who'd be more likely to discover a pension fund scam than the company's chief financial officer?"

Dante checked the time. He'd received that summons from the P.C.'s exec over ten minutes ago. "Gotta run. Christ knows how long this'll take." He told Jumbo to give a call if anything broke loose.

The usual herd of palace guard political animals loitered behind and around the various desks in the P.C.'s outer office when Dante arrived. With a contemptuous look at the wall clock across from his desk, the P.C.'s XO told Joe he was expected, and to go on in. As Dante walked through that door, he could see the writing on the wall. Gus was there, along with the loathesome chief of internal affairs, Jerry Liljedahl. So was an attorney from the Lieutenants' Benevolent Association, and a woman in a tweed jacket whom Joe didn't recognize. She was seated in a chair before Anton Mintoff's desk, a bespectacled guy in a charcoal suit at her side.

"How nice of you to grace us with your presence, Lieutenant," Commissioner Mintoff fairly sneered. A dapper, hawk-nosed man, he was alternately referred to by the job's rank and file as either "Big Tony" or the "Maltese Midget." Legend held that he'd bought his way into the police academy, pre–Knapp Commission, in a day when the job still had a minimum-height requirement. Raised in East New

York, Brooklyn, he was the son of impoverished immigrants, and hated to be reminded of that fact. Dante got along with him like hot grease got along with water. Always had. "This is Melinda Byers, U.S. Department of State. And Assistant U.S. Attorney Russell Jacobs, Southern District of New York."

When neither Jacobs nor Ms. Byers so much as nodded, Dante made no move to shake hands.

"We've always been able to keep our little problems with you confined to this department, Lieutenant," Mintoff continued. "Or at least within America's borders. Last night's incident could be the last straw. We've got the government of an entire sovereign nation calling for your head."

Joe looked at Gus. "Last I heard, we had a Constitution. Didn't we swear an oath to uphold it?"

Lieberman's look implored him to keep his cool.

"What am I missing here?" Dante asked the commissioner. He kept his tone measured and cool. "Or is a Kuwaiti prince not subject to our laws?"

Mintoff's face colored rapidly. He stared at Dante, furious that he might challenge him in front of outsiders. "Look here, Lieutenant."

"Just a minute, sir," Joe interrupted him. He turned to the woman from State. "Last night, I witnessed an incident where a woman was assaulted. In an effort to defend herself, she retaliated. When her attacker proceeded to press his assault, I intervened." He faced Mintoff again. "I did not use excessive force to subdue him. When two men in his company attempted to interfere, I had no choice but to neutralize their threat. Given that both possessed, and attempted to use, automatic weapons, the force I used against them was justified."

The room was so quiet when he finished speaking that conversations in the outer office could be heard through the closed door. Slowly, Joe scanned the faces of those present, then returned to the commissioner. "I did my job, sir." He refused to break eye contact until Mintoff eventually looked away.

"His Highness, Prince al-Mohmed, tells a significantly different story, Commissioner," Ms. Byers argued. "He and members of his party believe the lieutenant's attack was racial in motivation."

Dante's glare was cold enough to freeze alcohol. "Midtown North took statements from fifteen eyewitnesses. People who saw the entire incident."

The woman from State refused to meet his eye. She directed her reply to Mintoff. "I didn't come here to debate. Not with this man, nor anyone else in your—"

"Excuse me," Joe cut her off. "Racially motivated? You need to check my record. Talk to my chief. Talk to my partner of the past six years, who, by the way, is black. You want to make a charge of racism, find a racist to make it against."

"Man has a point," Mintoff told her.

Unable to believe his ears, Dante almost gaped.

"I was under the impression you had your facts in better order, Ms. Byers."

"It's Mrs. Byers," she said coldly. "We're faced with an incident that threatens to undermine the relationship between our government and a valuable ally in the Middle East, Commissioner. The emir, himself, has called the president to express his outrage."

Mintoff shrugged. "Sounds like his son broke the

law. And that I owe Lieutenant Dante an apology. He's sworn to uphold our laws, not Kuwait's."

Melinda Byers rose stiffly and turned her helpless anger toward the U.S. attorney at her side. "Are you going to just stand there, Russell?"

"What do you want me to do, Lyn?" the prosecutor replied.

Mintoff addressed them both. "You could make sure the prince is on the next plane home, for starters." He turned back to Joe. "I'm sorry about this, Lieutenant. I know you're a busy man."

Was that a twinkle that Dante saw in the corner of the Maltese Midget's eye? "Forget what I said about swearing to uphold the Constitution, sir," he said. "I know we're on the same page there."

"Get out of here," Mintoff said softly. "Go do your job."

Joe was in the hall outside the P.C.'s office when his cellular phone rang. It was Grover.

"A guy claimin' t'be Bennett just called, Joe. Wants t' meet, but only with you. Half hour from now. West end'a Bryant Park."

In all the years that Dennis Bennett had lived and worked in New York City, he'd never taken time to just sit and stare; to contemplate the mundane aspects of everyday life. Seated behind the wheel of his rented Dodge Neon, he watched the west end of Bryant Park from the far side of Sixth Avenue, where he was parked in a curbside loading zone. Dennis had never paid more than passing attention to this part of midtown, behind the main public library between 41st and 42nd streets. He was surprised to see how well maintained the park was, and how many separate business cultures intersected in this one vicinity. To the west, he was only a block from Times Square and the northern end of the Garment District. Just south a few blocks, on Fifth, was Lord & Taylor. He watched men in suits, women in sneakers and overcoats, homeless people with shopping carts, and workers in coveralls crisscross the avenue like so many industrious ants. There was so much of this city he'd left undiscovered, and here he was, ready to leave it forever.

Lost in thought, Bennett almost missed the light green Taurus sedan as it eased to the curb opposite. The car's occupant was halfway out of it before Dennis recognized him as the cop with Diana Webster in that picture in the *Post*. Lieutenant Dante. Almost as tall as Bennett's own six feet three inches, he moved with the easy demeanor of a man who owned the space he occupied.

Dennis made a note of the sedan's plate number and began to search the avenue north and south for the other policemen he knew would be hiding in the wings. He was surprised to spot only one other car, parked at a bus stop, a block back on Sixth. Search as he might, he could identify no others, and wondered if his feelings should be hurt. He was suspected of two homicides. Did they think this was a hoax?

He waited a full twenty minutes before Dante finally gave up on him. Then the lieutenant signaled that other car forward and its occupants climbed out. Two of them. They conferred on the sidewalk, heads down and hands in coat pockets. One of those new arrivals was balding, with frizzy, Bozo-the-Clown red hair. His partner was slender as a reed, in a camel hair coat that must have set him back a week's pay. All of them looked serious, and perhaps more intelligent than he'd expected. Good. These were worthy adversaries.

Bennett started his car. Now he knew what Dante's car looked like, and he had its license number. That would make him an easier target to find, and to follow.

Jumbo Richardson reached Dante by phone just as Joe had gotten under way again. The meet with Dennis Bennett hadn't happened.

"Somethin' strange goin' on here, Joey. No Andrea Hill. She didn't report t'her office today, and ain't answerin' her door at home. We ran a check on her credit card activity. She took a room downtown at the Vista last night."

All the time Dante had stood waiting for Bennett to arrive at Bryant Park, he'd had the feeling that someone was watching him. "Bennett's still in town, Beasley. He hasn't left for a reason."

"We called the Vista, Joey. They say she ain't checked out yet. Napier and me are headed down there now."

"I'll hook up with you," Joe told him.

"How'd it go with Big Tony?"

The question provoked a smile. "Son of a bitch surprised me. Implied the emir could go fuck himself, and told the State Department to back off."

"What kinda lines that gonna mean at the gas pump?"

Dante glanced at his fuel gauge, where the needle

rode in the red. "Which reminds me. I've gotta get gas."

"Might be your last chance," Richardson chided. "Think I'll fill my tank, too."

FIFTEEN

A check with the lobby desk at the Vista International revealed that Andrea Hill still remained registered there. Dante asked to see a manager, and moments later an anxious woman appeared. He showed her his tin and I.D., and moved quickly to put her at ease.

"This particular guest was expected at work today," he explained. "And didn't show up. Someone used her Amex card here. We don't know if it was stolen, or if she used it herself."

"You've tried the room?" the manager asked the desk clerk.

"She's not answering the phone, ma'am," the clerk replied. "The maid in that section, on nine, says there's a privacy card hung on her knob."

"We'd like you to come upstairs with us," Joe told the manager. "We'll want access if there's no answer."

Crisp and businesslike, the woman mulled over

the proposition and frowned. "Don't you need a warrant of some sort?"

"Not if we have reasonable cause. Concern for the well-being of a room's occupant could constitute it. If it's empty, and looks undisturbed, we'll leave."

Bennett had followed Lieutenant Dante to a filling station on the corner of Tenth Avenue and 45th Street, and then west the two blocks to the West Side Highway. Now, Dennis sat parked on the Battery Park City side of West Street, across from the Marriott Vista, and watched as a fifth police vehicle double-parked at the curb outside the hotel entrance. This car was occupied by that same pair of plainclothes detectives he'd seen with Dante earlier, midtown. An EMS ambulance, lights off and siren silent, pulled up behind them.

"The gang is all here," he murmured to himself. He was trying to figure how surprised he should be that they'd located Andrea's corpse as quickly as they had. Perhaps the maids at the hotel couldn't read simple English.

While Dante had filled his tank at that Hess station, Bennett had used the pay phone to call his new broker at Cooperman & Swift. He now had confirmation that the proceeds of his trades had begun to trickle into that new account, via electronic transfer. By Friday morning, the municipal bearer bonds would be cleared, and ready for pickup. Forty-eight hours from now, he'd vanish like a wisp of steam, in the cold winter air.

* * *

Whenever Joe Dante ran into this sort of purposeful killer, it shook his faith in the human species. There were several schools of thought on what motivated murder. Joe believed that a psychopath, for instance, devoured without any sense of the true horror he perpetrated because it was in his genetic makeup to do so. By some freak of nature, a psychopath was born haywired. But a killer like Dennis Bennett was different. He killed because homicide was convenient to his ends, not because his psychology drove him to it.

Dante stood with Richardson in the crowded Vista Hotel hallway outside the homicide scene. With his head thrown back, he leaned against the wall behind him and tried to make sense of the insane. "Four stiffs, four totally different M.O.'s, Beasley. A killer like this guy scares the shit outta me."

Napier was inside the room with the lab techs, watching their every move like a hawk. Don and Rusty had just arrived and were in there with him. Dante had left them to it just moments ago, so angry with himself, he could barely see straight. He'd hot-wired this woman with that interview yesterday, and yet he'd failed to see how imminent the outcome of it was. Rather than order a tap on her phone, he knew he should have ordered surveillance.

Richardson read him like cue cards. "You can't blame yourself, Joey. She was up to her tits in this, and holdin' out on us. If she'd wanted t' take herself outta the line of fire, she would'a had t' come clean. That, she didn't do."

"In midtown, an hour ago?" Dante murmured. When he pulled his gaze down from the ceiling, it had a faraway look in it. "You know how I get those hunches sometimes? I felt him watching me. He was there."

"He wanted t' have a look, Joey. Lots of 'em do. See who they're up against."

"Yeah, but toward what end? So far, he's killed one helpless pedestrian, a woman in her apartment, with a knife, an unarmed mailboy, with a gun, and now this one, apparently after fucking her. Does that sound like the kinda guy who wants straight-up confrontation?"

"Still, y'need t' be careful, Joey. Next couple days, you watch your back."

From somewhere inside the crime scene, Dante heard the chirp of a cellular phone. He checked to make sure he hadn't left his own unit behind, as Grover emerged from the room.

"That was the dead lady's secretary, Joe. This mornin', Rust and me contacted her. That investment she made into Bennett's Hi-Yield Fund was authorized."

"And?"

"It required two approvals. Bill Hoag was one. The other was Greg Nichols."

Dante was so otherwise preoccupied, Nichols had completely slipped his mind. He'd meant to ask Gus if Phoebe Michel's fiancé had been cut loose yet. "You find out if there's a document on file?" he asked.

"She says there's a standard approval form. This one's got both the necessary signatures, an' a note clipped to it. Says a copy was forwarded t' Foray."

"Let's get hold of it," Joe suggested. "She aware her boss is dead yet?"

"Nuh uh. But you know how fast news travels."

Dante addressed Richardson. "Not a word of this to Hoag. We need to locate Nichols. I assume he's been sprung by now. I want to see his reaction when we show him that signature of his."

"You think he might'a been in on it, all along?"

The notion had occurred to Dante. "I've tried to gauge men and been wrong before," he admitted. "But Mrs. Hoag made no mention of him."

Napier emerged from the room in the company of pathologist Rocky Conklin. With one of his cheaper, crime scene cigars clenched between his teeth, Rocky explained something about the angle and attitude of the victim's head and neck.

"You fix the time of death yet?" Dante asked.

"Ballpark? Between eight and ten last night."

"Her visitor ordered champagne sent up," Napier added. "Made his request from the clerk at the front desk."

"We get a description?"

"Not yet. That information's from computer records. The clerk won't come on duty until five. Cristal, no less. The guy's a prince."

The minute he reached home after his release from Rikers Island, Greg Nichols had stripped naked and made a beeline for the shower. It was close to an hour before he emerged, his new bar of soap worn to a sliver beneath the scalding spray. This was Wednesday. He'd been arrested Monday, and learned of Phoebe's murder, Monday night. Since New Year's Eve, an eternity seemed to have passed. Before last weekend, he'd been a young, rising star with his whole brilliant future still ahead of him. Marriage was on the horizon. There would probably be kids. A nice weekend house somewhere, as soon as they could decide between the country and the shore. Now, none of it seemed to matter anymore. Like a dud skyrocket, his rising star had fizzled and gone out. Seated in a living room chair, wrapped in his terry robe with the draperies pulled, he felt like the past seventy-two hours had aged him ten years.

Nichols had no idea how long he'd been sitting there, staring blankly into space, when a knock came at his front door. Two, three hours, maybe? He didn't even know what time he'd gotten home.

"Go away!" he yelled. It had to be someone from the building staff. The doorman hadn't buzzed him from the lobby to announce a visitor. If he'd flooded a tenant downstairs with his shower, screw them.

"Lieutenant Dante, Greg," a muffled voice replied. "We need to talk."

Fueled by fury, Nichols was suddenly on his feet. He threw open the door with such violence that it tore loose the stop mounted in the hardwood parquet. "Talk about what?" he snarled. "How you lock up an innocent man in a hole not fit for dogs? How the man you should have arrested was busy butchering the only person that I cared a whit about?"

Dante's oak-solid partner—Richardson—took half a step forward and lifted a huge hand to calm Greg. "It weren't his fault, Mr. Nichols. You know Bennett framed you."

Greg studied Lieutenant Dante's face. He thought he'd seen the tall cop wince as he hurled his invective at him. But any real pain was Greg's. He could feel hot tears begin to stream down his face. "You weren't in love with her, mister."

"That's true," Dante replied. "I never even met her. But I did meet Andrea Hill. Twice. Now she's dead, too. Let us in, Mr. Nichols. Please."

Greg realized his mouth had dropped open, closed it, then stepped aside to make way for them. "Wha . . . when? How?"

Dante wandered into the dimly lit living room, followed by his partner. Greg closed the door behind them and crossed to open the draperies. Sunlight flooded the room.

"We think it was Bennett," Dante told him.

Greg caught a glimpse of himself in a wall mirror and ran a self-conscious hand through his rumpled hair. "I don't understand. Why Andrea?"

Lieutenant Richardson produced a folded sheet of paper from an inside coat pocket. "We'd like you to take a look at this." He handed it across.

"Where'd you get this?" Greg murmured as he scanned it. "I don't understand." The document was a Telenet Employees Pension Fund investment authorization. A few dozen had come across his desk during his three-year tenure as the company's CFO. They were required when assets in excess of three million dollars were moved from one investment sector to another. "Wait a minute." He looked up, from one cop to the other. "What is this?"

"We were hoping you could tell us," Richardson said.

Greg stared at him. "This isn't my signature. I've never seen this document before."

"Do you have a sample of your signature somewhere, that you could show us?" Dante asked. "Anything. A credit card receipt. Canceled check."

Suddenly, Greg got it. He'd been so confused by

his signature's presence that he hadn't read the text of the document. Now, he saw how twenty million dollars had been invested by Andrea Hill in Dennis Bennett's Foray Growth Fund. He looked up. There was no way he would have approved a move of that size, into any mutual fund with earnings as weak as Bennett's had been of late.

"Dennis runs the Foray Group."

Dante nodded. "We know that."

"Phoebe worked in analysis for Pierce, Fair-brother. She must have spotted this."

"Did you and Miss Michel ever discuss your business?" Dante asked. "Would she have known that you didn't authorize this investment?"

A thousand different possibilities occurred to Greg at once. He frowned and shook his head. "Hardly ever. Discussed my business, that is. She might have noticed the size of this infusion. Then seen something irregular about what Dennis had done with it."

"Irregular like what?" Lieutenant Richardson asked.

"That's a two-hundred-million-dollar fund," Greg explained. "Twenty million would be ten percent of it. Hardly a drop in the bucket." As he spoke, he hurried to the table where he'd thrown the last three days' mail, including his most recent bank statement. He opened the envelope to paw through it. "Here," he said, producing last month's canceled mortgage check. "They're close, but that one's not mine. Look at the tail of the *S* in my last name. It's like someone drew it. It's not slashed, like I do it."

Richardson peered at the check in Dante's hand.

"Y'think Hoag's could be phony, too?" he wondered aloud.

"Let me see it again," Greg offered. And once they handed the authorization form back to him, he studied it for only a moment. "I've seen Bill's signature often enough, you'd think I'd know it on sight. Wait a minute. I can check." He handed the paper back and hurried down the hall to his bedroom. Moments later, he reappeared, a softball in his hand, and tossed it. "Catch."

Dante fielded it deftly and flipped it over. "What's this?"

"Our company team won a slow-pitch league we were in last summer. I play shortstop. They voted me MVP, and everyone on the team signed the ball."

The lieutenant stopped when he found Hoag's signature, then held the ball alongside the document. "Looks identical."

"Dead ringer," Lieutenant Richardson agreed. "Imagine that."

Despite the proximity of police headquarters at One Police Plaza to Manhattan's financial district, the Pierce, Fairbrother president, Oscar Lewis, had never been there. He'd met Police Commissioner Anton Mintoff at one or two civic functions, but had never had dealings with him in an official capacity. As such, he found Wednesday's urgent summons to a meeting at Mintoff's office unsettling.

It was late in the day when Lewis was shown into the commissioner's fourteenth-floor office and introduced to a five-man Special Investigations Division task force by Chief of Detectives Gus Lieberman.

Gus, he knew better as the husband of Cox, Cromwell heiress Lydia Cox. It put him somewhat at ease to encounter him here, in this otherwise alien setting.

"I'm not at all clear on what this is about," he told Gus as he shook a fellow named Dante's hand. "It's all very mysterious."

Any further exchange was interrupted by the arrival of the chairman of Telenet's board of directors, Thomas Nelson. Another man whom Lewis had met at various social events, the burly, energetic telecommunications maverick seemed as much at a loss as Oscar did. They greeted each other with brisk nods and looks of confusion. As Nelson was introduced around, Lewis turned back to Lieberman.

"Now I'm really baffled. I'd assumed this has something to do with that analyst of ours who was murdered." His face tanned after a week spent on the sunny slopes in Aspen, Lewis considered the pale, card-room pallor of the chief and wondered what could possibly drive the man to labor in such restricting harness. His wife was worth sixty million bucks. He could afford to go anywhere, do anything he wanted.

"Me'n my detectives'll explain everything, once we're all seated," Gus replied. "Gentlemen." He indicated a row of chairs, arranged in a crescent in front of Commissioner Mintoff's desk.

While Oscar and Nelson took seats alongside each other, and the five detectives sat partially facing them, Lieberman remained standing.

"I'm gonna let Lieutenant Dante explain details in a minute," Gus told them. "This is a bit of a dicey situation, and we want t' give you gentlemen time t' get some damage control in place. In exchange for that courtesy, we'd appreciate that nothin' you hear leaves this room."

"Sounds ominous," Nelson said. "You sure we shouldn't have corporate counsel with us?"

Oscar knew the man's reputation better than he knew the man himself. He'd started Telenet thirty years ago with the invention of a new computer modem that linked various work stations in different geographic locations, and had built his company into a major player on the international telecommunications scene. He was reputed to control over thirty percent of the company's stock.

"The false arrest of my CFO has done quite enough to tarnish my company's image already, don't you think?" Nelson asked.

From behind his big mahogany desk, Anton Mintoff steepled his fingers and fed the Telenet Chairman a cool, deliberate smile. "Gus?" he said.

"We'll let Lieutenant Dante take it from here," Lieberman replied. "Joe?"

Without rising, the tall, athletically built detective leaned forward to address Tom Nelson directly. "We've established beyond a reasonable doubt that Mr. Nichols was framed, sir. By a man he thought was a friend. Dennis Bennett."

Lewis gasped, not even attempting to hide his astonishment. "That's ludicrous!"

"We have evidence," Dante continued, and then proceeded to outline what they knew and what had transpired in the past twenty-four hours. When he reported the murder of Andrea Hill, Lewis felt Tom Nelson stiffen beside him.

"Oh my God," Nelson murmured.

Dante continued to speak directly to him. "We

have evidence that Miss Hill was involved with Bennett and your president, Bill Hoag, in a conspiracy to defraud your pension fund." He paused to nod to those two other detectives in the room. "Sergeants Grover and Heckman are working with the Securities and Exchange Commission, to determine the extent of it."

Mintoff continued to regard Tom Nelson with his deliberate cool. "We have Mr. Hoag's authenticated signature on a twenty-million-dollar investment authorization. The signature of Nichols, on that same document, is a forgery. That money was used to purchase over two million shares of Omnicom preferred stock."

"You say you have evidence of this purchase?" Lewis asked, his voice shaky. Damn. This was all craziness. How could Bennett hope to get away with it? "May I ask what that evidence is?"

It was Lieutenant Dante who answered him. "We've recovered data from the hard drive of Phoebe Michel's computer, sir. She was investigating recent Foray Group activity, in the hours before she was killed. There is a record of when those Omnicom purchases were made, and for how much."

The implication was clear. Bennett was involved not only in securities fraud, but murder. In Oscar Lewis's world, mutual fund managers didn't kill people. Miscreant drug fiends and motorcycle thugs did.

"Bennett's office tells us he left for two weeks vacation in Mexico last Friday," Dante continued. "We have reason to believe he never left town."

An agitated Tom Nelson rose from the chair beside Lewis to pace. As he walked to the big window overlooking the South Street Seaport and the East

River, he looked like a man trying to get air. "You say you've authenticated Bill Hoag's signature on this document?" he asked.

"We have," Dante answered him.

Oscar Lewis had never met Bill Hoag, but he'd had plenty of opportunity to watch Dennis Bennett. It was the same old story, here. Smart people playing with fire, believing they are smarter than everyone else in the game.

Tom Nelson still stared out at the world beyond as he spoke again. "To be frank with you? I'm astonished. And bewildered. Bill Hoag had a bright future with us." Past tense.

"We'll need your cooperation, gentlemen," the commissioner told them. He looked directly at Oscar. "That's what Chief Lieberman wants, in exchange for this little conversation we're having here."

"A run on Foray could scuttle us," Lewis replied. A shiver ran up his spine as he said it, really facing the possibility for the first time.

Mintoff glanced at his chief of detectives, and then back at the Pierce, Fairbrother president. "If I were in your shoes, I'd make an announcement, first thing tomorrow. Say Bennett has been replaced, and cite poor performance data or whatever."

"What if you run him to ground before that?" Lewis asked.

"You better pray to God that we don't."

Oscar realized he had little choice.

"We'll need one thing from you sooner than that," Sergeant Heckman told him. "Clear access to the Pierce, Fairbrother database. Not just for Foray Fund files, but everything. We're trying to figure out where that money went, once Bennett dumped his Omni-com shares, yesterday."

The idea of giving anyone free access to his bro-kerage's files caused Lewis to stiffen. They contained the confidential business dealings of a clientele with over ten billion dollars invested through his firm. The trust he was being asked to violate was a hundred and twenty years old. "How can you be certain he sold it all?" he asked.

"From records the SEC has already obtained," Heckman replied. "Bennett programmed a series of sell-offs, to commence at noon yesterday. All two-point-two million shares were offered for sale by noon today."

Numb, Lewis forced himself to push past it. "What, specifically, do you need, Sergeant? Perhaps we can help speed up your search."

"The records of every electronic transfer of funds made out of your brokerage, both yesterday and to-day."

"There would be thousands. Where on earth would you begin?"

"At the beginning," the sergeant replied. "If we follow the money, it'll lead us to Bennett. We'll check every last transfer made between now and then if we have to."

Dennis Bennett got a pretty clear idea of just how close Lieutenant Dante was getting when he saw Os-car Lewis emerge from a limousine outside One Po-lice Plaza. Minutes later, when Telenet's Thomas Nelson pulled up, Dennis felt the rumble of anxiety gnaw at his gut. It was a vivid reminder of the ulcer he'd nursed all last year, while he watched his fortune disintegrate with one failed speculation after another. He knew that a man's luck could always turn, but arrogantly believed himself exempt from the laws of metaphysics. He was charmed; one of society's annointed. *Fate* had stolen his fortune. Now, he contrived to steal it back, because wealth was his right.

The preposterous exploits of policemen in action movies aside, most evidence suggested that they spent more time running into each other than they did running criminals to ground. Bennett's plan counted, at least in part, on police ineptness. He counted on it buying him the time necessary to transfer his funds through a labyrinth of dummy accounts, and ultimately into the hands of Cooperman & Swift before noon tomorrow. The original idea was to give Sid Cooperman until Friday to purchase those thirty-eight million dollars' worth of bearer bonds, but Bennett realized now that he'd be cutting it too close. He needed to get his hands on those certificates no later than nightfall, Thursday. And if he didn't do something about this infernal police lieutenant dogging his heels, even tomorrow might prove to be too late.

SIXTEEN

For Dante, Sandy Pruitt's invitation to join her for dinner tonight had come as a pleasant surprise. In an abstract way, Joe considered himself something of a social scientist, too, and looked forward to swapping perspectives. It would be a welcome diversion. When the elevator appeared and Sandy stepped from it to collect him, she carried her coat over one arm. The wool tights she wore with short boots flattered her long, sculpted legs. An oversize sweater, belted at the waist, barely covered her backside.

"Wow," he greeted her. "Makes a guy think seriously about going back to school."

She took obvious pleasure in the compliment, and smiled. "You have gone back to school."

"Definitely not yours. My profs all run to plump and tweedy."

Earlier, she'd asked him to pick a restaurant. Now, as he took her coat to help her into it, he presented his choices. "I thought you might enjoy the

Golden Unicorn, down in Chinatown. Or my favorite little French joint in the Village. You got a strong preference?"

She tugged the coat closed to button it. "Is one of them any quieter than the other?"

"La Metairie. Definitely."

She took his arm as he led the way onto the elevator car. "Then let's go there. Drink a bottle of wine. Try to relax. You look like you've had another rough day."

On the way downstairs, he told her about finding Andrea Hill at the Vista. "Right now, we're hoping he either runs out of people to kill, or we catch him soon." On the sidewalk, he started them toward his car, the smell of her perfume heady in the crisp night air. "That might be asking too much, though. He's gotten the taste of blood."

Dennis Bennett was busy trying to figure out how to access the warehouse building into which Lieutenant Dante had disappeared, when the detective emerged again in the company of a tall, slender redhead. They crossed the sidewalk together, to where the policeman's Taurus was parked. Dennis watched him hold the passenger door for the woman, and then hurry around to climb behind the wheel. They'd appeared unexpectedly, and moved so quickly that Bennett could see no way to use his new Browning. Not without putting himself at too great a risk. Twice, since his arrival here, he'd been approached by prostitutes he'd had to shoo away. The area was crawling with them. Even if he was able to get a shot off, there were too many witnesses.

So what was this place, he wondered? Dante appeared to have used his own key to gain access, and minutes later, lights had come on behind windows, four floors up. There were already lights ablaze on the top floor, one up. But Dennis had seen no shadows of movement there. Moments before Dante reappeared, the lights on the fourth floor were extinguished again. So was this the woman's place of employment, perhaps? And if so, where had she been waiting for her date? She'd surely not been sitting in the dark.

The building wasn't big by warehouse standards; perhaps a hundred by a hundred feet square. Five stories tall. It was possible that it contained only one business, with offices on the higher floors. That would explain why all the lower floors were unlit, after normal work hours. A design studio, perhaps? Who knew? He was happy enough to see them leave it. This neighborhood gave him the creeps.

The policeman and his date drove south on Eleventh Avenue toward West Street, probably headed out to dinner. That thought made Dennis realize, as preoccupied as he'd been, that he hadn't eaten a thing all day.

Though always slightly crowded because it was small, La Metairie was still a wonderfully intimate eatery, with very good food. When Dante and Sandy arrived, their timing looked to be perfect. The early crowd of theatergoers had vanished, and the usual group of late diners was yet to arrive. After a first taste of her onion tart appetizer, Sandy explained that while Springfield was trying to attain some level of sophistication, it still had a long way to go. Good restaurants were few and far between. Dante was surprised there were *any* good restaurants in a city of just a hundred fifty thousand. He'd traveled to most of the major cities in America at one time or another on police business, but was woefully ignorant of small-town mid-America.

"The image I get when someone mentions the Ozarks is shacks with dirt floors. Li'l Abner and Daisy Mae. Not universities," he confessed.

"I was surprised by the countryside," she admitted. "Especially how beautiful the mountains and lakes are, down into Arkansas. It's not flat like Illinois. Not at all."

Arkansas seemed as foreign to Dante as Ireland had, before he'd vacationed there three years ago. "Pretty strong religious right through that region, no?"

She chuckled and groaned at the same time. "A prime rhinestone in the buckle of the Bible Belt. I find myself doing battle against some appalling ignorance, but hey . . ." She shrugged. "That's why I became an educator, right?"

Dante was getting the feeling, despite the wrong foot they'd gotten off on the other day, that this woman had a lot of her priorities straight. He could see she cared deeply about her work. There was no question she had ambitions, but she seemed to balance them against a strong desire to do good, quality work. She liked herself for what she was and what she'd accomplished. He liked that about her, too.

"So tell me something," she said. "Assuming you finish this thesis, what are your plans? What will you do with it?"

As Joe took a sip of his wine and let it linger on his tongue, he thought about his answer. "There was a time I thought I'd like to teach someday. Put in my twenty, retire on half pay, and move to some ivory tower. I never counted on the work getting into my blood. But I've got my twenty in now, and I can't imagine not going on for at least another ten, fifteen years."

He watched her remarkable green eyes probe his own, and felt most of the defenses he would usually put up, fading.

"I should have known that my sister wouldn't hang out with just any old flatfoot," she murmured. "Know what I assumed? When we met at the airport?"

"That I was some star-fucking leech. The kind you read about, who does favors and runs errands for the rich and famous, just to be seen with them."

She colored slightly, her eyes averted, and toyed with the stem of her wineglass. He watched her long, tapered fingers trace the length of it. When he raised his gaze, he found her studying him.

"You know," she said, "you could try your hand at teaching, just to see how it feels. I might be able to swing you a guest lectureship at my school. You'd bring a valuable perspective to the criminology debate."

A few years back, he'd taught for a time at the police academy. He'd missed the street, but a part of him had enjoyed it. "What kinda leave are we talking about? Four months?"

"About that. You'd probably want some decompression time, in between. We could rent a houseboat on the lake. The spring and fall weather is gorgeous down there."

Either he was mistaken, or she'd just said "we."

Outside the restaurant, it had started to snow. Huge, wet flakes drifted through streetlight to the sidewalk. By the time Joe finished the last of his duck breast, snow had begun to accumulate. "It's tempting, this idea of yours," he admitted.

"You could stay with me," she offered. "I've got a big house. There's plenty of room."

"What would I do with my cat?" he asked.

"No problem. I'd been thinking of stealing him, anyway."

While the policeman and his date dined at La Metairie, Dennis Bennett was forced to settle for slices of pizza and hot coffee. When it started to snow, he wondered how treacherous it would make the narrow Greenwich Village streets. To his relief, the couple didn't tarry late, but emerged from the restaurant at half-past ten. By that hour, close to an inch of snow lay across West 4th Street. Unimpressed by the handling of his little Neon in the best of conditions, Dennis found the pavement a bit unpredictable as he followed his quarry to Eighth Avenue. Then, because the wide avenue was more heavily trafficked, the going was easier. He drove, watching the car ahead of him, and wondering who the woman was. Of better-than-average height, she wore her hair cut short in a style similar to Andrea's. He couldn't imagine what kind of woman would find a policeman attractive. Any policeman. She was probably insecure, and subservient by nature. Policemen were of brutish, primitive sensibility.

Dennis was confused to see them return to the same building where Dante had gone to collect the woman earlier. It hadn't occurred to him that either of them might live there, and now he wondered if it was one of the many converted loft buildings that dotted the city. He had no idea how he was going to gain access to it, but knew he would likely think of something. There was a loading dock down at one end, on 27th Street, that no doubt led to a freight elevator of some sort. As he watched Dante park out front again, and the couple enter through the main 27th Street door, he eased the Neon around the corner to park on Eleventh Avenue. There was no fire escape in evidence here, either, which meant there had to be one somewhere around back, with some sort of access to it. The typical iron rungs of such a contraption would be slippery in this weather, but Dennis had come prepared. He'd worn sneakers, and brought along a pair of ski gloves.

The sidewalks adjacent to where he was parked were empty, the snow having driven all the whores to shelter. As he stepped from his rental car, the night was so quiet, it almost seemed as though he could hear the snowfall. Overhead, lights in those same fourth-floor windows had gone on again. The lights on the floor above were also still ablaze. He supposed that before he tried around back of the building, he should see if he could catch a glimpse of the building's lobby register. That would give him a better idea of just what this place was, and how many residential occupants it had, if any.

* * *

During the drive home, Sandy mentioned having purchased a bottle of good Armagnac that afternoon, and invited Joe upstairs to share it with her. He stopped off at his place to check his messages, and when he arrived, he found her with bottle in hand, looking confused.

"Snifters. I've looked high and low."

He crossed to the dining room and opened the bottom doors of an antique breakfront. "Not a big demand. Your sister keeps the esoteric stemware here." The cabinet was full of aperitif and cordial glasses, as well as large and small snifters. He removed two of the larger globes and carried them to a living room side table.

As Sandy handed the bottle to him, their hands touched, and she stopped. "The restaurant you chose was perfect. Thank you," she said. "I can't tell you how much I needed an evening like that."

"You say it like it's over," he replied, then lifted her chin lightly with a finger and leaned close to kiss her. He let it linger just long enough to make his point, then removed the bottle from her grasp to back away.

"Where do you think you're going?" she murmured. A restraining hand caught his wrist, and then she was in his arms, that first tentative kiss hungry now. By the time she broke it off, to bury her face in his shoulder, his heart thundered against the walls of his chest like a trip-hammer.

"Wow," he gasped.

"Sorry." It came out part muffled and part sheepish. "I've been dying to do that, ever since our appetizers arrived."

"Don't apologize. That's not the kind of spontaneity we want to discourage." With the bottle still in one hand, he wrapped her in his arms to hug her tight. "You do realize, we don't open this thing before we get carried away, we may not get around to it."

She jabbed sharp knuckles into his ribs. "Only a man would think of his stomach at a moment like this."

He grunted. "Believe me. My stomach is the last thing on my mind. I'm being considerate. Of your generous offer."

"Which one?" She lifted her face to kiss him again, more gently this time. Then she eased out of his embrace to pop the catch of that wide elastic belt around her waist, and sling it casually over one shoulder. "Hold that thought. I'll be right back. And while I'm gone, you might lose the gun. I'm not into pistol sex."

Sandy found herself slightly out of breath as she closed the door to the guest room and leaned with her back against it. Eyes closed, she asked herself if this was happening too fast, and if so, was it her fault. Most of it probably was, she expected. This guy was a close friend of her sister's, and she wondered how Diana would react when she found out. Then, as she shoved away from the door to cross the room toward the closet, she figured what the hell? She'd already come this far, and it wasn't like it was something she didn't want to do.

Stripped out of her oversize sweater, she studied herself in the closet's full-length mirror. Never one to flaunt her body, her fears had held her captive for years. It was something her ex-husband had complained continually about; how she wore things to hide her physique, even around the house. The first time she'd seen one of her brother-in-law's famous bronze nudes of her sister, in a contemporary sculpture exhibit at Chicago's Art Institute, she'd felt her ears burn with embarrassment. In a sense, she felt that Diana had betrayed her.

In the year and a half since her divorce from Carl Pruitt, Sandy had made some drastic changes. Two years ago, she couldn't have worn the pair of tights in public that she'd worn tonight. For fifteen years, she didn't own a bathing suit, never worked out at a gym, and hardly wore makeup. Then, over the past eighteen months, she'd had five carefree, barely discriminating affairs. None were deeply satisfying, but they had liberated her to a great extent. Now she wondered just how much. This thing she was about to do was different. Dante had reached out and struck a chord.

At five o'clock that evening, SEC investigator Marsha Hensley had arrived at the Special Investigations office of Don Grover and Rusty Heckman with a briefcase full of fresh information on Dennis Bennett's personal finances. It was, as yet, unanalyzed, and while Rusty continued to concentrate on Foray Group activity, Grover and Ms. Hensley worked to construct a picture of Bennett's relative financial health. They'd pored over bank statements, records of monies borrowed to cover loans that covered loans, mortgage-refinancing papers, and evidence of their suspect's ever dwindling personal assets. The hour was late now, they'd worked right through a dinner of take-out Chinese food, and as the picture they'd created came clear, it wasn't a pretty one.

Marsha, with her masses of permed dark hair, flamboyant dress, and ready laugh, was a tell-it-like-it-is gal who asked no quarter and gave none. While Grover refilled their coffee cups, she rose from her work to stretch the kinks from her back, and threw her pen at the rat's nest of paper on Don's desk in disgust.

"It's all smoke and mirrors, guys. Our mutual fund king doesn't have a pot to pee in, or a window to throw it out."

Across the cubicle, Rusty looked up from his computer monitor and rubbed his eyes. "Might not be quite the fund king he wants the world to believe either. Check this out."

Both Marsha and Don carried their coffee over and perched on edges of his desk as Rusty tapped keys and nodded at his screen. "It's like a sophisticated shell game he's been playing, transferring assets back and forth between his six funds so fast that nobody seems to have noticed. It's a pretty clever trick."

"Trick?" Grover asked. "How do y' mean?"

Heckman had some figures he'd scribbled on a pad at his elbow as he worked. He showed it to them. "It's happening so fast, sometimes three, four times a day, that even an internal audit hasn't caught it. But when you add the numbers up, what they claim each fund's got invested in it, and the actual total amount in all of them, combined, you come up a hundred twenty-eight million dollars short. At least that's the rough number I get."

Marsha leaned forward to peer more closely at Rusty's screen. "Son of a bitch," she marveled. "The sneaky bastard's been kiting money between his own damned funds."

The first thing Dante heard Sandy Pruitt say as she entered the living room, barefoot and clad in a short black silk robe, was, "Condoms."

"Yeah?"

"I don't have any. Do you? It's not the sort of thing you pack when you come east to bury your brother." She winced and shook her head, once she realized how bad that sounded. "Sorry. Into my brain and out my mouth. I do know how to set a mood."

"It's been years since I've gotten uneasy at the mention of death," he assured her. "Been too big a part of my life." He beckoned her close. "Relax. All it requires is a short field trip downstairs." He took her into his arms and let his hands glide down across the silk-sheathed curves of her back and hips. "We're not in any rush, are we?"

"I should say not." She pressed against him as they kissed. "No rush at all. We still haven't had our brandies."

One of her hands left his back to slide between them. "Ummm. Then again, we could have that drink later." Her eyes laughed with mischief as she found his belt buckle.

Simultaneous with a distant, muffled crash, the floor beneath their feet vibrated. Sandy froze.

"What was that?"

He touched a finger to his lips and strained to listen. The unmistakable sound of footsteps came from directly beneath them. "There's someone in my loft," he whispered. "Stay here."

He grabbed his gun from where he'd left it with his coat, and chambered a round out of reflex. Once he opened the back door off Brennan's studio and slipped into the dimly lit stairwell, Joe stood a moment to listen and let his eyes adjust to the gloom. The movement downstairs could be heard more clearly now. Someone knocked something over. It crashed as it hit the floor. He tried to remember how many lights he'd left on. One in the alcove next to the elevator in the living room. Where else? With the exception of the night-light in the bath, and an old exit light over the rear door off the kitchen, the rest of the place had been left in darkness.

Dante stayed as close to the wall of the stairwell as he could, to prevent the treads from squeaking. After a pause on the landing, halfway down, he continued on toward his floor. The back door to his loft hung ajar, the painted metal doorjamb scraped and twisted where entry had been forced. He approached to stand just to one side of it, and started to ease his head into the opening, when he saw the shadow of movement from the corner of one eye.

The short, heavyset individual in a black ski mask saw Joe at the same instant Dante saw him. He was poised with an automatic rifle held at the ready, and his surprise froze him for the instant Dante needed to shoot a stiff-fingered jab at his throat. Contact was made just as the man opened his mouth to call out. That cry was strangled in his throat as Joe surged forward to press the advantage. The intruder grunted as Dante hooked a foot behind his ankles and drove him backward to the floor. The force of impact, with Dante's forearm wedged hard beneath his opponent's chin, slammed that ski-masked head into Joe's arm and snapped the shorter man's neck. Joe rolled hard to one side as the dying man started to convulse, his attention already moving ahead to who else might be deeper inside his loft.

Back on his feet in a low crouch, his weapon extended before him in a two-handed grip, Dante strained to listen. A voice snapped a quick question in a language Joe didn't recognize. It came from the middle of the living room, beyond the kitchen doorway, and was answered by a second voice from what sounded like the direction of his bedroom.

"Ahmed!" the first voice snapped again.

Joe moved to crouch at one side of the doorway and drew a bead. A second ski-masked individual could be seen turning toward him. Backlit by the dim glow of that rear-door exit light, Joe knew how exposed he was. He had to act. Now. The report of his 9mm Walther automatic was deafening in the enclosed space as Dante's first shot caught the man mid-chest. The second was a head shot aimed at the mouth hole in the ski mask. It dropped his already reeling target like a bag of spuds.

At least one more intruder was lurking somewhere in the darkness of his loft, and Joe took no chances. He dove sideways to get clear of the doorway, and fired a third shot at that exit light to snuff it. Without a key to activate the elevator, the only way the third interloper had out of the loft was through the back door. Dante scuttled crabwise toward the breakfast nook at the far end of the room. From where he secreted himself, prone on the floor beneath his table, he had a perfect vantage of that last avenue of escape.

"Ahmed!" the high, panicked voice called out again. "Jabir!"

Joe heard quick footsteps, and then an anguished gasp of alarm. Suddenly, the darkness was ripped by muzzle flashes, the roar of automatic weapon fire like a lightning strike, it was so close at hand. The intruder let out a banshee wail, fired another burst, and made a desperate charge for the back door.

Hot lead, bits of drywall, splinters of wood and God only knew what else flew in every direction. Dante had to fight the urge to duck in order to stay with his target. When he saw the first shadow of movement outside the living room doorway, he sighted along the barrel of his weapon and slowly exhaled. With those deadly lead hornets tumbling overhead at supersonic speeds, the muzzle flashes from the shooter's gun helped outline him as he hurtled into Joe's line of fire. The pistol jumped in Dante's hands. As he aimed for the head, part of his target seemed to vanish. The automatic rifle continued to bellow and spit fire until the clip was empty, while the dying man's momentum pitched him twitching onto his side. For the next fifteen seconds, a partially deafened Dante could barely hear the scuffing shuffle of those death throes. Then all was quiet.

SEVENTEEN

From the corner of West 27th Street and Eleventh Avenue, Dennis Bennett watched from his rental car as muzzle flashes finally ceased to light the darkened interior of the building's fourth floor. He'd been on foot, in search of access to the fire escape around the back of the building, when a black Chevrolet Suburban had pulled to the curb on Eleventh, and three men in ski masks piled out. They carried automatic rifles and climbing gear. As he watched from concealment behind a Dumpster, the lowest rung of that fire escape had proven no obstacle for them. Two of the men had hoisted the third up to where he could scramble onto the lower catwalk. From there, he noiselessly deployed a rope ladder. Seconds later, all three of them had disappeared over the roof parapet. Dennis was pleased to find Lieutenant Dante had enemies other than himself, and was happy to yield the field to this team of well-trained assassins, whoever they were.

As much as Bennett wanted to savor this moment, he knew he didn't dare tarry long. Those assassins weren't likely to stick around for a post-event analysis. And they wouldn't look favorably on any eyewitnesses.

He started the Neon to proceed onto the avenue without lights. In the rearview, he took one last look at the black Suburban; an avenging angel's chariot. Two inches of snow had accumulated to slow his progress to a crawl, but Dennis couldn't care less. The police would need days to reorganize now. By the time they got their pursuit back on track, he would be only a name, vanished in the mist. An entirely other man, Randall Andrews, would be well on his way to a new life of sunshine and ease.

It was hard for Dante to judge how long he'd waited in the dark before he was satisfied that no one else lurked in ambush. As the first distant wail of a siren reached his numbed ears, he realized that Sandy had probably dialed 911. The unmistakable stench of cordite would have drifted up the back stairwell by now to mix with the heavy silence. On his belly, he eased himself forward from beneath his kitchen table, and stood.

"Sandy?" he called out.

"Joe?" He could hear relief and fear mixed together in her voice.

"I'm okay," he called back. "You don't want to come down here. Keep an eye out for Toby, will you? I'm gonna take the elevator down to the street." He walked on shaky knees to his broken back door. Up through the dim light of the stairwell, he saw Sandy's frightened face on the landing above.

"Wh-what happened?"

"I haven't turned on the lights to look yet. Don't think I want to. Hang tight, Sand." He could hear more sirens now. That first one seemed less than a block away. "It sounds like help has arrived."

Before he risked the trip downstairs, Joe raised the sash of a window that overlooked the street and stuck his head out. He hailed the two uniforms who'd just emerged from their cruiser, weapons drawn, and identified himself. Three more units had arrived by the time he unlocked the street door. A pair of cops were left on the front door to monitor traffic in and out. Two more were sent to scour for evidence outside. Dante took the remaining four upstairs.

When he flipped the bank of switches alongside the elevator, the light that flooded his living room reflected off an ocean of blood. Crimson and cranial matter were spattered across the wall outside the hallway to his bedroom and bath. A large, blood-soaked hole was torn out of the back of one dead man's ski mask, his facial features obscured. Dante knelt to carefully peel the mask back, and recognized one of the Kuwaiti bodyguards from last night; the one he'd tackled and kneed in the groin. A bullet had caught him dead center of his face and left a blackened 9mm hole at the bridge of his nose. His eyes were frozen in an expression of surprise and pain.

"Know him, Lou?" one of the uniforms asked.

"We met last night," Dante replied softly. As he rocked back on his heels and heaved himself to his feet, he was hopeful that sometime soon, his knees would quit feeling like rubber. "You probably heard about it on the news."

"Both these guys're dead, too," another uniform called from the kitchen. "Serious fucking mess in here. Jesus Christ."

Joe took another measured breath and turned to survey the damage. The burst of fire, sprayed inside his living room, had destroyed everything on the west wall shelves. His CD player teetered half off its perch at a crazy angle. The screen of his TV was shot out. Books, in ruins, were scattered all over the floor.

Dante and Brennan had lovingly fabricated all the cabinetry in the kitchen, and Joe was reluctant to survey the damage in there. Oak and mahogany raised-panel cabinet doors. Hand-made Italian tile backsplash and floors. The last guy had fired a burst of at least twenty rounds.

Dennis saw a light behind curtains covering one of his Baia luxury cruiser's portholes and a jolt of adrenaline started his pulse hammering. With the exception of faint security lights, fore and aft, the boat should have been dark.

Frozen in his tracks, he felt his pulse pound at his temples as he reached into his coat for his gun. Then, through the swirling snow, he saw the white scarf. It was tied to a mooring cleat at the stern. Their signal. Relief washed over him, quickly replaced by anger as he charged onboard. What on earth was she doing here now?

"Dennis?" he heard her call out as he stamped his feet and tugged the cabin door shut behind him. "In here. Where on earth have you been?"

It was snug and warm inside the cruiser's spacious salon as Bennett shook the snow off his coat and hat and tossed them across one of the butter-soft leather divans. In the cabin he'd outfitted as his library/office, he found Vivian Hoag curled in a chair, barefoot and wrapped in a skimpy satin robe. She had a drink on the low table at her side, and a map in her lap.

"What are you doing here?" he demanded. Her robe was left open to expose most of her right breast, the fabric just barely covering her nipple.

"I thought you'd be happy to see me," she pouted. "It's been days." She adjusted her wrap to reveal the edge of an areola, and yawned. Dennis had never been particularly attracted to diminutive women until he'd met this one, in a bathing suit at an Easthampton pool party, two summers ago. This one had changed his perception of tiny women for all time.

"You couldn't wait just one more day?" he complained. "We're so close now, Viv."

She persisted with that mock pout. "I thought it was two days."

"I've decided to push up the timetable, love. To move the pickup to tomorrow afternoon." He pulled his sweater over his head and sat in the chair opposite to remove his shoes. "Tell me how you got here. Walk me through it."

"You treat me like a child sometimes," she complained. "I took a cab from my place. To Grand Central. A train from there to Times Square. Another cab to Ninety-sixth, and then a cab to Riverside Drive. I walked, in this lousy goddamned weather, from there." She heaved herself to her feet, tugged the robe closed, and grabbed up her glass. "I'm having another drink. You?"

"Love one. Where's William?"

"Most likely passed out by now. In a pool of self-pity and puke. He was halfway through a bottle of bourbon by the time I got home from the office. The news about Andrea hit him pretty hard."

Sandy Pruitt was having coffee with the two policemen Joe had left with her when Diana and Brian returned home, a few minutes after midnight. Dante had been back upstairs twice to check on her. The building still crawled with police personnel, and her hosts had just run the gauntlet.

"What the hell happened? Where's Joe?" Brian was clearly shaken as he shrugged out of his overcoat. "The cops at the door downstairs wouldn't tell us a thing."

Sandy related what she knew. "Luckily, he was up here having a nightcap with me when they broke in," she concluded.

"Damn," Diana murmured. "All because he dissed some pissant prince?"

"I gather they're angry at the city's refusal to apologize."

"So they send a death squad?" Brennan scoffed. "Bit of an overreaction, don't you think?"

They heard a commotion at the back of Brian's studio, and looked over to see Dante, Beasley Richardson, and Chief of Detectives Gus Lieberman enter from that direction. The first time that Sandy saw Joe after the shooting, she'd hugged him and felt his body tremble. It was like an electric current was being run through his body. He still looked ashen.

"How badly did they wreck your place?" Brian asked.

"Might be easier to gut it and start all over," Joe replied.

"Meanwhile, you'll stay here," Diana told him.

He thanked her and glanced quickly at Sandy. "I've gotta go downtown; make a statement to the U.S. attorney and do an initial shooting inquest. God knows what time I'll be back."

"Don't worry about it," Diana said. "We'll get your bed made up."

Sandy almost told her not to bother. Then she considered what Dante had just been through, and realized this might not be the best time to begin a relationship, *or* to broach the subject with her sister.

Vivian let Dennis finish his drink and tell her the story of his day before she rose from her chair, hand extended, and asked him to take her to bed. He worried about the hour; that Bill would be alarmed by her absence. She assured him that Bill was so drunk, he wouldn't notice if someone pulled all his teeth.

"So tell me," she growled as Dennis stripped hurriedly from his clothes. Feet tucked beneath her, she knelt on the big master stateroom bed. "If she'd refused to invest that money, how long would you have continued to fuck her?"

Down to his socks and silk bikini briefs, he paused. "She didn't refuse, love."

Vivian peeled the robe back from her shoulders and let it fall to the crooks of her elbows. "I know you like my body better, but which of us was the better fuck, Den?"

"That's a trifle immaterial, wouldn't you say?" He tossed his briefs aside and sat on the edge of the bed to remove his socks.

"Indulge my curiosity. What did she have that I don't? The thing that made you keep going back?"

"Twenty million dollars." He stood to face her. "But yours is the much superior blow job. I hope that's some small comfort. I know it is to me."

"Get your ass up here," she ordered. "You're my small comfort."

"Small indeed," he complained. "You wound me, Vivian dear."

By the time Dante returned to his building, it was after two a.m. He rode the elevator past his own floor to Diana and Brian's place, where Toby the cat greeted him on arrival, followed by his hosts.

"How'd it go?" Brennan asked. "We at war with Kuwait?"

Joe was bone weary, and his sense of humor was shot. "The State Department's made it official. Prince Whatzizname is on the next plane home. I didn't know diplomatic immunity covered attempted murder. I guess it depends on how much oil you've got. Sandy turn in? How is she?"

"Your little adventure shook her pretty good," Brian replied. "She hit the hay about an hour ago."

Downtown at headquarters, Rosa had put in an appearance. She'd invited Joe to stay at her place. He'd taken a rain check.

"New toothbrush in the bath," Diana told him. "Bed in the other guest room's made up. How'd your dinner go, by the way?"

"We had a nice time," he reported.

"I can't believe the change in my sister. I think I actually like her, Joe."

Dante reflected on the conversation he'd had with Sandy over dinner. "We talked about me doing a guest lectureship at her school. Once my thesis is done." He saw Diana's eyes narrow, and reminded himself to be careful.

"In Bumfuck, Missouri?" she scoffed. "You'd hate it. You're a city guy."

He reached out to caress her cheek, and smiled. "It's just a thought. I'm gonna try to get some sleep. Full plate tomorrow."

"You want, I'll get hold of a commercial cleaning crew," Brennan offered. "I'm home all day. I can keep an eye on them."

Dante told him he'd appreciate it. "What's the status on the arrangements you've made for your brother?" he asked Diana.

She took it in stride. "There's not much point to a funeral," she replied. "We're the only family he had. Sandy's offered to fly out to San Jose with me, to deal with his estate. Sometime this summer, we'll take his ashes to Indiana, where our parents are buried."

Toby had vanished by the time Dante finished brushing his teeth. Beneath the bedclothes, with the night table lamp switched off, Joe closed his eyes and saw the darkness ripped by muzzle flashes. Crimson splashed across stark white walls. He'd stopped shaking a couple hours ago, and the sick, empty feeling in the pit of his stomach was fading. He was left with an anxious, wrung-out feeling, no longer able to make real, emotional contact with the horror of it. He guessed it was how witnesses to massacres had to feel, and what happened to rescue workers at disaster sites. The circuits just shut down.

He'd left the door slightly ajar for the cat. In the darkness, across the room, he heard it swing inward, then close again to click shut. The shadow of a slender female form emerged, his white cat cradled in her arms.

"Room for two more?" Sandy asked. "I need you to just hold me, Joe. We can pick up where we left off, some other time."

He lifted the bedclothes and eased to one side. With her backside nested against his stomach, he buried his nose in her hair. She smelled wonderful. "I thought you'd been asleep for hours."

"I just wanted to be by myself. Believe me, I haven't slept a wink." She flipped over to wrap her slender arms around his torso and hug him tight.

"Have I told you how beautiful I think you are?" he asked.

She shook her head. "I'm not. Your friend Rosa is beautiful. I'm moderately attractive."

"Bullshit."

In spite of himself, Dante's biology was slowly being gripped by an impulse of growing urgency. "Shit," he moaned.

She raised her head to peer through the gloom at his face. "Condoms?"

"I got a little sidetracked," he admitted. "They're still in my top dresser drawer."

A corner of her mouth curled in a wry smile. "How long can you hold this thought?"

"Huh?"

"Be right back."

She leapt from the bed to hurry from the room. On her return, she brandished a silver foil prophylactic packet. *"Voilà."*

"Where'd that come from?"

"I didn't snoop, I swear." As she said it, she grabbed the hem of her nightgown and whisked it over her head. "I just told the man on your back door that I'd left my reading glasses in your bedroom."

Her body, now revealed to him, was beautiful. "C'mere," he growled, and held back the blankets as she scrambled in again. "Moderately attractive, indeed."

"Resourceful, too," she murmured, and once again wrapped him in her arms.

EIGHTEEN

Don Grover couldn't pinpoint exactly when the idea had occurred to him. After twenty-three years trying to puzzle out the various problems thrown his way, he knew that any attempt to fathom his subconscious was fruitless. At six, he dragged his ass out of bed, barely awake, to take a cold shower. When that first icy blast of water hit him, there it was. The answer.

"I don't think the money ever left the fuckin' brokerage," he told Rusty on their way into Manhattan. "At least not directly. I don't know why it never occurred t' me before."

"How's he gonna get his hands on it, if it's still there?" Rusty countered.

"That's a question we still gotta answer. But him killin' the Hill woman can only mean one thing, Rust. That he intends t' run with the whole fuckin' take."

Last night, as they'd worked in their SID cubicle alongside the SEC investigator, they hadn't been able to determine where the principal and profits from the sale of those two million Omnicom shares had gone. But they had discovered the truth about Bennett's own financial health, and the scam he appeared to be working to mask the failures racked up by his funds. In recent months, it looked like he'd tried to liquidate everything he owned in an attempt to stay one step ahead of his creditors. Last night, a painstaking examination of recent Foray Growth Fund activity had revealed a series of rash speculative moves, made over the past eight months. Each had failed disastrously. By the clever kiting of liquid assets from one fund to another in a kind of high-tech electronic shell game, he'd been able to fool Pierce, Fairbrother's internal auditors so far.

"He intends t' cut and run," Grover continued with his theory. "But think about it, Rust. There's a sudden, huge demand for Omnicom, Tuesday. Bennett didn't have t' go nowhere t' dump it. The thing was done internally, in more'n fifty separate trades, all of 'em preprogrammed. Hell, he even had one'a his own funds buy some, at close t' twice what he paid for it."

"So what's your point, Donnie?"

"That he didn't have t' wait the usual three days for them trades t' clear. He keeps them all internal, everything he sells becomes instant cash."

"Yea-a-a-h." Rusty was catching his drift.

"He's already proven t' us he's the master of the bait 'n' switch. So. What d'we know that's fundamental t' every criminal mind we've ever run up against?"

"They get into a groove, they rarely depart from it," Heckman murmured.

"Fuckin' A they don't. Why should they? They're smarter'n everybody else."

Heckman had the ball, and ran with it. "He knew that if anyone caught on to his game, the gates would come crashing down. Transferring those funds off-shore would be risky. If Pierce, Fairbrother caught on, they might be able to block it."

Grover slapped the dashboard before him, really warming up to this now. "Exactly. But say, one'a the investors in his Hi-Yield Fund is a dummy client. Somebody he fabricated. If that guy wants his money out, all he's gotta do is ask. Bennett opens him another account, somewhere else inside the brokerage, an' transfers the money from the one account t' the other. What eyebrows would that raise?"

After last night's snowfall, the traffic into Manhattan at the west end of the Midtown Tunnel was all but at a standstill. Rusty's impatient fingers drummed the wheel. "Until," he mused, "John Doe, or whoever he is, decides to take his money out."

"And he will, Rust. Guaranteed. It's too fuckin' risky t' leave it there long. Sooner or later, some auditor's bound t' get wise."

"Question is, has he done it already? By the time we can pinpoint which accounts in his fund are fake, and where the cash from them's been transferred . . ."

"Don't forget. He's a clever guy. There's bound t' be a whole hoard'a them dummies."

"So clever, he's predictable," Rusty murmured. "Just like all the rest." He glanced over at his partner. "I like it, Donnie. Let's hope we're not too late."

Don met his gaze. "We gotta think positive, Rust. And remember. This mutt's cocky. Me? I gotta think about gettin' myself a doughnut. I'm starvin' t' death here."

* * *

Not an early riser, Diana surprised Dante that morning. She was up and had coffee made by the time he stole into the kitchen at seven-thirty. Showered and dressed, he carried his shoes in one hand to avoid waking anyone.

"No rest for the weary, huh?" she observed. "How you feel?" Dressed in sweats and warm shearling slippers, she'd only wet-combed her hair and wore no makeup. Over the span of their friendship, Joe had seen Diana this way much more often than in her MTV persona.

"Fair enough, considering," he replied. "I wish I could say we're hot on this asshole Bennett's heels. That would make me feel better."

"Fresh-squeezed juice in the fridge. Help yourself. So what's with you and my sister?"

Dante found himself a glass in an overhead cabinet. He turned toward the refrigerator. "Too early to tell. You uncomfortable with it?"

She wrapped her arms around her ankles, chin atop her knees. "No." She paused. "I don't think so. You like her. I can tell."

"What I've seen so far, I like a lot."

"And what about you and Rosa?"

He carried his juice to the table. "Good question." He pulled up a chair and sat. "We're in each other's blood. But my life's here, Di. Not in Washington. And not in the Ozarks, either. That doesn't mean I can't visit. Both places."

"So it wasn't just a one-night stand."

"I hope not. I'd like to see where she lives. Take a walk in her world."

Diana took one of Joe's hands in hers, and squeezed it. "You and my big sister." She shook her head.

"You okay with this?" He squeezed back.

She stared hard at him and he thought he saw the faintest bit of moisture accumulate at the corners of her eyes as she nodded. "Of course I am. Right now, she needs someone strong like you in her life."

When Bill Hoag awoke that morning, the sun streamed through his bedroom window and directly into his aching eyes. Vivian was not beside him, and even in his nauseous, post-bender fog, he realized he'd forgotten to set the alarm. It was late. Therefore, *he* was late. By the time he entered the kitchen, showered and dressed, it was nearly nine o'clock. Still no sign of Vivian. She hadn't even left him half a pot of coffee, had probably spent the night in the guest room and left for the office early. No doubt, she'd dumped what was left of the coffee out of spite. Bitch. He washed down three Advil with a glass of grapefruit juice.

When Bill contacted his secretary to let her know he was running late, she informed him that board chairman Tom Nelson's assistant had called looking for him. Twice. He considered a call to Nelson, but decided against it. His primary concern, as he rode down in the elevator, was how long he could keep that Advil down. Twice, he thought he might lose it, and his grapefruit juice, onto his neighbor's shoes.

The snarl of snow-slowed traffic delayed Hoag's arrival at the Telenet Tower on Lexington Avenue until almost ten o'clock. By that time, his pain reliever had gotten some slight hold on the worst of his head and body aches. Still, he felt positively green as he stepped off the elevator onto the thirty-eighth floor. His secretary glanced up from her work to do a double-take.

"You look awful, Bill. You should have stayed home in bed."

He tried to put on a brave face. "I know. Bad week to catch the flu."

"Well, breathe the other way," she begged. "Claire Wainwright just called again. Her boss wants to hear from you. ASAP."

Connie Blumenthal was the only secretary Hoag had ever had. She'd followed him every step of the way, from his first job out of Wharton, to this one. Over the twelve years they'd worked together, their relationship had become as comfortable as an old pair of shoes. At fifty-three, with two grown kids and three grandchildren, the portly dynamo could handle the workload of any Telenet vice-president. She also believed she could do a better job than ninety percent of them.

At his desk, Bill leafed through a stack of messages as Connie carried in a long-overdue first cup of coffee. Unless Claire called again, he was determined to finish it before he called Tom Nelson. He'd barely had a tentative first sip before the phone in the outer office rang. Seconds later, his intercom buzzed.

"Mr. Nelson, on two," Connie informed him.

He took a deep breath, determined to sound upbeat. "Yes, Tom," he answered. "Sorry I've been so hard to get hold of. Came down with a flu bug."

The board chairman's reply was decidedly remote.

"Something important has come up, Bill. I need to see you. Face-to-face."

Fifteen years Bill's senior, with a huge block of the company's stock under his control, Thomas Nelson *was* Telenet. Hoag might be a brilliant manager, but he was still only Nelson's hired gun.

Two minutes later, as Claire Wainwright greeted him and asked him to wait, he clearly felt a chill in the air. What the hell was going on? Tom remained seated and did not offer to shake hands as Bill entered his office. After yesterday's Omnicom coup, that seemed particularly odd. He suggested Hoag take a chair, and as soon as Bill's backside was planted, pushed several sheets of paper toward him.

"I'd like to have your comment on these," was all he said.

The instant Bill picked them up, an alarm went off in the back of his head. He recognized the top sheet, and quickly recollected the last time he'd seen that document. It was late afternoon, around the beginning of December, in Andrea's apartment. They were in a rush to get dressed. She had a meeting. So did he. No details of the investment on the authorization document had been filled in yet. She hadn't obtained Greg Nichols's signature yet, either. To save her a trip to his office in the morning, she'd asked Bill to sign it then; a routine permission that would authorize a shift of five million dollars from one batch of bonds that had matured, to a new issue. He knew Nichols would ask all the appropriate questions. Greg was a stickler for detail.

"I don't understand," Bill murmured. And he didn't. This was a permission to invest twenty million dollars, not five. As he thumbed the sheets beneath, his heart sank even further. They documented an investment made by the Telenet Employees Pension Fund, on December fifth, into the Foray Growth Fund, in the amount of twenty million dollars. The last sheet detailed how, over two weeks in December, Foray Hi-Yield had purchased two-point-two million shares of Omnicom preferred stock.

"That is your signature, is it not?" Nelson challenged him.

Bill swallowed hard and nodded. It wouldn't be difficult to authenticate it. "She changed the numbers on me," he croaked.

"I beg your pardon?"

Hoag looked at him, helpless with despair. "It's not an excuse. I've fucked up."

Nelson's expression remained cold and impassive. "I should say. If Greg Nichols couldn't prove that his signature there is a forgery, the entire Telenet organization would be implicated in an insider trading conspiracy of serious magnitude. This way, however, only you are."

Hoag spread his hands in helpless supplication. "Tom, please. I . . ." He stopped, at a loss for the right words. There *were* no right words. Andrea had defrauded him.

"For peanuts, Bill." Nelson said it with absolute disdain in his voice. "That's what I can't understand. You had your whole future ahead of you here. You could have made twenty million with two or three years' worth of stock options. More, if this Omnicom merger proves as profitable as it looks like it will. What was going through your mind?"

"The authorization was supposed to be for five." Hoag said it hollowly. "And not for investment in

Foray. That's her old boss Dennis Bennett's doing. And too obvious a conflict of interest."

Nelson grunted. "Bullshit, Bill. Your own wife turned you in. She told the police about the affair you've been having. She didn't want to be ruined by your recklessness."

Hoag felt the heat rise to prickle his flesh as his face flushed with anger. The stitched wound at his temple began to throb, the blood of his thundering pulse hammering at it. So this was all Vivian's doing. Just to get even. He was going to kill her. Right then and there, he swore a silent oath to that. The conniving, backstabbing little bitch.

Nelson stood, across the desk from Hoag. He looked down at the vanquished man and made no attempt to hide his disgust. "You've got exactly one hour to clean out your desk. Security will escort you from the building. I've called a meeting of all the available members of the board. To discuss whether or not we want to press formal charges. What the SEC decides to do is clearly up to them."

This short week had been an interesting one for Sid Cooperman of Cooperman & Swift. The market, in a downturn since the start of December, had shown signs of coming to life. That upturn was typified by an announcement made by the Telenet Corporation, first thing Tuesday. It had spurred furious interest in a company they sought to acquire, in a two-for-one stock swap. That had triggered buying in a whole host of software providers who stood to profit from the marriage. The high-tech sector, flat since mid-summer, was suddenly alive again.

To make this week even more interesting, Cooperman received a follow-up call, Wednesday, from his new big-talking client, Randall Andrews. Last Friday, Sid hadn't invested much faith in the claims Andrews made. No one at either Dun & Bradstreet or TRW had any record of an individual by that name. No one, at least, with that sort of wealth. But all the same, Sid had opened the account on the off chance. Thirty-five million in municipal bearer bonds would be the single biggest trade in his brokerage's history.

It came as something of a surprise, then, when Andrews called Tuesday to make sure they were still on for a Friday pickup. When the client mentioned he might want to increase his purchase by three or four million dollars, Sid assured him that the Federal Reserve vault downtown currently contained a stock in excess of two hundred million. A total buy of, say, thirty-eight million would put Sid and his partner nearly two hundred thousand in the black, only four days into the new year. All they needed, before they called the Brink's truck, was money.

That morning, when Sid arrived at the brokerage, his first item of business was to bring the Andrews account up on his monitor screen. To his delighted surprise, he found that not just part of the money was there, but all of it. It didn't matter to him that no one had heard of their client: not TRW, Dun & Bradstreet, the FBI, or the CIA. Randall Andrews could be a shill for a Chinese heroin cartel for all he knew or cared. In the eyes of the law, Cooperman & Swift had just one responsibility here. Once the trade was concluded, they were required to report it to the IRS.

At ten-fifteen that morning, the broker's secretary poked her head into Sid's office. "Mr. Andrews on line three, boss."

With a smile of satisfaction, Cooperman pegged the speakerphone button and eased back in his comfortable leather desk chair. He spoke at the ceiling. "We're in receipt of your transfer this morning, Mr. Andrews. Everything's in order."

"Excellent," the client replied. His up-market British accent inspired a mental image of unimpeachable prosperity. "I've encountered a bit of a bother, I'm afraid. My wife and I have been forced to change our travel plans slightly. Do you think our timetable could be pushed up? Just half a day?"

The sooner this deal was done, the sooner Cooperman & Swift locked in their brokerage fee. The logistics, now that the money was in hand, were no more complicated than a simple electronic transfer of funds to the clearinghouse. "I've scheduled an armored car pickup for nine tomorrow morning," Sid replied. "You'd like me to change it?"

"That's correct. Ideally, to late this afternoon. I have an insufferable amount of last-minute running around I simply cannot avoid. I'll have to send my wife. Would sometime after four suit you?"

"We usually close at five, but certainly an exception could be made. She'll be coming with your own security, I imagine?" Cooperman could *only* imagine. Wiry Asian thugs, with bulges under their jackets. Heavyset Colombians.

"An exception won't be necessary," Andrews replied. "You can expect her between half-past four and quarter to five."

"Been a pleasure doing business with you, Mr.

Andrews," Sid assured him. Indeed, he felt more smug by the second. Any time a client handed him a hundred ninety thousand dollars, gift-wrapped, he allowed himself a little smugness.

"Likewise," Andrews replied, and broke the connection.

By midmorning, Grover, Heckman, and Marsha Hensley had commandeered office space on the Foray Fund floor of the Pierce, Fairbrother building. While Marsha and her SEC team continued to focus on Dennis Bennett's web of deceit, Don and Rusty took their own, separate road. Given unrestricted access to the brokerage's database, they were concentrating on where that money from Tuesday's Omnicom sell-off had gone. Rusty was formatting their parameters into a specific database search request when Joe Dante and Jumbo Richardson put in an appearance at ten-thirty. It fell to Grover to attempt an explanation of their direction and progress. He tossed his pen onto the legal pad before him as the visitors took seats. Don yawned and ground the heels of his hands into his eye sockets.

"Okay. Assumin'—and that's the operative fuckin' word here—that Bennett dumped all two-point-two million shares between noon an' four, Tuesday, we've got the dollar amount we're lookin' for, pretty much narrowed down."

"If," Rusty cautioned, looking over the top of his monitor, "you're willing to accept a range of thirty-four to forty million as narrow." He had one eye on the new coffee he'd started, as the carafe approached full. "At a house that specializes in estate portfolio management, most of the ten-million-dollar variety, or more. That, and managing the assets of huge corporate trusts."

"Last guy I talked to says they've got two hunnerd seventy-eight accounts, all in the thirty-plus range," Grover added. "Besides them, we gotta consider he might'a dumped pieces of his profit inta several different accounts. With the access codes he's privy to, he could do that."

Richardson sipped the caffeine-free diet soda he'd bought from a machine in the company canteen. He took a swallow and held up a hand to slow Grover down. "Y'mean, he put cash in accounts where it don't belong? Then took it back out again?"

Heckman grabbed that one. "Either that, or created dummy accounts, and used them the same way. We're looking for deposits made Tuesday, and monies that were later transferred back out again, as soon as the trades cleared. Probably to one specific destination."

"Like where?" Dante asked.

"Could be a bank offshore," Grover replied. "But we kinda doubt it. Be too easy t' get on the trail of it. He can't risk the feds findin' it, and freezin' it before he can cash his chips."

Heckman told Dante and Richardson about a conversation he'd had with the detective captain who ran the Organized Crime Control Bureau's Fiscal Section. "He thinks Bennett would buy something negotiable," he concluded. "Right from jump street."

"Such as?" Richardson wondered.

Rusty stood, stretched, and crossed the room to fill his plastic foam cup with coffee. "Gold, maybe. Gemstones. Cash. Each of them has its own set of problems. Thirty million bucks in gold would weigh two tons. Cash wouldn't weigh that much, but think of the red flags you'd raise. That's three hundred thousand Ben Franklins. A million and a half Andy Jacksons."

Dante indicated Heckman's monitor screen, where a seemingly endless list of names and numbers scrolled past. "So where are you now?"

Rusty sat to sip his fresh java. "Still at step one. We've asked their people to isolate every stock trade made Tuesday, as it cleared. From that list, we'll attempt to track where the proceeds went, and then track the activity in every account we can pinpoint. For both yesterday, and this morning."

"What if he ain't moved the money yet?" Jumbo asked. "What if it's still here?"

"That's the gamble we have t' take," Grover told him. "That he wouldn't risk it. The man's wanted. For three fuckin' homicides. He's gotta be eager t' get outta town."

Beasley drained his diet drink and flipped the can into a nearby trash basket. "So you're bettin' the money's already gone."

Grover leaned over to peer at his partner's monitor screen as he nodded. He was proud of his little brainchild. As much as he wanted to rub his eyes again, he refused to allow himself. "It makes the most sense. The big question is: Where?"

Bill Hoag showed up at his wife's Madison Avenue law firm at eleven o'clock that Thursday morning. It was only a three-block walk across icy sidewalks from the Telenet Tower, but en route, he'd stopped at the first bar he'd encountered to toss back two straight-bourbon shots. After Tom Nelson's ultimatum, he hadn't bothered to return to his office and clean out his desk. What did a man whose life had been destroyed need with useless awards and mementos? To look at those framed photographs and citations again would only rub salt in his wounds. No, the only thing Bill carried away from Telenet was a fierce, unfettered hatred of the entire fairer sex; of Vivian, of Andrea, and of every other woman who hadn't yet had the opportunity to betray him. The bourbon got the monkey of last night's drunk off his back, but his leather-soled lace-ups were hardly suited for the treacherous post-storm pavement. He slipped and fell twice, which only served to sharpen his malice.

When Bill appeared in the doorway, Vivian's secretary started as if Freddy Krueger were standing there with his ax. "I-is there a problem, Mr. Hoag?"

"Where's my wife?" he snarled.

Along with the fear, she now registered confusion. "At home? She called in sick."

"Bullcrap!" he snapped. Up on the balls of his feet, he loomed menacingly before her desk. "Is that what she told you to say?"

Attracted by the belligerence in Bill's tone, one of the firm's junior partners stuck his head in the door. He was an athletically built guy who had once worked for the Brooklyn D.A.'s office. "Problem?"

"Who asked you to butt in?" Bill bristled.

The attorney took one look at Hoag and pointed to the phone on the secretary's desk. "Call security, Phyllis. Where's Vivian?"

"She called in sick. About nine. Said she was staying home."

His hands clenched into white-knuckled fists, Hoag slammed one of them down on the front edge of her desk. With a squeal, the secretary leapt back. She knocked over her chair in the process.

A bolt of searing pain shot all the way to Bill's shoulder. "She wasn't home at nine this morning!" he yelled. Then, as he stuck his injured hand in his mouth and saw the blood on his knuckles, something snapped. He suddenly realized how crazy he must look as he stared wide-eyed at Vivian's secretary for a mortified moment. The attorney in the doorway barely had time to register this sudden shift of mood, and leap out of the way, as Hoag hurtled past.

Unwilling to wait for the elevator, Bill raced to the emergency fire stairs and charged down the five floors to the street. When he lifted his arm to hail a cab, it sent another white-hot bolt of pain to his brain. Good God. He'd lost his head *and* broken his hand. What he needed more than anything right now was another drink.

Don Grover replaced his deli sandwich in its clear plastic tray and gestured excitedly to his partner. "Check it out, Rust. I think we're on to somethin'."

Heckman abandoned his salad to kick away from the table and roll over. "What's up?"

Grover tapped keys quickly and nodded at his screen. "That. A cash transfer made t' some outfit called Cooperman and Swift. 'Tween midnight an' three this morning. It's the third one I've spotted. This one's for a million six."

"Cooperman and Swift. Who're they?"

Still focused on his screen, Don shook his head. "Beats me. Try the phone book."

Rusty hurried off to find one. He returned less than a minute later to thumb the white pages. "Can you find those other two transfers again?" he asked.

"Gimme a sec. You got anything?"

"The pot of gold at the end of the rainbow," Heckman murmured.

Don tore himself from his screen. "Where?"

"Cooperman and Swift Investments," Rusty read aloud. "Fifty-eight West Forty-fourth."

Grover pointed at his monitor again. "Here's one'a the others. A transfer logged at two-thirteen a.m. Three million, seven hunnerd fifty thousand. Let's get over there. Three transfers, three separate names, three separate accounts."

"We don't want to risk spooking Bennett," Rusty cautioned. "It's possible he's got someone on the inside there."

Grover grabbed another bite of his pastrami on rye. His energy levels were suddenly on the rise. "So what's our move?"

"Do some quick research. See if there's someone on their staff we can trust." Rusty jerked his head toward the door. "You talk to Marsha, next door. I'll see who our people at Fiscal might know."

NINETEEN

From the start, Leo Swift believed this account Sid opened for that smooth-talking Brit last Friday had the stink of trouble all over it. It smelled like drug money, somewhere in the rinse cycle of a sophisticated laundering scam. The minute he scanned this morning's electronic transfer reports, he saw the worst of his suspicions confirmed. Nobody took three hours to dribble thirty-eight million into a single account. And if that weren't suspicious enough, every dollar was from just one brokerage house, downtown. All of it earmarked for the purchase of municipal bearers? Please. If it wasn't drug money, it was the product of some other piracy. It made Leo very nervous, and he wasn't at all surprised when just before lunch, his secretary told him that NYPD's chief of detectives was on the phone.

Thirty-odd years ago, Swift had worked as a fledgling broker for Cox, Cromwell, and cut his eyeteeth under the careful tutelage of Chief Lieberman's brother-in-law, Jim. Neither he, nor any of his co-workers, could believe it when the boss's little sister, Lydia, went and married some ex-jock cop. She was too cute and too rich to waste herself on a go-nowhere slob. Before Leo struck out on his own, to link up with Sid Cooperman here in midtown, he'd met Gus Lieberman on a dozen different occasions; at fund-raisers, cultural events, and even in the Cox, Cromwell box out at Belmont Park.

"Gus. What's it been? Twenty years?"

"At least that. Leo," Lieberman's deep baritone fairly rumbled. "Lissen. I need t' talk to you. In confidence. Somebody at your firm's gotten mixed up in something. Prob'ly unwittingly."

Ah yes. "This have anything to do with a series of cash transfers from Pierce, Fairbrother last night?"

"I'm in my car, headed your way," Gus replied. "Anyplace in particular you'd like t' meet?"

"Nobody here is trying to hide anything, Gus. We can skip the cloak-and-dagger." Leo looked at it philosophically. Most of the two-hundred-thousand-dollar paydays he'd seen in his life, he'd earned the hard way. "Feel free to come ahead."

"You got a name for me, Leo?"

"Our client's name is Andrews. Randall Andrews. Brand-new account, opened just last Friday. The name is probably as phony as a middle-class tax cut."

Through a pause down the line, Lieberman could be heard to mutter something to another occupant of his car. "Lissen, Leo," he then said again. "I can't say anything more until I get there. But do me a favor?"

"Sure. Keep it under my hat."

"You got it. We'll be there in ten or fifteen."

Wonderful, Swift thought. It would be just like old home week.

Four more fortifying shots of bourbon and Bill Hoag walked out of a Blarney Stone bar near Grand Central to flag a cab home. His damned hand was swollen to twice its size, but he was drunk enough that it no longer hurt so bad. When he reached his building on East 81st Street, he asked the doorman if he'd seen his wife.

"Jus' got back from my lunch break, Mr. H. But nuh uh. Ask Tommy. He had the door."

The concierge hadn't seen Vivian either. As Hoag rode up to his apartment, his rage continued to boil. At some point, as he sat in that darkened midtown bar, he'd decided that Vivian was to blame for Andrea's death. It just followed. She was trying to destroy him, wasn't she? In his apartment, he poured himself another drink from his dwindling bottle of Maker's Mark, and carried it to his bedroom to check Vivian's closet. The two biggest pieces of Louis Vuitton luggage were missing.

Bill needed to concentrate now, but was having difficulty. He needed to figure out how Vivian could have told those things to the police. How she knew. Andrea wouldn't have told her, and he didn't even know about them, himself. It seemed impossible.

Back in his kitchen, he killed the bottle of Maker's to build himself another drink, then filled an ice bucket with cubes and water. When he plunged his injured hand in, the intense pain of the cold did little to clear his head. Damn. Where had she gone? What wasn't he seeing?

* * *

Dante, Jumbo, Gus, Sid Cooperman, and Leo Swift were all gathered in conference at Cooperman & Swift. Dante was speaking; laying NYPD's cards on the table. Seated across from him at the big cherrywood table, Sid Cooperman squirmed nervously in his chair. Leo Swift looked resigned, as if he was already prepared to accept whatever the cops proposed. Dante needed their cooperation, and while this wasn't a bargaining session, he told himself to tread lightly.

"The way I see it, the only way we can lure Bennett—or Andrews—into our net, is to let the deal go forward," he told them. "Set up blanket surveillance here, and let him come ahead."

Cooperman eyed him warily. "You want us to go ahead. Broker the purchase of those bonds."

"That's correct."

"We keep our commission?"

Dante glanced to Gus, and shrugged. "That's usually the way it happens, isn't it?"

The wariness in Cooperman refused to budge. He turned to his partner. "Leo?"

Swift looked hard at Dante. "Two hundred thousand dollars isn't enough to risk getting my balls blown off, Lieutenant. Or to risk putting any of our staff in danger. I'm a chicken at heart."

Joe smiled. At least the guy was frank about it. "I understand your concern, sir. But I don't see where there's any danger on your end. This wife, or whoever she is, walks in here, picks up the bonds, and leaves."

"Bennett is using her as a decoy," Beasley explained. "To keep the score at arm's length. Wants to be damned sure there ain't any heat."

Sid Cooperman continued to scowl. "Let me get this straight. You're saying you intend to stand in the wings while we just hand it over to her? Thirty-eight million in negotiable instruments?"

"That's the plan, sir," Dante replied.

"And then you're going to follow her. Through midtown. During rush hour."

Gus Lieberman stepped into the conversation here, his voice calm and hands folded before him on the table. "That's our problem, Mr. Cooperman. Yours is more simple. All you gotta do is avoid spooking her."

"I hate this," Cooperman told his partner.

Leo Swift gave him an impatient scowl. "You hate your son-in-law and the Dallas Cowboys, Sidney. This, you can live with."

Fifteen minutes later, Dante loitered with Beasley and Gus on the West 44th Street sidewalk. Richardson glanced east less than two hundred feet to Fifth Avenue, and then west down the much longer stretch of street toward Sixth. He grunted and shook his head.

"Man's right, y'know. Coverin' the woman's escape is gonna be a bitch."

"Rush hour could help us," Joe contended. "The more pedestrian traffic we have as cover, the better."

"And what if she climbs on the back of a scooter?" Jumbo argued. "Or hands the bag off to a bike messenger? For all we know, she's some shill Bennett's hired. Somebody who don't know what the real score is."

"Either way," Gus interjected. "Joey's called the

right play. The more time we let tick off the clock, the less chance we have of runnin' this mutt t' ground." He checked the time. "Only four hours from now. We got work t' do."

Out of booze and out of hope, Bill Hoag knew which of those voids would be easier to fill. As much as he hated the idea of going back out into the raw January cold, he pulled on his coat and a pair of rubber boots. All the drinks he'd had since Tom Nelson gave him the sack that morning weren't enough to fill the hole of self-pity he'd dug. There was a liquor store over on Madison, a few blocks north. Too far to walk twice. He intended to stock up. Unemployed now, he would have plenty of time to figure a way to kill his wife. Later.

While Bill was away at the office, Saturday, Vivian Hoag had secreted her packed luggage in the basement storage bin of their building. Yesterday, her decision to visit Dennis at the boat basin was one of those impulses that a woman on the verge of a radical life change will indulge. She hadn't left until Bill was so drunk, he passed out. She'd planned to return before he awoke that morning. But then Bennett announced the change in their timetable, which prompted Vivian's decision to get a jump on her new life. She figured, what the hell? By the time the full implications of her disappearance hit home, she and Dennis would be in waters off the mouth of Chesapeake Bay.

At one-fifteen that Thursday afternoon, Vivian

stepped from a cab in front of her building, asked the driver to wait, and hurried across the sidewalk beneath the awning. As soon as he saw her, the doorman left the warmth of the lobby to hold the door.

"Afternoon, Miz H.," he greeted her. One finger touched the brim of his cap. "Your husband was just lookin' for you."

Her antennae went up. "When?" she asked.

"A little while ago. He was home, then left again. Wanted t' know if I seen you."

Vivian had to assume that Bill had rushed away from the office at lunch to check on her return. By now, he would have contacted her firm and learned she'd called in sick. "I'll give him a call from my office," she said. "I'm just here for a minute. I need some things from our basement bin."

"You need a hand?" he offered. A generous holiday tip had its advantages. So did her looks, she supposed.

"That would be nice," she told him. "Thanks."

The doorman asked the concierge to keep an eye on the lobby and took Vivian downstairs in the freight elevator. His curiosity was clear as he hefted those two bags. To diffuse it, she leaned close in an attitude of conspiracy. "I've got an anniversary surprise planned. Half the fun would be ruined if Bill saw our bags."

"Ah." He broke into a broad grin. "Your secret's safe with me, Miz H. I hope you're goin' somewhere warm."

Little did he know, she thought.

* * *

Bill Hoag carried a shopping bag loaded with four bottles of Maker's Mark in his good hand as he turned the corner from Madison onto East 81st Street. Down the block, he saw his doorman loading Vivian and two pieces of luggage into the back of a cab, and with a sudden surge of fresh anger, forgot all about his precious cargo. Abandoning it on the sidewalk, he broke into an ungainly run, hampered by galoshes and his overcoat. He managed to cover only half the distance to his building before the cab pulled away from the curb, headed for Fifth Avenue. His doorman spotted him out of the corner of his eye and stared openmouthed as Bill veered into the street between two parked cars. A cab with a lit roof light cruised so close, it almost hit him as he rushed to flag it, determined to chase his whore of a wife to the ends of the earth if necessary.

"That cab at the corner," he gasped to the driver. "The one turning left! Follow it!"

The heavyset cabbie came clear around in his seat to give his passenger a cool, appraising look. He took in the quality of the topcoat and suit, then focused on Hoag's raw, reddened eyes. "You seein' pink elephants, mister?"

Hoag jerked his billfold from inside his jacket. He winced as he struggled to cradle it in his injured hand while plucking out a crisp one-hundred-dollar bill. "Damn it, man! Follow it!" he roared, and threw the bill over the seat.

The hundred changed the driver's demeanor. He no longer cared how drunk his passenger was. He would drive him to Nova Scotia, as long as Ben Franklins kept coming.

The light at the corner held up Bill's quarry just

long enough to give him a fighting chance. The cabbie gave chase, balls to the wall.

"I hope you ain't expectin' no change," the man growled. "And any tickets I get, you pay."

The logistics of assembling a surveillance of the current proportions was a nightmare. Gus Lieberman was faced with mustering a legion of plainclothes officers, establishing a complex network of communications links, locating an unobtrusive command center, and getting it all up and running no later than three o'clock.

As a delivery truck vacated the last spot along the two hundred feet of curb opposite the entrance to 58 West 44th Street, three film-unit trucks, two motor homes, and five flatbed trucks loaded with 1950s-vintage automobiles were moved into place. Deputy Chief Frank Tomaselli of Support Services had suggested that rather than sneak around, considering the time frame, they go in bold. Last year, the city spent over two million dollars to put a dummy film location surveillance unit together, and hadn't had an opportunity to field-test it yet. Once the last truck was jockeyed into position, every individual seen scurrying up and down the sidewalk, pulling cable, setting up lights, and pushing dollies of equipment, was a cop. From inside one of the two motor homes, Lieberman and his special task force sat in chairs behind tinted glass. Chief Tomaselli's unit commander, Captain Oscar Duarte, was clearly proud of what he'd wrought.

"All those cars on the trucks? We let the guy who rents them to real movie crews store them inside city limits for free. He gets a break, and we get to use them, times like these."

"What about them location trucks?" Jumbo asked. "Big rigs like that cost a fortune."

"All smoke and mirrors," Duarte replied. "Except for the junk behind those couple of doors you see open, the trailers are empty. Those semi-tractors belong to Emergency Services. They don't care how we paint them, long as they run." He patted the table between them with an open palm. "This motor home is ours. The other one belongs to Communications."

Napier had been on the phone at one end of the motor home. He hung up to look their way. "No record of any Randall Andrews in any of the five boroughs. One in Hauppauge, on the Island. He's eighty-six and in a nursing home."

"Nothing to do but sit and wait now," Dante supposed. The clock on the console before him read 2:58. "And make sure every cop in the op's got a solid radio link."

While Vivian was away from the boat, retrieving her luggage, Dennis Bennett had several tasks to perform before his craft would be ready for the long trip down the Atlantic Coast to warmer waters. He'd had his extra-capacity fuel tanks topped up last week. Today, after so much time in port, he wanted to run the twin-turbo diesel V-8s up to high revs. He needed to fill the fresh-water tanks to capacity, do a grocery shop for perishables, and collect the dry cleaning he'd dropped off three days ago. It just wouldn't do to arrive at any of the Caribbean's luxury resorts without a closet full of clean, pressed clothes. And, of course, there was also Carnival in Rio next month. They might do some onboard entertaining, so he'd stopped at Zabar's for aged cheeses, several tins of caviar, and foie gras.

He was later getting back to the boat basin than he'd planned. As he left his cab, burdened with groceries, he saw that Vivian had returned. One of her bags was left dockside, presumably for him to carry aboard. Silly woman. Just because it was twenty degrees outside didn't mean that every thief in this fair city was home roasting chestnuts. He lifted his purchases into the stern well and turned to retrieve her bag. With one foot onboard the boat, he heard a thud and a muffled cry from inside the Baia's cabin. His mouth suddenly dry, he raced forward to find the stern cabin door left ajar.

Weaponless, Dennis went carefully ahead as he heard Vivian cry out again. In the dark of the cabin interior, it was hard to see more than frenetic movement at the far end of the salon. He nearly tripped over another of Vivian's bags as he stole toward where her attacker had her pinned to the deck. It looked and sounded like a rape in progress. Clearly, the animal had been lying in ambush for her as she came aboard.

Bennett grabbed the heaviest item he could lay his hands on: a large, hardbound world atlas. Vivian's attacker was on his knees, straddling her, one hand gripping her neck. With the snarls of an enraged beast, he lifted her head to slam it repeatedly into the thick pile carpet. Bennett took aim at his head and swung the book with all his strength. It caught the assailant flush behind the right ear and snapped the man's head sideways with a vicious jerk. In the next instant, poleaxed, the man pitched forward onto his face.

The moment Vivian could get air again, she began to choke. Bennett dragged the unconscious man from atop her and swept her up into his arms. Her chest racked with gasping coughs, he hugged her close.

"It's over," he crooned in her ear. "You're safe, love. I'm here." He felt his cheek become wet with her tears as her choking turned to great, heaving sobs. Slowly, he turned to look at the man he'd just subdued.

The quality of the attacker's clothing surprised him. What sort of rapist wore pinstriped suit trousers and a cashmere coat? The dress shirt cuffs were monogrammed. His eyes now adjusted to the darkness, Dennis read the letters there. "Good Christ," he murmured. Face buried in the carpet or not, there was no doubt in Bennett's mind who the man was. Now, a new kind of alarm gripped him. "He followed you here?"

Vivian had recovered enough to be helped to the sofa across from her husband. Bennett got a towel with ice in it for her neck. Bill didn't move.

"Is he dead?" she asked. With that towel wedged against her throat, she stared down at the body at her feet.

"I may well have broken his neck," Dennis replied. "I thought he was going to kill you. I gave it everything I had."

"He said he was going to," she murmured, a faraway hollowness in it. "More than once. He kept chanting it. Like a mantra."

"How did he follow you? Surely, you did as we've discussed."

She nodded and winced with the pain it caused her. "I did, Den. I swear. Three different cabs. But the bags were so damned heavy, I couldn't carry them very far, in between. I should have just left them, and bought new clothes down the coast."

"Ummm. When do you think he spotted you? When you left your building?"

"He must have. My doorman said he'd been looking for me. Around lunchtime. He probably heard I called in sick at work."

Bennett circled the built-in coffee table to crouch and press his fingers to the side of Hoag's neck. He spent several seconds probing about, and could find no pulse. "He's as dead as his business career," he said, and stood to look back at Vivian. "How are you feeling, love? We're only an hour away now. Are you up to it?"

She eased the bunched towel away from her neck and touched the area lightly. "What choice do I have?" she asked. "I'll wear a bulky turtleneck." She gestured toward her dead husband. "Get him out of here, Den. Please. The sight of him is going to make me sick."

TWENTY

By three-thirty that afternoon, the deployment of over fifty plainclothes officers in surveillance teams up and down West 44th Street was as ready for action as it was going to get. From inside the motor home command center, Joe Dante sat with one eye on the entrance to that building across the street. The rest of his attention was on the Metro section of Thursday's *Times*. The woman holding it was Lieutenant Melissa Busby, Chief Lieberman's recently appointed executive officer. She'd arrived just moments earlier from the Big Building, and brought the paper with her. Grover, Heckman, and Napier, her boyfriend, sat nearby in chairs. Jumbo was at Joe's elbow, field glasses trained through the tinted glass.

"I can't believe they've dug up so much detail on her, already," Melissa said. The article being brought to Joe's attention was coverage of the fund-raiser at Roseland last night. Inserted into the middle of the page, a boxed piece profiled the coalition's new candidate for Roberto Isabel's vacated congressional seat. It was accompanied by two photographs: one of Rosa and Jaime Ruiz at last night's event; the other from her academy graduation.

Dante studied that picture of the twenty-two-year-old Rosa, hair tucked up beneath her uniform cap. Her expression was so serious, it made him smile. "She told me they were doing this," he replied. "Ruiz is a master manipulator, Mel. You can bet he had a detailed bio from her before the ink was dry on this deal."

Melissa scowled. "Why are you being so cynical? She wouldn't cut a deal. She's no more crooked than you are."

Dante had mentored Mel Busby at Major Case. He admired her toughness, and her skills as a street cop, but what he liked most about her was her loyalty. "The deal doesn't have to be crooked," he countered. "But Ruiz is." He focused on the street again, where a Brinks truck had just pulled up out front of number 58. "You agree to take something from a mutt like him, he's gonna want something in return. That's the nature of the beast. He'll only want little favors at first, but over time, they'll have their corrosive effect."

Two uniformed Brinks guards emerged from the truck, one with an attaché case chained to his wrist. They hurried across the sidewalk to enter the building.

"She's going to get elected," Melissa said. "Look at this pedigree. And look at her. Every red-blooded male in her district will vote for her, just because he'd like to fuck her."

"Ah." Joe's eyes swept the opposite sidewalk,

alert for anyone who might be their quarry. "The fuck factor. I'm sure Ruiz figured it in. He thinks of everything, and of course she'll get elected. Who could beat her?"

"You don't sound eager to get aboard her band-wagon," she observed.

Before Joe could reply, Beasley stiffened beside him. "Wait a minute," Richardson murmured. "It's early, but a woman I'd swear is Vivian Hoag just walked in the front door of that buildin'."

Dante swung the mike of his headset into position and keyed the transmit button on his console. "This is location one. The star is on the set," he announced. "I repeat. The star is on the set. Everyone look sharp."

Outside the window of the motor home, he saw various clusters of cops doing some great imitations of loitering teamsters. Slowly, their clusters broke up. He was glad he hadn't called the alert when the armored car arrived. Their subject was so close on the delivery's heels that he had to assume she'd been watching for it. Vivian Hoag. He flashed on that meeting with her at Grand Central, Tuesday evening, and wondered if she'd worn that dress for his benefit.

Despite the handful of extra-strength pain relievers she'd swallowed before leaving the boat, Vivian's head was killing her. How many times had Bill slammed it to the floor? Four or five, before Dennis could stop him. Frankly, the brute power of her husband's outrage had surprised her. She'd always considered him a wimp.

Her turtleneck did a decent job of covering the

welts on her neck, and after half an hour spent putting herself back together, she looked as presentable as ever. Heck, she'd even incited a few wolf whistles from some macho asshole on that film crew. She felt the film shoot was one of those little extra bonuses that good fortune occasionally threw her way. It made her arrival at Cooperman & Swift seem even more incidental than it had last week, when she came here to scout the place. Now, she rode the elevator to the third floor with familiar ease, and pushed past the office doors into territory she couldn't risk entering the last time.

"Yes, ma'am?" a bored bleached blonde behind the front desk greeted her. She sounded like she had adenoids the size of golf balls. "What can I hep-chew wit?"

"Veronica Andrews," Vivian replied. "Here to see Mr. Cooperman. He's expecting me." She watched the woman's face for a sign that something was amiss. Instead, her new name drew a blank.

The receptionist placed a call to Cooperman's office, and nodded to the chairs and sofa that surrounded a low table piled with issues of *Fortune, Crain's,* and *Business Week.* "Y'wanna have a seat? His sec'tary'll be right wit' ya."

Vivian struggled to keep herself calm. She'd been over this plan so often, she knew it by rote. But the die was cast now, and all those mental rehearsals were little comfort. She wanted to get on with it.

A door to the left of the reception desk opened. A trim, well-dressed brunette stepped forward with her right hand extended. She beamed a businesslike smile. "Mrs. Andrews? I'm Tina Rosen. Mr. Cooperman's assistant." Her grip was cool and firm.

"He apologizes for being unable to meet with you in person."

What was this? "He's not here?" Vivian wasn't sure whether this was odd or not. In the Diamond District, just a few blocks north of here, millions of dollars in gemstones were routinely carried from dealer to dealer in plain paper bags.

"An educational foundation he's involved with called an emergency trustees meeting," Ms. Rosen replied. "But if you'd like to speak with Mr. Swift, I'm sure he can see you as soon as he's finished with the client in his office."

Vivian dialed down. "I don't think that will be necessary," she replied. "I assume Mr. Cooperman left you instructions?"

Ms. Rosen led the way toward her office. "Oh, yes. This will only take a moment, but I must see some form of photo identification from you. I'm afraid Mr. Cooperman was very specific about that."

One of Dante's cops was posing as a janitor in the hallway outside Cooperman & Swift. When confirmation was received that a blond woman fitting Vivian Hoag's description was aboard a lobby-bound elevator after leaving the brokerage, Joe gave final instructions to the teams of men and women up and down 44th Street.

"Whatever you do, don't crowd her," he warned. "We've got enough warm bodies, we don't need to. Wherever she goes, keep talking to me. She gets in a cab, don't panic. We've got it covered."

In one ear, the voice of another cop, in the building lobby, informed him that the subject was on her way to the street.

"Okay, people," Dante announced. "Showtime."

Vivian Hoag did not step off the curb to flag a cab. She went east on foot. Fifty feet along, surveillance reported that she'd donned sunglasses. Seconds later, another voice reported she'd reached Fifth Avenue, and was headed south. At 42nd Street, she veered off to descend subway stairs to the platform of the number 7 train. A lone plainclothes woman rode with her in the same car, while another six officers boarded cars front and back. Three minutes later, and one stop east, the subject disembarked onto the platform beneath Grand Central Station, a throng of early rush-hour commuters milling around her.

"What the hell's she up to?" Jumbo murmured. With a map spread on the table between him and Dante, he'd followed her path with a yellow highlighter pen.

"She ain't makin' no move for the street," the voice of a male cop reported. "Looks t' me like she's headed for the Lex line." There was a pause. "Wait a sec. She's stopped. She's waitin' behind some guy at a pay phone."

"Don't let that briefcase out of your sight," Dante warned. "And watch that guy on the phone, too."

"He just moved off, Lou. I didn't see nothing suspicious go down. She's got the case wedged 'tween her an' the box. She just dropped a quarter."

"Who else is in that sector?" Dante demanded. He glanced at the digital clock on the console and made a note of the time. It was four-twelve. Outside the command trailer, it was starting to get dark.

"I am, sir," a woman's voice replied. "Detective Kelly, from the One-Oh-Seven."

Dante conjured the face and first name of Detective Kelly, a stocky strawberry blonde with freckles. "Soon as you confirm she's cleared your sector, I want the number of that phone, Kathy. If it's not on it, call NYNEX."

Lately, the phone company had been removing the numbers from pay phones around the city so that drug dealers couldn't use them as beeper callback sites.

Before Kathy Kelly could respond, the male cop came back at Joe. "She's off the phone, Lou. Joined the herd again. Looks like she's headed for the Lex line platform. Still got that briefcase in her hand."

If her husband hadn't managed to follow her to the boat that afternoon, Vivian would have felt less paranoid and exposed than she did right now. The thirty-eight million dollars she carried made her very nervous. Before she left to make the pickup, Dennis had tried to reassure her. The police were at least a day away from stumbling on their trail, even if an internal audit at Pierce, Fairbrother caught something as early as Tuesday. They were home free. But his rationale did little to calm her as she emerged from the subway at Lexington Avenue and 50th Street. As she hurried west through the crowd of pedestrian traffic toward Madison Avenue, she glanced furtively at the faces of everyone she passed. They all seemed to be looking back.

At Madison, she turned south again in what amounted to nearly a full circle, from her 44th Street point of origin. At the corner of 47th and Madison, she darted into the lobby of the building that housed her law firm. While she stood and waited for the elevator, one of the firm's junior partners rushed in from the street.

"Viv. I thought you were sick," she greeted her.

"No rest for the wretched," Vivian replied.

"How you feel?"

"Not so hot." That much was true, at least. "But I need to finish the Honeycutt brief. Left some papers in my office. I wouldn't stand too close if I were you."

The warding-off worked. Her associate rode to the sixth floor wedged into the opposite corner of the car. They parted ways with something about the upcoming weekend, and Vivian headed off down the hall toward the ladies' room. As soon as the hallway was clear, she picked up her pace, skipped the washroom, and disappeared through a door leading to the internal fire stairs. The week before Christmas, she'd stolen a key from a cleaning cart. Now, she dug that key from her coat pocket, praying it would still fit. Two flights up, she strode with mock confidence onto the eighth floor, toward a janitorial alcove alongside the service elevator. Holding her breath, she inserted the key. The tumblers of the cleaning closet lockset turned without a hitch. Inside, the garbage bag containing her disguise was still hidden there, stuffed up high on the shelf where she'd stashed it.

"We've lost her, sir," a panicked male voice reported over Dante's headset. Twenty minutes had elapsed since Vivian Hoag was followed into the lobby of her law firm's building. At the height of rush hour, as scores of people poured from the building, she'd ridden upstairs and disappeared. Ten minutes ago, Dante had ordered every available member of the surveillance detail into the area. His feelings of wariness were fast turning to trepidation. Joe switched to another transmit frequency and hailed Don Grover, who was coordinating surveillance movements from a van parked a block away from the law firm.

"If she's hiding in there, we need to dig her out, Donnie. Time to flood the place. Commence a floor-by-floor search."

"Ten-four, Joe. But my money says she's already given us the slip."

Considering the time that had elapsed, Dante wasn't about to bet against him. He turned to face Gus, seated behind him with his own set of headphones. "Where are we with the phone company?"

"Should be hearin' back any second now. I told 'em we need all the calls made from that box 'tween four-oh-five and four-fifteen."

Joe took a deep breath. "It could be our only shot right now, boss." He tried to push his feelings of frustration aside. He'd underestimated Bennett's capacity for patient and creative planning, and he'd been outsmarted. The man had made a whole host of reckless mistakes, then somehow found a way to reformulate his overall plan to make it fit the current circumstances.

At Joe's elbow, Beasley Richardson grunted in disgust. "This party we just threw cost the city a fuckin' fortune. If there ain't no door prize, Big Tony's gonna need sedation."

* * *

In her three-inch heels and masses of fake brunet hair piled up another three inches, Vivian Hoag looked half a foot taller walking out of her law office building than she did going in. The dark stockings, heavy makeup, and black poncho-style coat gave her an art-tramp, downtowner look, a complement to the large, flat portfolio case she carried by its black plastic handles. The hair was the work of a top-notch theatrical wig maker. The clothes were East Village secondhand-store purchases, all of them down-at-the-heels enough to appear authentic. The coat was burned in several places by cigarettes—her own touch. After just two blocks, those stupid shoes were killing her feet.

She went north again, then west this time, toward Fifth Avenue and 53rd Street. An interminably long escalator ride took her down to the commuter-crammed subway platform, where she boarded a westbound E train. Once it started to roll, she began to relax. As strange as she felt in this disguise, it seemed to be working. That hideous feeling of being watched was fading as she walked here. Now it was totally gone.

At West 50th Street and Eighth Avenue, the doors of her car opened and Vivian stepped out, thirty-eight million dollars in hand, to stride confidently ahead toward a future with few limits.

Complicated by a computer room personnel change, between the day and evening shifts, NYNEX took over an hour to comply with NYPD's information request. By that time, Gus Lieberman had reluctantly called off his dogs. A search of the building where

Vivian Hoag was last seen had failed to find her. With the exception of their motor home command post, the rest of the phony film location equipment was being sent packing. Dante, Gus, Napier, and Melissa all waited impatiently while Jumbo took the NYNEX call, and scribbled. As he cut the connection, he tossed his headset aside.

"Durin' our time frame, there were six calls made from that phone. You noted the exact time as what, Joey? Four-twelve?"

Dante checked his notes. "Yeah. Can we narrow down those six calls?"

"To three. One made at four-oh-nine, one at four-eleven, and one at four-thirteen." Beasley scratched out the three that fell outside their parameters. "First one, to a number on Moore Street, in Tribeca. Second, to a pay phone at the Seventy-ninth Street boat basin. Last one, t' Brooklyn Heights."

Dante mulled this information and turned to the others. "Based on what we know about Bennett, either Tribeca or Brooklyn Heights would be reasonable places to hole up." The Heights was an affluent area overlooking the East River and the lower end of Manhattan. Tribeca was a trendy loft area popular with Wall Streeters, south of Canal Street on the downtown's west side. "But then, so would the boat basin. How off the beaten track is that?"

"At this time of year?" Gus was dubious. "This is a man likes his creature comforts, Joey. You freeze your ass, down there on the water."

"Maybe." Dante said it slowly. "But think a minute. He's killed three, maybe four people, and pirated close to forty million bucks. He knows it's creatin' some heat."

"You like the boat basin," Beasley murmured.

Lieberman looked back and forth between the two of them. "I still don't get it."

"Clearly, we gotta check out all three," Richardson replied. "But Joey's thinkin' Bennett's already anticipated that we'll throw a blanket over all the usual ways outta town. Bridges an' tunnels. Airports. Trains."

"But who'd be crazy enough t' leave by water, in January." Lieberman was catching their drift. "No question, mutt's gotta pair of balls on him."

"Mel and I can take Brooklyn Heights," Napier offered. "Don and Rusty can take Moore Street. That leaves you guys free to go fishing."

Dante closed his eyes and smiled; the pieces of the puzzle were falling neatly into place in his mind's eye now. Nowhere in any of the information they'd dug up on Dennis Bennett was there an indication that he'd ever owned a boat. One with some creature comforts, if Gus's presumption was correct. But what about Randall Andrews, the guy who just bought thirty-eight million dollars' worth of bonds?

It was a cold, still night on the water. Earlier, just as the sun set, the sky had cleared. The worst of an afternoon breeze out of the northeast had died. With the Verrazano Narrows now fifteen miles distant, Dennis Bennett stood in the Baia's stern well to stare back across the open waters. He could still see the lighted towers of the World Trade Center clearly, and the spire of the Empire State Building. The helm was set on autopilot, the luxury yacht's twin turbo diesels running at close to full throttle. Dennis and Vivian were making headway at over thirty knots.

If their fuel reserves were going to get them very far, their current speed was not one they could sustain for long. But Dennis wanted to put some quick distance between them and New York. No one who wasn't familiar with this craft's specifications would imagine that anything this big could achieve speeds even close to this. Plenty of runabouts couldn't run this fast.

"Anything you'd like to say?" he asked.

Vivian stood shoulder to shoulder with him and stared down at the shrouded corpse of her dead husband. Wrapped in a bedsheet secured with duct tape, its dead girth was strapped with a weighted diving belt. "He tried to kill me," she murmured. "I hope he rots in hell."

"All right then." Dennis wasn't going to take a stab at any phony remorse if she didn't. His initial plan hadn't anticipated the need to kill anyone. It began as an elegant concept, simple in design. Yet so much had gone wrong. He couldn't say he'd actually taken pleasure in killing any of them; not real pleasure. But all the same, they'd been in the way. "Care to give a hand?" he asked.

He squatted to grip the shoulders of the corpse and hefted it up out of the well while she grabbed the feet. Rigor mortis had done much to stiffen those limbs, which made the disagreeable task of handling twelve stone of dead weight much easier. "Ready?" he asked.

Vivian heaved with all her strength and her dead husband was flipped, head over heels, into the boat's churning wake. Bennett watched as the shrouded corpse tumbled in the whitened froth, then sank, to vanish in the gloom. While it disappeared, he clucked his tongue.

"So much anger, Vivian, love. Is it just because of his infatuation with Andrea? We did plan it that way, you'll recall."

"Only after he made the first play," she snapped. "After he'd made a laughingstock of me. You think that didn't hurt?"

"It's not as if he broke your heart, dear girl. You and I were having our own fun upstairs, remember?"

She barked a laugh. "What heart? He didn't marry me for my heart. He broke the business contract we had. Following you upstairs was payback. And all I did was fuck you, Den. I hadn't risen to the bait yet."

"Don't you think you're splitting hairs?"

She smirked at him, turned, and started back toward the warmth of the salon. "It's something you might keep in mind, Prince Charming. Even a heartless bitch like me has her pride."

Insulated from the Upper West Side by a wooded stretch of Riverside Park and the Henry Hudson Parkway, the 79th Street boat basin lay in secluded tranquility, a little waterbound world unto itself. Beasley Richardson had only been here once in his twenty-six-year career with NYPD. That time, as now, the improbability of the place had struck him; how far removed it felt from the metropolis that pulsed just blocks away.

This time of year, at least half the slips of the marina were empty. Tenants had either sailed south to warmer waters, or stored their crafts on land for the winter. There were fewer than a dozen cars parked in the tenants' lot, and only a handful of boats showed signs of life aboard. The administration office, operated by the city's Transportation Department, was locked up tight. A wavering light from an unseen TV screen could be seen inside a tiny guard shack.

At the shack door, Jumbo stood back, hands plunged deep into the pockets of his overcoat, while Joey knocked. A heavyset brother in uniform opened up. He had a half-eaten slice of pizza in one hand.

"Whadizzit?" he growled.

Joey showed him his shield and I.D. "Lieutenant Dante, Special Investigations. This is Lieutenant Richardson. Mind if we come in? We're freezing our asses out here."

Clearly in the middle of his dinner, the man grudgingly stepped aside.

The interior of the tiny eight-by-six structure was warmed by an ancient space heater. A *Baywatch* re-run played on the television, and most of a fourteen-inch pepperoni and mushroom pie was now ancient history.

Jumbo held up a photo of Bennett, cut from a Foray Fund annual report. "Ever see this man?" he asked.

The guard eyed it, and then him, with deep suspicion. "He s'pose t' be someone here? I only just started, first of the year."

"That a no?" Jumbo pressed.

It earned him a shrug. "Dunno. I ain't seen that many faces. I'm the night guy."

"Let me ask you this," Joey interjected. "Have any

boats pulled outta here tonight? Within the past couple hours?"

"One space-age cruise ship. That's 'bout it."

"Care to flesh that out a little?" Joey asked him. "Most cruise liners dock a little further south of here."

"This one's just about as big. Long an' sleek like them Cigarette boats they used t' have on *Miami Vice*, only huge. Go like a bat outta hell, I bet."

Richardson and Joey glanced at each other. "Creature comfort," Beasley murmured.

Dante turned back to the guard. "There some kind of tenant list you could get your hands on? Or a description of this boat? Name, registration, that sort of thing?"

"Prob'ly. But all of it be locked up, in administration. I ain't got a key."

Another means of gaining the information they were after would be to interview the tenants in residence. After thanking the guard for his time, Joe and Beasley headed off to see who was onboard their boats this evening. The first one they tried got them the boyfriend of the owner. She was away on business, and he'd only met her a month ago. As far as everyday life around the basin was concerned, he seemed to know very little. Another man, who lived aboard a sailboat, was more hopeful. The interior of the vessel's cabin was so impossibly cramped that Beasley got claustrophobic just looking inside. The man took one look at that annual report photo and shook his head.

"You got the wrong cat, you're looking for the owner of the Baia, man. Dude owns it has dark hair. Long as mine. Not around much. I did see him and his girlfriend this afternoon, though. She's hard to forget."

"Blonde?" Joe asked. "Good build?"

"Brick shithouse build," the sailor corrected him. "Itty-bitty thing, but serious hot stuff. Them rich dudes, they sure can attract them. Money's a magnet."

"What time did you see them?" Beasley asked.

"Couple times. First one, around noon. Leaving. Then she came back again, with a couple suitcases. Looks to me like old Randy was planning a trip."

"Randy?"

"Yeah. Andrews. Must've pulled outta here while I was doing my laundry. What? An hour and a half ago? Maybe two?"

TWENTY-ONE

The logistics of mounting a comprehensive air search after nightfall, in subfreezing temperatures, were formidable. The commander of the U.S. Coast Guard's seaplane base at Floyd Bennett Field in Brooklyn took pains to explain those problems to Chief Lieberman and his SID detectives. In detail. A boat the size of the one they sought was capable of making a deep-water run toward half the points of the compass. If it was headed south, as Dante believed, a search would include several thousand square miles of open ocean. If, to foil pursuit, Bennett chose to run northeast into the Sound, or due east along the south shore of Long Island, there were literally hundreds of anchorages into which he could duck. Depending on its configuration, a multimillion-dollar oceangoing luxury cruiser like the Baia was capable of speeds in excess of twenty knots. On fairly smooth seas, some Baias could sprint at nearly twice that.

Dante and Richardson opted to accompany the pilot assigned to scour the Intracoastal Waterway, where it ran south along the New Jersey shore. They had little more than a hunch on which to base their opinion, but Joe believed Bennett would head for warm waters. At this time of year, the further south he went in a boat like that, the better chance he had of blending in. If he got as far as Florida, which was possible in just three days, he could virtually get lost in the shuffle. If he ran east, it would be to lie low until the heat died, and then make the inevitable run south, to obscurity.

At eight o'clock that night, their pilot announced they were low on fuel and would have to turn back. By then, Dante was bleary-eyed with staring into the darkness out the starboard window of their pontoon-rigged Piper Cherokee. He'd scoured a hundred miles of Jersey shore, from Sandy Hook to Atlantic City, and was slightly nauseous. His eyes were being forced to adjust constantly to changing distances. During the two hours they'd been airborne, reports from other pilots in other search areas crackled in his headset. Every one of them had struck out, too.

Once they nudged back up against the main sea-plane dock on the waters of Jamaica Bay, a Coast Guard crew rushed out to tie them off. It was almost ten. Dante peeled his headset from his ears and turned to look back at his partner in the rear seat. "How you holding up?" he asked.

"Feel like I just spent four hours on a fuckin' Tilt-a-Wheel."

Their pilot chuckled. "Try it sometime when the weather's bad, Lieutenant. That'll really kick your ass."

"I'll pass," Jumbo growled. "What're you thinkin', Joey?"

"That the longer we wait, the further they can run. By now, they could be all the way to Cape May."

Beasley leaned forward to consult their pilot. "How 'bout you, Commander? You game for another run at it?"

The pilot checked the time, and shook off a yawn. "Take us another hour and a half, once we refuel, just to get to where we broke it off. Won't get back here until sometime after two."

"That a yea or a nay?"

"I like flying, Lieutenant. It's my life. How much more Tilt-a-Wheel can you handle?"

Beasley's impassive expression got hard. "We're talking about a murderin' shithead, Commander. We'll keep lookin', long as you keep flyin'."

When Napier had arrived at Bill and Vivian Hoag's East 81st Street address to question the husband about his wife's disappearance, he'd heard an interesting story from the doorman. On seeing his wife load luggage into a cab, early that afternoon, Hoag had given chase. In the process, he'd dropped the four bottles of excellent whiskey he was carrying. No one had seen him since.

Three hours of running at thirty knots was as hard as Bennett wanted to press his fuel supply. He cut back on the throttle and veered inland once he came within sight of Atlantic City. Convinced by then that they'd gotten clean away, he felt it would be safe to seek anchorage for the night. There were a thousand little towns along the Intracoastal Waterway; places where they could lie at anchor, just offshore, and not seem the least bit out of place.

He told Vivian his plan when she joined him at the helm to learn why they'd slowed. "I do think we should try to get some sleep, love. Did that ice help your neck?"

She rolled her right shoulder and grimaced. "I wish I had a muscle relaxant. Do you have a particular place in mind?" She leaned forward to get a better view of the chart, lit by the dim glow of the binnacle light.

"I thought we'd access the waterway here." He pointed. "Then motor south, toward Sea Isle City. It appears that there's plenty of open water, right along there. On the west side of the channel."

He felt her ease closer to him, to slide an arm around his waist. Even with the heater going, it had to be a good twenty degrees cooler here than it was in the cabin below, and she wasn't dressed for it. Not that he minded. Her cashmere sweater, with its deep-V neckline, afforded him a lovely view.

"I'll need help with the transom, and the name on the Zodiac," he told her. "Once we drop the hook."

"How's that?" It was muffled as she buried her face in the warmth of his chest.

"We need to change our name. As much as I liked *Buy and Large,* that was Dennis Bennett's boat. But a fun-loving couple like Ronnie and Randy? We need something with a bit more zip, don't you think?"

She pulled her face back to look up at his. "Such as?"

"You'll see." He slapped her fanny. "Now run below and put on a parka. You'll catch your death."

* * *

Fifteen minutes before Dante, Richardson, and their Coast Guard pilot took to the air again, Gus Lieberman and the seaplane base commander elected to call off the rest of the search until daylight. If Joe and Beasley weren't so adamant about making one last trip down the coast, the whole search effort would have been grounded until morning. The factor that convinced Gus not to fight them was the weather forecast. A nor'easter had dumped rain across the coastal southland as far north as Cape Hatteras, and snow in the mountains of North Carolina. By sunup, it was expected to have reached Philadelphia. When it did, all bets were off. Forecasters were predicting as much as a foot of new snow in New York City by afternoon rush hour, Friday.

For the second time that night, the bright lights of Atlantic City came into view. Moments later, they encountered their first turbulence from the leading edge of that storm. Over his headset, Joe heard Beasley groan. They'd switched seats and Dante leaned forward now. It was difficult to differentiate between the reflected glow from the instrument panel and Beasley's green color.

"You okay?" he asked.

"Fuck no, I'm not okay. Let's find this asshole. Then Sky King here'll have t' land this fucking thing. And let me out."

The pilot chuckled and pointed through the windscreen. "The waterway starts to snake quite a bit, in through here. More than it did along that last stretch, further north. Between here and Cape May, there must be a hundred little lagoons he could tuck himself away in."

Dante had a map in his lap. He could see what the pilot meant. But if this was the direction Bennett went, the prospect of finding him later, in either Delaware or Chesapeake Bay, looked even more daunting. "How long can you stay up, if the wind gets worse?" he asked.

The plane bucked violently. "This is nothing," the pilot replied. "Water's gonna get choppy, though. Could make landing a little dicey. Your partner might not be so eager to as he sounds."

From his rear seat, Dante watched the western shore of the waterway scoot past in the night. Their airspeed indicator was pegged at sixty knots. The altimeter read three hundred feet.

"Ocean City," the pilot reported. "New Jersey, not Maryland." He pointed out the port window, to the east.

Dante took a quick look, then returned to the view, west. Less than a mile off, he saw the occasional car on the Garden State Parkway. Down here along the coast, it was virtually empty. Most residents who wintered here were home in bed.

"Last tollbooth on the parkway," the pilot announced. He nodded out the windscreen in Jumbo's direction. "We're maybe twenty miles from the tip of the cape."

"You know this stretch of coast pretty well," Joe observed.

"I should. We've got a receiving station, mouth of Cape May inlet. Couple times a month, I'll fly someone from Governors Island, down and back. It gets pretty boring, you don't learn to enjoy the sights."

The long, sleek vessel, lying at anchor in a little sound, a minute or so below where those last toll-booths were, seemed uncharacteristically large, compared with everything else Dante had seen that night. "Whoa," he murmured. "What've we got there?"

Dennis had found a perfect anchorage, just beyond a two-lane bridge and causeway that connected the mainland to a tiny hamlet pretentiously named Sea Isle City. He and Vivian dropped the hook a few minutes after nine-thirty, and spent the next half hour warming the surface of the stern transom with a heat gun. It took that long to get the new boat name he'd had printed on vinyl to stick. In the end, he thought they'd done a pretty smart job of it. They also rolled new names out and affixed them to the gunwales of the twelve-foot Zodiac dinghy, rigged from davits to hang from the stern. An hour after they started, the boat was no longer the *Buy & Large NY, NY*. It was now the *Happy Go Lucky, Wilmington, DE*. Vivian suggested they christen their born-again craft with a bottle of champagne.

"Not broken across her beautiful bow, of course. Poured across ours."

Bennett inspected the deck to ensure that everything was securely lashed down, and then went below. He found his partner in just the sort of festive mood he'd hoped for; changed from her cashmere sweater and slacks into satin and lace. She lay stretched on the stateroom bed, a glass of champagne in each hand.

"I've secured the blackout curtains as ordered, Captain. I guess it's just you and me."

He advanced to accept a glass from her out-stretched hand and clicked it with hers. "To us, Ronnie love. By God, I think we've foxed their boxes." As he drank, he let his gaze roam over her.

"You think you'll miss it, Den?" she asked.

"Miss what? The Street?"

"Umm. The Street. The life."

"Bugger the Street. It already feels like a whole other life. By the way, it's Randy," he reminded her.

"I'll say it is." She took a sip of her champagne and reached out to drag nails over the bulge in the front of his trousers. "And it looks like it wouldn't mind a little air."

Bennett eased down onto the bed to kick off his shoes. He was setting his glass to one side when he heard the first, far-off drone of a single-engine plane. This was odd. With the wind kicking up like this, what was a small aircraft doing out so late? Earlier, they'd listened to a marine forecast that called for rain to hit the cape by midnight. Significant snowfall was expected inland. These winds were the leading edge of that storm, and the plane he could hear was flying south, right into it.

"Listen," he whispered.

"To what?" She had gotten his belt buckle loose, and was fumbling with his fly.

"Shhh!" he hissed. The drone of the aircraft grew louder. Perhaps it was the effect of being out here on the water, but it seemed to be flying awfully low.

"An airplane? So?" Vivian asked. "What are the chances that anyone is looking for us, way down here?"

Bennett wasn't listening to her. He'd leapt to his stockinged feet to kill the stateroom lights, then rushed into the salon to kill the lights there, too. Once the interior of the vessel was plunged into darkness, he risked a look out the starboard porthole just as the aircraft swept by. It was no more than a quarter-mile east and a hundred feet overhead. Though it was impossible to make out what sort of plane it was, Dennis wasn't going to rest until he was a good deal further removed from New York than he was right now. Fifteen hundred miles further removed.

Vivian crawled from the bed to stand at his side. "What is it, Den? What do you see?"

"Dunno," he muttered, deep in thought. "Just to be on the safe side, let's put the party on hold for a while, shall we?"

He could hear the fear in her voice when she spoke. "You're serious."

"An ounce of prevention and all that, love." He hurried to step back into his Top-Siders. "I'm going to rig the davits, just in case. If we need to put the Zodiac in the water, we'll want to do it quickly. You should get dressed."

The Baia's twelve-foot Zodiac dinghy was equipped with a twenty-five-horsepower Honda outboard motor. Ultra-maneuverable, quick, and relatively quiet, it was the same craft used by Greenpeace volunteers to harass whalers on the open ocean. To prep the boat for deployment, Bennett shrugged into a parka and ran on deck. Off to the south, he heard the pitch in the drone of the aircraft's engine change. It had started into a turn.

Damn! He'd do more than ready the Zodiac. It was headed over the side and into the drink.

* * *

His misery forgotten, Jumbo Richardson leaned forward to get a better view of the terrain below as their pilot dropped down to within fifty feet of the water. "It's gotta be them. How many big boats with those exact same lines could there be? Out in weather like this?"

"Looks like you guys just hit pay dirt," the pilot agreed. "Anchored out here in the middle of nowhere? It's about the right distance, if he motored down here, throttle wide open. You realize, the noise this thing makes, there's no chance of taking him by surprise."

"Do we care?" Beasley's tone said he clearly didn't. "Where can they go?"

Once they crossed the bridge and causeway that connected the mainland to the tiny hamlet of Avalon, the pilot dropped it down to almost skim the whitecaps. When he throttled back, it felt like they were hanging in air.

"Any slower than this, she'll flat refuse to fly," he warned. "You want, I can hit them with our landing light."

"Be just our luck, he sights up it and shoots us out of the sky," Dante countered. "You don't mind, I'd prefer we went in dark."

"Any problem, landin' this thing?" Jumbo asked. He never liked small planes, but hadn't realized how much until tonight. "Water looks kinda rough."

"I've put them down in rougher chop than this," the pilot assured him. "Couple hours from now, once it starts to squall, it could get a little hairy. But this? Piece of cake."

* * *

Vivian handed Bennett's Mark Cross briefcase across first, then reached to grab his steadying hand as she stepped from the ladder into the bobbing rubber boat. A part of her refused to believe that any of this was necessary; that there was any reason to abandon a perfectly cozy luxury cruiser in the middle of a bitter cold night, for this tiny open boat. Dennis was indulging a most uncharacteristic paranoia.

One of the first things that had attracted her to him, like a bar of steel drawn to a powerful magnet, was his absolute-zero cool. The attraction was so strong, she'd fucked him the first time they met. At an Easthampton party, with one subtle nod, he'd suggested she follow him into the house. Upstairs, he'd put her up against a wall in the empty nursery and gotten down to it with purpose. It was still the most memorable screw of her life; no soft warm mattress, no satin sheets and caviar, just animal urgency and arrogant cool.

The drone of the plane engine grew more insistent as it closed the distance between them. Dennis gunned the outboard's throttle to swing them in a wide arc and head them toward the waterway's western shore. When the plane broke through the gloom to roar past, so close she could feel the wind shift, Vivian's fear surfaced from cover. It was one of those aircraft rigged with pontoons, painted white, with Coast Guard insignia. It seemed impossible. They were virtually a needle in a haystack. Even the haystack shouldn't have been discovered for days yet, let alone the needle.

"The moment we hit the shore, run for the road!"

he yelled. With his free hand, he pointed to the causeway that led inland from the outer bank. "We need to find a car!"

Great, Vivian thought. Ronnie and Randy had just become Bonnie and Clyde.

TWENTY-TWO

Dante strained to watch the progress of that inflatable boat from the seaplane, while still on approach. It contained two occupants. When neither of them fired on the Piper, Joe wondered why not. There was no question now that the Coast Guard plane was in pursuit.

The pontoons of the plane touched water. The pilot kept the power poured on to send them skimming across the whitecaps like an ungainly catamaran. Dante leaned forward between the seats.

"How close can you get us to the beach?" he asked. "It looks like they're headed for that causeway."

"Depends." The pilot maintained his concentration, the rough water clearly making him nervous. "It looks like it's mostly rock up there. Either we find some sand, or you and your partner'll have to swim in."

He swung the aircraft around to enter the cove

where Bennett had anchored, still moving at speed. Joe and Jumbo searched the shoreline.

"Over there!" Beasley pointed to a white stretch, in an area on the opposite side of the inlet from where they wanted to go.

"Soon as you put us ashore, radio our position," Dante told the pilot. "Ask them to get in touch with the local cops. And the State Police."

The pilot nodded and gunned it toward shore while Joe took one last check of the map in his lap. That causeway ran beneath the Garden State Parkway to connect with U.S. 9 on the other side. A little burg called Ocean View sat beyond that intersection. It hadn't looked like much from the air, with only a few lights burning. He'd seen the fluorescent glow of what looked like a filling station plaza, but right now the raised parkway blocked any view of it. As far as he could tell, it was the only direction that Bennett and Mrs. Hoag could run.

The instant the floats of the plane nudged sand, Beasley had the side door open. He leapt out, with Joe close on his heels. They splashed into six inches of icy water, the freezing cold instantly filling their shoes and soaking their trouser legs as they slogged to dry ground. Joe took the lead to plunge into the underbrush and charge uphill toward the parkway.

"They've got a five-minute jump on us, at least, Joey." A four-mile-a-morning man, Richardson was in excellent shape, but he was breathing hard by the time they reached the road. "Let's hope they don't exercise too regularly."

Twenty miles away, the parkway dead-ended at the tip of Cape May. The traffic demands on it at that hour, at that time of the year, were minimal. All four lanes were empty in both directions as the partners broke into the open and raced onto the verge. His conditioning regimen notwithstanding, Jumbo didn't have Joe's natural speed. Dante had ten yards on him by the time Beasley reached and scrambled over the center guard rail. On the far side of the asphalt, Route 9 finally came into view. Dante could see the west end of the causeway underpass, an estimated quarter mile off. Two figures hurried, half running, along the shoulder toward the gas station he'd glimpsed from the air. Joe slowed to let Beasley catch up.

"The canopy lights are still on," he gasped, panting. "But the pumps are all dark. Place looks closed."

Beasley pointed. "That tavern down there don't. They steal a car, we're fucked."

They matched each other stride for stride as they scrambled down the embankment to a six-foot chain link fence. Both of them were Brooklyn boys. They'd grown up hitting link fences at speed and scrambling over them. But that was years ago, and what neither had lost in technique, both had gained in weight. Jumbo ripped his pants, going over the top. Joe held his breath as he leapt down, worried about his questionable left knee. He got lucky and managed an ungainly but effective shoulder roll. Seconds later, they saw Vivian Hoag and Dennis Bennett pause outside the roadside tavern, bathed in the glow of its neon sign. She waited where she was, as Bennett disappeared inside.

The blisters her spike heels had given her earlier were raising hell with Vivian's feet, even in her cushioned sneakers and socks. With each step, that last quarter mile, she'd been in agony. The adrenaline stimulus of pure panic kept her going. Dennis no longer had any plan but to run, and she wasn't sure how much more of that she could do. He'd walked breathless into this seedy bar she now hid behind, aiming to convince some drunk that his headlights had been left on. The car he'd selected was a Camaro, picked from those parked around one side of the establishment. Because it was purple, he was hoping it belonged to a woman. He'd told Vivian to stay out of sight.

So here she was, with thirty-eight million dollars, squatting behind a Dumpster. Even if Dennis managed to pull this off, he'd probably end up killing another pawn in his desperate game. That would make five. And who was to say that she wouldn't be his sixth? Or seventh? Now that the Coast Guard was on to them, it wouldn't be long before this stretch of shoreline was crawling with cops.

"Screw this," she murmured. She ran through a mental list of her options, and came to the inevitable conclusion. Slowly, she straightened from her crouch and drifted back into the night. She had her new passport in the briefcase, and if she was quick to use her Vivian Hoag credit cards, she could easily collect enough cash to sustain her for a week. It would get her to some airline hub like Cincinnati or Atlanta. Along the way, she'd buy another wig, or a bottle of Miss Clairol. She would watch the news. Much would depend on the heat, but she could fly to Miami first, rather than directly to the islands. Some street lizard down there would be happy to buy one of her certificates for ten cents on the dollar. That would give her enough to book a cruise, and keep her going for months, after she walked off the ship in Barbados or Jamaica. She'd never have to look back.

There was a paved driveway that ran behind the roadhouse. It emptied onto a side road that led back to Route 9. As much as further running pained her, Vivian wrapped her arms around that briefcase, clutched it to her chest, and bolted. There'd be another Dennis, somewhere. Sooner or later, there'd be another party, and another nursery wall. This time, she'd have his ass up against it, not hers.

"Where the hell'd she go?" Jumbo gasped. They'd fairly sprinted that last quarter mile. Both he and Dante were winded.

Joey kept his voice low. "I don't see her. You take that alley around back. I'll take the front of the place. If Bennett comes out, and I can't handle it, I'll yell."

Richardson veered off toward the shadow of a Dumpster and used the cars between it and him as cover. Where in hell were the local cops, he wondered? He didn't hear so much as a single distant siren.

As he followed the owner of that late model Camaro out of the bar, Bennett wondered if this was such a good idea. After all, the owner wasn't a woman, but a man, a whole lot bigger than any victim he'd envisioned, and nowhere near as drunk as he'd hoped. Close to Bennett's own height, the man outweighed him by a good two stone. He had long, scraggly hair, an unkempt beard, and tattooed forearms. Dennis could take only small comfort in the Browning he carried. This was the type of individual who might also be armed. His best bet was to make quick work of him. Shoot him in the back, before the man saw he hadn't left his lights on.

"Where you from, bud?" the big man asked as they descended the tavern steps. "You talk funny."

"Stoke on Trent."

The fellow glanced over. "What kinda fucking name for a place is that?"

They'd gone far enough. Bennett's target had thoughtfully dug his keys from a pocket of his motorcycle jacket, and carried them in one huge paw. It spared Dennis the time and inconvenience of having to locate them. Time was of the essence now. That aircraft had landed and taken off again, possibly to put someone ashore. The pilot had surely radioed the Baia's position. Once the police got organized, there wouldn't be a passable road for miles.

He slacked off a step, cleared the 9mm from his waistband, and brought it up level with the middle of the hulking bruiser's back. He'd grabbed the slide to rack a shell into the chamber when an unseen mass shot out of the shadows to knock his target reeling into the hood of a parked car. It so surprised Dennis that he froze for an instant. It was an instant too long; enough time for the man who'd attacked his target to throw a punch at him. It came out of nowhere. One moment Bennett held his gun. The next, he didn't.

Slammed into the hood of that car, the bigger man bellowed, shook himself like a wet dog, and came back with the resilience and speed of an experienced street fighter. The guy who hit him, and then turned to disarm Bennett, clearly didn't anticipate so quick a recovery. His attention was on Dennis when the tattooed hulk threw a fist at his head. Bennett was amazed at his adversary's quickness. The second man managed to parry part of the blow, while the force of what did land sent him reeling.

As those two locked in sudden, deadly combat, Dennis scrambled for the car owner's key ring, fallen to the ground underfoot. He then dove for his pistol. In the dim light, he caught a glimpse of the uninvited third party, but still had no idea who he was. Not that he much cared. All of his concentration was on that Camaro now. He wouldn't be able to keep it for long, but for the moment, he had fast, reliable transportation.

Dante had seen Bennett's plan, the moment that automatic appeared in the fugitive's hand. Unfortunately, the big guy Joe had to clobber, to save him from being shot, had no idea that he should be grateful. To make matters worse, he was one of those types who only got meaner, the further the chips were down.

"You an' your girlfriend picked the wrong drunk t' fuck with, dickhead," the big man snarled. "I'm gonna rip y'both new assholes." He circled to his left as he spoke.

Wonderful, Joe thought. Not only an opponent who didn't mind pain, but a southpaw. At least he could guess which hand he'd lead with, but Joe hated lefties. They were too unpredictable.

Out of the corner of one eye, a split second before the big man came straight at him, Dante saw Bennett recover the fallen keys. Rather than engage, Joe danced back. It only made his opponent more angry and frustrated, and therefore, wilder. Joe thought it a good bet that the guy had never done battle with a well-schooled fighter. He could hope. Once his opponent was forced to pause for breath, Joe caught him with a stinging jab, flicked at his nose. The enraged response was predictable, and Dante stepped inside a looping left hand to land a flurry of short, vicious punches to the man's gut and ribs. Joe's only intention was to disable him, and those blows proved more than enough. One kick to his opponent's knee, while he was in that suddenly frozen state, and he would limp for the rest of his life. But Dante backed off. Bennett had recovered the gun, and was on the run toward a purple late model Camaro.

His own weapon cleared off his hip, Joe dropped to a crouch. He sighted down the Walther's barrel and yelled. "Freeze, asshole!"

Bennett was bending over to unlock the car door. He jumped in surprise, whirled, and brought his gun to bear. Dante's shot caught him dead, in the middle of his chest.

Cape May County Deputy Sheriff Anthony Tarantino was five miles up Route 9 from Ocean View, parked outside Palermo on the lookout for drunk drivers, when the call came from the dispatcher. State Police units were converging on the causeway between Ocean View and Avalon. Details were sketchy, but two New York City detectives were involved, in pursuit of a homicide suspect. Anthony called in to report he was in the vicinity. Advised that he was the closest unit, he was told to go in quiet. Unless he observed officers in jeopardy, he was to wait for State Police backup.

To Tarantino, quiet didn't mean that he shouldn't put his foot in it. He hardly needed his siren at this late hour, anyway. Not in the dead middle of winter. He could fly.

When a pistol shot split the windy night air, Beasley Richardson had just caught sight of the Hoag woman. She darted furtively from one pump island to the next in that half-lit gas station. With a brief-case clutched to her bosom, that sharp crack saw her nearly jump from her skin. Then she bolted like a rabbit flushed from tall brush.

Fearful for his partner's safety, Jumbo gave up on his quarry to double back toward the bar. "Joey!" he shouted, his heart in his throat.

At the sound of Beasley's voice, the startled woman, halfway across Route 9 toward the sea, looked back. In her panic, she failed to see the county sheriff's cruiser as it bore down from the north. At ninety miles per hour, its headlights hit her and she froze.

On impact, Vivian Hoag was thrown a hundred feet through the air. The briefcase she held clutched to her breast exploded. Like large pieces of confetti, its contents were scattered to the winds of the on-coming storm.

"Mother fuck!" Dante's tattooed opponent gasped. His hands clutched his gut while his gaze moved from the dead man, sprawled in the tavern parking lot, to the tall one who'd just beat the crap out of him. Finally, he looked toward the crumpled dead woman in the road. The acrid odor of burning rubber from the cop car's skidding tires was as effective as smelling salts. He shook his head and blinked. Up the way, the engine fan of the cruiser was making a hellacious racket, its crushed radiator spewing hot, steaming coolant.

"I tried to pull those last couple punches," Joe apologized. "Sorry." He was somewhat stunned himself. "Man was setting up to shoot you in the back."

The guy eyed Dante warily, and watched as Joe holstered his weapon. "Who the fuck are you?"

Dante turned to regard the front of the roadhouse. "I'll explain in a minute." Other patrons were now starting to emerge and gawk, several with drinks still clutched in their hands. "How late does this joint stay open?"

TWENTY-THREE

When Don Grover told Wendy Sasser that he wouldn't get home until late that night, she said he could come over any time. He explained that in a cop's world, late might mean *late,* and she told him it was all right. She wanted to see him.

Headed back to Queens at five a.m., Rusty challenged Don to take the woman up on it. This was his life. He was too damned old to play games. Either she was serious, or she wasn't.

Don now lay with Wendy wrapped in his arms. Snowflakes tapped insistently at the window above their heads. She had a wonderful, musky smell, and he buried his nose at the nape of her neck to drink it in. "When we finally pulled outta there, they'd found thirty-seven of them thirty-eight million in bearer bonds," he finished his story.

"You mean, somewhere out there in this storm, there's a million dollars? Just floating around?"

"Prob'ly not floatin'. More like soakin' wet. But yeah."

She twisted in his arms to kiss the tip of his nose. "Must have been like an Easter egg hunt. You help?"

"Not much. By the time we flew down, it was like a fuckin' circus. And I was tired."

"Not too tired to come see me. I've got the day off tomorrow. You can sleep until noon if you want."

"I had my doubts about comin' over," he admitted. "It was Rusty who convinced me."

She ran fingers through the tuft of hair on his chest and chuckled. "Ah. I'm beginning to understand what you guys need partners for."

Once Gus and the rest of the squad flew down to collect Joe and Jumbo, they all choppered back to Manhattan again before heavy snowfall made further flight impossible. It had started to snow lightly by the time they landed, and half an inch dusted the sidewalk outside Dante's front door. The faint glow of dawn smudged the eastern sky as he fitted his key in the lock and nodded to the lone whore hugging herself at the corner.

"Early-bird rates, sugar," she called out to him. "Wanna have a good time?"

"Had about all the fun I can handle for one night." he replied, more to himself than her. The one drink he'd allowed himself at that Route 9 roadhouse had barely dulled the edges.

Upstairs, when he stepped off his elevator, Joe braced himself for the worst and was delighted to see what Brian's cleaning crew had managed. Gone was his favorite reading chair, half the stuffing shot out of it last night, and gone was his sound system, television, and all the carnage that had smeared his floors, ceiling, and walls. Broken shelves were propped back up, books replaced in neat, presentable rows. The odor of a pine-scented cleaning agent was heavy in the air. One hell of a week, he reflected. He knew he needed to be extra cautious right now; that the sorry sickness he'd witnessed all around him shouldn't be allowed to penetrate him, and eat at his soul.

Toby the cat appeared as Joe stepped over to his machine to check for messages. He scooped the furry guy into his arms and scratched his belly. There were two blinks.

· "Who called?" he asked the cat.

Toby gave him a look of contentment in reply. Presumably, Diana had left him a full bowl of dry food.

The first message was from Rosa. "Call me when you get in," she said in her typically blunt phone fashion. "You need a place to stay, you know the way. For me, tomorrow is looking like a fairly light day." Apparently, she'd turned in before all the headlines were made.

Joe thought about the longer trip he would soon have to make to Washington to see her as he waited for the next message to cycle through. He realized then that regardless of Jaime Ruiz, and how she voted on sugar price supports, Rosa *had* gotten into his soul. And he, into hers. For better or worse, they were stuck with each other.

The second message was from Sandy. "Hi. I'm up late helping Brian. We just heard what happened on CNN. I'm sure it'll be late when you get home, but if you need a shoulder, try mine."

Dante thought about the key on his ring that fit

Brennan's studio door. It would be easy enough to head upstairs. But no, not now. Sandy would be in town for another couple days before she and Diana flew to San Jose to deal with her brother's estate.

"If this is any indicator of what kinda year it's gonna be, maybe you and me ought to check out monasteries," he told the cat, then stooped to set the little guy on the floor. "Buy ourselves some time to sit and think."

In the kitchen, he found a bottle of his favorite Irish whiskey set out atop his shattered tile counter, a ribbon around its neck. Taped to its cap was a note from Diana.

Wish I had him back, it read. *Glad I've still got you.*

Friday wasn't working out at all the way Bob O'Brien and his wife, Jill, had planned. They'd had the bright idea that the best time of year to buy a little beach-front bungalow off Cape May would be the dead middle of winter. If any seller was feeling a money pinch, it would be after the holidays, when no one was thinking about sun and sand. Not this far north. They'd planned to make a long weekend of it, stop here and there to chat with the locals, and see the area when everything looked its worst. What they hadn't counted on was eight inches of snow.

Whenever Bob got a little uptight, he'd think back to that day last month when he brought home a Ford Taurus wagon from New York City's quarterly impound auction. With four flat tires and a busted windshield, it looked to be in much worse shape than it actually was. Once he'd washed away two months of accumulated filth, he found the paint had nary a scratch. A new battery was all it took to turn over an engine with thirty-four thousand miles on it. The damned thing ran like a top.

But that wasn't the best of it. Bob was a carpenter, with his own little finishing business in the North Bronx. He'd gone looking for a reliable second car that week, and towed home a gold mine. In the process of making it serviceable, he found two hundred thousand dollars, secreted behind the spare. Subsequent research revealed that the car's former owner was a murdered car dealer, from Queens, one who'd been involved with a Colombian coke smuggling ring.

That Taurus wagon was the very same car that Bob now labored to dig out of a snowbank in his motel parking lot. With each shovelful of heavy, wet snow, he focused on that moment of discovery again. He knew what it felt like to hit the Lotto, without there being anyone he could tell. Instead, he and Jill would take out a mortgage on whatever beach house they found, and pay it down each month just like normal folks. They'd agreed that Bob could buy a small boat, used, and pay the owner cash. The rest of the money would stay where it was, in a safe-deposit box at their bank, on Broadway, three blocks from their house in the Kingsbridge section of the Bronx.

Plastered to the front tire, beneath all that snow, the sodden leaflet must have blown into the motel parking lot during the storm last night. There'd been some sort of commotion up the road; cop cars speeding past, and even a helicopter landing at the gas station, half a mile south. By then, Bob and Jill were in bed, and weren't about to go out and rubberneck. They were from New York City, where that level of noise was almost routine.

Bob reached to peel that piece of paper away from the tire and wad it up. Then he stopped. It wasn't a leaflet. It was some sort of certificate. He straightened to stretch the kinks from his lower back, then smoothed the wet paper flat against his thigh. In bold, fancy script, it read:

THE CITY OF ALBUQUERQUE

Several little coupons along the bottom of it had been cut away. A dozen remained intact. The text beneath the heading declared this to be a bearer bond, issued in the amount of one million dollars, with an annual interest rate of nine-point-six percent. Interest was payable on a semiannual basis, when the attached coupons were submitted to the bond's paying agent. A million dollars, plus ninety-six grand a year, for the remaining six years to maturity.

For a very long moment, Bob felt so light-headed, he was forced to lean heavily on his shovel. He knew from experience that the light-headedness would eventually pass . . . and that Jill wasn't going to believe this. Heck, *he* didn't believe it. But there was one other thing he did know, with absolute certainty. No matter how old it got, or how many miles it had on it, he was never going to sell that car.